SEEING YOUR FACE AGAIN

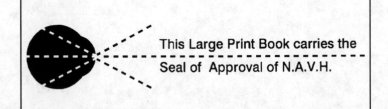

This Large Print Book carries the
Seal of Approval of N.A.V.H.

SEEING YOUR FACE AGAIN

JERRY S. EICHER

THORNDIKE PRESS
A part of Gale, Cengage Learning

GALE
CENGAGE Learning·

Farmington Hills, Mich • San Francisco • New York • Waterville, Maine
Meriden, Conn • Mason, Ohio • Chicago

GALE
CENGAGE Learning®

LIBRARY OF CONGRESS CATALOGING-IN-PUBLICATION DATA

Eicher, Jerry S.
    Seeing your face again / by Jerry S. Eicher. — Large print edition.
        pages ; cm. — (Thorndike Press large print Christian romance) (The Beiler sisters series ; #2)
    ISBN 978-1-4104-7195-6 (hardcover) — ISBN 1-4104-7195-0 (hardcover)
    1. Amish—Pennsylvania—Fiction. 2. Large type books. I. Title.
PS3605.I34S44 2014b
813'.6—dc23   2014018163

Published in 2014 by arrangement with Harvest House Publishers

Printed in Mexico
4 5 6 7 18 17 16 15

SEEING YOUR FACE AGAIN

ONE

It was almost dark as Debbie Watson drove her car down the icy road toward Verna's house. This visit was overdue, and her friend would be thrilled to see her. Of that, Debbie was sure. At last Sunday's meeting, Verna had said, "You haven't been over to the house in a while. Why don't you stop by sometime?"

"With the weather the way it's been, I'm just glad if I can get to work and back home in one piece. But I'll try," Debbie had said.

Now that Friday had arrived and the weather had cleared, Debbie decided to keep her word, even though the roads were still slippery. It would be good to see Verna again other than on Sundays. Before Verna had married Joe Weaver this past wedding season, Debbie had seen Verna every day at home. Debbie had moved in with the Beilers as a boarder last year. Now Bishop Beiler's house echoed with women's voices —

7

the two Beiler girls still at home, Ida and Lois, mingled in with those of their mother, Saloma, and now Debbie. But Verna was happy, so Debbie wouldn't wish her back home again. Verna and Joe were deeply in love. Debbie could see that every time she saw the couple together. They still had kind looks for each other, undimmed by the passing months. It was a love she hoped to experience with Alvin Knepp someday.

Debbie gripped the steering wheel tighter as she thought of Alvin. He still didn't pay her much attention, other than an occasional timid smile. But she shouldn't complain. Especially after the nice talk she had with him at Verna's wedding. *Yah,* Alvin was insecure, but beyond that, he was everything Debbie wanted in a husband.

Debbie's thoughts drifted back to Verna and Joe. If she didn't miss her guess, Verna was already expecting her first child. Such things weren't spoken of in the community, but still there were whispers. And then there was Verna's dreamy look at the Sunday services.

The car slipped a bit to the right on the ice, and Debbie corrected easily, looking ahead for the turn into Verna's lane. Joe and Verna had a tough time of it only a year ago, but now they had much to be thankful for. During the previous season, their wedding had been called off because Joe had been under a terrible cloud of suspicion. His *Englisha* girlfriend from his *rumspringa* days had brought a false accusation against Joe. The girlfriend claimed Joe was involved with her in a burglary ring. Joe had been charged by the police, and a trial date had been set. Only the intervention of a mysterious, last-minute witness had prevented a miscarriage of justice. Debbie was one of the few who knew that the hand of Henry Yoder, a man the Amish ministry had excommunicated for breaking the *Ordnung,* had helped Joe in the matter. He'd joined a liberal church after leaving the Amish community. A man in that church knew the truth, and Henry had brought it to Debbie's attention. This man's testimony exposed the lies of the ex-girlfriend and her accomplice.

So the last wedding season, Verna and Joe had finally married. Verna had been so faithful during that dark time, never wavering in her devotion to Joe in his time of trial. Debbie wondered if she would have done the same. Would she have stood by her man and seen the goodness in him when many others didn't? She hadn't been raised Amish, so the trait didn't come natural to her. It was one of the things that attracted her to these people. She was trying to practice with Alvin the wisdom she'd learned from Verna. Mostly it was the lesson of patience as Alvin continued to work through his fears. At least she hoped that was what was going on with him. He certainly had no misdeeds in his past like Joe Weaver had. The Knepp family was the model of perfection when it came to obedience to the *Ordnung.* Alvin's problem was his timidity around Paul Wagler, the man who was still determined to win Debbie's hand. Alvin couldn't seem to get past his family's low reputation among the community and Paul's well-respected family.

The image of Alvin as a poor farmer didn't fit her picture of him at all, but everyone had their opinion, she supposed. She used to drive past the Knepp farm before she moved in with the Beilers. She enjoyed catching glimpses of Alvin's broad shoulders as he worked in the fields. He handled the team of horses with such grace and power. Sometimes he even raised his arm to wave at her, even though he didn't know her. This was something not every Amish boy would do — pay attention to an *Englisha* girl while he stayed within the *Ordnung* rules. But Alvin had, which was one of the reasons she admired him.

Much later she'd learned from Emery, Bishop Beiler and Saloma's youngest son, that the Knepp family ran one of the worst-kept farms in all of Snyder County. Emery didn't think Alvin or his older married brothers were to blame. Their father, Edwin, ran things with an iron-but-incompetent hand. The results were disastrous. And keeping the *Ordnung* rules perfectly didn't make up for that in the eyes of the community.

Alvin's father's farm problems didn't bother Debbie, but they obviously did Alvin. There was one thing she had on her side. Alvin understood why she was here. When she'd told him, he'd seemed to grasp why she wished to join the Amish community — benefits that included the peaceful lifestyle and the depth of their faith. That was important to her — that Alvin understand her decision to join the community wasn't based on some spur-of-the-moment emotion. They'd talked about it when they had served as table waiters at Verna's wedding. She'd motioned toward the women with their *kinner* by their sides and commented, "I've always wanted to be a part of this — ever since I can remember anyway, when I was growing up next door to the Beiler farm."

"I'm glad to hear that," Alvin had responded.

Debbie had continued. "Life kind of stalled for me after college. Mom was pushing for me to get out of the house — getting 'out of the nest,' she called it. And at my age, I agreed. So I chose to board at the Beilers."

"I'm sure Bishop Beiler had no problem with that," Alvin had commented.

Debbie had almost bitten her tongue to keep the words in her mouth. She wanted to tell him that if it hadn't been for Lois's ever-present desire to join the *Englisha* world and Bishop Beiler's hope that Debbie's presence might influence Lois for the better, she wouldn't have gotten in so easily.

"Bishop Beiler had his reasons," Debbie had said instead.

"What did your *mamm* think about your move?" Alvin had asked.

Debbie grimaced. "Moving in with Bishop Beiler's family wasn't exactly what Mom intended, but it was 'moving out of the nest,' so she didn't fuss too long."

About that moment, Paul Wagler had sauntered across the lawn, as if he'd accidently passed by on his way to the barn. "Hi, Debbie!" he'd called — even with Alvin right there with her!

Debbie had felt her neck grow warm. Not because she cared for Paul in the least, but because this was an embarrassment. She'd given her assurance to Alvin earlier that Paul meant nothing special to her. Now here he was acting like they were old friends. And she couldn't be rude to him in public or say what she wanted to — that he leave her alone. Besides, Paul wouldn't listen anyway. At least he hadn't so far. Paul was a self-confident man who usually got what he wanted, especially when it came to women. That she didn't return his affections drove him to try even harder.

"Ignore him," Debbie had whispered in Alvin's direction when Paul was out of earshot. But Alvin had noticed her red face, Debbie was certain. And he'd taken a long time to compose himself. She knew that Paul was Alvin's greatest fear, even worse than his insecurity over his father's farming reputation. But Alvin had nothing to worry about when it came to Paul. Paul Wagler was like the *Englisha* boys who used to pursue her — confident, pushy, but with shallow character. She certainly didn't want Paul as her boyfriend. Ida, the second of the Beiler girls, was the one who had lost her heart to the dashing man. But that was another hopeless match. Paul returned Ida's affections about as much as Debbie returned Paul's.

"Ida likes him," Debbie had said to Alvin that day.

A slight smile had stolen over his face. Alvin knew the impossibility of that matchup. Not that it kept Ida from hoping things would change, especially after Paul had agreed to serve as best man in Verna's wedding. That temporary match had placed Paul in Ida's company for the day.

Debbie sighed and held the steering wheel steady as she pulled into Joe and Verna's driveway. Alvin had left her under the clear impression that afternoon that he would soon ask her for a date one Sunday evening after the hymn singing. But nothing had happened. Maybe he didn't wish to date an *Englisha* girl who wasn't a church member yet? The *Ordnung*-inclined Knepp family might have such thoughts, Debbie told herself.

Would Alvin's insecurity put an end to her hopes for a romantic relationship? Would it even shake her determination to join the Amish community? Debbie had always thought it wouldn't, but with the spring baptismal instruction classes ahead of her, the question stared her in the face. If Alvin wasn't the only reason she wished to join the Amish, why didn't she go ahead and join the class? There were many reasons to do so. For one, if she began the instruction classes this spring that would be about the time she'd graduated last year from college. Wouldn't that be a coincidence — and a fitting one at that?

Thankfully, Joe had cleared the lane of snow all the way from the road to the barn. Debbie pulled beside the barn door and parked. The soft glow of lantern light was visible through the dusty glass. Joe would be about his chores, no doubt. He'd want an early start before the winter's deep darkness set in.

Later in the evening, after supper, Joe and Verna would sit around the stove to read and spend time together. They lived their lives like the generations of the Amish faithful before them . . . and would do after them. These were not people tossed about by an ever-changing world. They were anchored in all that was good of the past. They embraced only what they found in the current culture that benefited their families, which was precious little. That was one of the reasons Debbie was here. She wanted this life — not the one she'd grown up in.

Debbie pushed open the car door and stepped out into the snow. True to her expectation, the front door burst open and Verna rushed out onto the porch with a shawl wrapped over her shoulders.

"Stay there!" Debbie called as she motioned with her hand. "I'm coming right in."

Verna looked like she meant to dash across the snowy lawn to greet her, but apparently she changed her mind.

Debbie hurried up the little pathway Joe had shoveled from the barn to the house.

"Oh, Debbie!" Verna wrapped her in a tight hug. "You've come to visit me."

"I said I'd try." Debbie laughed. "I wasn't sure the weather would cooperate."

"*Yah,* it's an extra-bad winter," Verna said. "Joe struggles to keep our lane open. But it's *gut* of you to stop by." Verna took Debbie's hand and led her inside. "I'll have hot chocolate ready for us in a minute. I even have cinnamon rolls I made today. Will you have one?"

"No rolls." Debbie held up her hand. "I don't want to spoil the supper I'm sure Lois will have ready at home."

Verna glowed. "You could stay, you know. I *can* cook."

"I'd love that," Debbie said. "But Lois and the rest of the family are expecting me." She followed Verna into the kitchen and sat down with a sigh. "You do have it cozy in here."

Verna beamed. "It's comfortable. And we get to enjoy our first winter together, just Joe and me. I can't tell you how thankful I am for all you did, Debbie. You know Joe and I wouldn't be together if it hadn't been for your help."

Debbie dismissed the praise with a wave. "There were others who helped besides me."

Verna shook her head. "You always play down your part, Debbie. That last witness was sent from *Da Hah,* but you were there to help get it through. And your college education didn't hurt either."

Debbie shrugged. What Verna said was true, but she didn't wish to dwell on the subject. She would help where she could, but it was small payment for all that the Beilers had done for her. They'd taken her in as a boarder even if she was *Englisha.* That wasn't exactly the accepted norm for the Amish community.

Verna poured steaming water into cups. "How are things at home? Is Lois enjoying having the bedroom to herself?"

"I think so," Debbie allowed. "I miss sharing a room with her, but it seemed senseless to go on that way, what with your room sitting empty across the hall."

Verna set the cup in front of Debbie. "Here's the bowl of cocoa. I'll let you add what you wish. Some days I like extra in mine."

Debbie dipped a heaping spoonful of the chocolate into her cup. She stirred it and took the first sip. "Winter makes things both darker and more peaceful, doesn't it?"

With a pensive look, Verna sat down beside Debbie. "*Yah.* The land rests in the winter and so does the soul. That's how *Da Hah* intended it. The world out there seems to rush through all the seasons, missing so many blessings."

"Yes, they do," Debbie agreed. "Like the Christmas season we've just been through. From what I was used to, it was such a change living in the community. Though I did go home to Mom and Dad's on Christmas morning, it turned out Mom had to work that afternoon. 'As a favor to a friend,' she said."

"*Yah,* though life lived our way has its costs," Verna mused. "But in the end it pays back . . . much more than most people can imagine. Like our quiet evenings together with the farm work finished early. It's truly a peaceful time, Debbie, with the quiet, snow-covered fields lying outside the living

18

room window. It heals the wounds of last year — some of which I didn't even know I had."

"You did well through all of that," Debbie said. "I don't think I would have kept faith in Joe like you did."

"That's just because you didn't know Joe very well," Verna said. "The man has a heart of gold. Steady and solid like a rock. I couldn't have wished for a better man — not in a hundred years of living. Still, the situation did hurt deeply. But *Da Hah* is healing us."

Debbie sat in silence, drinking her hot chocolate. Her earlier thoughts crept back. There was nothing she could do about Alvin's hesitation. In her *Englisha* world she had an option. There, she could ask a man out on a date, though she'd never done that. Here in the Amish world it wasn't even a dreamed-of possibility. She would have to practice patience and endurance like Verna had last year. Debbie would choose to believe that in the end Alvin would come around.

Verna tapped her arm, and Debbie glanced up to see her friend regarding her with raised eyebrows. "What were you thinking, Debbie? Your mind is somewhere else."

"Alvin . . ." Debbie said. Verna was one of the few people she'd unburdened her heart to on the subject of her interest.

Verna's brow wrinkled. "He still hasn't asked you home, then?"

"No, and I'm beginning to think he won't."

"You must keep up your faith." Verna smiled. "Look at what Joe and I went through!"

"I know. You shame me," Debbie said. "You were so patient, and here I go again complaining."

Verna shook her head. "Don't look at it that way. No situations are exactly that same. I was just trying to encourage you."

"Thanks," Debbie whispered.

Verna face lit up. "Should I have Joe say something to Alvin? Perhaps that would help."

"No!" Even Debbie heard the alarm in her voice. "You mustn't do that. It needs to come from Alvin . . . but thanks for the offer." She quickly changed the subject, and the two chatted on for another thirty minutes before Debbie got to her feet. "Well, it's time for me to go. Supper is probably about ready."

"You must come over more often!" Verna

said, following her to the door. "I miss our talks."

Debbie gave Verna a quick hug before she made her way down the narrow path to her car. After getting in and starting it up, Debbie turned the car around. Verna gave her a wave as she crept past. *She is a very dear friend,* Debbie thought. One she hoped she'd never lose.

Two

Fifteen minutes after she left Verna and Joe's place, Debbie slowed for Bishop Beiler's driveway. The Beiler home lay a few miles off Route 522. Here Emery, the youngest son still at home, had cleared a double lane of snow. Debbie slowed the car even more when she caught sight of Emery on the tractor, now backing the makeshift plow into the overhang behind the barn. He'd cleared a nice little spot for her car, the snow pushed into a heap against the fence. She would have to make a special effort to thank him. Debbie inched her vehicle into the spot between the drifts.

Emery appeared around the corner of the barn as she got out. He had his winter stocking cap pulled down tightly over his ears. "Like my nice lane?"

"*Yah,* thank you!" Debbie said with a warm smile. "Your lane is much nicer than Joe's."

Emery raised his eyebrows. "You stopped in at Verna's place?"

"Just to say a quick howdy. I don't get over there much with the way the winter weather is."

"How are things going for the young love birds?" Emery asked and then grinned.

"Wishing you were in their shoes?" Debbie teased.

Emery laughed. "I'm a little young yet. And where would I find a girl?"

"Now, Emery!" she scolded. "You're 20, and you know there are dozens of Amish young women lined up waiting for a word from you."

He laughed again. "I'm afraid you overestimate my Romeo powers. Isn't that what the *Englisha* call it?"

"Something like that," she said, humoring him.

"Plus I have to get all my sisters married off before I take the farm over. I wouldn't want to push anyone out into the cold."

"That's kind of you," Debbie said as she gathered her things together.

Emery wasn't through with his teasing. "I don't think you'll be lasting around here much longer. Not with the way Paul Wagler's carrying on."

Debbie stood upright so fast her head

spun. "I'm not interested in Paul, Emery!"

Emery cleared his throat. "I think you're showing the very spunk Paul finds so attractive. What's wrong with him, anyway?"

Your sister's in love with him for one thing, Debbie thought, but she didn't say it aloud. Ida didn't want her secret spilled to the world. And Emery probably knew anyway and was just as convinced the case was hopeless as she did.

"See?" he teased. "You're speechless. There's not one *gut* reason Paul Wagler shouldn't be arriving here every Sunday evening for sweet visits with you."

"Please." Debbie turned up her nose in exaggerated disdain. "That man is barking up the wrong tree. Plus, it sounds as if you're only trying to get me married off so you can take over the farm. That's quite a biased opinion in my book."

Emery didn't answer as he headed toward the barn with a pleased look on his face. He'd said what he wished to say, and he would now wait for his words to bear fruit.

Debbie knew Emery's push wouldn't help, but no one seemed persuaded of that except her. And if Emery teased her so openly about Paul's constant attention, no doubt there were plenty of others from the community who also had noticed. But what could she do? If she asked Ida for advice, she'd sigh with her meek spirit and advise resignation to *Da Hah*'s will. But surely the Lord didn't want her married to Paul!

Debbie made her careful way up the shoveled walkway and entered the house without knocking on the door. This had been, after all, her home for many months now. It had fast become the only life she knew, even with her *Englisha* car still parked out beside the barn. Bishop Beiler had tolerated the vehicle so far, especially since she'd proven so helpful with Verna and Joe's troubles last year. Besides, she wasn't Amish . . . yet.

The bishop bore a great burden for his family's welfare. Not just as bishop, but as husband and father. He wanted his wife happy and for all of his children to remain in the faith. This was an issue that had weighed heavy on his shoulders the last few years. Since her teenage years, the bishop's youngest daughter, Lois, had spoken of the time when she would leave the faith for the *Englisha* world. Things had become serious enough that the bishop had welcomed Debbie into his home in hopes of influencing Lois about the dangers of the world. He'd never stated that in so many words, but it wasn't hard to figure out. And so far it had worked.

Debbie's open admiration for all things Amish and her willingness to forsake so many things that Lois admired — her college education, her *Englisha* home, her *Englisha* boyfriend — had made an impression on Lois. Debbie thought it was almost like Lois and she had been switched at birth. In so many ways, Lois was the exact image of the daughter Debbie's mother had wished for, and Debbie was the daughter Bishop Beiler longed to see in Lois. It seemed like sometimes things got all turned around and no one could explain why.

Debbie pushed her thoughts away to peek into the kitchen. Lois and her mom, Saloma, were rushing about, surrounded by the aftermath of their afternoon's cooking. Several steaming bowls of food were on the stove, and dirty dishes were stacked everywhere.

"Well, look who's home!" Saloma said as she glanced up to give Debbie a kind look.

"I'll run right up and change so I can help," Debbie said. She dashed for the stair door.

Lois gave her a grateful look. There was no one in the Beiler family who could cook like Lois, but cleanup wasn't high on her priority list.

Debbie entered Verna's old room and

paused long enough to stash her purse in the dresser. Moments later she was back downstairs drying dishes for Lois.

"How did your day go?" Saloma asked.

"Okay. Nothing unusual," Debbie told her. "I stopped in at Verna's on the way home though. That's why I'm a little late."

Saloma's face brightened. "That was nice of you. I'm sure Verna appreciated it. How is she doing?"

"She looks all snugly in that new home of hers," Debbie said as she turned a dish over in her hands. "I think Joe and Verna are very happy together."

Saloma nodded but a sigh escaped her lips. "I guess that's the first one married, which we can be thankful for."

Lois gave her mother a quick glance but didn't say anything.

It went without saying that Saloma longed for a decent matchup for her other two daughters. If it didn't happen, Ida would survive as an old maid in the community. But Lois was another matter. With her desire for the *Englisha* world, there was little chance Lois would stay in the community if she were passed over by the unmarried Amish men.

"You don't have to be sighing like that *Mamm,*" Lois spoke up. "Joe's cousin Roy has been eyeing me for a while already. I'm not without my chances."

Saloma looked like she was about to drop the dish of mashed potatoes she was carrying. "Oh, Lois! Please keep your mind and heart open. Don't be doing anything foolish like turning down the man . . . if you get a chance. You know your words haven't been the best in past years. Many in the community have heard your sighings for the *Englisha* world. Few of our men wish for such a *frau* to stand by their side."

"*Mamm,* stop it!" Lois said. "What if I don't like the man?"

"Love can perhaps grow in your heart . . . if you get to know him better." Saloma sounded a little desperate.

Lois gave a little laugh. "And what is *Daett* going to say?"

Saloma was silent for a moment. Bishop Beiler was well known for his strict standards when it came to any man who wished to date one of his daughters. In the past, this reputation of the bishop's had as much to do with Lois's lack of romantic offers as her *Englisha* sentiments. "I will speak with *Daett* on the matter," Saloma said. She pressed her lips firmly together.

Debbie looked away. The truth was that the bishop wasn't as strict as he used to be.

At least when it came to Lois and her prospects. At this point Lois could probably bring home the wildest man in the community and get him past Bishop Beiler's inspection. Such was the urgency with which both the bishop and Saloma wanted their youngest daughter safely married into the faith.

For her part, Lois gave a little snort. "Save your efforts, *Mamm*. Until Roy asks me home, I wouldn't want word to leak out how desperate we all are." Lois's sarcasm was thick, but Saloma didn't seem to pick up the signal.

"That's not a nice thing to say, Lois," Saloma scolded. "At your age everyone is already wondering . . ." Saloma stopped. She apparently thought better of what she was about to say.

Lois was now lost in her own world and didn't notice. Her voice was dreamy. "Now if I had Debbie's chances, how happy I'd be! I'd be floating along on the arms of handsome *Englisha* boys like Debbie used to do in her college days. She probably had more offers than she could handle."

Debbie laughed. "You exaggerate, Lois. And I turned down those I had. It's not all that great out there."

"See, Lois?" Saloma clutched her daughter's arm. "Listen to the voice of experience."

Lois gave Debbie a quick glance. "Would you at least set me up with an *Englisha* boy — for just one date? I'd like to see for myself if I'd like it or not."

Saloma's face paled. "You must put such awful thoughts far from you, Lois! They aren't right in the sight of *Da Hah*."

"Oh well, just saying," Lois mumbled. "At least that way I'd know for sure."

Debbie spoke up quickly. "Amish men are every bit as handsome and charming as *Englisha* men, Lois. Plus the Amish know how to work hard. And they provide for their families and don't run off at the drop of the hat. Think about that. There are a lot of divorces out in the *Englisha* world."

"But our men aren't dashing, and exciting, and edgy, and thrilling," Lois said, her face glowing. "And they don't drive fast cars."

Saloma moaned.

Debbie glanced at her, but Saloma appeared unable to speak at the moment. Debbie spoke up. "Lois, you can have Paul Wagler if you want. He's dashing."

Lois giggled. "And break Ida's heart? The poor girl. *Nee.* Plus I don't like him."

"Then you might not like what's out there

in the *Englisha* world either. In some ways Paul is like an *Englisha* man."

Lois gave a little snort again. "I like the type, just not Paul. Though I'd let him bring me home just for the experience. And what do you know about Amish men anyway? What with your fixation on Alvin Knepp. His family is the farming joke of the community. That would be quite a come down from the life you're used to, you know."

"Maybe I look at the heart," Debbie protested. "That's what Verna did, and she turned out pretty happy."

Lois laughed. "I think you're mixed up, Debbie."

Saloma sat down on a kitchen chair, apparently at the end of her strength as she listened to such plain talk. She managed to whisper. "I have never heard such twisted thinking in my life, Lois."

Lois shrugged. "I'm just talking, *Mamm.*"

Saloma wiped her brow. Moments later she took a deep breath and got up. She rushed about to set the table.

The outside washroom door slammed, and Ida stuck her head through the kitchen doorway. "Hi," she chirped.

"Hi to you," Debbie greeted Ida. Even though her face wasn't the prettiest in the community, Ida had such a sweet spirit.

Why some boy couldn't see that, Debbie didn't know. Instead they'd passed up Ida all these years.

"Supper's about ready," Saloma said as she put the last of the food on the table. "I suppose the men aren't far behind."

"You still have a few minutes," Ida offered before she closed the door. Sounds of water could be heard splashing in the washroom as she washed up.

Debbie stacked the last of the mixing bowls on the lower counters. Ida soon dashed past moments before the sound of the men washing up could be heard. When Ida reappeared from upstairs in a clean dress, Saloma motioned for her to join them at the table. The women were waiting when Adam and Emery walked in. The food steamed on the table.

THREE

When the prayer was finished some minutes later, the spoken words directed toward heaven had produced a momentary hush around the supper table. The silence didn't last long though. Bishop Beiler spoke up. "It looks like another bad storm is moving in tonight."

"Well, *Daett,* I've got something that will help us forget this gloomy weather and all our troubles!" Lois said. "But you'll have to wait until you've cleaned your plate."

The bishop's eyes twinkled. "I'll clean my plate all right, but judging from what I smell coming from the oven, I'd better not take seconds."

"What is it?" Emery asked. "Cobbler? Apple Brown Betty?"

"Never you mind!" Lois said. "Just clean your plate."

Everyone laughed and seemed to eat a little faster than usual. Finally, Lois jumped to her feet to bring her prize accomplishment of the day from the oven. She slid the dish on the table, where it lay in all its delicious glory. "We have cherry pie tonight!"

Debbie smiled at Lois's antics, but they weren't without justification. Lois was the household's best cook. Her pie crusts were so moist and crumbly they melted in your mouth.

"There's no one like my Lois for cherry pie." Bishop Beiler beamed. "What will I do when *Mamm* and I are in our *dawdy haus,* and Lois is running her own household of *bopplis.* Will we still have your pies to make us fat and happy?"

"*Daett!*" Lois chided. "I don't even have a man bringing me home yet! And you know I'll always be baking pies for you."

Saloma spoke up. "*Daett*'s way too spoiled already. My pies will be just fine in our old age."

Bishop Beiler laughed, obviously enjoying the easy banter. He looked over at Lois. "Didn't I see Joe's cousin Roy making eyes at you the other Sunday, Lois? I hope you're seeing what I'm seeing."

"*Daett . . .*" Lois's face was flushed now.

"I want to let you know that Roy's a decent man. I have no objections about him."

Lois took a slice of cherry pie and put it on her plate before she looked at her father. "What's changing your tune, *Daett*? You used to chase most men off when they came anywhere close to your daughters. Has it been Verna's happy marriage or is there something else?"

The bishop thought for a moment before he answered. "Well, I'm always interested in my daughters' boyfriends, but perhaps Verna and Joe have mellowed me a bit."

Lois didn't look that convinced.

Ida quickly changed the subject. "There's a young folks gathering at the Wagler place this week. They might even have an indoor volleyball game in their barn."

Saloma didn't waste any time before speaking up. "I think that will be just the thing for these winter blahs. Do you think the Wagler barn will be large enough?"

"Of course the Waglers have room," Lois said. "They're the Waglers."

"The Waglers are decent and upstanding members of the community," Bishop Beiler said, having caught Lois's sarcastic tone.

Lois went on. "Speaking of upstanding church members, why has Deacon Mast been hanging around our place lately? Seems like I saw him here yesterday and today."

"Lois!" Saloma's voice had a warning in it. "You know not to ask questions about church work. The bishop's daughters will be told what they need to know just like the rest of the community."

Lois puckered her lip but offered nothing more.

Ida ventured a further question. "It's not something serious, is it, *Daett*?"

The family's drama with Verna and Joe last year had left them all on edge. This also explained the sympathetic look crossing Bishop Beiler's face as he answered. "*Yah*, it is something serious, Ida. But all church work is serious. Right now we're working through what needs to be done."

"Trouble, trouble. It seems like there's always trouble happening with someone or other," Lois muttered before taking a bite of her pie.

The bishop seemed lost in thought, his hand holding his fork suspended halfway to the plate. Finally he sighed. "Perhaps it's best if I do tell you. You'll know soon enough — probably at the first youth gathering you go to. In fact, I'm surprised you haven't heard already."

They all looked at him. Bishop Beiler took his time before he spoke again. "On Monday morning Alvin Knepp left for the *Englisha* world. He didn't run away, thankfully, so perhaps there is hope for him. His *daett* told Deacon Mast Alvin came home from the hymn singing on Sunday night, told them he was leaving in the morning, and packed his bags."

Shocked silence fell over the room. Debbie's spoon clanked against her plate. She looked away, trying to appear nonchalant.

"Did he say where he was going?" Emery asked.

The bishop nodded. "*Yah.* To Philadelphia. I don't know why that makes any difference. It's all the same out there — wherever you go."

"But how did this happen?" Saloma clutched her husband's shirt sleeve.

Bishop Beiler stared at Saloma's hand blankly for a long moment. "I wish I knew, Saloma. That's always the question we ask as a ministry, and I'm afraid we don't always find the answer. Alvin was the last person I would have expected to pull something like this."

Debbie's ears buzzed as the family's conversation continued around her. She heard the questions and speculations through a haze. Even her arms were numb from shock. How could this have happened? Alvin had left for her world? One of the

Knepps — the family known for never breaking the *Ordnung* — was going *Englisha*? He'd never shown the slightest inclination of such a choice . . . or had she missed something?

What about his interest in her? Did that mean nothing? Why hadn't she made an effort sooner to contact Alvin through Verna? She should have after all the silence these past months. Had Alvin interpreted her intentions incorrectly? Maybe he thought she wanted him to stay away. But how could he think that after the plain words she'd spoken to him at Verna's wedding?

Lois's words cut through Debbie's fog. "It sounds like a broken heart to me. That's the only thing that might cause a Knepp to stir himself to such effort. And to break the *Ordnung* on top of it."

"Lois!" *Mamm* scolded, but Debbie knew they were all looking at her, no doubt thinking she was the cause of this.

"But . . . I . . ." More words wouldn't come so Debbie lowered her gaze and stared at the table.

She could feel everyone staring at her.

The bishop spoke. His voice was kind, but the words cut to her heart. "Have you been toying with Alvin's heart, Debbie?"

Debbie shook her head. She didn't trust

her voice at the moment. How could they think this of her? She wanted to spill out words in her defense, to tell them of the efforts Verna and she had made at the wedding. How they'd invited Alvin to be a table waiter with her. How she'd spoken to Alvin afterward and tried to assure him that Paul Wagler meant nothing to her.

"Please, *Daett*." Saloma placed her hand on her husband's arm again. "Debbie isn't to blame for whatever Alvin is up to."

The bishop pressed on. "I could declare I heard someone say that Paul Wagler said something about . . ." Bishop Beiler paused.

Debbie waited a second before prompting, "Paul said what?"

Bishop Beiler took a quick glance around the supper table. "It might be best not to speak of such things here."

Lois snorted. "Come on, *Daett*. What you have to say can't be worse than what Paul says in public for all to hear."

"*Yah*, I suppose," Bishop Beiler allowed. "None of the Waglers can keep their mouths shut for the most part. And Paul is the worst. Word has it that he let on to Alvin that he wouldn't stand a chance with Debbie."

"He was speaking this around?" Saloma appeared horrified. "Debbie had nothing to do with this, I'm sure."

They all looked at her again. Debbie's mind spun. She was still an *Englisha* girl to them, and she couldn't blame the Beilers for being uncertain about her. What should she say? If Verna were only here, she'd know. But right now her silence convinced no one, so she blurted out, "I care for Alvin Knepp, and I wouldn't have turned down his interest. In fact, I would have welcomed it! I have no interest in Paul, and he is only saying such things to mess things up between Alvin and me."

"Are you sure about this, Debbie?" Bishop Beiler regarded her steadily. "It sounds to me like two of our boys are fighting over the *Englisha* girl among us. Is this at the bottom of Alvin fleeing the community?"

Debbie was sure she'd pass out any second. Bishop Beiler had never referred to her as "the *Englisha* girl" before. She'd always felt welcome in his home, even if she still drove a car every day. And hadn't she helped keep Lois from bolting into the *Englisha* world? And what about all the help she'd given Joe and Verna? Was the bishop forgetting all that? She met his gaze and allowed her plea for understanding to show.

Bishop Beiler gave a little nod. "You've always been a blessing in our lives, Debbie.

I wouldn't wish that to change. But losing a church member to the world is not something we can ignore — or any cause that might lie behind it."

Lois waved her hand around. "I'm sorry I brought up the subject. I shouldn't have been so quick to speak. And wake up, *Daett*. What's new about boys fighting over girls? I'm sure you had your competition for *Mamm*."

Debbie saw Saloma's hand reach over and squeeze the bishop's arm and caught a slight smile spring onto the bishop's face.

"I suppose that's true enough, Lois. But I'd still like to get to the bottom of this. My pursuit of your *mamm* didn't result in another man leaving for the *Englisha* world."

Silence fell. They were obviously waiting for her to say something. But how was she supposed to speak of things so close to her heart? Let alone in front of Ida since they concerned Paul Wagler. Ida must already be mortified and hurt beyond words to hear what Paul had been saying. Debbie stole a quick glance at Ida's face. The steady stream of silent tears that flowed down her face said all she needed to know.

Bishop Beiler was still looking at her, so Debbie felt she needed to answer him. She couldn't remain silent if she wished to

41

remain in the Beiler home. Debbie clutched the edge of the table. "Verna and I did arrange for Alvin to be a table waiter with me, and I did make a point of speaking with him at the wedding. I told him there was nothing between Paul Wagler and myself. Alvin gave me the impression he would ask me home after a hymn singing before too long." She stole a quick glance around. No one looked too horrified, and Ida had at least stopped her tears.

The bishop cleared his throat. "Paul's claim does sound unlikely if you and Verna took such measures. But you know that it's best if a woman waits for a man to come to her and not indulge in the *Englisha* way, where the woman pursues the man. That's not the way of our people."

Debbie nodded at once. This wasn't something she was ignorant of, but still the words stung. Had she in fact been wrong in her approach with Alvin? Perhaps the sad results spoke the answer. Alvin was gone.

Downing his last bites of pie, the bishop was quiet, and silence settled over the table.

Saloma spoke up first. "Then the matter's cleared on Debbie's end. She might have shown herself a little forward in speaking with Alvin, but she can't be blamed for what Alvin has done."

Bishop Beiler nodded as he used his napkin to wipe his mouth.

Debbie glanced his way and decided he didn't look convinced. But there was nothing more she could say. The Amish formed their opinions based on the end result of actions as much as the original intent. And her actions, however innocent, might have contributed to an Amish boy's dash into the *Englisha* world. So she was suspect no matter how much Saloma or anyone else tried to cover for her. In the meantime, her heart throbbed with the pain of Alvin's unexpected departure. And now, on top of that, her welcome in the community would be reevaluated and seen in a whole new light. How had this all happened? Suddenly the depths of this cold winter entered her heart.

"Let's give thanks for the food," Bishop Beiler said in his best Sunday-sermon voice. Debbie noticed that her hands shook as they all bowed their heads and Bishop Beiler led out in prayer again.

FOUR

Stillness settled over the farmhouse some hours later. Darkness lay heavy outside Debbie's bedroom window with snow thick on the sill. In the light that flickered from the kerosene lamp, Debbie checked her alarm clock on the dresser. Close to midnight. Why wouldn't sleep come? Though tomorrow wasn't a workday, Saturdays always contained plenty of jobs to do around the Beiler farm.

She'd tried to read herself to sleep, but to no avail. Ida's sorrowful face after the discussion around the supper table still haunted her. It just wasn't fair how Ida pined after a love that was denied her. Now, with the news about Alvin leaving the community, it appeared Debbie had joined Ida. Perhaps she was mourning for herself as much as for Ida. And she had the added trouble of the bishop's suspicions that she might have contributed in some way to

Alvin's venture into the *Englisha* world. How upside down things had become. The wrong man was determined to win her affections, and at the same time her reputation in the community might turn into that of a troublemaker.

Debbie got up. There was no sense in an all-night stew over her troubles. She couldn't drown them with a book. Perhaps she could offer a measure of sympathy to Ida. Ida hadn't said a word while they washed the supper dishes. An offer of help might comfort her troubled spirit. Saloma had asked her daughter repeatedly what troubled her, but Ida had done nothing but shake her head.

Unless Debbie missed her guess, Ida was in her room across the hall still awake, mulling over the turn of events just as she was. Why not pay Ida a visit? Debbie pushed open her bedroom door. A dim light coming from under Ida's door guided her steps down the dark hallway. Debbie tapped on the door.

"Come in," Ida's weak voice called out.

Debbie turned the knob and slipped inside. Ida stood beside the window, apparently transfixed by the snowflakes swirling on the other side of the windowpane.

Ida turned around, a slight smile on her face.

"May I sit?" Debbie motioned toward the bed.

"Sure." Ida didn't move away from the window.

Debbie cleared her throat. "I'm sorry about Paul, Ida. Believe me, I'm not making any attempt to court his attention. I don't like the man in the least."

Ida's small smile vanished. "I know you aren't doing such things, Debbie. You have a *gut* heart. It's not your fault Alvin did what he did. And I wish *Daett* hadn't doubted you the way he did."

Debbie pressed back the tears. How like Ida to quickly turn this visit around to one of offering comfort. And all the time Ida's own heart had to be throbbing with pain.

"I should be comforting you, Ida," Debbie whispered. "Not the other way around."

Ida's look was kind. "You think so, I suppose, but that's because you don't know how much trouble you may be in."

"What?" Debbie sat up straight.

"Yah." Ida stared out into the darkness. *"Daett* will not soon forget his suspicions, and Minister Kanagy will only make them worse once he hears what's going on. And *Daett* will have to tell him what he knows

46

and suspects."

Debbie tried to look skeptical, but her heart was pounding.

Moments later Ida added fuel to the fire. "You remember how Minister Kanagy was with Verna and Joe? He would have had them both excommunicated if *Daett* hadn't stood in his way."

"But surely not . . ." Debbie let the words hang.

Ida shrugged. "*Daett* will stick up for you, but you could help him by doing something for yourself."

When Ida didn't continue, Debbie asked. "And what could I do?"

Ida turned to look out the window again. "You could accept Paul's offer to court you."

"Ida!" Debbie leaped to her feet to grab Ida's hand. "I'm not going to do that. Even if I knew you didn't care for him, I couldn't do that."

Ida turned around, sorrow written across her face. "Paul's never going to return my affections, Debbie. And neither is any other man. Don't let my situation stand in the way of your decisions."

"I'm not!" Debbie protested.

"I know you haven't been returning Paul's affection, but wasn't it a little bit out of

47

consideration for me?" Ida's face was etched with pain.

"No — and that's the truth. Well, perhaps just a little, but I'm really not interested in Paul."

Ida thought for a moment. "Okay. But perhaps you should consider changing your mind. Word will get out. It will be said that Alvin left because of you. That won't sit well with the community. I know them better than you do, Debbie. *Daett* has protected you for most of last year, but it won't be like that anymore. Not once they find out that a man has left the community because of you. And, on top of that, you're turning down one of the most eligible bachelors in our district."

"Then I'll put away my car at once, and I'll tell your father I want to join the instruction class this spring." Debbie squared her shoulders. "That should settle the matter."

"It's a little too late, I'm afraid," Ida said.

Debbie stared at Ida's figure as it cut a sharp contrast against the darkness outside. Had the winter weather affected Ida's mind and cast her spirits so deeply in the doldrums that she thought only the worst? Other than the talk tonight around the supper table, Bishop Beiler had never given any indication that she wasn't welcome. In fact, he'd always gone out of his way to make her feel at home.

Ida regarded Debbie again. "This thing that Alvin did will put thoughts into Lois's heart. She may even join him in Philadelphia."

Debbie clutched the edge of the bed. "You have to be wrong about this, Ida. Your sorrow about Paul's rejection has affected you more than you realize."

Ida didn't move. "I sorrow, *yah.* But Lois isn't above using Alvin's actions to justify her own."

"I hope you're wrong." Debbie's emotions sank fast. What Ida said made much more sense than she wished to admit. That must have been the real reason Bishop Beiler had regarded her with such concern at the supper table. He'd been thinking of Lois more than he was of Alvin's situation. And the bishop wouldn't want to say something like that in front of Lois.

"You can wait and see what Lois does," Ida continued. "But if you wish to continue in the community, you'd better start returning Paul's attention."

"I will do no such thing." Debbie wanted to say more, but she couldn't think of anything else.

Ida glanced at her. "Remember, Debbie,

Paul's never going to ask me home. Not if I wait a thousand years. So don't feel bad for me."

"I . . ." Debbie paused. She did feel sorry for Ida, but she was also horrified that she might even consider this outrageous suggestion. Even now thoughts raced unbidden through her mind. She'd dated this kind of man before, and maybe she could do so again. It didn't mean she had to marry him. And Paul did have good looks and a charming personality. His witty jokes weren't unpleasant, and they conversed with easy rapport. No one in the community would doubt them as a couple. In fact, they might well be considered among the community's best-looking couples. And who knew, maybe Paul would eventually tire of her and move on to someone else. Surely the community wouldn't hold that against her.

"I'll be glad to see you get Paul." Ida sent a brave smile toward Debbie. "My heart will heal with time, and you'll get someone who is decent way down inside. I know it's a little hard to see sometimes, but Paul's a kind and compassionate man."

"You must stop saying things like this." Debbie kept her voice firm. "I don't love the man, and you do so we'll let the Lord work everything out."

Ida's smile went thin.

A sharp knock came on the door before Debbie could think of what else to say.

"Come in!" Ida called without hesitation.

Lois appeared in the doorway. "I thought I heard talking. Are we sharing secrets tonight?"

"None that you can't hear." Ida gave Lois a sweet look. "Come in and sit down."

Lois entered and closed the door behind her.

Debbie wasted no time. "How is this thing with Alvin affecting you?"

Lois gave Debbie a sharp look. "You mean with my wanting to go *Englisha*?"

"Just tell her the truth," Ida said.

"Maybe I don't want to," Lois snapped.

"Have you two been talking?" Debbie motioned between them.

Lois shook her head. "Ida knows me well enough to guess. And the fact that I didn't run my mouth tonight must have tipped her off. I'm seriously considering finding out where Alvin went. Maybe he would help me set up an apartment and find a job wherever he's working. I know his family can't farm worth a hoot, but I'd imagine even the Knepps can handle themselves in the *Englisha* world. Everything is easier out there."

Wild protests rose in Debbie's mind. The

world out there was anything but easy! Lois would find trouble she never even imagined existed. But Debbie bit her tongue. It didn't seem like the right thing to say at the moment. Lois wasn't in a mood to listen anyway.

Ida regarded her sister. "You know you're going to break *Mamm* and *Daett*'s hearts. Plus put a real black mark on *Daett*'s standing in the community, what with Alvin having just left."

Lois turned up her nose. "What can the community say worse than 'the bishop can't keep his own daughter in the faith'? *Daett* can survive that."

"Don't be so sure," Ida said.

Lois tossed her head. "That's always the story you and Verna give me. I'm tired of it. I'm twenty-two years of age, Ida. Time is passing me by! I don't want to live here in the community all my life, always wondering what's out there. I want to know, Ida. I want to taste the things of the world for myself. I don't want to believe what Debbie says they are. I want to see for myself. And Debbie survived that world, didn't she? So why shouldn't I be okay?"

Ida had turned pale in spite of her earlier warning that Lois had exactly these plans.

Debbie grasped for a solution. "Okay, if

I'm the one who's at fault that Alvin left, maybe I can be the one to win him back. I'll visit Alvin in Philadelphia and talk some sense into him."

Lois laughed. "Your *Englisha* ways aren't going to work this time, Debbie. *Daett* will blame you for sure if you go gallivanting to Philadelphia after Alvin."

Debbie stole a look at Ida's pale face before she answered. "It was just an idea. I admit I'm not quite sure what's acceptable."

Ida ignored the comments as she straightened from leaning against the wall. "I think we should all get some sleep now. Morning will be here before we know it."

Lois grunted as she glanced at the clock on Ida's dresser. It was long after midnight.

Ida had used the tried-and-true tactic the Beiler family turned to when arguments failed with Lois. They moved the discussion to other subjects, and things usually simmered down. This time that might not work. Debbie stole a quick look at Ida's face and saw she'd arrived at the same conclusion. Ida was grasping for straws tonight.

Lois had a forced smile on her face as she bid them *gut* night at the bedroom door.

Debbie lingered for a moment. Should she have one more quick word with Ida? Perhaps they could give each other a last word of comfort, what with all the weighty things they'd discussed tonight. But Lois stood outside in the hallway and showed no inclination to leave until Debbie came with her.

Debbie moved toward the doorway, whispering a *gut* night over her shoulder. She said *gut* night to Lois, crossed the hallway, and entered her own room. She shut the door, blew out the lamp flame, and walked to the window. The storm outside had increased in intensity. Snow was blowing everywhere, and the wind was howling under the eaves. Bishop Beiler's weather prediction at the supper table had been right. But his guess about the storm outside couldn't hold a candle to the storm Debbie was feeling inside.

FIVE

The following Monday Ida sat in front of the sewing machine, the gas lantern hissing above her. She ran the pressed edges of the soft, dark-blue dress material under the needle. She paused and glanced outside at the glowering skies. The heavy feel of the day reminded her of the heaviness the entire Beiler family was experiencing.

The snowstorm had raged for most of the weekend, and the roads were still drifted over. The community had barely been able to gather for church yesterday, though the buggies usually could go where *Englisha* vehicles couldn't in the snow.

Emery had plowed the lane for Debbie's car before he worked on his barn chores. When Debbie had seen Emery out that early on the tractor, she'd donned her boots and heavy coat before running outside to protest. But Emery had continued to clear the lane, so Debbie's pleas had fallen on deaf ears. After the *kafuffle* last Friday with Lois, Emery was probably trying to soothe their spirits with a little extra kindness this morning. Still, there was the reality that Lois's vow to leave for the *Englisha* world had cast a pall over the household.

After their talk Friday night, Debbie had appeared remarkably peaceful on Saturday morning. When she'd come in from doing the chores, Lois was the one who appeared disturbed. She'd remained downcast at the breakfast table, though she hadn't expressed further plans to leave the community. But something had definitely changed. Always in the past Lois would speak of her admiration of all things *Englisha* but would back down when *Daett* or *Mamm* reproved her. Now Alvin's departure for the *Englisha* world had made a difference. Ida feared Lois might well continue to draw strength from his example. She paused and listened to the sounds of Lois and *Mamm* working in the kitchen. Lois was perfectly capable of baking bread on her own, but *Mamm* must be feeling the same uneasiness. She felt a need to be with Lois. No wonder, really. Lois was walking around in silence for the most part, which usually meant she was thinking things she shouldn't be thinking.

Ida sighed and ran another edge of the

dress through the sewing machine. There was little she could do about Lois. *Daett* and *Mamm* would have to deal with her. Debbie was the one she was more concerned about. Lois had always been the way she was, and it made sense that things would eventually get worse. Debbie, on the other hand, had her heart set to join the community. It simply wasn't fair that her plans might be waylaid through no fault of her own. And the only solution she could see to this problem was for Debbie to accept Paul's attention. That would solve so many problems.

This would destroy her own chances to attract Paul's attention. Ida laughed at the thought. What were those chances in the first place? Next to zero, if she were honest. *Yah,* she'd allowed her hopes to soar at Verna's wedding when Paul had served as the best man. They had sat together during the ceremonies, and she'd stolen more glances at Paul than were decent. She hadn't been able to help herself. Oh, if Debbie only realized how thankful she should be that a man like Paul paid her attention. But what would have turned Ida all shades of red seemed to have no effect on Debbie. Maybe Debbie just needed encouragement in Paul's direction. If so, Ida knew she could supply that.

Paul was the perfect gentleman. She knew this because he'd been nothing but nice to her the whole day of Verna's wedding. Paul had made small talk with her at every opportunity. There had been no teasing comments about her constant blush, and Paul had to have noticed. He had, after all, sat only inches from her for most of the day. The man had tried his best to give her a *gut* day. It was as if he knew what she so desperately wanted. And though unable to give his love, Paul had given what he could — kindness for the day, compassion for her bumbling ways, and even a couple of smiles. He wasn't mean. Ida was sure of that.

Paul had wanted to give his *gut* friend Joe a *wunderbah* wedding day. So he had made the best of things — including sitting next to a girl he would never give a second notice to on any other day. *Yah,* for his kindness Paul was a man who deserved a sparkling girl like Debbie. And Debbie deserved a dashing boy like Paul. On her part, Ida would have to be sensible and move on with her life.

Ida finished one side of the dress and turned the cloth around. She held it up to the lantern for a better look at the thread line. The job was pretty *gut.* She might have gotten it a little straighter if more light came in the window, but this was okay. The dress would be ready to wear next Sunday, and she was happy with the outcome even if it was slightly flawed. Was that not the attitude one should have?

Ida started the clatter of the sewing machine again and thought about her future without Paul . . . possibly without a man at all. The answer lay in *Da Hah*'s hands, and in the end there was little one could do to change things. But a person could miss opportunities, that much was plain. And wasn't that exactly what Debbie was doing with Paul? Not that Debbie intended to miss any *gut* thing *Da Hah* gave her, but her life among the *Englisha* had for some reason blinded her to Paul's *gut* qualities. Ida thought long on that fact, and the sewing machine clatter died down. Then something interesting occurred to her. *Nee,* there would be no Paul Wagler in her life, but what about someone else? Was it possible *she* was missing an opportunity just as she was accusing Debbie of doing? But *who* would that be?

Her mind raced through several single men in the community, all of whom had never looked her way or whose way she'd never looked. But then hadn't Minister

Kanagy's brother, Melvin, cast a glance or two her way at some Sunday meetings? Those momentary glances had been sharp and possibly filled with intent, though she'd noted his gaze had only briefly lingered on her. The fact that the looks had come from the married men's bench might have been partly the reason she'd ignored them. But Melvin wasn't married. Well, he *had been* to that beautiful Kline girl from the other end of the community. They'd been married enough years to have six children before Mary passed away from a brain tumor a year or so ago.

Ida's thoughts paused on the idea of Melvin Kanagy. She didn't know that much about his situation. Someone from his family helped care for his young children, she thought. Maybe it was his younger sister, Lily, who went to his house on weekdays. Didn't Lily have plans to marry this fall? One never quite knew such things for sure, but Lily and her boyfriend, Mahlon, had dated for over three years now. The expectation of a fall wedding was reasonable enough. Could Melvin be thinking of marriage again? Could his glances have been . . . *Nee*, of course not! But then why not? He'd married a beautiful girl in Mary. Perhaps in a second marriage beauty might not be at the top of his list. Not with six children. A woman who would make a good *mamm* would surely be more fitting, wouldn't she?

Ida gasped. Her thoughts about Melvin shocked her. She . . . Melvin Kanagy's *frau*? She didn't even care for the man. He was handsome enough, unlike his nervous brother, Minister Kanagy. He looked better fed too, and his arms and shoulders were filled out. Ida clamped her hand over her mouth. These were not decent thoughts to have! Melvin had been another woman's husband and had borne six children with her. How could she ever think of Melvin as her own husband? Ida drew in her breath. Mary was gone, was she not? That freed up Melvin. And what if this was *Da Hah*'s will for her? What if she, like Debbie, was failing to see His will because of her own blindness? Ida felt her face heat up at the thought.

Suddenly the sewing room door behind Ida opened, and *Mamm*'s voice asked, "How's the dress coming, Ida?"

"Okay, I think." Ida's voice squeaked a little. "It's a little dark in here."

A chair scraped on the floor. *Mamm* sat down behind her, but Ida still didn't turn around.

"Has Lois been speaking with you?"

Mamm asked.

Ida breathed a sigh of relief. At least there would be no questions about the color of her face.

"What do you mean?" Ida snuck a quick look at *Mamm.* The concern written there caused her to turn all the way around and face her *mamm.*

"It's not that hard to imagine," *Mamm* said. "Since Friday evening has Lois said anything more to you about her dreams of joining the *Englisha*? Or of contacting Alvin Knepp in Philadelphia?"

Ida hung her head and didn't answer.

Mamm clutched her arm. "Oh, Ida, tell me it's not as bad as I fear!"

"Lois spoke quite a bit with Debbie and me," Ida said.

"So she's going to follow Alvin to Philadelphia? She is, isn't she?"

Ida reached over to squeeze *Mamm*'s hand. "We don't know that for sure."

"How can Lois do this?" *Mamm* didn't wait for an answer before she continued. "It must be that school Debbie went to that still draws Lois — all that higher learning, which only leads so many people downhill. That's what has Lois fascinated the most. We thought she'd forgotten all about it this past year, but it's all coming back now with

Alvin's leaving."

"Debbie's not to blame," Ida whispered. "You can't be thinking that, *Mamm.*"

Mamm moaned and held her head in her hands. "I don't know what to think anymore, Ida. My youngest daughter is about to make a horrible mess of her life. She's throwing away her heritage. She's counting as nothing the price our forefathers paid to give us simplicity and closeness to *Da Hah.* My heart is breaking."

"You can trust Debbie," Ida said.

Mamm stared out the window. The clouds outside seemed to press in on the room. Surely tonight it would storm again, just like the storm raging inside this house. Who would have thought this winter would be so disruptive? Usually the cold months passed peacefully and gave the soul much-needed rest after the rush of the summer. *Mamm*'s fingers dug into Ida's arm again. "I will speak with *Daett* tonight. Perhaps he can convince Lois before she does something foolish."

"I hope so." Ida tried to smile.

Mamm rose and opened the door. She left, shutting the door behind her.

Troubles began and ended in the heart of man, Ida knew. And only *Da Hah* could work some of those out to a satisfactory end. She breathed a quick prayer. "Please help us, dear *Hah.*" She turned back to her unfinished dress and worked the sewing machine's foot petal until the clatter of the machine filled the room. Staying busy would help push back the dark thoughts about Lois. And she couldn't do anything about Melvin Kanagy, even if, indeed, he planned to show interest in her. Warmth spread up her neck again. *Nee,* she mustn't think about Melvin! Yet the image of his piercing eyes wouldn't go away. Ida forced herself to focus on the line of thread in front of her. *Da Hah* would work things out . . .

SIX

On Tuesday evening, Alvin Knepp threw his duffle on the motel bed. He walked over to the window and stared out at the bustling Philadelphia street. Dirty snow lay along the street, and automobiles streamed past. Unfamiliar smells surrounded him. His head throbbed with a severity that almost blinded him. What had possessed him to flee the community? Alvin wondered for the hundredth time. He wanted to run away from his problems, there was no question about that. What a coward he was! And now he couldn't bring himself to return home.

The truth was he'd lived a sheltered life so far. Wasn't it about time he faced life on his own terms for a change? And why not in Philadelphia? Nasty as this big city seemed once he'd arrived, hadn't he wanted something he had never experienced before? Well, this was it. He sighed. *Yah,* his thoughts were logical and true, but that didn't ease the sick sensation in his stomach. Nor did it lessen his knowledge of his own faults. He'd made a horrible mistake and must now live with it. And at home on the farm, *Daett* would likely lose the place. Not because his son had left. *Nee,* the loss of the farm was going to happen anyway, and that had been the final straw in Alvin's decision to leave. That and the knowledge that his dream to be better than Paul Wagler was a hoot. How could he think he would ever be worthy of Debbie Watson's affections when Wagler was in the picture? Against Paul, Alvin believed he couldn't win her heart. *Nee,* he wasn't man enough. Not when Paul could charm the socks off of any girl he chose to lay his eyes on. How could Debbie not be affected? All the rest of the girls in the community were. She had to be! As *wunderbah* a woman as she was, Debbie couldn't be the only female who could stand up to Wagler's charms.

And once the community learned that the Knepp farm had gone under, Alvin could never live long enough to see his reputation restored. And Debbie, despite her assurance to him at Verna's wedding, wouldn't desire any further association with him. He'd wanted to tell her of the worsening financial condition at home, but the words had stuck in his mouth. He kept telling himself there still was hope. A portion of the corn crop had still been in the fields. They'd been late getting it in, as always, but that was expected. Their reputation as lousy farmers was well established in the community, so that shame didn't burn deep. What he hadn't expected was the early winter and the lighter yield on the lower 40 acres.

He'd told *Daett* what lay ahead, but *Daett* had claimed the samples of corn Alvin had brought in from the fields weren't representative of the truth. How could you open a few ears at random and get a true sample of the whole? And *Daett* didn't want any further investigation either. *Da Hah* would do what He wished, *Daett* said. They would bow their heads and accept the result.

So it had been for years when it came to *Daett* and his farming ways. Alvin had been the last of a long line of brothers, all of whom had never raised a complaint over how things were done on the home farm. There on the slopes east of the city of Lewistown, farming was the height to which any Amish man could aspire. Farming was in their blood, and land owners who didn't know how to farm were pitied and eventually scorned. Especially if they didn't profit from the help others offered. Advice in these valleys was eagerly sought after and usually followed. That was true for everyone except Alvin's *daett*. *Daett* had his ways, and that was it. Nothing would change his mind. Let the others talk of the latest farming techniques, such as when it was best to get in the crops, based on information someone gleaned from a talk with the old timers in the community. Knowledge that might point to a dry summer ahead or an extra cold winter. All this was mulled over and discussed in great detail after the Sunday meeting. Alvin listened but it was useless to try to apply anything he'd learned at home. *Daett* ignored the talk after the services or got in an occasional snort of derision. This year he'd sat on the lawn and chewed a grass stem while the others made plans to get their corn crops in early. At times the consensus had been so strong that Alvin had dared raise the issue the next day at the breakfast table.

Daett had laughed. "I won't listen to old wives tales, Alvin. It's the same thing whether the man at the *Englisha* tractor dealership says it or if Old Mose thinks his bones are aching. There's nothing to it. And we'll not stir ourselves to run around like chickens with our heads cut off over the spring planting. It will happen when it happens. *Da Hah* does all things in His own time, and man can do nothing about it."

And that had been the end of the subject — only it hadn't been the end. Their corn crop had gone in later than anyone else's, even though a little hustle would have put the seed in the ground before the week of vicious thunderstorms set the planting back by another two weeks. And the early winter had caught them with corn still in the fields, which gave a yield that fell far short of what they needed to break even. Now winter had set in, and there was no money for next year's planting. Nor was there money to pay the mortgage payments. *Daett* had continued to borrow small amounts — for years now. No complaints from Alvin had changed his *daett*'s ways. With the economy the way it was, the banker had informed *Daett* last summer that there would be no more loans given. They needed to pay down on the loan amount, not increase it.

Alvin paced the floor of the motel room. There was no reason to even have a mortgage on the place. It had been a point of contention between him and his *daett* for years. Most of the other farmers were out of debt, and the Knepps should have been too. Especially with a farm as well established as their place was. On that point *Daett* had hung his head, but he'd done nothing to bring the problem under control. It was as if he were incapable of anything different, and he was too stubborn to let his youngest son try. There had been nights Alvin had lain in bed and wondered if they could make it until *Daett* retired. He would then take over the farm and change things. But "retirement" wasn't a word in *Daett*'s vocabulary.

Beyond this there was Debbie. He was so unworthy of her. He'd told himself that a thousand times, but his feelings for Debbie wouldn't leave. To make things worse, she was such a *wunderbah* woman. Alvin figured he would never be satisfied with another woman, even one who was at his same station in life. Debbie deserved so much more than he could supply. With the farm on the brink, he was stuck with no place to go. The plan to bring his future wife home and have *Daett* and *Mamm* move into a *dawdy haus* was lost.

And what else could he do? He only knew how to farm. Without his own farm, he would be little more than a hired hand who worked on someone else's place. He'd get paid hired-hand wages, which weren't enough to support a family. In fact, these last six months he'd taken no pay. He hadn't needed it, he'd told himself, because he could never marry Debbie. And who would hire him with the Knepp reputation? Shame burned in his heart. He shouldn't have left Debbie like he had. The least he could have done was tell her goodbye. But he couldn't bring himself to speak the words, let alone face her. Even when his conscience throbbed, this decision had appeared to hurt less. Now he wasn't so sure.

Alvin stopped pacing. At least he hadn't stooped to asking *Daett* for money before he left. He would have a hard time surviving on the little money he'd saved since he'd turned twenty-one, but that was the way things were. He'd known the world out here wasn't anything like the farm at home. Things wouldn't be easy. But difficult or not, this was better than what would happen at home this spring. He didn't want to face that. *Daett* would no longer be able to hide the facts of the farm's failure when planting time came, and they couldn't afford to let the land lie dormant for a year.

Some Saturday afternoon, about the time the snow began to melt, *Daett* would make the trip to see Deacon Mast. The deacon would listen with bowed head. He would nod and express sympathy, but nasty repercussions would follow. A committee would be appointed, chosen by the harsh Minister Kanagy, if Alvin didn't miss his guess. *Daett* would lose control of his checking account. Changes would be demanded in his farming practices. Changes that Alvin had asked for many times and had been refused. *Daett* would nod and agree, but he would do what he always had done once the men drove out of the driveway — *nothing*! After a time the committee would catch on. They would send in a hired hand, but still there would be no change. The best hired hand in the world wouldn't be able to watch *Daett*'s every move or change what the years had solidified in his soul.

If Alvin had stayed, the blame would also descend on his shoulders. "Alvin should have known better." The whispers would make their rounds. "After all, isn't Alvin twenty-one and a man?" "You can't teach one of Edwin Knepp's boys anything," they would say. And there were his brothers to prove the point. All of them had left farming when they married. Wallace and William, the twins, had taken construction jobs with crews who specialized in pole barns. Amos had a small harness shop outside of Beaver Springs. The business didn't do that well, but it was better than Amos's farming skills. Alvin had been the only brother left to take the farm into the next generation.

If he hated farming, the matter might have been easier to bear, but Alvin didn't. He loved the work, the early morning rising before dawn, the dew fresh on the grass, the neigh of horses eager to work, the smell of freshly mown hay in the summertime. He even liked the howl of the winter wind outside the house and the knowledge that the animals were safe and secure in the barn.

His love for the farm was really why he left, Alvin told himself. He couldn't bear the pain of losing the place. It tore at his emotions. He couldn't bear to see so much drift away when it could have been prevented. And his attraction to Debbie had made things worse.

His first glimpses of her had been exactly that — brief sightings of her car at first. He hadn't known who was in the car that repeatedly drove slowly past the farm. He'd expected an older, local couple. Perhaps someone fascinated with Amish farms. The car came by too often to have been the usual drive-by tourists. Alvin knew what they thought, even though he seldom heard them from his perch on the rusty seats of his horse-drawn farm equipment.

"How quaint these people are!"

"It's like living in the seventeenth century."

"Such thrifty people!"

Alvin flopped on the bed and stared at the ceiling. Debbie's face had seemed like an angel's when he'd seen his first sight of her through the car window. She had apparently considered herself caught and had rolled down the window to wave. He'd waved back. She was an *Englisha* girl and more beautiful than he'd ever thought a woman's face could be. At first he'd told himself it was his imagination, that his backwards upbringing caused him to see what wasn't really there. He told himself that *Englisha* girls naturally appeared more attractive than their unadorned Amish neighbors.

But he wasn't able to convince himself. And then Debbie had continued to drive by. Apparently she felt comfortable with his acceptance of her presence. He'd tried to convince himself he would never see her again, that she was not from his world, that he must think about an Amish girl when it came to love. But she'd haunted his dreams at night, and some days she was all he could think of while he worked the fields. And with how Mildred Schrock had used him after they both joined the young folks — how she'd turned up her nose at him after their schooldays crush on each other — he had plenty of reason to consider a girl outside the community.

Alvin was at Bishop Beiler's farm one afternoon when Debbie walked out of the barn. He'd stayed in his buggy for fear his tongue would stammer and stutter. He'd dared ask Bishop Beiler who she was though — after Debbie had driven out of the lane and given him the usual brief wave and quick smile. Bishop Beiler hadn't seemed too curious about his questions, and strangely enough the bishop seemed to have friendly feelings toward the girl.

"She's Debbie, our neighbors' girl," the bishop had told him. "She's been coming over ever since she was a child. She's *gut* friends with my girls."

So there was more to Debbie's frequent trips past his place than touristy curiosity. Still, he knew he should never think of an *Englisha* girl with romantic notions. Then the unthinkable had happened. Debbie had moved into the Beiler household, and the whispers around the community were that she planned to join the faith. Her trips past his place had stopped about the same time.

Paul Wagler was soon enamored with the charming *Englisha* girl. This didn't surprise Alvin. He might have been able to get over

75

Debbie eventually if she hadn't asked him to wait on tables with her at Verna's wedding. There she'd taken it upon herself to assure him that she wasn't interested in Paul. After that talk he'd almost convinced himself that he could ask her home some Sunday evening after the hymn singing. In fact, he had promised Debbie he would do so soon.

But in the end he couldn't. Not with the farm situation. He loved Debbie too much to ask her to walk with him through that shame. There would be plenty in the community who were willing to remind Debbie how great this disgrace would be — Paul Wagler being the first in line. *Nee,* it was best if he found his own way in this world, far from the community and his unchangeable past.

SEVEN

The Friday-night Amish youth volleyball game in the barn was well underway. Paul Wagler dominated the front row at the moment, sending one spike ball after the other over the net, flashing triumphant looks toward Debbie in the spot next to him after each success.

He was good, Debbie admitted to herself. And he was handsome. Most girls here tonight — now that Alvin was gone — would look at Paul and her with new interest. Yet they would be wrong. Paul would make some girl a decent husband someday — just not her.

From the other side of the court, Ida sent a smile of encouragement. Ida was a dear, but she only made things worse by her not-so-veiled attempts to push Debbie straight into Paul's arms. What had come over the girl? Ida knew the depth of loss she'd experienced with Alvin's departure. Did Ida wish to sacrifice her own affections for the handsome Paul for another's perceived benefit? It seemed so. She'd whispered in Debbie's ear tonight, just before the game began, "I don't have a chance in the world to catch Paul, so don't you be holding yourself back now." Debbie had been horrified but her expression hadn't deterred Ida in the least. She'd just given her a sly smile in return.

Paul interrupted Debbie's thoughts with another triumphant look. The man was the limit tonight. He seemed emboldened by Alvin's absence and was moving in for the kill. Since Paul was one of the team captains, he'd not only chosen Debbie for his side but had placed her next to him in the play rotation. The man either had no shame or he considered her a gone goose and unable to resist his attentions. That idea raised her hackles.

He glanced over at her and said, "Thanks for agreeing to play beside me tonight."

She'd done nothing of the sort, so she gave him what she thought was a piercing look. But it only produced a hearty laugh from Paul as the ball sailed toward them again. At least he was a gentleman, Debbie noticed. He stepped back to give her a chance to play. But when the arch of the ball drew close, Paul shouted, "Set it up for me! Over this way!" *Self-serving man,* Debbie thought, but she still bounced the ball toward him in a high arch. Paul leaped into the air and pounded the ball into the barn floor on the other side of the net with seemingly effortless ease.

"Good one, Paul!" someone called out over the groans heard from the other side of the net.

Paul pranced about for a moment enjoying his success but saying nothing about her part in the score. Now he looked at her expectantly, obviously wanting her to comment on his prowess.

"Not bad," she said, avoiding his gaze.

"Come on, you can do better than that, can't you?" He stepped closer and tilted his ear toward her.

"You're a great volleyball player!" she hollered.

A satisfied look spread over his face. "That's much better."

Moments later Paul got another spike in. Mary Yoder, who played across the net from them, scrambled out of the way rather than attempt to block the ball. She blushed red as Paul teased, "I didn't mean to endanger your life."

Mary replied, "I only had to duck a little.

I was ready for that anyway. You know, playing across from you I've learned."

"I'll be more careful next time," Paul said with the same kind of wide grin he'd been sending Debbie's way. Mary blushed at the attention, and Debbie looked around for Ezra, Mary's boyfriend. But it didn't really matter, she realized. Paul's effect on girls was well-known. No doubt Ezra would take it in stride. Most Amish boys seemed practical about such things. Obviously Alvin didn't fit that mold. He'd left the community with a broken heart over her. At least that's what was being said. What other reason could he have had? None. Which didn't speak well of Alvin's courage. On the other hand, how could she blame him in the face of Paul's overwhelming charisma and manipulation?

Debbie tried to push thoughts of Alvin away, but his absence hung over the gathering tonight. Thoughts of him wouldn't go away no matter how hard she tried to ignore them. Thankfully no one else had mentioned anything so far. If they did, Debbie didn't know how she would respond. A thought raced through her mind and stung as it went by. Perhaps the young people shared Bishop Beiler's suspicions that she was to blame for Alvin's actions?

Debbie held still for a moment, the game continuing around her. Paul sent his charms her direction again, but she ignored him as she processed her emotions. Surely no one would think she should also leave or that she'd join Alvin in the *Englisha* world? Didn't they know that neither Alvin nor she would be happy out there? She wouldn't. And she was sure Alvin was a man firmly rooted in the community, regardless of his current action. Wasn't the Knepp family among the most faithful church members around? Bishop Beiler had told her so himself. Somewhere there was a problem with Alvin that no one else knew or had addressed yet.

"Hel–lo!" Paul shouted near her ear. "Wake up, Debbie. The ball might come your way. This is our last round in the front line for a while, and I need spikes set up for me."

Debbie stared at him blankly, but when the ball came her way moments later, she set it up perfectly for Paul. While Paul celebrated his successful spike, Debbie's thoughts drifted back to Alvin. Could she have done more to assure him of her affections? She couldn't see how. Things were done differently here. A girl could be considered too aggressive. And she had done her part. She'd tried to get across to Alvin at Verna's wedding that Paul meant nothing to her. Yet look at her tonight. She was playing beside Paul in the front row. Did Alvin perhaps know more about her than she did? Come to think of it, she hadn't protested Paul's maneuvers out loud. A protest would have caused a scene, and one didn't do that with Paul. Maybe that's what Alvin had seen — the inevitability of Paul. Perhaps Paul's persona had acquired a life of its own in Alvin's mind and driven him to hopelessness.

Debbie stole a glance at Paul's handsome face. He could be more persistent than men like Doug had been. She liked it in a way — this inability to bend a man's mind once he had it made up. That response came from deep inside of her, unbidden and without her permission. It seemed like a primordial instinct that lingered from an era when a woman chose the strongest man in the clan and wed him out of necessity, not love.

Paul's voice cut through her thoughts again. "Your turn to serve, beautiful. Get on back to your place."

His tone commanded and condescended at the same time.

"I'm going!" she snapped.

Paul laughed.

The man infuriated her! But she dutifully took her place behind the serving line. She mustn't let him get to her. Her whack at the ball sent it on a crash course to the outer barn wall, well out of bounds.

"Hey, don't do that!" Paul scolded.

Debbie ignored him. If he hadn't distracted her, she wouldn't have made such a bad play. Volleyball might not be her best game, but she was reasonably proficient.

Paul cheered up when the following serve by the opposing team landed in the net. The serve changed again, and the ball was now in Paul's hands. With a confident whap, he sent the ball over the net in a high arch. It landed just inside the boundary line without a hand touching it. He gave Debbie a sharp look as if to say, "Now that's how it's done."

"I know that!" Debbie wanted to shout at him, but she didn't. What Paul thought of her didn't matter in the least. She watched as he served again and gained two more points. He lost the next serve when their teammate Betty Miller hit the ball out of bounds.

While they waited for the serve from the opposing team, Paul turned his attention back to Debbie. "I heard your little boy left the community."

She gave him a fierce glare.

He laughed. "Don't blame me. I had nothing to do with it."

"Yes, you did!" she wanted to snap back, but she kept her mouth shut.

He leaned over to whisper, "I suppose your date card — or whatever you *Englisha* call it — will be open now."

"And I suppose you're wanting to fill it?" This time the words didn't stay inside.

"I see my eligibility has not escaped your esteemed notice." His smile was triumphant.

"You don't have to talk so high-brow," she whispered back.

Paul's smile widened. "Just letting you know I'm both available and suitable for a fine lady educated in the ways of the world — not like someone else we both know."

"The ways of the world? So you're also thinking of leaving?" Debbie shot back. She wished at once she hadn't. Paul had her more rattled than she'd thought possible.

Paul assumed an injured look. "You wound me to the heart, Debbie. I'm as solid as a rock. You need to get your evaluation sheet in better order."

Debbie forced herself to laugh. "I think it's in perfect order, thank you."

Paul raised his eyebrows. "Then why is a certain someone wandering off in no man's land? What happened to your evaluation sheet on Alvin Knepp?"

When Debbie didn't answer, Paul kept going.

"You know, we Amish never settle down out there. Men who leave the community are doomed to roam the earth, forever neither this nor that. And then there's the church's highest displeasure of course, and she can be most severe. I'm expecting Bishop Beiler to have the boy placed in the *bann* before too many Sundays are past."

Debbie tried to keep the spin out of her head. Excommunication was something no one at the Beiler household had said anything about, but then they might have been careful not to say anything in front of her. Alvin was a church member, so of course the *bann* was on the agenda.

As if he read her mind, Paul smirked. "The inept boy was a church member, you know."

"And he was a man!" she almost yelled, but she caught herself in time. Paul was trying to get under her skin on purpose, and he was doing a pretty good job of it. It was time she took control of the situation.

"I liked *that* boy," she responded.

The words came out a little louder than she intended, and Betty Miller in the next row glanced back at her, a displeased expression on her face.

Paul shrugged as if he was puzzled. "I'm sorry I'm not more likable." He turned his charms on Cindy, who had also glanced back. She grinned at him and turned around again.

Paul had gone for a haggard and contrite look, and it was working with Cindy. But that wouldn't work on herself. Of that, she was sure. Still, Paul wasn't deterred because he turned his attention back to her. "It seems to be the bane of my life that the one girl I admire the most gives me nothing but the cold shoulder."

"Maybe you should try a different approach," she told him.

Paul perked up. "I'm open to instruction, you know. And what better teacher for a poor Amish boy than a woman educated in all the wonders of the world?"

"You talk too much," Debbie said, unable to stop herself.

Paul looked pleased. "See, you're doing a *gut* job already. We'll have to do more of this — later."

The ball sailed toward them in the back line before Debbie could retort. Paul had stepped away and given her the floor even though he could have easily returned the ball.

His charms aren't going to affect me! Debbie told herself as she set the ball up for a front row spiker. The boy spiked it — not as cleanly as Paul would have done it, but good enough to score the point.

"Nice set up," Paul complimented Debbie.

Debbie sighed. She'd been through this before with men. Doug was supposed to be the last man who did this to her — give shallow compliments, be manipulative, and demand compliments. This was what had helped her decide to move into the Amish community. She'd been tired of the foolishness, and now she was right back in it again. "Thank you," she said without looking at Paul. She could see his face glowing in her side vision. Clearly he would have to find out the hard way that his advances were useless. Someday that would soak into his thick head. And the day couldn't come soon enough for her.

EIGHT

The following Monday night Debbie sat on the couch in the Beiler living room with a hamper of clean clothing beside her. The only sounds in the house were the ones Lois and Saloma were making in the kitchen. Debbie folded the clothes as her mind drifted back to the game Friday night. Paul was probably still gloating over his supposed advances in his plans to conquer her heart. Oh, if he only knew the truth. She took a deep breath. She shouldn't think about Paul right now. There were other things more important. For one, the house was in a bustle tonight. She'd come home from her job to find the basement full of drying wash.

"We kept the wash on the outside line until twelve or so," Ida told her. "Then it became obvious the sun had done all it could. When the wind picked up, *Mamm* helped me transfer everything into the basement."

Then the two women had fired up the small woodstove they used for such occasions. Wash in the basement was a winter's inconvenience that all Amish women faced. The Beiler women had taken the extra work in stride without a grumble or complaint. Debbie had joined in, helping fold most of the clothing once it had dried while Ida helped with the chores in the barn. Lois and Saloma had begun supper preparations soon after Debbie had arrived home.

Debbie's efforts seemed like a small contribution when she considered the amount of work the Beiler women did to keep the place running. It made her hours at work at Destiny Relocation Services, where she answered phones and managed the moving crews, seem insignificant. Maybe she should quit her job and stay "home" full-time now that Verna was married. The problem was that Saloma and Ida had already made the necessary adjustments. Between the two of them and Lois, the workload was usually covered. The extra strain only showed on cold, winter days when the wash wouldn't dry in the usual time. But that was the weather's fault. On normal days, Ida and Saloma could handle things at home fine without her.

Debbie folded the last of Emery's denim

pants and pressed out the crease the best she could. "Such things aren't necessary," Verna had told Debbie. "Our men don't need creases in their work pants." Verna had laughed at the very idea. But this was one of the few instincts from her past that still stayed with her. If — and that was a big if — she ever married an Amish man, she would always be tempted to take the time to iron his work pants. But she wouldn't. She didn't want her husband to stand out from the other men. That was a matter of great importance in the community. No man should lift himself above the others in word, deed, or clothing.

Debbie let her mind wander. She thought about life as a married Amish woman. There would be lots of children, she was sure of that. Once they began to arrive and with all the work in the house, there would be no time for such frivolities like ironing work pants. Debbie pulled her thoughts up short and felt her face burn. She rarely indulged in such intimate dreams. And with Alvin gone, there was even less reason to do so. For a moment she felt like crying about her lot.

It must be the winter weather, Debbie decided. Another storm was ready to howl outside tonight. Perhaps she was in denial about Alvin and just couldn't accept that the winter of her soul had arrived. Instead, she wished for spring. She found pleasure in thoughts of marriage and sweet babies. She couldn't let go of the hope of spring when the soil and the soul would bring life forth again.

A shiver ran down Debbie's back. She really was in denial. She should run from her fears like Alvin had. And she had a ready excuse. She was at great risk right now. She could easily lose her welcome at the Beiler home plus any hope of someday joining the community.

While living across the road from the Beilers for most of her life, Debbie had longed for their quiet life. Even in the moments when she forgot the desire, it had been there, ready to exert itself for the smallest of reasons. The sound of distant horse hooves beating on pavement, the clang of horse-drawn machinery in the fields, or the smell of freshly mown hay drifting into her open bedroom window was enough to turn her thoughts toward Amish life. Then there was Alvin. Alvin was the crown that could have held it all together. But now, even with him gone, the pieces were still there like they always had been. She must readjust. But how? That was the question. Should she pursue Alvin in Philadelphia? Amish women didn't do that. And that course of action seemed foolish and impossible at the same time. He wouldn't listen to her anyway. Perhaps she should weather this storm in her soul. Hunker down and wait and not draw attention to herself.

That was the best route, Debbie decided as she folded one of her dresses. She looked and acted like an Amish woman in many ways now. Verna and Ida had assured her of that many times, so it must be so. Ida might be inclined to indulge in a biased point of view, but Verna would have told her the truth. Verna was practical in that way. Ida let her kind heart get in the way of total honesty sometimes.

Right now Ida was clearly on a mission. She wanted to help quiet down the community's whisperings over Alvin's departure and eliminate the resistance Debbie had to Paul's attentions. Ida meant to solve the first with the second, and she gave up her own hope for Paul in the process. Debbie sighed. No doubt Ida found a certain satisfaction in her self-sacrifice, but her soft heart was the real reason behind Ida's actions. And for that Debbie couldn't slight Ida in the least. But the girl's efforts were wasted when it came to Debbie's affections toward Paul.

"Look how he likes you!" Ida had said on the way home Friday night. "I haven't seen Paul so impressed with a girl in a long time."

Debbie wondered how she could make Ida understand that this placed her right back where she'd been in her college days. She'd dated several boys, Doug being the last one. All of them were of the same type. They dashed about with outgoing personalities and plenty of charm. Debbie knew a part of her was drawn to that. When she moved in with the Beilers, she'd thought she was rid of that tendency. Now it was back and perhaps even made worse by Paul. He made Doug and the others look like amateurs in the "smooth" department, which said a lot.

There was no way Debbie would settle for Paul. She hadn't left her own world to fall further into her relationship weakness. What she wanted was a man with depth and mystery. Alvin might think he'd lost her with his sudden departure from the community, but the truth was that it made Debbie more attracted to him. If Alvin was able to strike off on his own and succeed, that said more about him than he probably realized. The man had a mystique about him that she liked.

Debbie studied one of Lois's dresses she'd pulled from the clean clothes hamper. She draped it over the back of the couch. What Alvin's real problem was right now, she couldn't imagine, but it had to be something besides her presence and the issue with Paul. No, there had to be more. But what? All she knew was what she'd gleaned from community speculation. She'd overheard conversations among the women and girls at the Sunday services. No one made any effort to hide them from her. None of the buzz about Alvin had deterred her heart.

"Alvin comes from such a solid family," someone said. "How could he leave like this?"

"His *daett* and *mamm* must be devastated . . . their last son, and now he's gone."

"Alvin never was much for *rumspringa*. Maybe that's the problem," Minister Kanagy's wife, Barbara, had opined.

"I say that's a warning for us all," said Lavina, the woman Barbara was speaking to. "Thinking one is so holy that the world has no attraction is a great pride."

"*Yah,* we must all test our faith," another added. "But it's best done as the forefathers did this, not by how these spiritual giants amongst us think best."

"Such pride is an awful thing."

The older women had nodded, as if that supplied the answer. But Debbie wasn't convinced. She couldn't imagine that a man would leave so much that he loved because he was afraid of her rejection. Doug never would have, and Paul certainly never would. Alvin was different, but still . . .

In the meantime, Ida's efforts would bear little fruit, as would Paul's confident advances. His boldness Friday night had continued on Sunday because Ida had volunteered Debbie to help serve the unmarried men's table. When she'd dropped off the peanut butter bowls, Paul had taken the opportunity to tease her.

"Is this a special *Englisha* mix?" he asked with a straight face.

"You haven't even tasted it yet," she said, unable to hold her tongue. "It might not be any good."

"Oh, it'll be good. I was waiting for special service from your hand!" Paul quipped, garnering low chuckles from the others at the table.

"Maybe she wanted to serve us first," a boy ventured. "She looked like she was headed in *my* direction."

"That's when my handsome looks distracted the poor girl," Paul said. Louder laughter followed this time.

"I'm going to put this peanut butter bowl right on top of your head pretty soon,"

Debbie retorted.

"Now wouldn't that be a sight!" one of the men hollered from the end of the table. "I'd like to see that."

"Debbie wouldn't harm a flea, let alone plop peanut butter over my head." Paul gave her a sweet smile. "She's just trying to demonstrate how much she cares about me."

"Woo hoo!" the man who sat beside Paul hooted. "We've got live courting going on right before our eyes. Are you showing us how it's done, Paul?"

Ida pulled on Debbie's arm, apparently satisfied with her work at the moment. "Come, we have to get more food from upstairs."

"She looks like she's fleeing!" a man's voice proclaimed as Debbie followed Ida up the stairs.

Ida gave Debbie a quick look when they walked into the kitchen. She whispered, "He cares a lot for you, Debbie. And you're doing very *gut* yourself."

Debbie kept her mouth shut, which only encouraged Ida to whisper, "It's not useless, Debbie. He'll be asking you home soon. Don't give up so easily."

What a confused mess! Debbie tried to straighten out Ida's thoughts on the way home. "Ida, *I don't like Paul.* He's not my type. Paul's like the boys I used to date out in my world, and that's one reason I came to the Amish community."

Ida hadn't appeared convinced in the least.

At the hymn singing that evening, Debbie tried a different tactic. She took a seat among the second row of girls. Her usual place was on the front row, but she hung back and kept herself busy in the kitchen with the last few dishes on the counter. By the time those were put away — at a slow rate of speed — the first bench was full of girls. She slipped into a back row and stayed out of sight of Paul's searching gaze. When he finally found her, she shifted a bit and used Minister Kanagy's eldest daughter, Wilma, as a shield for the rest of the evening.

As she'd suspected, this only made things worse. Paul made a beeline for the outside door right after the hymn singing. She figured his plan was to wait for her near the washroom door. What he intended to say, she didn't have any question about either. Probably a proposition that she allow him to take her home the next Sunday evening . . . or perhaps even that very night. An invitation she had no intention of accepting. But she didn't want word leaked out that she'd turned down the handsome Paul Wagler either. Not right now when her position in the community hung by a thread. She slipped out the front door and walked clear around the house to avoid him.

The last piece of laundry folded, Debbie let out a sigh. She had to ride out this storm. The weather would clear as it always did. Spring would come . . . eventually. She stood and walked over to the front window for a peek toward the barn. The windows there glowed with soft warmth from the gasoline lanterns. Likely Ida would appear in the barn door soon with one of the lanterns in her hand. She didn't have to worry about whether she could stay in the community. Ida was born Amish. In a way, none of this situation was fair, and yet Debbie had to trust that God knew all things. In the end this would turn out like it was supposed to.

Debbie tucked her loose hair under her *kapp.* She turned to walk into the kitchen where Saloma and Lois were placing the last of the supper dishes on the table.

"Finished with the wash?" Saloma asked, looking up with a pleased expression. "You've been such a help today, Debbie. *Danke.*"

"I'm the one who should thank you," Debbie said as she busied herself with work in the kitchen. She wondered how long she'd have to endure the present situation before God revealed His will.

NINE

Debbie stood at the kitchen sink over an hour later as Lois dried the dishes beside her. The soap suds came up to Debbie's elbow, creating a chill on her forearms where the cool air from the window reached in. The kitchen stove still gave off a warm glow from the cooking Saloma and Lois had done as they prepared supper. To Debbie, her cold arms and warm back reminded her of the conflicting emotions that swirled inside her. On the one side there was the comforting presence of the Beiler household she'd become so used to. On the other hand, there was the trouble that had blown in with Alvin's departure.

Winter weather never won out, Debbie decided, comforting herself with the thought. Spring always came regardless of how cold the storm blew. Would not this trouble with Alvin end in the same way? How that would be, she had no idea, but there had at least been a little good news tonight . . . even if she had to imagine it.

Bishop Beiler had told them at the supper table, "Deacon Mast stopped by to tell me that Alvin has let his parents know that he's safe in Philadelphia."

"The deacon made a special trip for that?" Saloma was surprised.

"Deacon Mast knew I was concerned," the bishop replied, but he fell silent after that.

From the look on Saloma's face, Debbie could tell there was more to it. Maybe what church discipline was on tap for Alvin. Perhaps that was part of the reason for the deacon's visit too. Deacon Mast probably consulted with the bishop on what his first contact with Alvin ought to consist of now that Alvin's whereabouts were known. Excommunication was likely not far away, even though such a public rebuke wouldn't reflect well on Bishop Beiler's leadership. If he lost a member to the *Englisha* world in such a fashion, it wouldn't be an easy matter for him to resolve. She could tell from the looks on all their faces that the situation was serious. Even Henry Yoder's excommunication last year hadn't produced such troubled expressions around the supper table.

Lois wiped the dishes beside her with quick motions, apparently lost in her own thoughts.

Debbie gave her a little smile. "Sorry. I haven't been meaning to ignore you. I was just thinking about Alvin's leaving."

Lois nodded. "I understand. It's a troubling thing for the community. And for you. But perhaps he'll come back."

"Thanks," Debbie whispered. She doubted Lois really had much hope in Alvin's return, but the sentiment did count. And what concern in her own life was Lois thinking about right now? She had a faraway look in her eyes. Should she ask?

While Debbie pondered the question, Saloma came in from the living room and cleared her throat. "Are you girls about done? *Daett* wants to have the prayer and Scripture reading soon. He's retiring early tonight."

"We'll rush," Debbie said. Saloma withdrew, and Debbie decided the bishop was even more troubled than she'd imagined. He seldom retired well before nine o'clock. But then perhaps the winter weather was getting to him. She ought to stop her thoughts about things and retire herself for a long winter's sleep. Things might look different once spring weather arrived. And if she thought about spring long enough, she could almost imagine the first of its warmth. The warm breezes would melt the drifts of snow along the road. The horses would run in the barnyard with full vigor. This renewal might also happen for Alvin and herself. She just had to keep her faith in the Lord's guiding hand. He'd brought her this far. He wouldn't fail her now.

Lois interrupted her thoughts. "I should tell you something. Debbie. You won't like it though."

Debbie glanced at Lois, who had her gaze glued on the plate she'd just dried. Lois looked downright guilty.

Lois continued. "I was over to speak with your *mamm* and *daett* on Sunday afternoon." Lois let the words hang.

"Yes?" Debbie remembered Lois had gone for a walk after they came home from the church services. She'd thought at the time it was a little strange. Lois usually stayed around the house on Sunday afternoons. But with the trouble in the community about Alvin, and Debbie's own worries of the evening ahead when she'd have to face Paul, she hadn't thought more about it.

When Lois walked down the drive, Debbie and Ida had both given a little shrug as they watched from the upstairs window. The bishop and Saloma had been taking their afternoon naps at the time, asleep in their rockers. They probably hadn't noticed anything unusual.

"Well, it's like this, Debbie. I'm moving in with your parents for a while."

Debbie jerked her head toward Lois. "You're doing *what*?" she almost shouted.

"I spoke with your *mamm* at length," Lois said, her voice low. "They're giving me a place to stay for the time being. Until I get my feet on the ground and find a job. In fact . . ." And here Lois's face lit up. "In fact, your *mamm* said she would help me find work and give me help with all the things I'll need out there — a driver's license, some schooling. Your parents are very *wunderbah* people, Debbie."

Debbie tried to speak, but nothing came out.

"I'm moving this weekend," Lois continued. Her face took on a glow as she spoke. "This is what I've always dreamed of, Debbie. And now I'm going to get a chance to live it. Even though I hope for your sake that Alvin comes back, I'm still so thankful to him. His leaving gave me the courage to finally make the plunge. And you gave me the way it could be done. For so long I've wondered how I'd ever get going out there in that *wunderbah* world, sheltered as I've always been. Then I saw the way open up for me by your coming here, Debbie. It was like seeing the path through the Red Sea that the children of Israel traveled on when the Egyptians pursued them."

"Lois!" Debbie almost shouted. "You're not thinking straight! What I did *is not* what you're doing."

Lois looked over her shoulder. "That's what you say, but your *mamm* had a totally different take on it. I could see her eyes shining when I told her what my plans were. She thinks what I think, Debbie. And I know we're right. It is the same as what you did. You walked away from your world, so why can't I do the same?"

"That world is not what you think it is!" Debbie knew the attempt was doomed to failure before she even said the words. Lois had finally gone over the edge, and she had provided the way out. Well Alvin and she had. Now Bishop Beiler would not only mourn the loss of his daughter, he would also surely hold her accountable. Oh, how quickly things changed!

"You don't have to look so downcast." Lois sounded almost chirpy. "I say it's a fair trade, really. And your *mamm* seems to think the same thing. You're becoming

Amish, and I'm going *Englisha.* Everyone's happy."

Debbie said nothing, but she could imagine how the conversation with her mother had gone. No doubt Mom would look at things exactly how Lois described them, though her mother had always disapproved more than mourned her decision to move into the Beiler household. If her mother's pain came from anywhere, it came from the rejection of her way of life. She'd always dreamed her daughter would follow her into the world of business. Lois would fill that dream in a belated sort of way. Mom was practical, Debbie thought. She'd think better late than never. And Lois had swerved into the one person who would be the most helpful on her venture into the outside world.

"It's actually going to happen!" Lois sounded ever more cheerful.

"Have you told your dad and mom?" Debbie asked.

A cloud passed over Lois's face. "*Nee,* but I'm moving anyway."

Debbie sensed Lois's hesitancy. "You'd better tell them before you go," she said, pressing her advantage. Perhaps there was still a way to persuade Lois to change her mind before she told her parents her plans.

But Debbie knew that even if she succeeded and Lois was temporarily persuaded, the way was open now. As the Amish often said, "Get a cow's head through the fence, and she'll find a way out sooner or later." It was why they worked so hard at prevention. They strove to keep even an inkling of desire for the *Englisha* world from a person's heart, rather than depend on persuasion once a person had decided to leave or had actually left. Debbie washed the last bowl and tried one more time. "Lois, please don't do this. You're making a huge mistake."

Lois said nothing, but her face was pinched with resolution.

The dishes finished, both girls silently went into the living room.

"There you two are!" Saloma said, looking up with a smile on her face.

Debbie sat on the couch, and Lois took a seat beside her.

Saloma stood and called up the stairs, "We're ready, Ida!"

Quick steps followed Saloma's words, and Ida appeared in the doorway. She rushed over to sit down. The bishop cleared his throat and opened his Bible.

Debbie stole a quick glance at Lois's face, but it appeared calm. That was good. Lois would say nothing tonight about her plans.

Of that, Debbie was certain.

Bishop Beiler read from Psalm 31 in his deep voice. "In thee, O Lord, do I put my trust; let me never be ashamed: deliver me in thy righteousness. Bow down thine ear to me."

The scripture verses couldn't be better selected for tonight, Debbie thought. The Lord Himself was talking to her through His Word. She prayed silently as Bishop Beiler continued to read. "Please, Lord, help me. Don't let me harm these people. I know I'm not perfect and I don't always do what is right, but I really did come to the Beiler home with pure motives. Now it seems as if everything is turning around, and I won't be able to justify what's happening. It does look like everything is my fault. First Alvin leaving, and now if Lois really moves in with my parents, there will be no explaining that away. I may have to leave. I don't want that to happen. I thought I was following Your will by moving into this community. Dear Lord, be my fortress and strong tower right now. And be with Alvin wherever he is in Philadelphia. Comfort his heart and show him that I do love him. Lead him back home again. And talk to Lois. Help her see the sorrow she's about to bring to her parents' hearts. Show her how unwise this choice really is."

Bishop Beiler finished the Scripture reading and closed his Bible. "Let's pray," he said. He knelt beside his rocker without further words. He lifted his head toward the heavens and spoke. "Now unto you, O Lord, all merciful and compassionate Father. Look down upon us tonight and remember us, your frail and broken creation. Of all the things Your hands have made, we are the ones who bring You the most grief and sorrow. We ask that You forgive us our sins and remember our iniquities no more, just as we likewise do for those who trespass against us."

Lois sobbed, and her *daett* paused. When no more sounds followed, he continued, "Remember our community tonight, O Lord, and the trouble we have amongst us . . ."

Debbie listened to Bishop Beiler's voice. This was what she wanted for herself someday. A home of her own with a man who had spiritual depth and strength. If she needed any confirmation as to who that man could be, she received it this very moment. She couldn't imagine Paul Wagler, the jokester, at prayer like this. Perhaps he would learn to do so in time, as all Amish men she'd met seemed to eventually, but she didn't want to take the chance. Alvin praying like this? That didn't take much imagination at all. Even though she'd never heard him pray out loud, she was certain he prayed from his heart. "Lord, please don't take this away from me," Debbie pled quietly.

TEN

Later that week, on Saturday morning, the breakfast dishes had been cleared away and the house was quiet. The winter weather had cleared, and sunshine made the snow glisten through the kitchen window. In Debbie's mind it was the calm before the storm — at least inside the house.

"Next week the *gut* weather will hold," Bishop Beiler had declared at the breakfast table. "There might even be a warm spell coming our way."

"Winter's far from over though," Saloma reminded him, as if one needed such a qualifier with the deep drifts that still lay along the road.

To Debbie, Saloma's words had double meaning that spelled trouble for her.

Lois had remained silent all week about her plans to move out, which was unlike her. She usually readily spoke up when she had something to say or big plans.

Debbie hoped Lois had changed her mind.

As if Lois knew what Debbie was thinking, she appeared in the kitchen doorway. "Debbie, may I speak with you in private? Outside?"

Saloma gave them both a worried look as Debbie followed Lois through the washroom door and outside.

"What are you doing?" Debbie asked once they were out of earshot.

"I need you to tell *Mamm* and *Daett* what's going to happen today."

"Today?" Debbie asked. "You're doing this today? And without having informed your mom and dad?"

"I'm not going to wait any longer, Debbie. I've lived this life for twenty-two years. I'm absolutely suffocating. The longer I put it off, the worse it will be. Today is the day."

"Well, don't count on me to tell your parents." Debbie allowed disappointment to sound in her voice. "I was hoping you'd forgotten about your harebrained idea."

"My suitcase is packed and under my bed," Lois said, her voice firm. "That's all I need. I'll be getting new clothes anyway."

The girl had thought things through, which explained her silence all week. What Debbie had feared was actually going to happen . . . and today. But Lois would have to tell her parents her news. Debbie knew she'd get enough blame for this without being the one to announce it to the Beiler family.

"Then I'll tell them myself," Lois said, obviously understanding Debbie's attitude. She took a deep breath. "Will you at least come with me?"

If she stood by her side while Lois broke the news to her parents, Debbie knew that would look like she was supportive of this move. And she wasn't. But it felt mean and cruel not to. Lois waited with an expectant look on her face. "Are you coming, Debbie?"

With a silent groan, Debbie nodded. Somehow she'd have to make it plain to the Beilers that she had no hand in this matter.

Lois pushed open the washroom door, and announced their return with a shrill, "I need to speak with all of you."

Saloma looked up with shock on her face at Lois's tone.

Ida reached over and squeezed Debbie's hand.

Thank you! Debbie almost whispered, but she didn't. At least she had one ally, and Ida didn't even know what Lois was going to say. Surely they all expected it though. Well, except Emery perhaps. And he wasn't inside, having gone back out to the barn after breakfast.

Bishop Beiler had stayed at the kitchen table for a few moments to read the latest copy of the weekly *Budget.* He glanced up. "Is something wrong?"

"Apparently Lois has something to say," Saloma offered.

Lois remained silent.

Perhaps there was yet hope, Debbie thought, since this was always the place Lois backed down in the past — when she had to face her parents. But seeing the determined look on her friend's face, Debbie knew the words would find their way out.

"You have something on your mind?" Bishop Beiler regarded Lois.

Lois glanced at the floor, and the words came in a great rush. "I'm leaving home today, and there's nothing anyone can do to change my mind, and it wasn't your fault, or anyone else's fault. And no one encouraged me in any way, including Debbie." Lois took in a huge breath of air.

Saloma collapsed on a chair, ashen.

"You're leaving?" Bishop Beiler slowly rose to his feet. "Where are you going?"

Lois didn't look at any of them. "I'm going down to Debbie's parents' place. Her *mamm* said I could stay in Debbie's old room. She said she'd help me get a new start in life. And I don't want any complaints about it either. You took Debbie in, so how is that different from them taking me in?"

The arrow went deep. Debbie could see that from the look on Lois's dad's face.

"But, Lois," he protested, "Debbie didn't go running out into the world. She was seeking *Da Hah*'s will for her life. She was leaving the world behind."

"And I'm doing the same thing in reverse," Lois shot back. "You know how long I've yearned for what *Da Hah* has for me other than living in this house. You've all been *gut* to me, *yah,* but I've always felt there is more for me than what lies in the community, *Daett.* Can't you see that? Out there in the *Englisha* world there's learning from books, and from people, and from experience. I don't want to miss out on all that. And if I don't take the door *Da Hah* has opened up for me, I'll never get out of here."

Saloma sobbed quietly.

Bishop Beiler glanced briefly at his wife before he turned his attention back to Lois. "You're my daughter, Lois. My youngest, and we love you dearly. How can we lose you like this . . . to the *Englisha?*"

"It's no more the world than this is the world." Lois waved her hand around to include the house and farm. "It's all the same world, *Daett.* You just call it something else, and make things harder. Perhaps we do that so we can feel like we're suffering for the faith. Well, it's not for me."

"Did you have anything to do with this, Debbie?" Bishop Beiler's eyes were piercing as he stared at her.

Debbie clutched the kitchen doorway frame, but Lois spoke before she could answer.

"Debbie's the reason I stayed this past year, *Daett.* And she tried hard to talk me out of this. Don't blame her."

"But her *mamm* and *daett* are taking you in," the bishop said. "How can that be?"

"Last Sunday I walked over to visit her *mamm.* That's when I told her what I wanted to do, and she agreed to help. Debbie didn't know anything about it until I told her later. Don't go blaming her, *Daett.* You've known this was coming for a long time."

But you are using her parents as your way out. Debbie could see the words written on Bishop Beiler's face even though he said nothing.

Saloma reached up to cling to her hus-

116

band's arm. She wailed, "Our daughter is leaving, Adam! Do something, please! Talk to her! Tell her this is forbidden!"

"There will be no more talking," Bishop Beiler finally stated. "I've said all I have to say. I've said it for many years now, and it is enough. Lois knows what she's doing and what it means." He guided Saloma into the living room, and they sat down on the couch. His chest heaved.

Lois stayed where she was for a few moments, and then she dashed upstairs.

Would she really come back down with her suitcase in hand? After what had just transpired? Debbie wondered.

"Come!" Ida whispered in Debbie's ear. "Let's go speak with her."

They climbed the stairs to the soft sounds of sobs from the living room. Lois was already out of her room when they arrived on the landing. She was dragging her suitcase.

"I want to hear no more words," Lois said before Ida could open her mouth. "Will you help me with this suitcase?"

Ida stepped back. "I will have nothing to do with aiding your departure, Lois. Let's make that clear. If you walk out of this house, you'll have to do so under your own steam."

"And yet you helped Debbie move in," Lois shot back. "You welcomed her, even knowing her parents were disappointed with her choice to change her life."

"It's not the same, Lois." Debbie found her voice. "Sure mom was disappointed with my decision, but this is different. It really is. My mom wanted me to move out . . . expected me to move out . . . told me to move out."

Lois took off down the stairs. The suitcase cleared each step except the last one, banging down with a loud clatter.

Silence hung for a few moments.

Ida clung to Debbie's arm as Lois grabbed the suitcase and moved forward. They heard the front door slam. Ida rushed into her bedroom and headed for the window facing the front lawn. Debbie followed, and the two pushed the drapes aside to watch Lois make her way down the snowy sidewalk. The girl paused for a second to glance back, but then turned and continued toward the plowed lane.

Emery appeared in the doorway of the barn. He sized up the situation and ran to Lois. He came to a stop, and in his haste his arms flailed for balance on the icy ground. He was obviously firing questions at Lois from the looks of things, and Lois was answering him. Lois soon set the suitcase on the ground to gesture with her hands for emphasis. It didn't take much imagination to figure out how that conversation was going — or how it would end.

Moments later Emery turned on his heels and marched back into the barn.

Lois stood still for a second before she wiped her eyes with the back of her hand. She picked up her suitcase and continued down the drive.

"I can't stand this!" Debbie said, her voice cracking. "I don't care what happens to me, but Lois can't walk over to my parents by herself. I'm driving her."

Ida squeezed Debbie's hand. "You do that. I know *Daett* would wish it, even if he can't say so himself."

That was a bit of a stretch, but Debbie attributed it to Ida's kind heart. She rushed downstairs and paused for a moment in front of Bishop Beiler and Saloma to explain. "I'm taking Lois over to my parents'. It will look better to my parents, and it might keep some of the bitterness out of Lois's heart. I don't like what she is doing, but this has to be hard on her even if she's acting like it isn't."

Bishop Beiler nodded. "You do what you think best, Debbie. Our hearts are too torn right now to think straight."

Saloma had her face buried in her husband's shoulder, but she glanced up and attempted a weak smile through her tears.

Debbie wiped her own eyes as she went out the door. These were all dear people and close to her heart. Why they must experience this day when their hearts were so torn was beyond her.

Lois was already on the blacktop by the time Debbie got into her car and caught up with her. She pulled up alongside Lois and pushed open the passenger door. "Climb in, Lois."

Lois continued to stare straight ahead as she marched along with her suitcase.

Debbie called louder, "Lois, get in!"

Lois paused and turned her tear-stained face toward Debbie. "And where's everyone else?"

"Throw your suitcase in the back and climb in," Debbie ordered. "You're making a scene."

Lois finally responded, but her face still looked determined.

Debbie sighed as she drove the short distance to her parents' place. "What did you expect, Lois? You knew your parents were going to take this hard. That's why you haven't done this for so long. We don't come from the same world, so your family isn't going to get over this right away. And the Amish community will suffer too. This is going to cause major trouble for everyone. My leaving the world didn't result in those things. That's the difference between what you're doing and what I did. And you know that."

Debbie stopped the car by her parents' garage. She gave Lois a direct look. "Will you let me take you back before it's too late? I'll run in and tell Mom. She'll understand."

Lois considered it for a moment, but resolution set in. "I'm not going back. Not ever. I don't care what anyone says. Thank you for bringing me over. It was nice of you."

"I don't want Mom to think the Beilers and the Amish are heartless," Debbie said. "She won't understand how deeply this is hurting your parents."

Lois looked away.

"Are you going inside?" Debbie asked. She waited for a response.

Lois opened the car door and climbed out. She grabbed her suitcase.

Debbie got out of the car too and led the way to the front door. It opened before they arrived.

"Good morning, Mom," Debbie said.

"*Gut* morning, Mrs. Watson," Lois said.

"Good morning girls. And Lois, you're to call me Callie."

"I'll try," Lois said. "It will take some getting used to."

"Yes, dear. I think there will be a great many things you'll need to get used to. Now tell me, how was it at home? Was there a little . . . what do you Amish call it . . . a *kafuffle* over your decision?"

"You can't imagine the half of it," Debbie said.

Callie shrugged. "They'll get over it. I did."

It's not the same! Debbie wanted to say, but she held back her words. Her mother wouldn't understand.

"Well, come on in, girls," Callie said. "Lois, your room is ready."

"I think I'll run on home," Debbie said, taking a step back. She immediately realized the impact and awkwardness her use of "home" would be to her mother. "Lois will settle in on her own. I'll stop by sometime next week to see how she's doing."

"You do that." Callie nodded. "I assume your dresses are fair game for her use."

"Of course, Mom." Debbie turned to go. "I don't need them any longer." She realized those were brave words at the moment. She didn't know how long her welcome at the Beilers and in the community would last after today. Debbie walked back to her car and climbed in. Starting her vehicle, she allowed the tears to come. The world had just gone from difficult to impossible, and she had no idea what she should do about it. "Please help me, Lord," she whispered.

ELEVEN

The next day was Sunday, and Minister Kanagy preached the main sermon. He was a short, thin, nervous man and walked with quick steps back and forth in front of the minister's bench. He was in full cry since beginning some 15 minutes ago.

His high-pitched voice is grating, Ida thought. The man was clearly agitated, as he should be, she decided. *Daett*'s news of Lois's departure yesterday couldn't have done anything but unsettle the ministers, as it had the entire Beiler family. She'd been surprised that *Daett* hadn't reported the matter to Deacon Mast yesterday, if only to soften the blow and give the ministers time to take in the news before the church services.

Saturday had been a devastating day at their house. *Mamm* had walked around as if preparing for a funeral. Every once in a while Ida had gone to the kitchen window to take a peek toward the house across the fields where the Watsons . . . and now Lois . . . lived. There had been no sign of her sister, even when a car left the driveway to head toward Lewistown. Lois could easily have been inside and ducked her head until she was out of sight. She would do that, Ida thought. And Lois would also wish to head into town at once to enjoy her new-found freedom.

Ida interrupted her sad thoughts long enough to steal a look at the married men's section. Normally she wouldn't look over there, but she now had a reason to. The widower Melvin Kanagy had glanced her way earlier. Ida was sure she saw intent in his gaze. At the moment he was busy with his youngest daughter, Lisa. Ida was certain she'd felt his gaze more than once this morning . . . and also last Sunday at the meeting. She hadn't returned his attention so far. Her spirits had been too low to think of romance, and she'd been too focused on Paul. And yet now that she'd resolved to consider Melvin, she felt he might give up if she didn't respond before long.

Her heart certainly didn't pound at the thought of a smile sent by Melvin, nor did she blush when she considered him. That might come in time, Ida told herself. She mustn't judge the matter too quickly. And if those feelings didn't come, was a red face and weak knees something one *had* to have? None of that had helped her with Paul Wagler. At her age she should be thankful she even had a suitor — well, a prospective suitor hopefully.

What a sorry mess, Ida mused. She turned her thoughts back to the happenings at their house yesterday. Debbie had stayed out of sight all day. She'd hardly shown herself except at mealtimes. And then she looked like she was the one who had run away from the Beiler household instead of Lois. Debbie clearly took a large portion of the responsibility for what had happened. That wasn't right. When Debbie had gone upstairs after supper, Ida had approached *Mamm.* "You surely don't blame Debbie for any of this?" she asked.

"*Nee,* of course not." *Mamm*'s tone had been mournful. "Lois has been talking of this since she was a teenager. I had my hopes up that she would grow out of it. And with Debbie's coming and her appreciation for our way of life, we let our hopes get even higher."

"Perhaps you should go tell Debbie this," Ida encouraged. "She feels horrible. What with Lois down at her parents' place, I'm sure she believes she's to blame. Or at least that you and *daett* hold her responsible for some of Lois's decision."

"Lois would eventually have thought of a way to go." *Mamm*'s voice caught. "*Yah,* I will speak with Debbie."

Ida had sighed with relief as *Mamm* went up the stairs. What *Mamm* told Debbie, Ida never learned. The two were together for some time before *Mamm* came back down again and joined *Daett* in the living room. *Mamm* didn't look upset, so the conversation must have gone well.

Minister Kanagy now waved his arms around with quick motions and grabbed Ida's attention. "And in our battle with the world and the devil — we all know that not everyone is always victorious. This is a sad situation that weighs heavy on our hearts — when a brother or sister falls into error. This grieves us more than we can find words to express. In those times it is up to the strong among us to bring both correction to the fallen and comfort to the ones left behind. And we wish to do this today. As our dear bishop himself has told us over the years, *Da Hah*'s vineyard needs much work to upkeep it. And this is not always easy or pleasant work. I hope that we are all praying today — and in the days ahead — for those who have strayed and for those whose hearts are bleeding from their great fall."

It wasn't hard for Ida to figure out that Minister Kanagy was speaking of Alvin Knepp and possibly Lois. The first step of Alvin's discipline would no doubt be on the agenda today. This was already a heavy burden on *Daett*'s shoulders, and now he had the added weight of his own daughter's flight into the *Englisha* world. When the whole community found out, the shock would be great. *Mamm* had sent her over in the buggy yesterday afternoon to break the news to Verna. Even now Verna sat in the married women's section in tears. People would think she was crying for Alvin's sake. But if they only knew . . . well, they soon would. Ida wiped tears from her own eyes.

After she'd told Verna the news yesterday, her sister had clung to her for a long time barely able to speak. "I had so hoped Lois had outgrown this thing."

"I know," Ida said. "Especially with Debbie at the house."

"How's Debbie doing?" Verna asked as she lowered herself onto the couch.

"Troubled, I suppose. She takes a lot of the responsibility on her own shoulders." Ida's sadness wrinkled her face.

"I will speak with her after church," Verna

said. "Debbie mustn't think this is her responsibility at all. Lois has been talking about doing this since she was young."

Verna was right, Ida thought, but the community would likely not see things that way. As she sat in church this morning that point was being driven home. Perhaps it was the way Minister Kanagy spoke or the tone in his voice. He would surely look for a reason why these things had happened. And Debbie would make an easy target. It made too much sense to those who didn't know everything that had transpired at the Beiler household. And explanations would do no *gut* . . . even if it was decent to speak of family matters in public, which it wasn't.

Minister Kanagy paced back and forth with his hands by his sides. "I bring this time to a close now, beseeching each and every one of us to search our own heart. Do we have the love of the world hidden away in even the most secret part of our lives? If we do, let us not think this won't be found out. The pressures are simply too great to hide such an awful thing. We might think the shame of others knowing our secret thoughts too much to bear, but it's better if we confess our thoughts and actions to each other than to let them build and then perish in the coming storm. And a tempest is coming into all our lives. As surely as the winter follows the fall, and summer follows spring. *Da Hah* Himself has told us of this thing. We are to build on the foundation of His Word, not on the shifting sands of the world's opinion. Those are established today and changed tomorrow. Oh how those sands move about when storms come. And how great is the fall of that house. Brothers and sisters, be not one of those whose house is caught off the foundation of *Da Hah*'s Word. Confess your sins today and seek forgiveness. This is the only way we are ever to survive in this present evil day."

Finally, Minister Kanagy took his seat looking quite distraught. He asked for testimony on what he'd said from several of the older men. They spoke, saying they agreed with everything that had been preached. Ida's mind drifted again as she felt Melvin's gaze upon her. She wondered if all girls could feel such a thing. It was something she hadn't felt in a while. Not since *Daett* had forced her to turn down the last man who had asked to take her home from a hymn singing.

Those bygone days when *Daett* was so strict with his daughters seemed a long, long time ago — even though it wasn't really. Verna's successful courtship and marriage to Joe had changed *Daett*'s thoughts on the matter. With all the trouble Verna and Joe had run into, they'd persevered and everything had turned out okay.

Would Lois's departure change all the *gut* Verna had accomplished? Would *Daett* recoil in fear if she mentioned that Melvin Kanagy might have an interest in her? She'd better not say anything until Melvin actually asked her home from the hymn singing. But if he did, surely *Daett* would allow it. Melvin was a decent man, and he'd never shown any love for the *Englisha* world. And that would, no doubt, be *Daett*'s biggest fear.

Ida didn't blame *Daett* for the way he felt about it. The thought of the *Englisha* world did make one's spirits sink. How could she give Melvin some encouragement before the service concluded and everyone went home? It would be good to do before he found out Lois had left for the *Englisha* world. If Ida had known that was going to happen this soon, she would have paid attention to Melvin sooner. That way their relationship might weather the shock when he found out the awful news.

Ida snuck a quick glance toward the married men's section. Melvin was indeed looking at her. His daughter Lisa sat straight beside him. Obviously she anticipated the close of the service. Ida dropped her eyes for a moment and gathered her courage. She looked up again and attempted a sweet smile in Melvin's direction. It came off tense, and Ida chided herself. But she consoled herself with the fact that Melvin looked pleased in those seconds before she'd dropped her gaze. Well, it would go better next time — if there was a next time.

The silence after the finished testimonies interrupted Ida's thoughts. Someone shouted out a song number, and they all joined in. When the song was over, *Daett* stood and said, "That concludes our service today, and we can be dismissed with *Da Hah*'s blessing. We would appreciate it if those who are members will stay behind for a meeting."

This was followed by the usual dash of the younger boys for outside. They weren't old enough to understand the seriousness of what happened when their parents stayed behind. They would know before long. Their turn would come to shoulder the responsibilities of the church. Ida intended to do her part, though there wasn't much a woman could do. She would show her support for her *daett* today. And she would leave the world a better place in the end, while those who chased the things that lay out in the world would be left with only the possessions and emotions that soon passed away.

Ida wiped a tear away as *Daett* got up to speak. All the nonmembers had gone outside, including Debbie, who had disappeared into the kitchen. This was something Debbie had experienced before, and she knew to offer her help to the younger girls as they set up a table in the basement and fed the younger children while the members talked of church matters.

"Please help us all, dear *Hah,*" Ida breathed as her *daett* informed the members that a letter had been sent to Alvin Knepp reminding him of his church member responsibilities and asking him to return and repent of his error. Alvin's *mamm* sniffled over in the married women's section.

Daett stood for a moment with a bowed head. "And now, I have something I must say that also tears at my heart. But you need to hear this from me. My own daughter Lois left our home yesterday to live with an *Englisha* family. I know she was not yet a church member, but I wish to tell you what's happening because as your bishop I'm responsible to lead the church and keep you informed of what is necessary. With that said, you can all be dismissed."

Feet shuffled as some of the men rose to leave for the barn. The full implications of what *Daett* had said didn't register on their faces yet. Maybe it wouldn't until they arrived home and spoke with their wives. The women, however, seemed to fully understand the implications. A few gathered around *Mamm* and whispered encouragement in her ear. *Daett* hadn't said who the *Englisha* family was that Lois was staying with, but it wouldn't be long before someone asked or figured out it was Debbie's parents. Poor Debbie would be caught unfairly in the fallout.

Ida stole a quick glance toward the place Melvin had been sitting. He was still there, and he gave her a warm smile. She tried to smile back, but she was afraid it came across crooked. Still, Melvin looked pleased. Hopefully he was still interested in her — at least for now. Maybe he also didn't understand fully what it meant that the bishop's daughter had left for the world. With a sigh Ida walked to the kitchen. She would help serve dinner to get her mind off her family and herself.

TWELVE

On Thursday evening of the following week, Alvin opened his mailbox at the Park Heights Apartments. He was on his way in from work and had walked several blocks from the nearest bus stop. It wasn't the best arrangement, but Mr. Rusty, the motel manager where Alvin had stayed first, had suggested the place. Alvin figured he didn't know much about the wild world of the *Englisha,* so if Mr. Rusty said this was a *gut* deal, then it probably was. And Mr. Rusty, who ran the Hyatt downtown, had proven himself an honest man in his business dealings with Alvin. That he did know something about.

Alvin had made no secret of his past when he'd asked at the front desk of the motel for employment opportunities in the area. The man at the desk had summoned Mr. Rusty, who had conducted a job interview on the spot. Their relationship was based on trust.

"If you grew up around old farm machinery, you might be just the man I'm looking for," Mr. Rusty said. "And the Amish have a reputation for being honest, right?"

Alvin nodded and thought about the "old machinery" comment. He hadn't expected his farming background to carry much weight. In fact, he'd thought it would be a negative in the *Englisha* world.

"Then why don't we give it a try!" Mr. Rusty had given him a slap on the shoulder. "Handymen are hard to come by, especially in the winter when everything's breaking down. I'll start you out at a decent wage and give you all the overtime you can handle. What do you say?"

"That's fine." Relief flooded through him. And the wages — once Mr. Rusty had named an amount — had been much more than he'd dared hope. How *Da Hah* could bless him after he'd done such wrong was hard to imagine, but Alvin was still thankful.

Now Alvin squinted into the mailbox. At first he saw nothing because the letters had been set up on edge. They fell over just before he closed the lid and caught his eye. Alvin reached in and took them out. He turned them over to see Deacon Mast's return address on one. The other one was from *Mamm.* So things had come to this so quickly, he thought. *Mamm* had written a letter last week too. And she must have given the deacon his address. Not that he'd asked her not to or made any effort to hide. That would have been a useless endeavor anyway. Church discipline was what it was, and one couldn't postpone things for long. Even if a man hid out in a big city, things happened at home at their usual pace.

Alvin took the elevator to the fifth floor. He held the letters in one hand, and with the other he found his key and let himself inside. The room was plainly decorated. Mostly bare walls. He didn't have any money to splurge, he'd told himself. Besides, it felt more like home this way. His life in the *Englisha* world still had a painful feel to it. This feeling might never go away for all he knew. His heart throbbed at moments like this when he came home to an empty apartment. It was a different feeling than the pain the deacon's letter in his hand would surely cause. *Mamm*'s letter would make the other ache return too. He already knew that.

Homesickness was a common affliction everyone suffered. But he found that wasn't a very convincing argument. If this was homesickness, he might die from it before this was over. He should be able to bear up better, but the truth was that the things of home ran deep in his heart and soul. What he wouldn't give for some of *Mamm*'s cooking right now, meager though it had been the past few months. Homemade cornbread smeared with butter would taste like heavenly manna, to say nothing of *Mamm*'s bread, fresh from the oven. Those things would always be at home regardless of how bad the financial situation became. The community would see to that, which was one of the problems really.

Alvin believed he couldn't bear the shame of his *daett*'s downfall, and yet he wasn't holding up well in his escape to the *Englisha* world either. *I must do it!* Alvin told himself. He pulled a chair out from the kitchen table and sat down. He might as well begin with what the deacon had to say. Cutting open one end of the envelope with a kitchen knife, Alvin unfolded the single page.

Our dear brother Alvin:

I need not tell you, I suppose, what the purpose of this letter is. I and the others of the ministry are deeply grieved in our hearts and troubled in our minds by the news of your departure from home. We have joined your parents in mourning this great tragedy, and we pray fervently that *Da Hah* might begin his *gut* work in your heart and draw you back to the truth.

As you know, *Da Hah*'s vineyard needs much work. If we have failed to minister to your needs or if anyone else in the community has done so, we beg your most heartfelt forgiveness. We hope you will remember that we are all frail human beings and subject to mistakes like anyone else. May *Da Hah* grant us all grace to live better lives than what we are living.

I hope this letter finds you well and not too settled in where you're staying. Our hopes are that *Da Hah* and home will be calling you soon, and that we will see your face again.

Whatever happened, Alvin? You seem to have left without telling even your parents what the problem was in your life. Please don't allow this matter — whatever it is — to bring a gulf between you, your parents, and the community. Perhaps *Da Hah* will need much time to repair the hurt, I don't know. But we want you to know that you are welcome back, as you always will be. Coming home would be as simple as giving us your confession of failure, which you must surely know by now has occurred. How can leaving for the world do anyone any *gut,* Alvin?

Please consider returning and making things right with your dear parents. Their hearts as well as ours would have a great burden lifted from them. The church was told of this matter on Sunday, and they were also notified of this attempt to reach out to you. I don't need to say what will happen, Alvin, if you don't respond with repentance and return. It grieves me unbearably to even say such words, but *Da Hah*'s rod is with us for a purpose.

The Holy Scriptures say, "Thy rod and thy staff they comfort me." Allow *Da Hah*'s comfort to reach you, Alvin. Return home and visit me. Not that much damage has been done yet. Nothing that a few words spoken and a heart turned from wickedness cannot make right.

Think on these things, Alvin, and do not throw them away lightly.

Yours truly,
Deacon David Mast

Alvin closed the letter, and slid it away from him. He'd expected something like this, but the pain still cut all the way through him. How did Deacon Mast know exactly the words to say to drive his point in the deepest? He could almost see last Sunday morning's meeting when the announcement was made at church — the sober faces, the tears in *Mamm*'s eyes, the burden on Bishop Beiler's shoulders. Deacon Mast managed to bring that picture and a thousand thoughts to his mind. All Alvin had to do was return home and express his sorrow. They would forgive him and take him back with open arms. If not, then surely the *bann* was only weeks away. Deacon Mast hadn't said that, but he didn't have to.

Alvin stood up and paced the floor between the kitchen table and the window that overlooked the parking lot. He paused and gazed out at the vehicles. Most of them were dirty from being driven through the snowy streets marred by the city's grime. Snow here didn't look the same. It wasn't pure like the snow at home. There the fields didn't leave stains on the flakes. The farm animals made a mess in the barnyard, *yah,* but clean straw and hay lay inside the barn. Here the earth didn't reach one with its soft touch preserved from last summer's sun-kissed fields. Here there was concrete and asphalt that covered much of the earth, and the buildings and his apartment smelled of things he had no names for.

Perhaps he should repent and return home. Yet how could he? It would be one more failure on his record. *He tried it out there in the world and couldn't make it.* Paul Wagler would snicker at this idea and make no attempt to hide his disdain after services or at the Sunday dinner table. And it would be true. Alvin had tried something new, something out of desperation, but had changed his mind. *Yah,* but this was entirely his own decision for once.

He wanted to at least stick it out for a year or so. Deacon Mast and the ministry would have *Daett*'s financial situation well under control by then. Alvin wouldn't have been the one required to reveal the truth of his *daett*'s poor farming ways. *Nee,* Alvin couldn't run back home before that problem was solved. He might have to bear the pain of excommunication. They would release him from the burden and shame when he returned and repented. And perhaps this experience would help make him the man he wished to become. *Yah,* he should have done this during his *rumspringa* time, but his family was known for their objection to *rumspringa* and their strong support of the *Ordnung* so Alvin had minimized it. He'd wanted to please his *daett.* But even in that obedience, he'd failed.

Alvin cut open the second letter and unfolded it. Tear stains were clearly visible on the bottom edge. *Mamm* must have cried as she wrote. Alvin bit his lower lip as he read.

My dear, dear son, Alvin,

I need not say that you are often in our thoughts and prayers because you know you always are. I struggle with my health at times and lie awake at night thinking about where you might be and what trouble you might be facing. I cry out to *Da Hah* for your safety. I ask that you might be protected from the evils of the world. Oh, if you would only come home, Alvin. Whatever the problem is, it can surely be worked out. There is nothing on this earth that could have been so bad that you had to leave home. Surely there wasn't, Alvin. I refuse to believe there could be even for a moment.

I suppose you have received a letter from Deacon Mast. It was announced in church today that contact with you would be officially attempted. You know what that means. I hope you will have sense enough to straighten things out with Deacon Mast before you are lost to us in spirit also. Such a thing is unimaginable to us, Alvin — you being shut out into the darkness by yourself. Please come to your senses and return home. Our hearts do nothing but ache and long for you.

Your *daett* is almost out of feed this week — as you know, I'm sure. I'm not saying that's your fault because it isn't, Alvin. We'll make it somehow. He will have to ask for help soon, and Deacon Mast will see that your *daett* gets what he needs for the spring planting — if things come to that. *Da Hah* knows we try our best, but for some reason we are not blessed as others are even if we have some of the best farmland in Snyder County.

I've been wondering, Alvin. Did *Daett*'s farming methods and troubles these past years have anything to do with your leaving? I think it must have, and I can't quite forgive myself for not seeing that possibility before. Now that I look back, I think you've been troubled for some time.

I thought it was only about that *Englisha* girl you took such a shine to, but I believe that is another subject entirely. You really need to get her out of your mind, Alvin. I've heard that Paul Wagler is making quite a fuss over her. I say Paul can have her.

We've been faithful church members for generations now, Alvin. What's gotten into you that you have made such a change? That you have done this to our family? Was it that Debbie? Did she put ideas into your mind that shouldn't have been there?

I fear this is true. I'm sure you haven't heard yet, but Bishop Beiler's youngest daughter, Lois, also left for the *Englisha* world. Although that is no comfort to you, it might make it easier for you to return. People will not see your leaving in the same light. They will be extra glad because you chose to come back.

Come home, Alvin. We can work things out. I'll speak to *Daett* about giving you more charge over the farm. That will make things better for you, won't it? You could even try some of those new farming methods you kept talking about. Again, I'm sorry I didn't see how much this troubled you before. Consider the matter well, my son. I trust you will not make the wrong choice.

Your loving *Mamm*

Alvin stuck the letter back into the envelope. So *Mamm* didn't like Debbie. He wasn't surprised even though she hadn't protested his interest up to this point. Perhaps that was because she thought nothing would ever come of his love for Debbie. Now *Mamm* was striking at what she thought could be the second root of his problem — the failing farm. Well, *Mamm* was partly right, but her solutions wouldn't make anything better.

So it was true that Paul was making progress in his advances to Debbie. Well, so be it. What could he do about it? Alvin set his chin firmly and began to prepare his supper. It wouldn't be much, but after those two letters he needed the comfort food might bring.

THIRTEEN

Debbie awoke with a splitting headache. Even Emery's soft footsteps as he crept past the bedroom doorway on the way to his chores vibrated in her head. And the squeak of the stairs as he descended was even worse. She held both hands to her face, and got out of bed. With care she lit the kerosene lamp and then pushed aside the drapes. A full moon hung low on the horizon. Already the rough surface of the round orb was dimmed by dawn's rays in the east that gave the snow banks in the west a soft, red glow. Before long another February winter day would be upon them and the duties of farm life would continue. At least it was a Saturday, and she wouldn't have to go to her job.

Two weeks had passed since Lois had left for Debbie's parents' place. No one from the Beiler household had visited her, and her absence hung like a heavy quilt over the house. They were all trying their best to ignore it.

Debbie groaned. It wasn't Lois who had sent her head into this blistering ache. No, it was the tense talk with Paul last night. That and the worry of what would happen if she turned down his offer to bring her home Sunday evening. Debbie sat on the bed and ran through the incident in her mind. She'd told herself time and again to be ready for the moment, yet she'd been so unprepared once it arrived.

The youth had played volleyball last night at the Waglers, and Paul had made no effort to have her situated beside him during the game — even though he was captain and could have done so easily. Perhaps that was what had disarmed her and raised her hopes that he'd seen her resistance to his attentions and accepted her decision. That had been dashed after the game. Paul had stepped out of the shadows of the barn when Debbie was leaving. His fingers had brushed her arm.

"Debbie, may I speak with you for a moment?"

She was walking beside Ida at the time. Paul must have wanted his attentions noted. That would be so like him. In fact, she was surprised he hadn't commenced the conversation in front of the whole youth group.

Debbie knew that her bad attitude was quite inappropriate for a young Christian woman. She couldn't imagine any of the other girls harboring such feelings. And to make matters worse, she'd seen the look of brief sorrow that had flashed across Ida's face. Debbie turned to follow Paul away from the buggy.

"I hope you've enjoyed the evening," Paul said, turning toward her.

I did until this moment! Debbie wanted to snap. She smiled instead. "It's been a good evening."

Paul returned the smile. "I always enjoy these winter volleyball games. Spring will get here soon enough." He paused.

She waited in silence for him to continue.

His smile didn't dim as he said, "Spring is also a *gut* time of the year, although I do so love winter and the slowing of the rush from summer." His face had brightened as he paused for a moment to think about what he would say. The words came out more of a statement than a question. "You'd consider it a *gut* thing, Debbie, if I took you home on Sunday evening, *yah.*"

The dreaded moment had arrived. Why was she so tongue-tied? She had rehearsed her answer for when this moment would finally arrive. She hesitated. She was about

149

to stammer her answer, when Paul took her hesitation in exactly the wrong way.

He nodded. "I thought so. Well, I'll be looking forward to it then, Debbie. I know this thing with Alvin Knepp must still weigh heavy on your heart, so I didn't wish to rush things too much. But surely you've seen by now what kind of stuff Alvin is made of. And his *daett,* of course, the problems he's having with that farm."

"Ah . . . I . . ." she tried to interrupt, but Paul had already rushed on.

"I think you know which buggy I drive and how we do these things. You've been in the community long enough to know. And tell Ida she needs to get a ride with Emery, but I guess she knows that since you both drive with him now that Lois is out in the *Englisha* world."

He was worse than any man she'd yet encountered, Debbie decided. So in charge. So confident. He clearly didn't expect no for an answer. In a way she could almost let herself go along with his self-deception. It would be like falling asleep on a raft afloat on a fast-moving stream. The only problem was there were rapids ahead, to say nothing of the falls just down the river.

Paul had already turned to go, when she pulled on his shirt sleeve.

"Umm, Paul . . . wait." She took a gulp of air and plunged ahead. "The thing is, I can't do this. I just can't."

He couldn't have looked more thunder-struck. "You're . . . you're saying *nee*? You're saying *nee* to letting me take you home?"

"Something like that, yes." The words came out squeaky.

Paul studied her face for a moment. "You surely know Alvin's not coming back, Debbie. He wasn't the man for you anyway. You have to know that by now . . . or was it worse than I thought and you need more time to heal?"

She tried again. "I'm saying *no,* Paul. Like in *never.* It's not about needing time for me to heal." Her words didn't register.

"You can't be serious! What are you doing here in the community then, Debbie? You surely know you can't go on like you are. Not with Alvin gone and Bishop Beiler's daughter out in the world. And she's stay-ing at your parents' place. Do you know what that means, Debbie?"

"You would force me into a relationship with you?" she managed to whisper. It was the wrong thing to say.

"Of course not, Debbie!" Anger crossed his face as he stared. Then he relaxed and began again. "So, do you want to drop this question for a while? Maybe that would be wise. I see you do need to heal more, and I'm sure the people of the community will understand. Sometimes things take a little time."

She should have screamed *no* or stomped her feet or done something to drive home the point that she would never consider going out with him as her boyfriend, let alone her husband. But it was easier to say nothing. She looked at him and then stared at the ground.

Paul gave her arm a quick squeeze and walked her back to Ida. A few of the girls who stood nearby glanced their way. They had soft smiles on their faces. Everyone approved of the match apparently, Debbie thought. And Ida was among them. She gave her the warmest smile of all.

Ida's attitude affected Debbie the most and almost brought tears to her eyes during the ride home. Her friend couldn't have forgotten her feelings for Paul, and yet once Ida decided something was the right thing to do, she proceeded ahead with such a sweet spirit.

"I'm so happy for you!" Ida had whispered as Emery drove them through the chilly darkness.

"Ida, I turned him down," Debbie said.

Her friend was unable to say anything for a moment.

"Turned who down?" Emery asked as he pulled back on the reins to stop at an intersection.

"You're blind as a bat, Emery!" Ida scolded. "Don't you see anything?"

"Paul Wagler," Debbie offered in Emery's direction. There was no reason to keep this hidden. They'd been seen together, and the news would spread anyway.

"Paul Wagler?" Emery stared at her for a moment before he slapped the reins to urge the horse forward. "You turned down a date with him?"

"Is that some kind of sin?" Her anger had finally returned, but it was a little too late. And besides, she shouldn't make Emery the target.

Emery laughed. "Turning Paul down right now is dangerous, that's all I say. Though I kind of like it."

"Emery, don't say that!" Ida said.

"I still like it." Emery chuckled, and Ida fell silent. Her silence hung over them until they got home. They unhitched the horse, and Emery led her to the barn. Ida even remained silent on the walk to the house. Debbie and Ida went inside, said good night to the elder Beilers, walked upstairs, and then parted in the hallway with a mumbled "Good night."

The memory of last night faded as Debbie rubbed her throbbing head with both hands. A soft knock sounded on the door, and she got up and opened the door.

Ida greeted her with a too cheery, "Just thought I'd check to see how you are this morning."

"I have a splitting headache!" Debbie said as she sat on the bed again.

Concern flashed on Ida's face. "I'll get aspirin for you. Do you take two or three?"

"A dozen," Debbie mumbled.

"Just give me a minute." Ida disappeared and the squeaking stairs seemed to pierce Debbie's skull. A few moments later Ida came up again with two aspirins and a glass of water.

Debbie washed the pills down quickly.

Ida sat on the bed and placed a hand on Debbie's shoulder. "Is last night bothering you?"

"Ida, why don't you take Paul, and put me out of my misery?" Debbie groaned. "You like him. I don't."

Ida gave a little laugh. "That's over, Debbie. Surely you know that. Paul has no interest in me, and I think *Da Hah* is opening other doors for me. Even with the awful things Lois has done, I think I'll be offered a chance at love. So you mustn't turn down Paul out of respect for me."

As always Ida expected the best motives in others, Debbie thought. "Ida, please believe me when I say I have no feelings for Paul. Actually that's not true. I don't like him. Why can't anyone understand that? My answer to Paul will always be no — even if you no longer want him."

"You don't think that's a mistake?" Ida asked, her tone insistent.

Debbie met her gaze. "Ida, dear, please. Paul *is not* the kind of man I want. That's not to say he wouldn't be great for someone else . . . for you. I'm just not interested. I hope that doesn't hurt your feelings."

"I suppose we all do have our own taste." Ida shifted on the bed. "I wish you the best then, especially with what the community will say about this."

Debbie winced. "That's what Paul said. And he didn't take no for my answer either. He's planning to ask again 'after some time,' he said."

"Then there's yet hope?" Ida's face lit up. "You must have given him some reason to wait."

"I don't know what runs through Paul's

feverish brain," Debbie muttered. "I seem to have that effect on men. It's happened before, believe me, and no matter how hard they've tried, I haven't changed my mind. It's never worked with *Englisha* men, and it's no use for Paul to persist either."

"But Paul is a *gut* man," Ida said. "He might be different from the *Englisha* men you knew before. Have you considered that?"

Debbie held her aching head for a moment. "I don't think so, Ida. And no offense to your high regard for the man. I'm sure he'll make some Amish woman a decent husband someday. As for me . . ."

Alarm was back in Ida's face again. "Debbie, you wouldn't let this mess cause you to leave us? You wouldn't give up? Surely there's some way out of this!"

"I don't want to leave. But the question is whether I'll be asked to leave." Debbie glanced at Ida's troubled face.

Ida turned a shade whiter, and the words came out in a rush. "Perhaps I spoke out of turn. I shouldn't have said that."

"Will your dad ask me to leave?" Debbie persisted.

Ida shook her head, saying without hesitation, "*Daett* would never do something like that."

"Then how will I be in danger? I was thinking your father would be forced to evict me. Isn't that what all of you keep referring to?"

Ida glanced out the window. "It's more complicated than that, I'm afraid. I heard *Mamm* and *Daett* talking the other evening while I was in the kitchen. *Daett* won't ask you to leave, no matter what Minister Kanagy and the others say on the matter. On this he plans to hold his ground."

Debbie gripped Ida's arm. "But they could try, and the pressure I'm sure will be severe."

Ida shrugged. "*Daett*'s the bishop. He doesn't have to change his mind."

Debbie squeezed harder. "But he'll suffer a lot of damage to his reputation. Is that what you're saying?"

Ida thought for a moment. "You could put it that way. He will suffer, *yah.*"

"Dear God, what am I going to do?" Debbie whispered.

"I will pray for you," Ida offered.

"Thank you." Debbie held Ida's hand, as a thought ran through her mind. Something about the look on Ida's face brought the question out with force. "Is there something you're not telling me, Ida?"

Ida looked down.

Debbie reached over and pushed up Ida's chin. A tear trickled down her friend's cheek.

"It's nothing," Ida whispered.

"You must tell me," Debbie ordered.

"This is all about me, Debbie, so it really doesn't matter. Melvin Kanagy has been giving me attention for some time, and I've been returning it. Melvin is Minister Kanagy's brother, and Minister Kanagy will be the hardest set against you, Debbie. He was the one who made all that trouble for Verna and Joe, remember? Now I'm afraid he'll seek to break up any potential relationship between Melvin and me before it even takes root."

Debbie groaned out loud and pressed her hands to her head again. "I think I'd better move out tonight."

"*Nee,* you will do no such thing." Ida clung to Debbie with both hands. "We'll speak with *Mamm* after breakfast and the chores. If we talk to her now, we won't have her full attention. Besides, it's already late, and I have to get to the barn."

"I'm not sure your *mamm* can change what has to happen." Debbie tried to appear upbeat. "It won't be so bad. Besides, if I leave, maybe I can have an influence on Lois — to help bring her back.

"*Nee,* you are *not* moving out," Ida said. "We will talk to *Mamm* as soon as we can get some time with her.

Debbie offered a weak smile but remained unconvinced.

FOURTEEN

After breakfast that morning and after the bishop had said the prayers in the living room, Ida and Debbie were doing dishes. Suddenly Ida pulled on Debbie's elbow. "Come! We must speak with *Mamm* now. *Daett* has just left for the barn."

Debbie kept her groan silent. She really shouldn't sink this deep into despair. It wasn't like her at all, but that was the effect Paul had, she figured. At least on her. He was a reminder of her old life that she didn't want to return to.

Ida entered the living room first with Debbie close behind her. Saloma was sitting in her rocker, staring out the window at the snow-covered fields. Ida took a seat on the couch closest to Saloma.

"*Mamm?*" Ida said quietly.

Saloma turned her head. Tears were streaming down her face.

"What is it?" Ida asked. "What's wrong?"

Saloma just shook her head.

"Mamm?" Ida repeated, alarm in her voice. "What is it? Has *Daett* said something?"

Saloma shook her head. "It's been two weeks now, and Lois hasn't stopped by. Do you think she's okay?"

"I'm sure she is." Ida moved closer. "Do you wish to visit her this morning?"

"You know I can't do that." Saloma's voice caught in a sob. "As much as my heart would rush down there if it could. Oh, my baby daughter. What could she be in to?"

Ida clung to Saloma's arm for a moment, and Debbie walked around to the other side of the rocker. She placed her hand on Saloma's shoulder. "I'll go down and check on her if you wish."

Instant relief flooded Saloma's face. "Would you, Debbie? Is that asking too much of you?"

"I'm glad to help out."

"But, Debbie . . ." Ida protested.

Debbie cut Ida off with a shake of her head. Now wasn't the time to think of her own problems. That could come later. And it felt good to function in her role as helper around the house. This was what she knew — both the world out there, and the world in here. Why not continue to serve as a bridge between the two even though her

161

time of welcome in the Beiler home might be short-lived?

Ida seemed to understand and rose. "I'll get your coat."

Debbie followed her into the washroom.

Ida took Debbie's coat from the wall hook and handed it to her. "You'll tell Lois how much we miss her, and that she's welcome back anytime, right?"

Debbie nodded. "Of course."

"And one more thing," Ida added, "tell her about Melvin's interest in me. I want her to know."

"Okay," Debbie agreed. "But maybe Lois will come home to visit soon, and you can tell her more about Melvin yourself."

"*Yah,* perhaps." Ida's eyes filled with hope. "She might even visit today, if you ask really nicely."

Debbie smiled. "I'll do what I can. I'm sure your mother also wishes to see Lois."

"She does." Ida's face had fallen again. "Lois knows we can't visit your parents' place. It wouldn't be proper."

Debbie nodded and then headed outside. Ida was conniving more than she thought she would. Her friend clearly hoped to draw Lois home with news of what she was missing out on. The tactic wouldn't work. If Debbie didn't miss her guess, Lois was quite full of her new life right now. This was something she wouldn't mention around the Beiler household. Their hearts were already torn apart enough.

Debbie headed down the driveway and walked down the road. The snow banks still stood high along each side, but they would be gone soon. A warming trend had begun this week and would likely increase. She couldn't be happier that this winter would be over soon. Debbie made her way to the front door of her old home and knocked. She would normally have walked on in, but this morning she felt like a visitor. Was it because Lois was staying here or because her heart had grown separated from her childhood home? She knew one thing for sure. If she did have to leave the Beiler household, she wouldn't move back here. She simply couldn't. The pain would be more severe than she wished to admit. She couldn't watch her mother's joy each day while Lois became increasingly the daughter her mother had always wanted.

The door opened. Her mother said, "You knocked? You didn't need to."

"I know. Coming home just felt different this time." She hoped her mother would understand, but it was unlikely. Debbie stepped inside. "Is Lois home?"

"Of course." Callie raised her eyebrows. "We haven't sold her into slavery, you know. It's good to finally see that someone's concerned. The poor girl. I don't understand how she's not a bundle of tears every day with the way her family is treating her."

Debbie gave her mother a sharp look. "Has Lois been complaining?"

Callie half smiled. "No, but I have eyes."

"And did you come visiting when I moved in with the Beilers?" Debbie tried to choke back the bitterness in the barb but failed.

Her mother winced. "Well, that was different."

The words rushed out of Debbie's mouth. "No, it wasn't. But who would have guessed the tables would get turned on all of us?"

"Justice is blind they say," Callie quipped. "If one can believe that, anyway. Your father and I have been enjoying Lois to the fullest. Here she is now!"

Lois rushed down the hall to wrap Debbie in a tight hug. "I'm so glad to see you. Did *Mamm* and Ida also come along?"

"You know they couldn't," Debbie said. "But I have come on their behalf."

Debbie was glad neither Saloma nor Ida had come. Lois had on one of her old dresses. The hemline barely came halfway to the knees. She wasn't wearing a covering on her head, either. Her hair had obviously been done up by her mother's hairstylist. Debbie had always resisted doing that. Lois clearly had no such qualms, and the price couldn't have been cheap — well above anything Lois could afford. Her mother must have footed the bill. That was no surprise.

Lois noticed her interest. "Do you like it?" She flicked her short hair with one hand, her smile a bit crooked.

"It's nice," Debbie allowed. There was no sense in being rude about this, and it was true. In fact, Lois looked stunning. But Debbie wasn't about to admit that.

"I'm so happy here, Debbie!" Lois gushed.

Debbie glanced at her mother, who was clearly pleased with Lois's enthusiasm. Lois was indeed becoming the daughter her mother had always wanted. A sharp pain ran through Debbie's heart, one she was familiar with. She mustn't hold this against her mother. Things were simply what they were. And she'd left home last year for a world her mother didn't approve. Apparently this had hurt her mother more than Debbie had realized.

"Are you working yet?" Debbie asked Lois.

Lois's face glowed. "*Yah* . . . I mean, yes. I

work at the McDonald's in Mifflinburg. It's such fun. I get to meet all these people, and even some Amish." Lois rushed on as if she hadn't heard Debbie's groan. "Most of them don't know me. Especially looking like this." Lois motioned toward her short hair and dress. "But Minister Kanagy's eldest daughter, Wilma, stopped in the other day with some of her friends." Lois smiled at the memory. "They must have been shopping. Anyway, I'm sure she recognized me, and I gave her a wink so she'd know for sure. I guess the uniform does change a person quite a bit."

There were a thousand things Debbie wanted to say about that. Like what in the world did Lois think she accomplished when she flaunted herself like that? Did the girl have no idea the damage this was doing to her father's reputation? Didn't Lois care or think about such things? Debbie turned and directed a question toward her mother. "Why do you have her working at Mc-Donald's?"

Callie shrugged and said, "She has to begin somewhere, and the girl has no education."

She's not stupid, Debbie wanted to snap. But Lois could defend herself if she were offended.

Lois's glow never dimmed. "I'm studying for my GED. Your *mamm*'s helping me. It's harder than I imagined, but I'm not giving up. Not in a thousand years."

"She has quite the spirit," Callie said, speaking as if Lois weren't in the room.

"Unlike me, I suppose."

Callie didn't appear ruffled. "You had spirit too, Debbie. Your problem was you didn't know in what direction to profitably invest it."

Debbie glanced away. There was no way to come out ahead in this discussion. She knew her mother considered her life in the Amish community a waste. But for some reason working at McDonald's was great — as long as a person was going in the right direction. Debbie pushed the bitter thoughts away. She'd come to speak with Lois and convince her to visit at the house, not fight with her mother.

"Shall we go in and sit down? No sense in chattering in the hall like magpies."

Her mom apparently was ready to make peace. "I came over partly to see if Lois wished to visit at home." She turned to Lois. "Perhaps today?" She might as well come right out and state the purpose of her visit. Otherwise they'd maunder around for twenty minutes of conversation none of them would enjoy.

A look of alarm flashed across Lois's face. "Go home? Visit today? I couldn't go looking like this!"

At least Lois hadn't taken total leave of her senses, Debbie thought.

Even Callie joined in. "I agree, Lois. You should visit, but in one of your old dresses. And with something on your head."

Lois's hands fluttered about for a moment. "I'll be right back then. I guess it would be *gut* to visit."

Lois turned and dashed down the hall toward Debbie's old bedroom.

Debbie turned towards her mother. "Did you have to allow her to change so fast? You know Saloma will see what's happened. The poor woman is suffering enough already."

Callie sighed. "Do you think you could have held back that girl under these circumstances? Well, you couldn't. She's like one of Bishop Beiler's calves they let loose after a long winter."

Debbie felt a smile creep across her face despite the seriousness of the situation. Her mother's description fit perfectly. Calves turned loose in the spring nearly turned the barnyard upside down as they dashed about with hooves kicking every which way. It did put Lois's actions in a different light. Not

168

that it was any easier to bear or would cause Saloma less tears.

Silence fell between them. Debbie shifted on her seat. Her mother wasn't trying to make trouble, she told herself. *Mom has her own ideas about life, and they don't mesh well with the Amish way of thinking.* But who could blame her mother for that? She'd never been Amish and never planned to be.

Lois interrupted Debbie's thoughts when she rushed back down the hall. How the girl had changed so quickly with all the pins involved, Debbie couldn't imagine. After all her months with the Beilers, she still stuck herself while she dressed. *I guess that's one advantage of growing up in the Amish faith,* she supposed.

"Ready to go!" Lois's face was glowing.

"Take care then." Callie opened the front door for them. "Will you be back for lunch, Lois?"

Lois didn't think long. "I doubt it. Maybe I'll just make it a day at the house. Cheer *Mamm* up a bit."

Callie nodded. "You do that. I'll see you when you get back."

Her mother clearly had no fear that Lois would decide to stay at home. She probably believed Lois would never go back to the

Amish way of life.

"Life is so *gut* to me right now," Lois chattered. "And your *mamm*. She's *Da Hah*'s gift from heaven for me. The things she does for me! I couldn't begin to mention all of them. She drives me to work each day and picks me up. I plan to get my driver's license." Lois talked away as they walked out the driveway and down the road. Finally she said, "But enough about me. Now fill me in on all the news from home."

"There are mostly troubled hearts right now," Debbie admitted. "I'll let the others fill you in on what's going on."

Fifteen

Before Debbie and Lois were halfway across the Beilers' lawn, Ida came running out of the front doorway.

Lois squealed and raced forward to grab her sister in a tight hug. The two clung to each other for a long time.

Debbie waited. She'd expected something like this, but even so, the reunion brought tears to her eyes.

"Look at you!" Ida held Lois at arm's length. "You still look Amish."

Lois frowned. "I put on one of my old dresses and my *kapp,* but this is not who I am now."

Ida took Lois by the hand. "I thought you might come in your *Englisha* clothing. This is better, and I'm thankful. Now come. *Mamm* will want to see you."

Lois held back for a moment. "Ida, did *Daett* say I could come? I didn't think of that until just this moment."

"We all miss having you around, Lois. I'm sure *Daett* will be okay."

Lois didn't look convinced as she followed her sister up the front steps.

Debbie tagged along behind them. Ida didn't pause as she led Lois inside, and Debbie caught a glimpse of Saloma on the rocker as the door swung open. There was welcome written on Saloma's face even though she hadn't come to the door. The first sight of her daughter in a while might be a shock Saloma preferred to take sitting down. Debbie was glad Lois had changed. Saloma would eventually see her daughter dressed *Englisha,* but that didn't have to happen today.

Lois approached Saloma, her step a bit hesitant. "*Mamm,* I'm home for a visit."

Saloma rose and reached out with both arms. Lois flew into them, and the two hugged each other.

Ida wiped her eyes in the silence that was broken only by Saloma's soft sobs.

"Are you home to stay?" Saloma asked hopefully as she let go of Lois.

Debbie figured Saloma knew the answer, but she still had to ask. That was a trait of an Amish woman Debbie hadn't fully acquired — the hope they possessed at times, even in the face of great difficulty.

"You know the answer to that, *Mamm*. But I can at least come home at times to visit . . . can't I?"

Saloma's voice caught as she agreed. "*Yah,* Lois. And I'm glad you've come today — and in decent clothing with your *kapp* on." Saloma reached up to tuck a strand of hair back under Lois's *kapp*.

Lois blurted, "*Mamm,* you need to know I'm not going to hide the way I'm living. It's what I've wanted all these years. And it's so *wunderbah* I have no words to describe it. It's like I'm finally free. But if it makes you feel better, I will come home looking like this for a while yet."

"You've cut your hair, haven't you?" Saloma asked as she tucked another strand of Lois's hair under her *kapp*. The effort had little effect because the section of hair floated loose again.

Lois's voice turned timid. "*Yah.* And since I don't have that much money yet, Callie — Debbie's *mamm* — insisted on paying. She said I'd look more *Englisha* and fit in better."

A tear ran down Saloma's cheek. "You're cutting your hair like a horse in the barn, Lois. How can you do such a thing after being raised so decent all of your life?"

"*Mamm,* please!" Lois took both of Saloma's hands in hers. "Let's not fight about this. I came over to see you and to tell you how much I've been missing you. I want to hear all about what's happening here at home."

"My precious daughter . . ." Saloma apparently couldn't let go of the subject. "This is so wrong, Lois." Saloma sighed. "But let's not speak of it anymore. Come sit, and we can talk." She motioned toward the couch as she took her seat on the rocker again.

Ida sat down beside Lois as Debbie slipped into the kitchen. She would busy herself while they conversed. She wasn't really part of the family, and Saloma needed time alone with Ida and her youngest daughter. Debbie paused to look around as a stab of pain ran through her. For the first time since she'd moved in with the Beilers she no longer thought of herself as part of their family. With Alvin's and Lois's departures, the dream of being part of them seemed far away and slipping further away with each passing moment.

In the living room, the low voices of the three women rose and fell as Debbie's thoughts drifted over the past few weeks. Alvin and Lois had made their decisions to leave the community. Paul Wagler's attention toward her had increased to the boiling point. And in a way that bothered her, it seemed her parents had turned against her by welcoming Lois into their lives in her place. What was to become of her? Debbie bolted out the washroom door and gasped for air. Was this some sort of panic attack? Or was she just realizing that she didn't seem to have a home anymore. Not really a Beiler, and not really a Watson either. Who was she?

Perhaps she needed an honest talk with the bishop. That would make more sense than if she spoke with Saloma as Ida had proposed. The women were occupied inside the house and would be for some time. What better time than right now? Debbie placed her thoughts in action. She approached the barn and pushed open the creaky door. The dim interior pulled her in. She took deep breaths of the musty air that smelled of hay and cows and well-cared-for horses. The back door was open with a manure spreader backed up against it. Emery and his dad were bent over their pitchforks as they cleaned out the horse stalls. Debbie approached them with soft steps.

Emery noticed her first. "Well, look who's come to help us!" he sang out.

Bishop Beiler looked up with a start.

"Debbie! I'm surprised to see you. Is the Saturday hanging heavy on you?"

"I suppose so," Debbie allowed. "May I help you?"

"I wasn't serious." Emery laughed.

"Well, I am." She gave him a warm smile.

"Right over there." Bishop Beiler pointed toward another pitchfork. "And there's still room on my side. We should have this first load up before long."

Debbie sank her fork in the gathered pile the men had moved from the stalls. She could take considerably less each swing than the two men, but that didn't surprise her. She worked slowly but steadily alongside them in silence until the manure spreader was filled. She leaned against the barn wall and caught her breath. Emery drove the team and manure spreader out of the barnyard and over to a snowy field.

"I'm guessing you didn't really come out to help load manure," Bishop Beiler said once Emery was out of earshot.

"No, I didn't." Debbie searched for words to continue.

"Troubled about what's going on?" Bishop Beiler leaned on his fork. "I see you took Lois inside the house a moment ago. Were you expecting me to come in and speak with her?"

Debbie shook her head. "I didn't really know what you'd do. I knew you saw us go in. That's why I didn't say anything."

Bishop Beiler nodded. "I couldn't help but notice with all the shrieking going on." He smiled briefly before his smile faltered.

"I understand," Debbie said. "It must be unsettling for you."

He appeared weary now. "You spend your life training up your children, working with the church, hoping things will turn out okay, and then this."

"Lois did give you plenty of warning." *Now where did that boldness come from?* Debbie wondered. Now seemed the moment to speak her mind though.

The bishop lowered his head. "I was hoping you'd help me out in that area. And you did for a while."

"Are you disappointed in me?" Debbie heard her voice catch.

Bishop Beiler stroked his beard. "Not in you. Maybe in the plan I had. I guess when Alvin left . . ." He paused. "Debbie, you didn't have anything to do with that, did you?"

"Not unless liking him is a sin." Debbie didn't meet his gaze.

Bishop Beiler managed to laugh. "I think that's a virtue more than anything."

Debbie ventured a chuckle. "I don't think the others in the community will see things that way."

Bishop Beiler took his time before he answered. "I suppose you want me to speak plainly, Debbie, since this morning seems like that kind of day. Well, *nee,* the community won't tolerate things as they are going for very long. How long, I don't know, but there are rumblings already. The time will run out soon, I'm afraid."

"So I'll have to go?" Debbie's voice broke.

Bishop Beiler gave her a sympathetic glance. "Not on my part. But I'm not the one who will make the call. There is only so much a bishop can do . . ."

Debbie finished the sentence for him, ". . . when there is an *Englisha* girl in the midst who might be leading people astray."

"I didn't say that because I know that's not the case. And I will tell them so. But our people tend to go by how things look." The bishop paused, and his words hung in the air.

"It doesn't look good, does it? My fingerprints are all over both cases. I give a young Amish boy impossible dreams so he rushes out into the world. I open the way for the bishop's daughter to do the same. My own parents even take her in. People will believe

I helped set that up even though they know I tried so hard to talk her out of it. I guess that won't be accepted as a very good excuse."

"You are a wise young woman." Bishop Beiler frowned again. "You see how things stand."

"If I married Paul all would be forgiven. Is that not true?"

Bishop Beiler shrugged. "Nothing like love to cleanse sins. *Yah,* I'm afraid that's true, though it doesn't make me happy in the least that things stand like that."

"I *can't* do that though. I don't love him. In fact, he's an example of the type of person I'm trying to avoid out there in my world." Her response was heated, but she couldn't help it.

Bishop Beiler raised his eyebrows. "You're sure of this? Paul Wagler has quite an upstanding record among the people. He's not a man any of our young women would turn down, Debbie."

"And yet I have," Debbie snapped. "He comes on too strong for my taste. I'm just not attracted to him." There were nicer ways she could have said this, especially to the bishop.

Bishop Beiler studied the tines on his pitchfork. "I suppose there are many things that must be decided in the future. But let's don't rush into them, Debbie. Please take your time. There are those who will seek to hurry things along, but our people believe a person needs to take all the time that's necessary — even if it seems time is running out. Perhaps you'll come to see the wisdom of returning Paul's attention now that Alvin is gone."

Debbie bit back a quick retort. "Do you think Alvin is really gone for good then?"

"He hasn't responded to Deacon Mast's letter." Bishop Beiler studied the ground. "But there's always hope. Yet I must tell you this, Debbie, simply because you're so closely involved. I fear there is false hope stirring in your heart. Alvin apparently has some serious problems he's running away from."

Debbie stared, unable to speak.

Bishop Beiler continued. "Alvin's *daett* has come to Deacon Mast for financial help. Seems like there isn't enough feed in the barn to last the winter, let alone money in the bank for the spring planting. And yet Alvin left with a large amount of money, we believe. Why would he leave his *daett* in such straits?"

Debbie struggled to find her voice. "Alvin *stole* family money? Is that what you're saying? That he abandoned the farm? Is his father making this claim?"

Bishop Beiler winced. "Edwin is speaking only the best of his son, but Deacon Mast fears the facts may be otherwise. Already men have been assigned to look into the affairs of the Knepp farm. This is a great shame among us, Debbie. And that may be what Alvin is running from."

"Alvin's no thief!" Debbie protested. "I refuse to believe it."

"No one is saying he is." The bishop looked up as Emery rattled into the barnyard on the manure spreader. "I'm only telling you this because it wouldn't be fair to hide the matter from you. You need to know."

"Thank you," Debbie managed to say. She turned and stumbled out of the barn and into the chilly air outside. Now the world had really fallen in on her. Alvin was suspected of theft!

SIXTEEN

Alvin labored over his letter to Deacon Mast. The paper and pen were spread out on the kitchen table in his little apartment. It was high time he got the thing written and in the mail or Deacon Mast would draw his own conclusions based on his non-response. Not that the letter would produce a different ending, but it was better this way.

He'd struggled a few days over the issue and thought about what it would mean. He knew in his honesty that the sorrow it would cause his parents was what held him back more than anything else. That and Debbie's disappointment in him, but he didn't wish to think about her right now. *Mamm* and *Daett*'s heartache was enough pain to bear. That pulled at his heart even as he tried to tell himself there was no other way this could be done. If he returned to the community, *Mamm* and *Daett* would rejoice, as would most of the community, but their compassion would soon turn into pity and, from there, to scorn. He was certain of this. The people might not desire to have such emotions, but how could they feel otherwise? With the failure of *Daett*'s farm, Alvin would be just another boy who couldn't succeed in any venture. He couldn't even successfully leave home for the *Englisha* world.

How this would be put back together later, he had no idea. But perhaps he didn't need to understand. Life had settled into a muddled sort of existence. It went on day to day with ever-lessening stabs of homesickness. He never thought he'd like city life — and he didn't. But perhaps it was the noise and the soot in the streets that was helping deaden the pain in his heart. In a way he was thankful for even the ugly things in life.

Alvin clenched his jaw and picked up the pen.

Dear Deacon Mast,
I received your letter and am thankful for your concern and words of advice. I wish there was a way things could be otherwise, but right now there isn't. I will not be returning home anytime soon — not until I find peace in my heart on

some matters. I understand that such a move isn't acceptable to you or the community, so you may do what you wish. If *Da Hah* ever straightens things out where I can return, I will beg for your forgiveness and understanding for having caused the grief that I have. Until then, I wish you and the community nothing but the best.

Yours truly,
Alvin Knepp

Alvin folded the letter and slid it inside an envelope, sealed it, and then grabbed a thin coat and headed into the hallway toward the elevator. There was really no reason he had to mail the letter right this moment, but he wanted to. It was as if he needed to get the deed done and out of his hands so he could move on with life. How that would be done, he wasn't sure, but this felt better than if he left the letter in his apartment a moment longer.

He needed a breath of fresh air anyway. Back in the apartment he still couldn't bring himself to turn on the television — except for very short periods of time. He felt little interest in what he saw: people who chattered about world news, intense conversations, movies he could make little sense of, and baseball games that went on forever.

He knew he was strange in that way, but it was a subject he didn't own up to at his job. Not that many people asked, but Carlos, who worked with him in maintenance, had this love affair with the New York Yankees. Alvin had embarrassed himself terribly when he asked who they were and Carlos had been shocked.

"The Yankees! You don't know who the Yankees are?" Carlos thought Alvin had lost his mind.

Which he probably had, Alvin thought with a wry smile. *Yah,* he'd left his mind back at the farm. There he knew about life even though his *daett* wouldn't let him run the farm efficiently. He knew how to fix the machinery when it broke down, and he knew where he belonged. Here, well, he tried, and that was the best he could do.

The elevator pinged its arrival, and the doors opened. Alvin walked in. The halls were usually empty this time of the night. Getting out on the ground floor, he dropped the letter in the lobby mailbox. He didn't want to go back upstairs — not yet. Not when he knew the letter would head back to the community in the morning. This was a stressful-yet-momentous occasion. The letter was necessary, but it was also final and, thus, painful.

Alvin pushed open the front door and stepped outside. The coat he had on did little to cut the chill, but he'd experienced worse at home on winter days when he worked outside. He hadn't been raised pampered, he thought as he headed down the street with his chin up. He was a hardy farm boy. It finally dawned on him that the direction he was walking was going away from his usual bus stop. Maybe he wanted new scenery tonight — as if that were possible in the city. Every street and sidewalk looked like the one before.

His brisk walk soon brought him to a gray, pillared entrance to a park. Alvin stopped and stared. Was it possible? A large expanse without buildings in the city? *Yah*, the *Englisha* did keep such things, now that he thought about it. That way they could experience a little of what *Da Hah* gave country people to enjoy every day. It wasn't the farm, but it was better than the sidewalks! Even with the dusting of snow on the ground Alvin thought it was wonderful.

He walked past the pillars, and once he was away from the street he stopped and wiped snow from a stone bench. He sat down and allowed the peacefulness of the area to settle his spirit. He would have to come here more often. It certainly beat anything offered on the television. Here things were as they should be. Here the world showed only the work of *Da Hah*'s hands. In the summertime there would likely be more people around, but that didn't matter. They would come for the same reasons he came, and he would consider them friends.

In the distance the forms of a man and woman came into focus. They came up the same path he'd been on. They nodded and smiled to him as they passed seemingly absorbed in their conversation. Alvin shifted on the cold bench as the thought of Debbie flashed in his mind. He pushed it away, but it persisted. Her face was coming to him from the apartment complex or somewhere near. Only it wasn't Debbie after all. *Nee,* it was the woman he'd seen in the apartment building who reminded him of Debbie. Was he feeling drawn to her . . . just as he'd been drawn to Debbie?

Even if he were drawn to her, she was still an *Englisha* girl and forbidden to him. He had seen her a few times when she walked in and out of the building with her dog. The beast was a special breed. Large. A Saint Bernard? Maybe. He didn't know much about dog breeds, and his attention had been taken up with the girl, not her dog. She'd hardly given him a sideways glance — and that was *gut*. That way temptation wouldn't go beyond comparisons to Debbie at home.

No doubt Paul was already taking Debbie home from the hymn singings. Why was he still thinking about Debbie anyway? She was surely gone from his life by now. Was that girl like Debbie? Sweet and charming and wholesome? Her name was Crystal — if he trusted the name stenciled on her purse she always carried over her shoulder. She'd gotten off on the fourth level the one time they'd been in the elevator together. He'd never seen her with friends, but he could have missed them.

Having these thoughts wasn't right. He would have banished thoughts of her from his mind the first time they came if Crystal hadn't looked so like Debbie. Somehow that justified thinking of her. What were the chances that he would run into a girl in this huge city who lived in the same building and resembled the girl he was in love with? Not very high. Maybe that meant *Da Hah* had a hand in the matter.

Alvin pushed away his thoughts as the couple again appeared on the path. They were chatting away and passed him without notice. Alvin figured he'd blended into the stone bench by this time. He was half frozen to its surface in the falling dusk. It was high time he got back inside the apartment and warmed up before he took sick with a cold or worse.

He rose and put his hands in his pockets. He followed the couple out of the park. When they turned left after the stone pillars, he headed right. Bold thoughts raced through his mind. Things he'd never dreamed of before. He would speak with that girl — Crystal! He would knock on her apartment door and introduce himself. Or maybe he would just smile and say hi the next time they rode together in the elevator.

His determination sent shivers of anticipation through him. Alvin quickened his walk. Was there something wrong with him? He'd rarely spoken with Debbie at home. He always left the moves up to her — even after Debbie had spoken of her feelings for him at Verna's wedding. He hadn't dared take the relationship onward. Paul Wagler was to blame for that, but Alvin's own fears were at the root of his hesitation. Perhaps this choice to enter the *Englisha* world and do something on his own for the first time was the right one. He needed courage, and here of all places he'd found it.

Alvin squared his shoulders. He would find which apartment the girl lived in, and he would call on her. Wasn't that what *Englisha* people did? Well, they might call on the telephone first, but he didn't have a phone and he didn't know where to find her phone number. He could find her apartment number much easier. Tenant names were listed in the front register on the wall in the lobby. He hurried his steps. If he waited too long he might lose his nerve. What if he passed out when she answered the apartment door? Alvin gave a nervous laugh at the thought. He glanced around, but the few people out tonight were busy with their own worlds. The man ahead of him walked even faster. If the fellow had heard him, he might figure a crazy man was loose on the street.

Alvin suppressed a smile as he entered the apartment complex and stopped in front of the list of names. "Crystal Meyers" was among them, with a fourth-floor number. Alvin's hands shook as he stepped into the elevator. This was right, Alvin told himself. He must move on just like he'd done with the letter to Deacon Mast that had to be written. The elevator door opened and Alvin stepped into the fourth-floor hallway. Crystal's number was just around the corner.

He approached and knocked.

Moments later the door opened with a chain latch still attached. Crystal stared at him. "Yes?"

"I'm Alvin Knepp from the fifth floor." Alvin pasted on a nervous smile. "I've seen you a few times . . . in the hall . . . and thought I'd stop by to say hi."

"Oh . . ." The door closed and opened without the chain. "Alvin, is it?" She returned his smile. "Do you want to come in?"

"Sure." Alvin stepped inside.

Crystal wore a comfortable-looking gray dress spotted with pale-red flowers. She didn't look much like Debbie up close, so maybe he'd imagined that. But she was still beautiful. She must have recognized him from earlier to give him such a nice welcome. Maybe *Englisha* girls were all like this. He hadn't known very many of them. He clasped his hands in front of him like Bishop Beiler did when he was preparing to preach a Sunday-morning sermon. He pushed thoughts of Bishop Beiler and his Amish life away when Crystal's dog came up and sniffed his hands.

"Saint Bernard?" he asked, taking a guess.

She laughed. "No. He's a Labrador retriever."

Alvin rubbed the dog's head. "Maybe we could all go for a walk in the little park I found tonight. Sometime, that is."

"Clovery Park?" She raised her eyebrows. "You know of the place?"

"I guess that's what it's called. I found it tonight when I was out on a stroll to clear my mind." The words came out easily enough.

"I walk Brutus there often. He likes it."

Alvin didn't know what to say.

"You work in the area?" she asked, studying him.

"I work for Mr. Rusty. Downtown . . . at the Hyatt." Alvin met her gaze. "He's a nice man to work for."

She shrugged. "How about we take that walk tomorrow afternoon then, around two? It's a Sunday."

Alvin nodded. "That sounds fine." He backed toward the door. "I suppose I'd better go now." He was suddenly nervous at how easy it had been to meet this *Englisha* girl.

"Well, okay," she said. "It was a very short visit, but I'm glad you stopped by. Come again tomorrow at two for that walk."

"I will," Alvin said as he twisted slightly to open the door and then backed out into the hallway.

When Crystal closed the door behind him, Alvin wiped his brow with the back of his hand. He'd spoken with an *Englisha* girl! He'd handled himself well. And she had agreed to go out with him! His heart now pounded like crazy, but how bad was that? It felt *gut,* in fact.

SEVENTEEN

The following day, soon after lunch, Alvin tried on his best Sunday suit — the same one he wore to church services. He clipped in the hooks and eyes while standing in front of the bathroom mirror. As he looked at his reflection, he thought, *Nee,* this simply wouldn't do. Way too Plain. He didn't plan to hide his past from Crystal, but if he showed up like this he would scare her for sure. He undressed and pulled on his work jeans and a shirt. Over that he put on his heavy work coat. Crystal would have to see him like he usually was. If she didn't like it, that might be for the best anyway. Last night and this morning he'd been racked with a horrible guilt. How could he go out with an *Englisha* girl? What if his *mamm* and *daett* found out . . . to say nothing of Debbie. Yet what did it matter? The worst would soon happen at home anyway — the *bann.* And his relationship with

Debbie was finished now that he'd left the community. He told himself this over and over again. Debbie was surely dating Paul by now. No girl could turn down that kind of charm for long. Wasn't that one of the reasons he'd doubted Debbie's profession of interest at Verna's wedding? There was simply no way someone of Debbie's quality wouldn't choose Paul over him. And what if she did choose to marry him for some reason? There would surely be regrets on her part later. And he simply couldn't live with that.

Why Crystal had agreed to go out with him begged an answer. But she must have done so because she thought nothing serious would develop from their time together. That's how things were out here in the *Englisha* world, were they not? He didn't know that much about *Englisha* dating, but it did seem so. Back in the community a man dated and planned to marry. Here in the world, everyone seemed more like friends without making deep commitments.

Alvin paced in front of the mirror and peered at his drab clothing. He looked a sight. It made his heart sink. Surely Crystal wouldn't reject his company because of what he wore. Not like the community back home rejected him. Out here in the *Englisha* world people thought differently. Look at Mr. Rusty, for example. The man gave him respect Alvin had never felt from his *daett*. Already Alvin was head of maintenance. That wasn't such a great accomplishment, but it was a start in the world. Carlos worked under him, along with some part-time help. It felt strange to have his suggestions followed. Alvin had never been the boss of anything. And his suggestions worked like they would have worked at home — if *Daett* had only accepted them. Alvin dismissed the bitter thought. *Daett* did the best he could and must not be blamed.

Alvin glanced at the clock and rushed out the door. He took the stairs one floor down and approached Crystal's door and knocked.

"Come in!" she called out.

He opened the door and stepped inside.

Crystal appeared from the kitchen for a brief moment. "Have a seat. Smile at Brutus. He likes that."

"Hi!" Alvin said, but Crystal had disappeared already.

Alvin sat on the couch and eyed the dog, who did the same back at him. *Daett* had kept a cur around the place since Alvin was a teenager. A smaller dog who kept the rats down in the barn. Brutus didn't appear quite as friendly. Alvin leaned forward. "Hello. How are you, Brutus?"

Brutus growled.

"Not the friendly type, huh?"

Brutus lay down and stared at him. At least the dog didn't bark or lunge at him. So far so good.

Crystal bustled through the kitchen doorway. "I packed a little something. I thought we might get hungry."

Alvin smiled. "Sounds good to me. How far are we going?"

She eyed him for a moment. "I thought you said the park?"

"Of course. I was just . . ."

"Joking," she finished for him. "Don't mind me. I'm used to being alone and having only Brutus to boss around."

She handed Alvin a paper bag and snapped the leash on Brutus's collar.

"Are we ready?" she asked.

"I'm ready." Alvin jumped to his feet. He opened the door, and she marched through with Brutus in the lead. They took the elevator down in silence, much like they had the other time he'd ridden with her. Elevators didn't lend themselves to conversation, Alvin decided. There was no reason he should be nervous.

They got out in the first-floor courtyard. Alvin hurried ahead to open the door. Brutus strained on the leash, and Crystal almost had to run to keep up.

"Want me to take the leash?" he offered.

A grateful look crossed her face as she handed the leash over. "Thanks. He needs a strong hand on these walks, which is why it's a struggle to take him out."

Alvin hung on. Brutus seemed to have forgotten his earlier hostility toward him. No wonder Crystal had accepted his offer of a walk so readily. She needed a strong dog walker more than anything else!

"Weather's turning nicer." Crystal gave him a warm look. "I thought for a while there we'd be in drifts ten-feet deep with how it kept snowing every week."

"*Yah,* the farm back home was taking it hard too." He gave her a quick glance. He hadn't planned on giving out such personal information.

She smiled. "I know you come from Amish country. Mr. Rusty told me when I asked."

He almost stopped. "Do you know Mr. Rusty?"

She laughed. "Not well, but I made inquiries. I grew up around here. It's not that hard to find things out about people . . .

when you're interested."

Warmth rushed through him. Did Crystal mean something special by that comment? She would have had to make inquiries *after* he'd talked with her last night. And Mr. Rusty was off on Sundays unless there was an emergency, so this took some effort on her part.

"I like Amish country." Crystal gave him a kind look as if that explained everything.

And it might, Alvin thought. If she knew he used to be Amish, this might explain her easy acceptance of him. How many *Englisha* girls would go for long walks with men they barely knew . . . even if they lived in the same apartment building? Not many. But Crystal had accepted his offer before she'd spoken to Mr. Rusty.

Alvin hung on to the leash until they reached the park pillars.

"You can let him run," Crystal told him. "He knows enough to stay within the park area. If not, I can call him."

Alvin unclipped the leash, and Brutus was off with great bounds.

Crystal watched her dog run among the trees. "I can't let him run that much during the summer. He bothers people — or rather people are bothered by him."

"It must be difficult keeping such a dog in

an apartment," Alvin said sympathetically.

She laughed. "Better than the alternative — getting mugged or robbed. The city's not the safest place for women, shall we say. And I don't have a husband or boyfriend."

Alvin glanced away. He wasn't about to comment on *that* subject.

Crystal seemed to have no such compunction. "Do you have a girl back in Amish country? Or a wife, as far as that goes?"

Alvin laughed. "A wife! I wouldn't be here if I did."

Her gaze held great interest. "Loyal, huh? I heard you Amish were like that."

Alvin shrugged. "We try."

"I heard you don't divorce. Is that true?"

Alvin didn't hesitate. "No one from my community has left his wife in my lifetime. Or from any of the other districts. I would have heard if they had."

"That's quite a record. I'm impressed."

Alvin nodded. "It comes from our obedience to God's Word and our love for each other, I suppose. We stick it out."

"So why are you here?" She regarded him with a skeptical look. "Seems kind of far from home."

"I have my reasons," he said enigmatically.

"Family stuff, huh?" She smiled. "But no girl anyway?"

"Well . . ." Alvin ducked his head. He felt the heat burn on his neck. There was no way he would lie. But he wasn't going to tell her about Debbie.

Crystal chuckled. "Someone steal her from you?"

That was close enough, Alvin figured. He glanced away and still didn't say anything.

Thankfully Brutus bounded in, and Crystal bent over to rub his head. She muttered sweet nothings to him. Moments later Brutus disappeared into the trees again.

Alvin didn't wait for more conversation as he stood and moved deeper into the park. Hopefully Crystal would forget her question. At least she hadn't said anything by the time he found the bench he'd sat on last night. It was still clear of snow, and even the frost had melted off the stone from the morning sun's rays. "Have a seat," he offered. He waited while Crystal sat down before he did so himself.

"So what do you plan to do with yourself?" she chirped. "Other than keep Mr. Rusty's motel running."

"I haven't thought that far." He stole a glance at her.

She leaned forward and looked intently at the snow in front of them.

"Deer droppings." Crystal pushed snow

on top of the offending particles. "There seems to be more of them every year. I sure hope Brutus doesn't run across one. He'll chase deer, and I don't have the energy today to track him down." Crystal stood and whistled. Brutus appeared at once. "Stay around here," she hollered at him.

The dog seemed to understand. Brutus kept his next run to a broad circle within sight of the bench. "He's an obedient dog," Alvin commented.

"Yep, you can train them." Crystal's voice was clipped, like she didn't think some things in life could be trained.

They sat mostly quietly with a few moments punctuated by small talk until Crystal said, "Well, I'd better get back. Mom and Dad have a get-together with some old friends tonight, and I'm supposed to be there."

"Why don't you live at home?" Alvin winced as soon as the words came out of his mouth. How stupid that question sounded! Things were different out here. Older, unmarried people didn't live at home.

Crystal didn't seem to mind. "Little birdies are supposed to fly the nest at a young age. Don't yours?"

Alvin hesitated. "Well, we do. When we

marry, that is. Except for the girls who never . . ." He let the sentence hang.

She smiled. "I understand."

He went on. "Well, it's just very different out here. Believe me, you don't know how different."

Silence followed.

Has Crystal ever been married? Alvin wondered. He didn't ask though. How could she have been married? He couldn't imagine that Crystal would leave a man who loved her, which any man would. He was certain of that. Alvin stole a quick glance at her face.

As if she knew his question, she gave him a warm smile. "Don't even ask," she said.

The words came out in a rush. "I didn't mean to imply anything."

"It's okay." Her smile didn't fade. She whistled for Brutus. When the dog trotted up, Alvin snapped on the leash. Brutus strained and pulled him along as they headed for home. Crystal walked beside them on the sidewalk.

She broke the silence. "I work for the government, in the tourist department. We handle the downtown area, though we're not busy this time of the year, of course."

He spoke before he thought. "What's there to see downtown? Every day I see mostly ugly old buildings sitting around."

She regarded him for a moment. "You really don't know?"

He grew warm under his coat. What had he said now that was stupid? He muttered, "I'm sorry. What did I miss?"

Slow comprehension dawned on her face. "I guess you do come from Amish country."

"Yes." He pulled himself together. "You still haven't told me what's in downtown Philadelphia."

Her laugh was short. "Only a little thing like the original copy of the Declaration of Independence and the Liberty Bell, to name a couple."

Alvin swallowed hard as his mind rushed back to his eighth-grade social studies class. Of course! How could he have forgotten? The lessons hadn't seemed real or important back then. That had all been in a book, and this was a big city. He managed a grin. "That's 'Amish farm boy' stupid, I guess."

She shrugged. "At least you admit it, unlike half of the country, it seems. The schools have gone to pot, in my opinion. They don't teach history like they should."

"The education was there," he said at once. "It was me."

She took the leash from him. "That's sweet of you to admit, Alvin. You want to do this again some evening?"

He held open the front door of the apartment building for her. "I'd love to."

They rode the elevator in silence and parted with a smile and a nod when she got off on the fourth floor. They'd made no arrangement as to when they'd meet again, but Alvin knew it would work out. This friendship seemed destined to progress.

EIGHTEEN

At the Sunday night hymn singing in Snyder County, Debbie lagged behind when the line of girls filed through the serving line for supper. She watched Paul Wagler finagle his way in the men's line to where he wanted to be — right across from her. No doubt he'd crack his first joke soon — and after her sleepless night on Saturday due to her concern over her future here she was in no mood for jokes.

The man didn't appear too happy right now, Debbie thought. Probably because she'd stepped out of line for a moment and threw off his timing. He was now in the men's line at least four people ahead of her. Debbie kept her head down. Hopefully her maneuver would discourage Paul from attempting conversation. But the man was known for his determination. If he did engage her, she would have no choice but to respond the best she could. A scene was the last thing she needed right now.

Her thoughts drifted to yesterday and her conversation with Bishop Beiler as they cleaned stalls. He'd been more than kind to share with her the information about Alvin. She was thankful for his efforts, but Bishop Beiler had no idea the agony the revelation had caused her. Kindhearted Ida had noticed even though Debbie had tried to hide her feelings. Her friend had come into her room after supper.

"What is it?" Ida asked as she sat on the bed beside her. "Has Lois's coming today disturbed you?"

Debbie winced. "No, I'm glad Lois could come. I enjoyed every minute of it." That wasn't quite true. She'd felt sorry for Saloma and imagined how she must have felt as Lois chattered on about her new life among the *Englisha.*

"Then what is it?" Ida's hand reached over to squeeze hers. Her face was full of compassion.

"I'd rather not talk about it right now. I've got to think things through."

"You know I'm here anytime you want to talk." Ida stood to leave.

"Thanks," Debbie said.

Ida headed to her own room.

How could she share her disappointment

that some folks in the community might be suspecting Alvin of being a thief? Debbie wondered. And this from his own father! No, that just wasn't possible. She knew him too well. Alvin was insecure, yes. But he wouldn't stoop to dishonesty. Even Bishop Beiler had to know that. She could tell by the look on his face. But evidence was what it was. And from the talk after the church services today, the bishop hadn't exaggerated. The woman at the first table Debbie had served talked of little else, and others joined in.

"*Nee,* he's not replied to the deacon's letter yet."

"I don't know what his answer could be, other than coming back at once and repenting of his sins."

"How is the man supporting himself out there? You know that life among the *Englisha* isn't cheap."

"*Yah,* and my Matthias told me an *Englisha* machine can cost ten thousand dollars easily. Where does that kind of money come from?"

"We now know his *daett* doesn't have any money."

And then the final comment that always brought the conversations to a tight-lipped halt. "I heard Alvin's *daett* visited Deacon

Mast this week. Seems like Edwin's run out of feed, and the winter isn't half over."

This was always followed by gasps and comments.

"You don't say!"

"I can't believe that!"

"The family is so upstanding with the *Ordnung*!"

And then silence would fall.

Debbie had finally fled to the kitchen even though her hands still held a peanut butter bowl. When she had collected herself enough to return, shocked silence still hung over the table. Only a few whispered conversations had begun again. And things had been that way all afternoon.

Paul's voice brought Debbie out of her thoughts with a jolt. "Hello there, Tweetytweet. What's the long face about?" He stepped out of line and reached over to touch her arm.

Debbie almost slapped his hand but caught herself in time. The girls around her giggled. They obviously would love to have this much attention from the handsome Paul Wagler. And none of them would understand if she openly rejected him.

Debbie cooed back, "I was thinking wonderful thoughts about you."

There was loud laughter from the men's

line. One of them spoke up. "That's telling him *gut*."

Paul shrugged off the implied insult. "At least she's thinking about me, which none of you handsome dudes can stake a claim to."

"Hey, what about that!" Several of the men slapped each other on the back. "He says we're handsome."

Paul laughed and stepped back in line. He gave Debbie a sharp glance.

Clearly Paul wasn't through with her tonight, Debbie thought. No doubt he wanted a positive answer on his question of whether she'd allow him to drive her home tonight.

The line moved forward again. Debbie filled her plate with food. She hadn't been hungry, with all her thoughts and worries from the last few days, but the meat casserole and the canned corn steaming in the bowl made her mouth water. Debbie took large portions. To compensate, she took a smaller piece of shoofly pie when she reached the end of the line.

Paul was waiting for her by the side of the kitchen doorway. He smiled and whispered, "What's Melvin Kanagy doing here tonight?"

"How would I know?" Debbie asked.

Then she added, "Maybe he's after me."

Paul glared at her. "Ha, ha. Why would he show up out of the blue at a youth gathering? Melvin's a married man."

"His wife has passed on, hasn't she?"

Paul glared even more. "*Yah.* How do you know that?"

"It's not like it's a secret. Everyone knows." Was Paul jealous? If so, Debbie couldn't let the moment pass. "He *is* quite handsome, isn't he? And he's the minister's brother. Maybe he's here to ask to drive someone home."

Paul's glare turned into shock. "You?"

"I didn't say that . . ."

Paul surveyed her face. "Ah, so you're teasing."

At least he knew her well enough to figure that out. But it had taken him a moment. "So what *is* Melvin here for?" Paul hadn't moved. Several people had to walk around them.

"You're creating a scene," Debbie whispered.

That seemed to convince him, and he moved on with a perplexed look still on his face.

Why *was* Melvin Kanagy here? Debbie wondered. She glanced toward Ida, who was already seated at the table. Melvin had just taken his place in the food line and a smile lingered on his face. If she didn't miss her guess, Melvin had directed that smile in Ida's direction. Hadn't her friend said something about Melvin glancing at her during the meeting? Was that why he was here? Because of Ida? Paul was right. Melvin wouldn't show up like this unless he had a good reason.

Well, that about took the cake, Debbie thought as she took an empty seat. Wasn't that a little fast? She would have to speak with Ida the first chance she had. That chance came twenty minutes later when they'd finished the meal. Ida was standing by herself toward the back of the room.

Debbie stepped close. "So, Ida, what's going on with Melvin Kanagy?"

Ida didn't answer, but she turned pink and then red.

"You should have *told* me," Debbie scolded. "When were you going to break the news?"

"Sometime." Ida's voice squeaked. "Besides, he only asked me home this afternoon."

Debbie gave Ida a quick glance. "Are you happy about this? You like the man?"

"Why wouldn't I? He's quite decent and godly." Ida looked away. "It's just embarrassing, that's all. I've never gone home with a man."

Debbie touched her arm. "Relax then or someone's going to notice you're nervous. You'll be okay."

Ida took a deep breath. "I'll try."

Debbie forced a smile. "So, I'm going home by myself with Emery tonight."

Alarm flew into Ida's face. "That's not a problem, is it?"

"Of course not!" Debbie didn't hesitate. "I'm glad this is working out for you."

A motherly look crossed Ida's face. "You know Paul can take you home if you're uncomfortable being alone with Emery."

Debbie laughed. "I like Emery. Enjoy your evening, my friend. You have a right to, you know. That is — if you really want this man."

Ida lowered her head.

She'd be okay, Debbie figured. Melvin *was* a decent man, if she was any judge of men.

Moments later Ida made a beeline for the kitchen to help with the dishes. Debbie knew she should offer to help too, so made her way to the kitchen. Girls were already lined up on both sides of the counter with towels and washcloths in their hands. Ida had somehow worked her way into the center of it all and was busy with dishes at the sink. She was so efficient and sweet.

Debbie hoped Melvin Kanagy would treat her really nice. If he didn't, Debbie wasn't going to speak with him ever again. She sighed as she took a seat at a table again. She figured she might as well sit down rather than stand around while everyone waited for the hymn singing to begin. The clock on the wall showed the time to be a quarter after seven, so there was still fifteen minutes to go.

Thoughts raced through her mind. Why couldn't she date Paul and postpone the inevitable for a while? She'd been in a similar situation before with Doug and several others. The relationships didn't work out in the end — and this one wouldn't either, but Paul wouldn't know that. He was too taken up with his own world and what he wanted. Just like Doug and the others had been. Paul would have to deal with the shock down the road when she cut off the relationship. It might help Paul get over himself and give Alvin and her time to clear their names.

Debbie silently groaned. She couldn't live that way. She couldn't give a man encouragement when she knew she wasn't serious about him. It seemed okay out there in the world, but here in the community things were run by a different standard. And she wanted to live like they did, regardless of the cost. So what was to become of her if she didn't return Paul's affections? Nothing good. She'd be asked to leave. Something had to be done. She couldn't just stand by and watch her heart's desire to join the community go down the drain.

Debbie jumped when Paul whispered in her ear.

"Did you find out what Melvin's here for?"

"Nothing I'm going to tell you." She glared up at Paul as he laughed.

"As long as it has nothing to do with you, I'm happy." He smiled and moved on.

The man has nerve! Debbie thought. *Such nerve!*

NINETEEN

Ida slipped out of the washroom, wrapped her shawl around her shoulders, and closed the door behind her. Emery had left some time ago, and Debbie had gone with him. Now she would be taken home by Melvin Kanagy. She'd never imagined life would turn out this way for her — that she would go home on her first date with a man who had been married. But many other girls had done so, and there was no shame in the matter since Melvin was a widower. It's just the way *Da Hah* worked things out sometimes.

Melvin's frequent glances toward her all evening had kept her feelings up, so there was no reason she should sink into despair now. For the first time she would get to speak at length with Melvin. He was a *gut* man, and though she might not love him yet, there was no reason that couldn't change. Maybe she'd get over her embarrassment soon and stop all the blushing. At least no one had teased her tonight. Maybe they hadn't noticed, although that was hard to imagine. Maybe the thought of her with a date seemed too impossible to imagine. Either way, she was now dating and might soon be a married woman, if she didn't miss her guess.

Ida made her way down the snowy sidewalks. A few snowflakes brushed past her bonnet. She shielded her eyes with her hand and peered at the line of approaching buggies. Melvin drove a dark-red horse — if she remembered correctly. How embarrassed she would be if she climbed into a buggy with the wrong man. And with her nervousness, that might be exactly what she'd do!

"Chilly night," commented Susie Schmucker, who stood in line beside her.

"*Yah,* it is," Ida agreed. "A storm must have blown up suddenly."

"It won't be too bad." Susie smiled. "Well, here's Jonas with his buggy. You have a *gut* evening now."

Ida allowed the warmth of Susie's words to run all the way through her. They certainly were meant to include more than the comment about the storm that brewed in the sky. Susie had noticed Ida and was telling her she cared and that she approved of her going home with Melvin. *What a wunderbah thought*! Ida told herself. It must be a terrible thing to have the disapproval of the community on one's head — like Alvin and Debbie had right now. She felt so sorry for them, but it couldn't be helped. Alvin had left the community, and Debbie should face the facts. But her friend was stubborn about such things. Paul had sent glances her way all evening during the hymn singing, but from what Ida could see, Debbie hadn't returned one of them.

For a moment Ida let a thought linger in her mind. What would it be like to have a man like Paul pay attention to you? She pushed the thought away. It was a dream out of her reach, and she would accept her lot. She must never think about such a thing again. Melvin was a decent man, and he was taking her home tonight. She would be grateful for his attention and seek to open her heart to his love.

Ida moved forward with quick steps as the next buggy pulled up. The horse was the right color, and the faint form of the man in the buggy had a beard. It couldn't be anyone but Melvin. Married men didn't pick up their wives and families this early in the evening. With a quick pull of her hand on the side of the buggy, Ida was up and onto the seat.

"*Gut* evening!" Melvin's deep voice came from beside her.

"*Gut* evening," Ida whispered back, lest her voice quiver. Melvin didn't need to know how nervous she was. Hopefully he didn't know she'd never done anything like this before.

Melvin gently slapped the reins against his horse's back, and they were off.

"The weather's turned kind of nasty," he said as he pulled out of the driveway and onto the blacktop road.

"*Yah,*" she agreed. "I had snowflakes flying in my hair while I waited for your buggy." He said nothing, and she glanced up at his face. Had she said something wrong? Was the comment about the snowflakes in her hair too personal? Did he think such an intimate image inappropriate for the first time in a long time that he took a girl home? She settled back in the buggy seat. Melvin had been married and had six children. He wouldn't think such a thing, she decided. "How are your children tonight?" Ida finally asked when Melvin still said nothing.

He smiled, obviously pleased with her question. "My *mamm* is taking care of them for me. My sister Lily's dating herself tonight." He gave a little laugh. "Young people, you know. They have to see each other."

What should she think of that comment? Wasn't she young? Melvin was taking a girl home tonight, but maybe he didn't consider himself young any longer.

"*Mamm* was most helpful when I asked," Melvin continued. "*Daett* stayed too so I don't have to drive her home even though I offered." He shrugged. "Old people don't mind lost sleep, I guess. But they don't want me to lose more of mine than necessary."

It almost sounded like taking her home was a burden, Ida thought. But Melvin wanted another *frau,* so he must feel he had to do certain things for her — like stay up later than he normally would and ask his parents for help. Ida stared off into the darkness. Her heart pounded. Perhaps this was a mistake?

"Is something wrong?" Melvin shifted in the buggy seat beside her.

Ida tried to speak but the words wouldn't come. Was she suddenly tearing up? She couldn't believe this! What would Melvin do with a girl who sobbed on their first date? He'd likely drop her off right here beside the road!

Melvin waited for her to reply. His voice

finally rumbled in the darkness. "I'm sorry, Ida. I didn't mean that like it must have sounded. It's a great honor that you're allowing me to take you home tonight. The children just need . . . well . . . a lot of attention."

Melvin's hand touched her arm for a moment in the darkness.

Ida rushed out, "Thank you. I understand. I really do. It's okay. And you don't have to stay late tonight if you don't wish to. I don't need much . . . much attention."

His laugh was soft. "Don't undersell yourself, Ida. You're a *wunderbah* woman."

"Don't say things you don't mean." She glanced up at his face. His silhouette was outlined in the dim buggy lights.

His answer came at once. "I'm not, Ida. But *yah,* maybe I'm speaking too plainly for our first time together . . ." He let the sentence hang.

Ida hesitated. "It's not that, Melvin. I'm just not used to . . . things like that being said about me."

"Then it's time to begin." His held the reins in both hands. "You are easy to love, Ida, and my heart has already opened up greatly to you. I hope you will soon feel the same about me."

Ida took a deep breath. This was plain talk

and plain thoughts for a first date, but then she'd never been on one before. And Melvin had been married. And she was older than most dating girls. No doubt he'd said such things to his *frau,* Mary. No wonder Mary had always seemed so in love with him.

They rode in silence for a few moments until Melvin cleared his throat. "My children — they don't bother you?"

Ida jumped. "Of course not! I love children. Well, I don't know yours very well — yet. But the youngest, Lisa, she's a picture of cuteness. And she's so well behaved."

"I have six of them." He turned his head to look at her.

"That you have children makes no difference. Not for me. I know there are many problems that one can have with children in second marriages. But I'm okay with working through any that might arise."

As he guided his horse onto the Beiler driveway, Melvin said, "I didn't know how you would react, Ida. I'm glad to hear your thoughts. I love my children."

"They are *wunderbah* children." Ida smiled as the buggy came to a halt beside the hitching post. She climbed out. In the light of the buggy lamps, Melvin gave her a kind look, and Ida felt heat burn up her neck. She waited while Melvin got out and tied up his horse. Her heart pounded, but not quite like it had before. He was a comforting presence. He wasn't stern like she'd expected — although he probably could be.

"What is your horse's name?" Ida asked as a gust of wind blew against her bonnet.

"Red Rover." He came to stand beside her. "Are you ready to head for the house?"

"Shouldn't he have a blanket?" Ida asked, motioning toward the horse.

He smiled. "You're a thoughtful woman! I didn't bring one along because I didn't expect this storm."

Ida glanced toward Emery's buggy. "I'm sure there's one in Emery's buggy. He won't mind if you borrow it."

Melvin seemed agreeable enough. He returned with the blanket moments later and threw it over Red Rover's back.

Ida helped Melvin fasten the straps underneath. Then the couple headed toward the house. Ida clasped her hands in front of her. She'd never considered herself confident around men, but she had clearly made an impression on Melvin — and she hadn't really tried. The thought sent warm circles around her heart. Paul could make her hopes leap into the air, but Paul had never generated this kind of emotion. She had longed for his attention, but had never obtained this level of consideration. Ida pinched herself. Paul was a most inappropriate subject at the moment!

Melvin opened the front door, and waited while Ida went inside.

As Ida removed her shawl and Melvin undid his winter coat, she said, "Over there's fine" as she motioned toward the woodstove. "You need to be warmed up."

"Are you always this helpful?" He was regarding her with an interested look.

"I guess you'll have to ask other people." Ida winced. She wasn't about to sing her own praises, not even to get another loving look from this man.

Melvin relaxed and smiled. "That's a *gut* answer. I'll take it as a *yah.*"

"I didn't say that!" she protested. "I'm sure I can be quite a pill at times."

He smiled and motioned toward the couch. "Shall we sit?"

"Of course!" Ida wrung her hands. "I'm forgetting all my manners. Let me get some pie from the kitchen for you. I'll be right back." Ida raced off.

Melvin grinned when she came back with pieces of cherry pie and glasses of milk. She paused before she set them down. "Is this okay? We do have shoofly — if you'd rather, but it's a few days old. This is fresh from yesterday."

He laughed. "Cherry pie? I couldn't ask for anything better, Ida. And please don't take any further bother. I'm happy just to speak with you tonight."

Heat rushed up her neck again. She sat on the couch beside him and hid her face for a moment before giving him a quick sideways glance. His voice reached her like a soft breeze blowing over her soul.

"You'll have to tell me, Ida, if I speak too plainly since I'm not used to these things anymore. I haven't dated for a long while, you know, or spoken of heart matters with a woman who wasn't my *frau*."

Ida nodded but didn't face him.

He continued. "I've been trying to make my intentions known at the church services." He paused for a moment. "Is it too much to read a welcome of my attention into your responses so far, Ida?"

"They are welcome." She met his gaze. She was redder than a summer beet, she knew, but he might as well get used to her reactions. She would be calmer as she became used to him. And he was a mighty decent man. She could clearly see that. "Your attentions are an honor to receive." She didn't add that it would also be an honor to live as his *frau.* That would be too plain of talk for her on a first date.

He seemed happy with her response as they ate their pie and the clock ticked on the wall. His voice broke the silence. "This is almost more than I could have expected, Ida. I can't tell you what this means to me — that you would return my affections and allow me to bring you home. I do hope we can continue so we might get to know each other better quickly."

Ida gathered her thoughts. She might as well tell Melvin what he apparently couldn't bring himself to say. Perhaps it might also help decrease her frequent blushes. And she did need to learn to speak her mind with this man if she hoped to be his *frau* sometime in the future. Her voice trembled. "I understand what you're saying, Melvin. You're worried you may not court me like I might expect. I know you can't do all the typical activities with your six children at home to care for. And you have been married before. I know that makes it different too. But, Melvin, it's okay. I don't expect to be pampered or treated like I just finished school."

He looked startled and surprised.

"What I'm saying is true," she said.

"Thank you, Ida, for understanding," he

spoke at last. "I'm unworthy of such a blessing. Twice in my life *Da Hah* has given me more than I could have imagined. After Mary's passing, I never thought to find another woman I could . . ." He let the words hang in the air.

"I'll never be Mary. I want to be clear on that. I'm not worthy to fill her shoes."

His smile was soft. "I don't wish that, Ida. You're quite *gut* enough as your own person."

She ducked her head and felt warmth fill her face.

He didn't seem to notice. His voice was hesitant when he spoke again. "I hate to bring this up at a moment like this. But does your family know what a problem Debbie is causing the community right now?"

She glanced at him. "Are you saying Debbie's situation might come between us?"

He shook his head. "You know I wouldn't let that happen, Ida. I'm just concerned."

"I appreciate that." She looked away.

He touched her arm. "It's your *daett* I'm most concerned about."

She met his gaze. He looked sorrowful enough and deeply troubled. He was being honest, and he was right to bring the subject up. They needed to clear the air. "I hope you will make no requirement about Debbie leaving our house before you see more of me."

He didn't say anything for a few seconds. "I take it that's a *yah* to my bringing you home again and coming to visit sometimes?"

Ida met his gaze. There was a twinkle in his eyes, and Ida felt the heat rise into her face again. She couldn't get any words out. Melvin was saying he wouldn't make an issue out of Debbie's situation *and* he wanted to see her again.

"So it's a *yah*?" he persisted.

She nodded.

He found her hand and gave it a gentle squeeze. "Thank you for letting me come over, Ida. I must be going although it's still early." Melvin got to his feet. "Other than mentioning Debbie, I have greatly enjoyed myself tonight. And I may come again — right?" The twinkle was back in his eyes.

"*Yah . . .*" Ida managed as she rose and followed him to the front door.

"I'll throw the buggy blanket back where it came from." He reached back to brush her arm with his fingertips. "You don't have to come out in the cold." He paused on the porch for a quick wave.

She watched him from the window until he'd driven out of the lane. When the weather warmed, she would go out and see

Melvin off in person, Ida told herself. But this was *gut* enough for the first evening. She was going to love this man. Of that much she was certain. Now if Debbie could be convinced to return Paul's affections, the world would be back in order again. Ida's heart had already begun to open wide.

Twenty

On Friday evening, nearly two weeks later, Debbie pulled into Verna's driveway and came to a stop beside the barn. She was on her way home from work. She should've stopped in a long time ago, Debbie told herself. But Alvin's departure had taken the heart out of her plans to ask for Verna's help. Now it seemed useless. What could Verna do that the others at the Beiler household couldn't? Still, this would be the time for a long talk with Verna. A talk far away from the bustle after Sunday service. Then they'd only have a few minutes alone before someone interrupted. And here at Verna's house no one would overhear if they wished to discuss Alvin in detail.

Ida would probably object to this visit if she knew about it. She'd be afraid Verna's advice would be different than what she'd said in the past two weeks. Actually, pressure was what Ida applied, though Debbie was sure she meant no harm. Ida was sincerely concerned, and who could blame her? Paul was still persistent, trying to persuade Debbie to accept his offer of a relationship. He'd looked quite impatient this past Sunday, and she expected another contact with him before long. The man wouldn't look kindly at another brush-off from her. Of that she was sure. Nor would other people in the community. Once it became clear to people like Minister Kanagy that she'd turned down the most eligible suitor in the community, her welcome in their midst might end. She might appear as little more than a troublemaker at best and a danger to community beliefs at the worst. Yet was that the truth? She was certain Bishop Beiler understood her heart, even though he too would struggle to understand why she continued to turn down Paul. The real problem was Minister Kanagy. His brother Melvin had brought Ida home from the singing on Sunday night again. If Debbie read the signs correctly, Ida planned to marry the man before too long. How her troubles impacted that situation she wasn't sure. And whether Ida's choices helped her own, she wasn't sure either.

Ida told her Melvin was much more sympathetic to her cause than his brother was. Did Debbie trust Ida's evaluation of Melvin? The man might sweet talk Ida to stay in her good graces but say something else to his brother.

How had everything that had gone so well at the beginning turned so much toward a likely inglorious end? She'd never hear the end of it from her mother if she had to leave the Beiler place in disgrace. And Lois would be even more solidified in her determination to never come back to the community — if there was any hope of that.

Debbie sighed and walked briskly toward Verna's front door. The first of the spring thaws was starting, and Debbie paused to breathe deeply. The cool, clean air encouraged her heart and energy stirred inside of her. The change of the seasons usually affected her this way. Perhaps there was hope for her future even if she couldn't see where the path was leading. She climbed the front steps and knocked. She heard footsteps at once, and the door was soon flung open.

Verna rushed out to wrap Debbie in a tight hug before she could even get out *"Gut* evening!"

Debbie laughed once she could breathe. "With that kind of welcome I should have come sooner."

"*Yah,* you should have." Verna led the way

inside. "Have a seat on the couch, and I'll bank the fire in the kitchen stove so the food won't burn. It'll only take a minute."

"No, you won't!" Debbie declared. "I'll come into the kitchen and help you if I can."

"Oh, *nee*!" Verna protested. "I'm well ahead on making supper."

"Then I'll sit in the kitchen, and you can keep working. You don't stop food preparations right in the middle." Debbie pulled out a kitchen chair. "Lois taught me that much."

"How is Lois?" Verna asked, a slight frown crossing her lips.

Debbie winced. "Other than that Saturday when she came home for a visit, we haven't seen anything of her. I'm afraid she's taking well to my former world."

"That's such a shame." Verna pulled out a chair to sit down. "Let's talk about something a little more cheerful."

"I could use it." Debbie grimaced. "If there is anything more cheerful."

Verna sounded chirpy as she said, "Well, Ida's dating Melvin. That looks like a sure relationship. That doesn't help with Lois's situation though. But we have to be honest and admit that her decision was coming for a long time. And there's Alvin, of course. That isn't *gut* either."

"I know." Debbie groaned.

Verna reached over to give her friend a quick hug. "*Yah,* but don't take all this responsibility on your own shoulders. It wasn't your fault Alvin and Lois turned out like they did."

"Then whose fault was it?" Her voice was way too bitter, but she couldn't help herself. "Minister Kanagy sure seems to think it was mine."

"Minister Kanagy doesn't know everything!" Verna protested. "I'm depending on the *gut* sense of the community to see you through this situation."

"Even if I turn down Paul Wagler . . . maybe for the final time if it finally soaks in?" Debbie glanced sharply at Verna.

"I suppose that will make it harder," Verna allowed. "The Wagler family won't take the rejection kindly."

"Well, now you do see." Debbie fell silent.

Verna touched her arm. "Perhaps you're considering Paul just a little bit?"

Debbie groaned again. "Not you too, Verna. I came over here for sympathy, not more pressure for something I can't do."

"Then we will say no more about it." Verna set her lips firmly.

Debbie wrinkled her brow. "Even your father thinks I should accept Paul's attention. Am I wrong, Verna?"

"You said you didn't want any pressure." Verna glanced at Debbie. "If I think you're wrong, that's just more pressure."

"But do you really think I should?" Debbie moaned before the words were even out of her mouth. "I really value what you think. You know me better than anyone else here."

Verna laughed. "With the type of an attitude you have now, *nee* . . . you shouldn't. I'd feel sorry for Paul."

Debbie sat up straight. "Paul! Now I've heard everything. I'm the one who should be felt sorry for."

Verna's face appeared pensive. "What I really think is that you should visit Alvin in Philadelphia. Speak with him. You may be able to talk some sense into his head."

Debbie gasped. "That's a sudden change of subject. I don't even know where he stays. And going there by myself . . . wouldn't that just make it worse? An Amish woman — or would-be Amish woman chasing a man?"

Verna shrugged. "It wouldn't be indecent in your world, and that's where Alvin is right now. And I don't think things could get much worse for you here. Even if someone from the community found out about it."

Debbie searched Verna's face. "It'll confirm what they're all thinking."

"*Ach . . . yah . . .* it would." Verna waved her hand about. "But nothing risked, nothing gained. That's what I say."

"*You* can say that." Debbie glared at the wall for a moment. "You're safely married and living with the man you love. And you're expecting." Debbie glanced at Verna's mid-section.

Verna turned bright red. "I know. It's no longer a secret. I'm showing early, it seems."

"You must be thrilled!" Debbie beamed.

"I am." Verna laughed. "It's one of the most *wunderbah* things to ever happen to me. It's going to be a boy *boppli,* I'm sure. He'll look just like Joe. Oh, Debbie you must not lose heart! Not that long ago I thought things with Joe were over forever. But *Da Hah* saw us through, and here we are as happy as can be. And I'm to have Joe's *boppli* this fall sometime." Verna's voice ended with an excited giggle.

"I knew I came over for a reason," Debbie muttered. "You do lift a person's soul to higher ground."

"Debbie, it's so *gut* to hear hope in your voice again," Verna said. "Remember how we schemed at my wedding to get you and Alvin together? Well, why can't we do the same thing again?"

And you can see how that worked out, Debbie almost said. But she must not cast cold water on Verna's plans. Debbie took a deep breath. "So you think I should visit Alvin? I could go tomorrow. It's Saturday."

"*Yah,* I do." Verna was serious now. "It's really your last chance, before . . . before . . ."

"Before what?" Debbie looked up sharply.

"Has *Daett* or *Mamm* talked to you about Alvin?" Verna's face was creased with concern.

Debbie clutched the edge of the tablecloth. "I have no idea what you're talking about, Verna."

"Alvin is to be placed in the *bann* on Sunday." Verna's voice caught. "I was praying this morning that I could speak with you before then. In fact, I thought of driving over this evening after supper. But now I don't have to." Verna thrust a piece of paper toward Debbie.

"What's this?" Debbie asked as she took the offered note with care.

"Alvin's address. I asked his mother for it." Verna had hope written all over her face.

Debbie unfolded the paper and read the writing in a quick glance. "So you've been planning this? That I should go see Alvin

237

for some time?"

Verna looked guilty. "*Nee,* well, last week it came to me. But what we did at my wedding worked, Debbie. Don't tell me it didn't even though events overran our plans. That Paul Wagler! He's the limit is all I can say. He'd intimidate any boy, let alone Alvin."

"So you think that's why Alvin left . . . because of Paul?" Debbie studied the paper. Verna hadn't said anything about the possible theft of money. Did Verna not subscribe to that theory or had she even heard it?

Before Debbie could ask, Verna leaped up to attend to the soup pot. She spoke over her shoulder, "I'm afraid it's worse than that, Debbie. Alvin left partly because of the state of his *daett*'s farm."

"And stole his father's money?" Debbie asked, keeping her gaze glued to the floor. She might as well say the words. Verna likely thought them anyway.

Verna wrinkled up her face. "I don't buy that at all. And his *daett* isn't saying that. He claims he's been paying Alvin a fair wage since he turned twenty-one. That's a few years now. And if Alvin didn't waste it — which I don't think he did — there's no reason he wouldn't have the funds for an adventure like he's on."

Debbie sighed. She hadn't known how much she wanted someone else to believe in Alvin's innocence. Not that Bishop Beiler willingly accepted the charge against Alvin, but he had at least entertained it.

"So this is an *adventure* of Alvin's?" Debbie kept her voice steady. The thought troubled her. Alvin had caused a lot of grief for an adventure, and it didn't seem like him really.

Verna's look was intense. "Maybe it's a journey of self-discovery — that kind of adventure. I don't know, but I think Alvin was tired of being under his *daett*'s thumb."

Debbie was all ears. "What do you mean?"

"Well, the farm has been going down the tubes, that much is for sure." Verna had her back turned toward Debbie as she stirred the soup. "Deacon Mast isn't saying much, which he shouldn't, but I have my sources. The Knepp farm has been run into the ground by Alvin's *daett*. It comes down to his refusal to upgrade his farming practices and general stubbornness. Things are so bad now the Knepps will need community and ministry help to plant this spring. Alvin might have wished to skedaddle before that happened."

"And run away from the problem?" Debbie didn't like the sound of that in the least.

Perhaps she was missing something. She waited while Verna framed her response.

"I can see where you might think I'm saying Alvin is a coward, but it's not like that in the community. A son who contradicts his *daett* — that's the worst shame. And Alvin would never do such a thing. In that lies his real courage, Debbie. If he stayed, he may have had to speak badly of his *daett.*"

"So his *daett* is Alvin's problem?" Debbie asked.

Verna winced before she spoke. "Alvin would never admit this, but his *daett* isn't one for taking responsibility. Edwin's been blaming Alvin for running the farm down, but most of us know that's not true. However, with Alvin gone, what can Edwin say when the committee of men Deacon Mast assigns to run the farm tells him what he needs to do? He'll have to face things and change his ways. There'll be no one around to blame but himself if things don't get done right."

Debbie took a deep breath. "So it is that bad then?"

Verna shrugged. "I don't know for sure. I'm guessing . . ."

"And your guesses are often right," Debbie added.

"You mustn't tell anyone what I told you." Verna forced a smile. "I meant to encourage you, that's all."

"And send me on a mission?" Debbie held up the address.

"*Yah* that." Verna admitted. "It may do some *gut,* but you must go tomorrow before the *bann* is in place. If you wait, you'll be violating the *bann* if you visit him. That would really spell the end of your hopes for joining the community."

TWENTY-ONE

In the early morning hours of Saturday, Debbie rose and made her way out to her car in the partial darkness. Neither Emery nor Ida were up yet for chore time, so Debbie had successfully sneaked out of the house without waking anyone. She wasn't trying to hide anything she told herself. If it wasn't for the upcoming *bann,* she wouldn't be in such a hurry to take the risky chance of going to see Alvin in Philadelphia. Besides, Saloma and Ida knew of her plans.

Last night Debbie had told Saloma and Ida her intentions, and they understood — especially when she told them about her conversation with Verna. They had voiced no objections even when Debbie was frank about what her intentions were — that she wanted to speak to Alvin about returning to the community. Any chance at success in that department was apparently worthy of pursuit in their estimation. Ida had even stopped her constant hints that Debbie give a *gut* answer to Paul's next request to drive her home from the hymn singing.

At the first rest stop she came to, Debbie changed into an *Englisha* dress. She dared not put it on at home in case someone from the Beiler family should see her. Now well down the road, she felt it was the right thing to do. She drove and hummed one of the hymns the young folks sang at the last Sunday-evening hymn singing. She'd learned the tune, which was a faster melody attached to the community's German favorite *O Gott Vater, wir loben dich.* Debbie tried a few lines, and even spoke the German words out loud. She sounded decent, Debbie told herself. At least close enough for an outsider still learning the language. She must take comfort in any progress she made right now. The thought that her venture into the Amish world might not continue was too painful to dwell on for long. If her trip were a success today . . . but what were the chances of that? The question darkened her brow. She'd already been over that ground a hundred times. She'd lain awake late last night and thought things through again. No other answer had come. There was one thing she knew for sure. Verna had been right with her assessment of Alvin at her wedding. And Verna was probably correct this time.

Alvin must have left the community as much to spare his family from shame, as for his own sake. That and to find his own way for a change. His father sounded like quite a pill. Debbie had come from a home where she didn't fit in, so she could understand what Alvin must have experienced with his father — at least a little. Only Alvin did the opposite from what she'd done. He'd left the community while she'd sought to join it. Yet, in the end, they were versions of the same thing. The thought comforted her.

Perhaps if she shared this with Alvin it would help him understand his own journey and see his way back. Alvin must be made to understand that this was where their journeys parted ways if he didn't return home. Debbie would never go back to her former life — even if the community rejected her. She hoped Alvin would come to the same conclusion — to stay within the community. In fact, Alvin might already be there and she might only have to help nudge him homeward. Perhaps he'd even return with her this afternoon! The thought sent chills up and down Debbie's back. What an accomplishment that would be! It would silence the wagging tongues in the community. It might even convince Lois to see things in a different light. Alvin would have stories he could tell from his experiences that might speak to Lois better than what Debbie had shared. Yet, who did she think she was? She didn't have that kind of power over Alvin. She ought to be thankful if the man even spoke with her once she arrived unannounced. He might not appreciate her efforts to influence his life.

And were these not her *Englisha* ways that were pushing their way forward again? Verna hadn't thought of that angle, but things were as plain as day now. No Amish woman would act like this — visit a boyfriend she'd lost. What a conflict this caused! Debbie was no longer one thing but not yet another either. She'd tried hard to live a suitable life for a future Amish and possibly an Amish *frau* for Alvin. She'd lately even used Ida as her example. She watched as Ida gave up her dreams of love with Paul and willingly accepted what she saw as the Lord's leading toward Melvin. And Debbie had to admit that Ida had bloomed. Whatever Melvin told her on their Sunday evening times together had brought Ida out of her shell.

Debbie brought her thoughts back to the subject at hand as the suburbs of Philadelphia came up. The speed limit on the

Pennsylvania Turnpike dropped, and Debbie slowed down. She checked the directions she'd written out. She had the map open on the passenger seat. Philadelphia wasn't familiar to her, but the apartment where Alvin stayed was close to an Interstate. It couldn't be that hard to find. She let her mind wander as she turned off the turnpike onto Interstate 422. The miles continued. How had Alvin lived since he left the community? Had his bashfulness gotten in the way out here in the big, wide world? She couldn't imagine him in Philadelphia. She'd always seen him in plain clothing busy at work on the farm or silently seated on a church bench at Sunday meetings. Even at the church dinner tables or at the hymn singings Alvin never joined in with the jokes. If someone addressed him, he responded of course, but that hadn't been very often. Alvin was the silent type. But she'd always sensed an untapped strength that ran deep inside his stillness. And no doubt in the *Englisha* world Alvin would have to rely on that strength. He would either grow into a better person or fall apart. No one could survive out here without some source of strength. No doubt Minister Kanagy would think her a heretic to even entertain such thoughts. How could one become a better person in the *Englisha* world? But she couldn't help it. It seemed like the truth.

Debbie took the correct exit and stopped at the intersection. She turned right and looked at the street names. The sight of Park Heights Apartments and the area that surrounded it brought a pleased look to her face. Already she had evidence that Alvin hadn't fallen apart. He must have found a decent job to afford the rent on an apartment in this well-kept area. Unless, of course, Verna and she were wrong and Alvin had used stolen money to afford such a neighborhood. The thought burned through Debbie's mind, but she pushed it away. Alvin was a decent man and no thief. He wouldn't steal money, nor would he survive on credit.

Debbie pulled into the parking lot and took the elevator to the fifth floor. Now that she was here, her heart was pounding. Her boldness also left her, but at least she wasn't drawing undue attention since she was wearing *Englisha* clothes. That choice had been the correct one. She tried to still her beating heart as she knocked on the door. She waited. When nothing happened, she knocked again. When there was still no answer, she checked the number on her paper. It was the correct one. Perhaps Alvin was at work — wherever that was. She couldn't imagine him anywhere else.

Well, she would wait for him. If he didn't come home before lunch, she would find a place to eat and then continue to wait. Alvin would surely be home by four at the latest. When he returned, their talk wouldn't take that long. She should be back to the Beiler farm by midnight, at the worst. Perhaps she should knock on a few of the adjoining doors to ask if Alvin Knepp lived here, just to make sure. A better choice, Debbie decided, was to check the lobby downstairs. Tenant names were probably listed somewhere — on the mailboxes at least. She took the elevator down and checked the names for the fifth floor. Alvin's was there, right where it was supposed to be. Debbie sighed and waited in the lobby for a few minutes. When a couple people gave her strange glances, Debbie retreated to her car. She'd be able to spot Alvin from here, so she'd just relax and wait.

As the minutes passed her thoughts drifted back to the community. Ida and Saloma would be busy in the kitchen by now. She should be with them to help out, but right now this was more important. She shouldn't feel guilty. After twenty minutes or so, Debbie noticed a couple coming down the street accompanied by a huge dog. They walked across the parking lot, laughing at something the woman had said. Just as she was beginning to turn away, Debbie looked closer. Was the man Alvin? How could it be? Alvin with an *Englisha* woman? And laughing with her like he had no shyness left in his body? "It can't be!" Debbie whispered. Her hand raced to the door handle, and she almost pulled it open. She was ready to leap out and call after him. What she planned to say, she had no idea. But they were stopped now, and she could see the man's face clearly. It *was* Alvin. There was no doubt about that.

Debbie couldn't see the woman's face that well because she was wrapped up in a bright red scarf. But the woman was beautiful — that much she could tell. Alvin laughed again at something she said, even throwing his head back in obvious delight. Deep stabs of pain ran through Debbie. Her hands turned cold. Alvin had found a girlfriend out here in her world. The truth was plain to see. It was there right in front of her eyes. He'd never been that comfortable with her.

Debbie stayed put, her hands back on the steering wheel until the two disappeared inside. She couldn't help but notice how they walked closely side by side. She stayed frozen for long minutes in the car. Part of her wanted to rush out and demand an explanation from Alvin. Why was he doing this to her? Hadn't she made her feelings plain? But those words had been said to the Amish Alvin. This man was someone else entirely. His hair had been cut short, and he had on *Englisha* clothing. That she'd expected, but the woman? No, it couldn't be — and yet it was.

Debbie clung to the steering wheel as great sobs burst out. She wanted to leave, but she couldn't see to drive. She wanted the comfort of the Beilers' living room, the soft murmur of the household as people stirred around her.

"How could you, Alvin?" She practically screamed the words. Long moments later, Debbie gathered herself together and drove out of the parking lot while brushing away the tears. A car swerved away from her, its horn blasting. Debbie raced off, in which direction she didn't care. Finally, she noticed a city park. A parking place was available. She pulled in and turned off the engine. She was in no condition to drive. Not until she could get control of her emotions.

Sobs racked her chest as she stumbled into the park and found a bench to sit on.

Now what was she going to do? This was something she was going to have to bear alone. She couldn't tell the Beilers. They would think Alvin all the more hopeless, to say nothing of how they would question her judgment. Here she thought she could drive up to the city and snatch Alvin from the jaws of the world. *Hah!* How full of herself she'd been.

"We were wrong, Verna," Debbie said into the open air. "Alvin's in love, and it's certainly not with me. He's never coming back."

TWENTY-TWO

While Debbie was in Philadelphia, Ida was cleaning her bedroom upstairs. She heard a car drive in the lane. She rushed over to the window and saw an *Englisha* girl climb out of her car that was parked by the hitching post. Ida couldn't see the girl's face, but there was something familiar . . . but what? Who would be arriving on a Saturday afternoon for a visit without her knowing? Perhaps *Mamm* was expecting someone but had forgotten to mention it? Ida left the broom and dust cloth and hurried downstairs. *Mamm* was already at the front door when Ida arrived in the living room.

"Is this someone you're expecting?" Ida asked.

Mamm didn't answer as she opened the door. She gasped and stepped back, letting go of the door, which swung shut with a snap.

Ida ran to *Mamm*'s side and took her by

the arm. "Who is it?"

Her face white, *Mamm* clutched Ida for support. There could only be one explanation — but surely not that. It couldn't have been Lois. Ida would have recognized her sister, even with only a side view. Still, from *Mamm*'s reaction Ida asked, "Was it Lois?"

When *Mamm* didn't say anything, that was answer enough. Ida helped *Mamm* to her rocker, and then heard a quick knock on the front door.

"Please answer the door," *Mamm* managed to whisper. "Lois is still our daughter, even if she looks like an *Englisha*."

Ida pulled the front door open. Lois's concerned face peered at her. Ida stared. Everything about her sister had changed. Lois's hair was uncovered and cut short, with curls wavy around her head. Her dress was one of the most colorful *Englisha* ones Ida had ever seen. Its length stopped well above the knees. Lois's shoes were bright blue. Ida brought her gaze back to Lois's face. "What are you doing here dressed like that? You scared *Mamm* badly."

A momentary look of grief flashed across Lois's eyes, but it vanished in seconds. "It's a free world, isn't it? And *Mamm* said I could visit."

"Not like this!" Ida gave Lois another

sharp glance. "You look like something, well, *awful*. And what have you done to your beautiful, long hair?"

"It's even more beautiful now, isn't it?" Lois ran her fingers through the cloud of curls before shaking her head to make them bounce.

"Maybe the *Englisha* think so." Ida didn't move from the doorway. "But you knew what *we* would think. You should have known better. And you should have at least worn a covering."

Lois shrugged. "Where's *Mamm*?"

Daett came across the lawn at a fast clip, too late for Lois to flee even if she wished to, which she obviously didn't.

"You're being awful to me this morning," Lois said, sounding hurt.

"It's *Daett* I'm worried about now."

Ida's gaze over her shoulder finally caused Lois to turn around and look toward the barn. "Oh no!" She groaned. "Maybe I should leave."

"It's a little late for that." Ida stepped out on the porch and closed the front door behind her. *Mamm* might as well be shielded from what was about to happen, even though she would still be able to hear clearly from her seat on the rocker.

Daett came to an abrupt halt at the bot-

254

tom of the porch steps and stared up at Lois. "Is this who I think it is?" He didn't wait for an answer, but turned and motioned toward the car. "And you're driving a car?"

"What did you expect I was going to do?" Lois's voice was clipped. "I've joined the *Englisha, Daett.* That's what they do."

Daett came up the steps and faced Lois. "Then you can get right back into that car of yours and drive back out the lane. I will not have you here like this."

Lois's hands shook.

Ida couldn't speak. What had Lois expected from *Mamm* and *Daett*? A red carpet? But then Lois always had been a little scatterbrained.

"But Debbie's here all the time, and she drives a car," Lois said, her voice rising.

"You are *my* daughter. And Debbie doesn't act like this." *Daett* motioned with his hand toward Lois's outfit. "And *she* dresses decently."

"I *am* decent!" Lois wailed. "You're just throwing me out because I don't plan to stay Amish. That's why you like Debbie over me."

"That's not true," *Daett* said at once even though he winced. "I love you. You are my daughter, Lois! But I will not have you bring the world into our home. Please leave."

255

"I can't even come home to visit?" Lois had tears running down on her face.

"We'll see about that later," *Daett* said, standing his ground. "Right now you can start by dressing with modesty. Surely the *Englisha* people have some semblance of that. Most don't look like you do now. At least Debbie never did."

"There you go!" Lois wailed. "You're comparing me with Debbie. Don't you understand, *Daett*? I'm not Debbie. I'm my own person."

"Then you should try to be more like her." *Daett*'s voice had softened. "This conversation has gone on long enough. We've tried and tried to talk sense into your head over the years, Lois. I'm sorry for where I've failed you, but you can't come home and be in the community looking like this. I'm ashamed to have to even speak of this with anyone, and yet I must because we do not hide our faults and our trials from one another. You know that. You grew up in the community. Or have you already forgotten even that?"

Lois didn't answer. She stumbled down the porch steps toward her car. Ida went with her, steadying her until they reached the car. Lois climbed in, and Ida waited until she'd closed the car door before she

256

stepped back. Lois started the car and turned it around. She didn't even wave as she drove down the driveway.

Ida couldn't help but think that Lois should have known better. She just refused to learn that her actions had consequences.

Ida turned back to see *Daett* sitting on the top porch step. He held his head in his hands. He sighed. "I've failed, Ida. Miserably failed. I'm supposed to be the bishop of the flock, and my own daughter doesn't know better than to act like she just did. I can't believe how she was dressed."

"You did the best you knew raising her." Ida sat down beside him. The front door opened behind them. They turned slightly and watched *Mamm* come out. No one said anything as she joined them on the steps. They stared down the road together.

Ida broke the silence. "I don't know why Lois never had much sense in her head."

"She's not like we are. We mustn't blame her too much," *Mamm* said.

"I will not have this." *Daett* rose to his feet. "It's also obvious that we can't allow Debbie to have a car here any longer."

"But *Daett*!" Ida leaped to her feet. "That's not fair! Just because of Lois?"

"It might not be fair, Ida, but neither is life. We must look at this sensibly. When the ministers hear Lois arrived at our house in that outfit and driving a car, they're going to make a connection between Lois's behavior and having an *Englisha* living here. Debbie's going to have to go, I'm afraid."

"But she's close to accepting Paul's offer." Ida clutched her *daett*'s arm. "Once she gets Alvin out of her thoughts."

Daett smiled slightly. "Really, Ida? I'm afraid you have your hopes much too high. I don't think Debbie will allow Paul to bring her home anytime, let alone soon. She's got her heart set on Alvin, and Alvin's not coming back."

"You're just bitter," Ida said. "Please don't say such things, *Daett.*"

"They're true," *Mamm* said as she stood up too. "This is a wake-up call for all of us, Ida. We'd better pay attention."

"So you're going to throw Debbie out?" Ida let the horror sound in her voice. She frowned. "Just like that you're going to sweep her away — and just because Lois shows up on our doorstep dressed indecently."

Daett sighed. "It's more than that, Ida. It's time we moved on. Lois is gone, living with Debbie's folks. And they're obviously having a bad influence on her."

"And we can't go on like we are," *Mamm* added.

"Then let me speak with Debbie." Ida knew she sounded desperate, but this had happened so suddenly. "It will be such a disappointment to her."

"Perhaps we should take this slowly." *Mamm* glanced over at *Daett*.

He frowned. "We don't have much time. Minister Kanagy will have enough to say about what happened here today, to say nothing of your own interests with Melvin, Ida."

"Melvin's fine." Ida didn't hesitate. "He understands about Debbie."

Daett shook his head. "Then it comes down to me, Ida. I'm no longer comfortable with how things are going around here. We'll tell Debbie tonight that things have to change. I don't want to chase her out, but I don't know what else to do." *Daett* looked at *Mamm.* "By the way, where is Debbie?"

Ida gave *Mamm* a quick glance.

Having seen the look, *Daett* repeated, "Where is she?" Alarm rang in his voice.

"Debbie went to pay Alvin a visit in Philadelphia," Ida said.

"With his excommunication scheduled for tomorrow?" *Daett* paled. "What was the girl thinking?"

Mamm reached for his arm. "Debbie kept me informed. I'm sorry I didn't tell you, but I didn't see anything wrong with the visit. I was going to tell you. Debbie's trying to persuade Alvin to return to the community."

Daett appeared thunderstruck.

"Verna advised the trip," Ida said.

"Now I've heard everything! A woman going to instruct a man on his shortcomings! How do you expect that to work?"

"No one else seemed to have much success," Ida offered. She saw by the look on *Daett*'s face that she should have kept silent.

"Are we *Englisha* now?" *Daett* exploded. "That we use whatever means lies at hand to accomplish a task. This is as bad as Lois showing up dressed . . . dressed like she was. I can't believe you didn't see the error in this, Saloma!"

Mamm hung her head. "I'm sorry, Adam. It seemed like the right thing at the time."

"We've fallen far indeed." *Daett* stared off into the distance. "Minister Kanagy was right after all. I've been slipping in my leadership at home and didn't even know it. I see I will need to make my own confession tomorrow at the service before I can deal with anyone else. As the Scriptures say, "Cast out first the beam out of thine own eye, and then shalt thou see clearly to pull out the mote that is in thy brother's eye." *Daett* turned and walked slowly toward the barn. He didn't look back.

"What does he mean?" Ida asked as *Daett* disappeared into the barn.

Mamm sat on the porch step and wept.

Ida sat beside her and waited.

"I don't know what all he means, Ida," *Mamm* said. "But a bishop doesn't lose his daughter to the world without the people of the community becoming concerned about his leadership. Lois is now past the grace period in which we hoped she'd come back. And no daughter comes home looking like she did unless she's got her mind made up about how and where she wants to live. We've been deceiving ourselves thinking Lois doesn't know what she's doing. Lois knows exactly what she's doing."

"So why does Debbie have to go?" Ida's voice trembled.

"Something has to change." *Mamm* got to her feet. "I support *Daett* totally, Ida. I want you to know that. So don't go getting any ideas. Now, let's get busy with our work before the evening gets here and we aren't done."

Mamm disappeared into the house, but Ida stayed seated on the step. She would go help *Mamm* soon. Right now she was too weak to trust her own feet. How *Mamm* could turn on Debbie like this was beyond her — to say nothing of *Daett*. Still, the shock of having Lois come like she did wasn't a light matter. That's why her parents were taking this so hard. Lois had moved into the world, and there was nothing any of them could do about it.

And poor Debbie was caught in the middle. Ida breathed a quick prayer. "Please, *Da Hah*, let Debbie see the wisdom of accepting Paul's offer." But her heart sank even as the words came out. Debbie would never allow Paul to bring her home from the hymn singing. Ida decided that she too needed to be honest about the facts and quit her daydreams. With a sigh, she got up and went inside.

Twenty-Three

Late that evening, after darkness had fallen, Debbie parked her car in its usual place under the overhang next to the barn. She'd taken her time coming home. Her tears hadn't stopped for a long time. If she showed up at the Beilers' home with tear-stained cheeks, that wouldn't help anyone, herself included. It would accent the failure of her mission and make the situation worse — if that were possible. Alvin would be excommunicated tomorrow. She decided the news of how he was cavorting with an *Englisha* woman was something no one needed to know — at least from her lips.

Debbie choked back another sob. She wouldn't break down again if she could help it. Enough tears had been shed already. How she could have been so wrong about Alvin she couldn't imagine, but her eyes hadn't lied to her. Alvin was thoroughly enjoying that woman's company, and it was clearly more than a casual friendship. Debbie wasn't stupid enough to think otherwise.

And the woman had been beautiful, so who could blame Alvin? Yet Debbie so desperately wanted to find an excuse for him. That impulse surprised her more than anything. Her heart ached, but it also wanted to understand. Maybe there was a reason for what Alvin had done. Maybe she should have approached Alvin and asked. Instead, she'd fled. If she hadn't, she would only have embarrassed him, to say nothing of how she would have felt. There was no way she would throw herself at a man. If Alvin wanted a relationship with another woman, who was she to stand in his way? From now on she would stay in the community and mind her own business.

Debbie got out of the car and walked toward the house. As she turned the corner, Emery stuck his head out of the barn doorway. Debbie pasted on a quick smile. "Howdy. How are you doing?"

"Okay," he smiled back. "Where have you been all day?"

"I'm surprised you missed me," Debbie said, but she didn't slow down.

He grunted something she couldn't hear and retreated back into the barn. She wouldn't be offering information on her day's outing. Her lips were sealed; her heart was broken. She didn't want to think about it anymore lest the tears start again.

Ida met Debbie at the front door with a worried look on her face. "How did it go?"

"It didn't." Debbie kept a stiff upper lip.

"Oh, you poor dear," Ida consoled. "Was he hardheaded?"

Debbie didn't reply. She wouldn't lie; she just wouldn't offer all the information. Ida didn't seem bothered by her silence, but she fidgeted with her hands and looked like she had something on her mind. "Ida?" Debbie reached out to touch her friend's arm. "What's wrong?"

"We'd better go up to my room," Ida said. "I have something I must tell you."

Debbie followed Ida through the house, glancing into the kitchen as they went past. Saloma was busy at the stove, but she looked up with a pained expression on her face. *Was this about the trip to Philadelphia?* Debbie wondered. Surely she hadn't done anything that wrong when she went to see Alvin. Ida and Saloma had seemed supportive before she left. Sure, Debbie hadn't talked to Bishop Beiler, but she supposed Saloma would pass on the information. Once he was told, had he disapproved of the trip?

Ida didn't offer any information on the way upstairs, and Debbie didn't ask. She followed Ida into her room and sat on the bed. Ida took the chair and faced Debbie as she sat down.

"I'm sorry to have to tell you, but something terrible happened while you were gone," Ida said.

Debbie's heart sank even lower. "The bishop is angry because I interfered with Alvin?"

Ida nodded. "Yes, but it's more than that. Lois stopped by today driving a car and dressed in clothes that were quite indecent. *Daett* ordered her off the place. Lois isn't to come back until she shows more respect by coming without a car and dressing more appropriately."

"Oh, I'm so sorry to hear this." Debbie touched Ida's hand. "This must be an awful shock to your family."

Ida winced. "That's not the worst, Debbie. *Daett* says that with Lois raising such a stink and because she's living with your parents, you have to move out. When the people of the community are told what's been happening, that will be the last straw for you. *Daett* needs to be the one who makes the first move. It will look better for him."

"So I'm to blame for Lois's behavior?" Debbie heard the bitterness in her voice.

"I know you're not to blame," Ida said. "But this is how things are. That's the way it goes in the community sometimes."

"And I suppose the only way I can stay is by accepting Paul Wagler's advances?" Debbie's anger was obvious. She wished it wasn't there, but this day had been tough and long. And she wasn't a saint.

"I don't know about that now." Ida's looked very serious. "I've been thinking about things a lot since Lois was here."

"And?" Debbie cut in, not waiting for Ida to finish.

Ida took her time before she continued. "*Daett* has given up hope on you and Paul. We're sure Minister Kanagy will blame you and your parents for leading Lois astray. He's also going to suggest you had something to do with Alvin's sudden departure. At the least, that you put the thought in his mind through your *Englisha* background and influence."

Debbie stood and paced the floor. She wasn't going to leave without a struggle, she told herself. But what could she do? She was clearly out of ideas, and she didn't think like these Amish people — as much as she admired them. Debbie stopped and faced

Ida. "Help me out here. What can I do that would persuade your *daett* and the community that I'm serious about staying here? That I mean no harm and want to embrace living in the community."

"Date Paul? I'm not sure that would work at this point, but it would be the place to start."

Debbie didn't hesitate. "I can't do that. I'm not interested, and I don't love him."

Ida's brow furrowed, but moments later her face lit up. "I know what you can do. You could live like we do — completely. Like get rid of your car tonight yet, quit your job, and embrace all our traditions and the *Ordnung.* You could apply to join the baptismal class this spring."

"Wow!" Debbie turned to gaze out the window. "That's radical."

Ida rose. "It would counteract the shock-wave Lois set off today. I think the plan would work. And I could speak to Melvin on Sunday evening about you. He has more influence with his brother than people know. After Melvin's talk with him, Minister Kanagy might give you more time."

Debbie took a deep breath. "Then we'd best tell your *daett* the new plan."

Ida hesitated. "Don't you need more time to think about it?"

Debbie shook her head. "Why would I? I'm committed to this way of life, Ida. I want to be part of the community all the way. I need to move forward, especially after today . . ." Debbie let the words drift into the air.

Ida eyes grew wide. "What about your car, Debbie? Will you bury it in a field?"

Debbie laughed. "Ida, people don't bury cars! They give them away or sell them."

"There's no time to sell it. For this to work the car has to be gone by tomorrow." Ida waved her hand in the air like Cinderella's fairy godmother.

A hint of a smile played on Debbie's face.

Ida regarded her strangely. "Have I said something funny?"

"No, I was just thinking about something else." Debbie wiped the last bit of smile off her face. "So let's see. The car. I could give it to my parents. What kind of vehicle was Lois driving today?"

"I don't remember," Ida said. "I was too busy looking at Lois. You should have seen her, Debbie! She had more than half of her legs out for the world to see. I blushed myself at the sight."

"I can imagine." Debbie stifled another smile. Why did she see so much humor in this tragic situation? Likely it was from the stress of the day and the shock of seeing Alvin with that woman. Instant soberness filled her heart as she remembered the image. "We should go tell your father now," Debbie said. She moved toward the doorway. She wanted this over with to quiet the fear that was rising in her heart. There was no guarantee Bishop Beiler would approve this plan. If he didn't, she would have to leave soon. That would break her heart in ways even Alvin couldn't do.

Ida led the way down the stairs without another word.

The bishop was seated in his rocker reading the latest copy of *The Budget.* He lowered his paper when they appeared. "Hello, Debbie. It's *gut* to see you back."

His words seem genuine enough, Debbie thought. Perhaps selling Ida's proposal wouldn't be too difficult after all.

"I'll get *Mamm,*" Ida said.

"Please sit, Debbie." The bishop motioned toward the couch.

Debbie sat down and folded her hands in her lap. The sudden image of herself in her *Englisha* dress as she drove to Philadelphia flashed in her mind. Intense guilt followed. She'd indeed pushed the line, and she was tired of life like this. In a way it would be a relief to make the final plunge — if it wasn't already too late.

"*Mamm* said you were in Philadelphia today." Bishop Beiler laid his paper on the floor beside him. Clearly he planned to have a lengthy conversation with her, and from the sober look on his face, it was the same one Ida had given her earlier.

"Did Saloma tell you before I left?" Debbie asked.

He shook his head.

Ida rushed back from the kitchen with Saloma in tow. The two sat on the couch.

Ida wasted no time. "*Daett,* I already told Debbie about what you said, and we've come up with a plan. Debbie wants to tell you about it."

Bishop Beiler raised his eyebrows. "A plan? And what would that be?" He sounded skeptical.

"Tell him." Ida looked at Debbie.

"Not so fast," Bishop Beiler interrupted. "I'd like to hear what Debbie thinks about the problem we have."

Debbie took a deep breath. "I think you're perfectly justified in asking me to leave. In fact, I'm ashamed of myself that I've not thought more about how things appeared to the community. So the plan is — if you'll allow me — I'm going to get rid of my car — maybe even tonight. Next week I'll hitch

271

a ride to my job until I can give Mr. Fulton my two weeks' notice. I'm ready to make the final plunge and join the church — and put in my application for the spring baptismal class."

"I see." Bishop Beiler seemed a little stunned. "This is rather quick."

Saloma stood and walked over to give Debbie a hug. "That's the most *wunderbah* news I've heard all day. Surely, *Daett,* that will satisfy those of the people who still have questions about Debbie's character."

"And what about Paul Wagler?" Bishop Beiler regarded Debbie with intensity. For a moment, Debbie wavered. The temptation from the other Sunday evening at the hymn singing returned. It would be so easy to promise to see Paul. No one would know that she wasn't serious. That way she might weather the storm until things had calmed down. But she couldn't do it. That was how she used to live in her world. In the community she was determined not to live like that. Not even if it cost her Bishop Beiler's approval. If he asked her to leave, then that was how things would be.

"I don't love him, and I'm not interested in him. I can't see the man — not in that way," Debbie whispered.

"That's what I thought." Bishop Beiler

settled into his rocker. "Well, we'll have to think about this. I will speak with the ministers tomorrow, but in the meantime don't do anything about your car, Debbie. I wouldn't want you to get rid of it and still have to leave. That wouldn't be right."

"You can't decide now?" Ida's voice trembled. "Debbie has to stay, *Daett*. She's one of us."

"I agree." Bishop Beiler nodded. "I feel so too. But it's not all up to me, you know."

"It's okay," Debbie said to Ida. Peace ran through her heart, which surprised her. Bishop Beiler's kind face had helped. He looked like his reasonable self again, so surely something could be worked out. The community was full of decent people, and they would judge her correctly. She wouldn't begin to doubt that now.

TWENTY-FOUR

The following Monday evening Debbie knocked on the door of her parents' home. Her car was parked in the driveway in its usual spot, only this time the vehicle would stay there when she left. Now that the moment had arrived to permanently leave this part of her life behind, it was even easier than she'd imagined. Her dream to join the Amish community was, after all, what she'd wanted for years. Her only sorrow was for Alvin and what had happened yesterday — the horrible excommunication. But she wouldn't think about that now. Rather, she'd dwell on the thankfulness that bubbled up when she thought of how hard Bishop Beiler must have worked so she could continue to stay in his home. Minister Kanagy had grudgingly given his consent yesterday to the plan, but at least he'd given it. Debbie was determined to not disappoint the bishop anymore.

She knocked again and peered through the glass in the door. She couldn't see anyone, and yet her mother's car was parked in the garage. Debbie tried the doorknob and went in when it turned.

"Mother?" Debbie called out as she paused in the foyer.

"Hello!" her mother's voice answered from the back of the house. The sound of footsteps soon followed, increasing in intensity.

"Am I interrupting something?" Debbie asked when Lois and her mother appeared.

"Oh, no!" Callie was all smiles. "I heard you drive in, but we were trying on Lois's new dress. We're going out for the evening, Debbie. Doesn't she look splendid?"

Debbie gave Lois a quick look. "She does, mother. You always know how to do such things."

"Thank you." A look of regret flashed across her mother's face. "But you never wanted any of it. But now . . ." Her mother paused as she turned to give Lois a glowing look. "Isn't she just something, Debbie? All that beauty buried under those awful clothes. I say it's a crime hiding away what the good Lord gave the girl."

"Mom!" Debbie exclaimed. "It's not exactly like that. We believe a woman's beauty is for her husband's benefit, not for everyone's."

Callie waved her hand dismissively. "I disagree. This is what a woman should look like." She continued to beam at Lois, who had begun to turn a little red. Lois wasn't used to all this attention, even though she enjoyed it to the fullest most of the time.

"Well, don't come over to the house looking like that." Debbie addressed Lois directly.

"So now you're one of them," Lois snapped. "I used to think you were my friend."

"I'm sorry," Debbie said at once. "That may not have come out right. Your appearance on Saturday hurt your family a lot. Can't you be a little more understanding about how they feel?"

Lois didn't look happy. "I can't come over anyway for a while. *Daett* forbade it."

"Isn't that just the most intolerable thing you ever heard?" Callie spoke up. "How can you be a part of that, Debbie?"

Debbie sighed. "Look, Mom, that's what I want. And it's not how you think it is."

Callie gave her a quick glance. "I see you're looking and talking more like one of them all the time."

"I guess I am," Debbie allowed. She

thought about what she'd said earlier. She had included herself when she defended the Beilers. Maybe she had made more progress than she imagined. No wonder Bishop Beiler went to such efforts to help her.

"So why are you here, Debbie?" Callie asked. "Is this an official visit or just a friendly chat?"

Debbie knew her mother had no interest in a friendly chat. She and her mother had been at odds over most things in life — unlike Lois who was the spitting image of what her mother thought a daughter should be. Debbie pushed the bitterness away. She'd been accepted at the Beilers as if she were one of their own girls, so she shouldn't complain if her mother lavished her affections on someone else's child. Still, it stung.

"I've come to drop off my car," Debbie said. "Since Lois drives now I figure she can have it." Debbie directed her look toward Lois.

"You're giving your car to me?" Lois couldn't have sounded more astonished. "But I can't afford one. I'm working at McDonald's, and it doesn't pay that much."

"I'm *giving* it to you," Debbie said.

Her mother didn't appear convinced. "Is the car payment too much, Debbie? A car payment right now on Lois's salary would be difficult."

"I've paid the car off." Debbie tried to keep the disappointment out of her voice. Did her mother really think she'd unload something she didn't want onto Lois? What had she done to cause everyone to question her motives? Her mother didn't believe her, and some members of the community thought she was the cause of Alvin and Lois leaving the faith.

Her mother didn't say anything for a moment. "Oh. That's different. But why?"

Debbie shrugged. She had no plan to explain this. "I have to move on with my life, and you know the Amish don't drive cars."

"So you're joining the church?" Lois's face showed her disapproval.

"That's what I'm doing." Debbie tried to keep the tremble out of her voice.

Lois looked teary-eyed for once. "I suppose *Daett* will get the daughter he wanted after all. I know I never could be that for him."

"It's not like that at all." The words rushed out of Debbie's mouth, but Lois didn't change her expression. That was because Lois had spoken the truth. And Lois must feel the same pain Debbie was experiencing with her mother — being rejected because

278

she couldn't live the life that had been planned for her. "I'm sorry," Debbie said to Lois. "I really am."

Lois wiped her eyes. "You don't have to give me your car, Debbie. I'll pay for it when I can. Would that be okay?"

Debbie thought for a moment. She'd planned to give the car away outright, but Lois might be offended with such a large gift. That was something she hadn't thought of in her rush to find a way she could stay at the Beilers. She nodded. "You don't have to, but you can if you must."

"That's great then!" Lois made an attempt at being her usual bubbly self. "May I take a look at my new car?"

Debbie led the way outside. Lois had seen her car many times, but the first sight of it when Lois knew the car was her own would be a different experience. Lois ran her hand up and down the length. "It's so beautiful, Debbie. I can never thank you enough."

Debbie hid her grimace. "It's just a car. I've tried to take good care of it."

Lois opened the door and climbed behind the wheel. "If you ever want it back, it'll be here for you."

"I won't," Debbie assured her. She wouldn't even if she had to remain forever an old maid among the Amish. Last night after the hymn singing she'd given Paul another firm *no.*

Paul had responded with a clipped, "You'll stay an old maid forever, Debbie. That's what will happen to you." He'd sounded like he was describing an awful disease.

She'd stayed firm in her insistence that her answer was *no* and would always be *no.* And so far she had survived. Chalk that up as victory number one. And she would continue to stand on her own two feet.

"Debbie!" Her mother's voice cut through her thoughts. "Do you have the title with you?"

"Yes." Debbie focused and handed her mother the paper. "I signed it over today at the notary."

Callie took the paper, and glanced at it. "Efficient as ever, I see."

At least her mother admired one thing about her, Debbie thought. She told them goodbye and turned to walk away. They were still standing by the car when she glanced over her shoulder. She was surprised that Bishop Beiler hadn't objected to her gift of the car to Lois. That could be construed as a helping hand for Lois in her *Englisha* ways, but no objections had been raised even though Debbie had made sure the bishop knew her plans. Maybe he figured Lois had made her mind up to leave and nothing would persuade her anyway.

Debbie walked faster. It felt strange that no car awaited her under the barn overhang. Her world had shrunk greatly in size. Yet, this was what all the Amish people felt, and she would get used to it. In fact, she already liked it. Home seemed closer, more intimate in a way that it couldn't have before. Sure, she'd always been happy at the Beilers', but she would be even more so now. If only Alvin were here to enjoy this moment with her! A pang ran all the way through her. But Alvin had jumped the fence into the *Englisha* world and was even dating an *Englisha* girl.

Debbie had been so sure of her estimation of his heart. How could she have been so wrong? Perhaps that question couldn't be answered, and agonizing over it wouldn't help. Clearly she traveled in one direction, and Alvin and Lois in another. She might catch glimpses of their faces in the years ahead, but things would never be the same.

Yesterday, Alvin had been placed in the *bann.* Since Debbie wasn't a member, she hadn't been inside to see it happen, but Ida had shared the details afterward. There had been plenty of tears among the women, and Alvin's mother, Helen, had wept openly.

The strain might prove too much for Helen, Ida told her, since Alvin's mother already struggled with her health.

Alvin would not come back — unless the *bann* worked like Ida claimed it would. Debbie doubted that somehow. Yet what did she know? All she knew was that she must not pin her hopes on Alvin. That had been a recipe for disaster so far.

Debbie put on a cheerful smile as she walked up the Beilers' front steps. She still had much to be thankful for, and she ought to act like it. Bishop Beiler had allowed her to stay at his home. That was a great and blessed honor indeed.

TWENTY-FIVE

Ida slipped through the washroom doorway after the Sunday evening hymn singing and joined the line of girls waiting for their boyfriends' buggies to pick them up at the end of the sidewalk. She still wasn't used to this, Ida thought. She had to admit she was falling in love with Melvin Kanagy. At the thought, Ida blushed in the darkness. Recently Melvin had become ever bolder at the meetings with his glances toward her. She couldn't blame him really. He had lost Mary, the *frau* he'd loved. Ida did like receiving his attentions. She hoped no one would think them indecent by the time they wed.

Ida pinched herself. She shouldn't think about marriage, but it was difficult not to. Melvin seemed so sure of himself. Paul Wagler drifted further from her thoughts with each passing day. She should never have allowed her heart to dream of Paul's attention anyway. Paul was not for her, and he had demonstrated that further by the way he'd acted today. Paul had made quite a scene at the unmarried men's dinner table. He had joked with several of the girls who had steady boyfriends. Usually he confined his attentions to the ones who dated. Apparently Debbie's rejection of him had hurt more than even she would have guessed.

Ida had been surprised when Debbie shared how her conversation had gone with Paul. How she'd told him, "There is nothing between us, Paul, and never will be, regardless of what happens." That statement was brave of Debbie, Ida thought. She wouldn't have dared turn down Paul's attention even if she'd wanted to. Debbie seemed determined to make her own peace with Minister Kanagy and the community without Paul's help. And it seemed to be working. She'd gotten rid of her car and told *Daett* plainly that she planned to attend the first baptismal instruction class scheduled to begin two weeks after communion. Still, Ida decided she'd speak with Melvin about Debbie tonight. Surely that wouldn't hurt, and it might even help Debbie since Melvin was Minister Kanagy's brother. Melvin should be open to what she had to say, and he might pass on the information. Every little thing she could do to help Debbie was worth the effort.

Ida turned her attention to Susie Schmucker, who stood in front of her in line. Susie whispered over her shoulder as her boyfriend Jonas's buggy came to a stop. "Have a *gut* night Ida, and the best to the two of you."

"*Danke,* and the same to you." Ida watched as Susie climbed into the buggy. The door closed, and Jonas's horse dashed off into the night. Melvin's buggy pulled into the line several places toward the back, and Ida headed that way. She wouldn't wait until he came to the end of the sidewalk.

"*Gut* evening," Ida sang as she pulled herself up to sit beside Melvin.

"It's *gut* to see you again." Melvin's deep voice filled the buggy.

Ida clasped her hands in front of her as thrills ran down her back. Melvin guided Red Rover out of the line, and they were off. Ida hung on as they passed the other buggies still waiting at the end of the sidewalk. She straightened herself on the seat once the ride smoothed out.

"How are your children?" Ida asked as Red Rover's hooves beat steadily on the blacktop.

"*Mamm*'s taking care of them tonight

again — and *Daett* too of course," he said. "They don't mind. Especially knowing the *gut* woman I'm with."

Ida felt her neck grow warm. Melvin sure knew how to turn the most innocent question into kind words.

Her silence must have worried him because he glanced at her. "I do like taking you home, you know."

Ida wanted to hug him, but she stared over the buggy door instead. She really should turn this conversation in another direction. She turned to smile up at him. "I'm sure your children are well behaved for your *mamm.* I would understand if you didn't take me home every Sunday night. We could skip a Sunday . . ."

"Tired of my company already?" He gave a little laugh.

"You know that's not true, Melvin." Ida reached over and touched his arm.

He leaned toward her. "I wasn't sure. I'm not as young as I once was."

"You must be having a bad day." She looked up at him.

He laughed. "Nothing unusual. Amos did fall and skin his knee this afternoon, but let's not talk about that right now. You always cheer me up, regardless of my mood."

"Was the fall anything serious?"

Melvin didn't seem too concerned. "*Nee.* Amos was just sliding down the haymow ladder. Boys do that all the time."

She wondered about that. Melvin might not be aware of how much his children were hurt. Men were like that.

He glanced down at her with a grin on his face. Melvin must know she was thinking of his children's welfare, and he seemed to like it. What man wouldn't be concerned with what the woman he dated thought of six children?

They rode along in silence for a few moments. It was peaceful enough, Ida thought. One should be able to spend time without words with the people one loved. She took this as another *gut* sign. They seemed to belong together.

"How's Debbie doing?" Melvin asked as he guided Red Rover into the Beiler driveway.

"Okay." She let go of his arm.

A tease played on his face. "Maybe I shouldn't have interfered, but I spoke with my brother about her. I told him Debbie's trying and that he should back off a bit."

She stared at him. "You did that for Debbie? Before I even asked you to consider it?"

"So . . . you were going to ask me." He smiled. "Well, I beat you to the punch! And I was glad to help out." He pulled to a stop and climbed down from the buggy.

Ida followed him as he tied Red Rover to the hitching post. Her words tumbled over each other. "I can't thank you enough, Melvin! You didn't have to do that, but it was very nice of you. Debbie's intentions are very honorable! And it is true that she's trying. Debbie plans to join the baptismal class this spring, and you know she got rid of her car. She's very serious about joining our community."

He grunted and pulled the tie rope tight. "You don't have to convince me, Ida. How's Lois doing?"

"Not well." Ida caught her breath at the sudden change of subject.

Melvin shook his head. "I'm sorry for your family when it comes to Lois. These things cut deep when someone we love leaves the faith. And the community isn't always certain why it happens."

Ida breathed easier again. "I appreciate your confidence, Melvin. *Daett* blames himself plenty, but I can assure you Lois was always this way." Melvin might as well know their family troubles, she figured — if he planned to take her as his *frau*.

Melvin reached for her hand, and his fingers closed around hers. "I'm not trying to say anything, Ida. I don't doubt you or your *daett*. Let's be clear about that. I love you already more than I wish I did."

Ida felt her hand tremble and figured Melvin must feel it too. He would know that she was timid on the inside — if he didn't already know that. And he would also know that she wanted this to work. She wanted it more every time she was around him.

He pulled her closer to him. "Let's not let church trouble keep us apart, Ida. I don't know much about Debbie, other than that you like her, and I trust your judgment of a person. But the ministry can take care of any problems should they arise. In the meantime, I love you, Ida."

Her fingers tightened in his. "You know how I feel about you, Melvin."

"Can you love me enough, Ida?" His voice caught. "Enough to want to spend your life with me and my children?"

She leaned against his shoulder. "Why else would I let you bring me home like this?"

He turned to face her. "I'm asking you to be my *frau,* Ida. Do you love me that much?"

Ida's head spun. Had she heard right? Had Melvin asked for her hand in marriage right out here beside the buggy? *Yah!* Her knees would buckle under her at any minute. Thankfully Emery and Debbie were already inside the house. What an embarrassment if a buggy pulled into the driveway right in the middle of a marriage proposal.

Red Rover neighed beside them, and Melvin's hand touched her face. "Will you marry me, Ida?"

Her voice shook. "Melvin, *yah.* Of course I will. I'm willing!"

"Even with my six children . . . even then you will have me?" Both of his hands found her face.

She trembled as his callused fingers gently touched her soft skin. "I will love you and them with all my heart, Melvin. It would be a great honor . . . to be your *frau.*"

His hand slipped around her waist, and he pulled her close.

She lifted her head to meet his. Wild thoughts raced through her mind, and time seemed to stand still. A man was ready to kiss her. She would die from the excitement if it didn't happen soon. Ida closed her eyes, as his lips touched her. He smelled of Ivory soap and barnyard hay. It was sweet . . . and so was his mouth. She'd never imagined how this would be, but it was beyond her wildest thoughts. Even if she'd tried, she never would have come close to how *wunderbah* kissing the man who would be her husband would be.

His beard brushed her face as he pulled away.

Did he like her kiss? Ida searched his face for affirmation in the dim light. Had he enjoyed her touch? Even after he'd kissed Mary so many times over the years?

As if he heard the questions in her heart, he bent his head and whispered, "You're the sweetest woman, Ida. So fresh and pure." His mouth sought hers again.

Now she would die, Ida thought. Even the thought of heaven had never seemed better.

"This is enough." Melvin lifted his head. "You're too *wunderbah* for the likes of me."

"I'm not!" she protested and tried to breathe.

"We must set the wedding date," he said. "Tonight yet, if you don't object."

She clung to his hand. "Of course I don't. I told you earlier . . ."

His hand touched her face again. "*Yah,* I know. But when will you wed me?"

She laid her hand on his chest. "I'm not one to boldly think of such things, Melvin. But I will say the wedding vows whenever you wish. I don't need pampering."

He took her hands in both of his. "You're

more than I could ever have hoped for, Ida. Shall we go inside?"

She laughed. "It might be easier to make plans there." A great happiness swelled up inside her. How quickly things were moving along! But was that not *Da Hah*'s way? Doing *wunderbah* things that no one thought possible.

"We will have to tell the children." His voice was a little worried. "I do so hope that won't be a problem. They're all small yet and shouldn't complain of whom I choose as a *frau*. And with you, I'm sure there shouldn't be any problem at all."

"It'll be okay." She opened the front door for him. "What's Willard's age — the oldest? About nine?"

"You're right, nine." He was impressed. "You took the trouble to ask around to find out?"

"I'm a woman," Ida told him. "That's what we do. Especially if we love children."

She held the door for him, and he entered and sat at his usual place on the couch. When she made to walk past him toward the kitchen, he motioned for her to sit beside him. "I want to look at you right now, Ida. I don't think I can get enough of you."

She sat down and knew heat was rising in

bright streaks of red up her neck. He saw her discomfort and took her hand. "It's okay, Ida. I know I'm still a little strange to you, but I love you. I hope that's enough."

She met his gaze. "It's all I need, Melvin."

He grinned. "So about that wedding. When can it happen?"

"We can get ready by May perhaps," she said. "Is that *gut* enough? Of course, I should speak with *Mamm,* but I'm sure she'll understand."

He made a sad face. "I suppose I can wait that long."

"You'll have to wait that long." She jumped up as he looked ready to kiss her again. "I'd better get that food out in the kitchen."

His fingers lingered on hers as she pulled away and scurried into the kitchen.

TWENTY-SIX

The following Monday Ida cleared away the breakfast dishes, humming as she worked. In the basement the washer motor had run since well before daylight. *Mamm* was down there now with a few more loads of the weekly wash ahead of her. The rest was already out on the line. Only minutes ago, Debbie had left for her job at Destiny Relocation Services with her friend Rhonda, who also worked there. Rhonda lived near the town of Penns Creek. She could easily pick up Debbie in exchange for gas money. The way Debbie made the adjustments necessary to her new life without an automobile was so *wunderbah,* Ida thought. Debbie had such a cheerful attitude, and *Da Hah* blessed her for it. There was no doubt about that.

Melvin's face was still in front of Ida's eyes as she worked. She could still see his smile after he'd kissed her goodnight beside the buggy. Ida blushed at the thought, and the dish in her hand clattered to the table. She bent over to pick it up, her thoughts still fixed on Melvin. He had asked her to be his *frau*! And in May already! How fast things moved. And how would they ever get ready in time? That's what she ought to be thinking about. Instead, her head was up in the clouds, and all about a kiss. But that's what people in love did, didn't they? She felt the heat rise to her face again.

Ida rushed to clear the rest of the table. She must speak with *Mamm* about the wedding the first chance she had. Maybe after all the wash was on the line. Ida paused to catch her breath. She really couldn't be blamed for her mixed-up state this morning. A man had never kissed her before. Melvin wasn't as dashing as Paul Wagler, but Paul had only been a fantasy, not unlike a young schoolgirl's idle dream. Melvin, on the other hand was real, and he loved her. What more could she ask for than that? And he had already done the family a great favor when he stuck up for Debbie. That gesture alone made Paul look like a shadow of the man Melvin was. Paul was too consumed with himself to think of such a kind action.

With a quick step *Mamm* burst into the kitchen with an empty hamper in her hand.

"Another load down and two to go, I think." *Mamm* paused to glance at Ida. "You're awful dreamy this morning."

Ida kept her face turned away. Now that the moment had come, she really didn't want to tell *Mamm* about the proposal. It had all been so sudden, and she wanted to savor it a while longer. But *Mamm* waited, so she had to say something. "Melvin spoke up for Debbie with his brother. That's why there hasn't been the trouble we expected."

Mamm didn't say anything for a moment. "I didn't know Melvin had so much influence with Minister Kanagy."

"Apparently he does," Ida said.

Mamm muttered something Ida couldn't hear and disappeared toward the bedroom. She was back moments later with the hamper full again.

Ida stopped her. "I have more I want to say. The kitchen work is almost done anyway. And Melvin . . ."

"I guess I'll have to stop." *Mamm* sank to a kitchen chair with a sigh. "These old bones don't take to work like they used to."

"*Mamm,* don't you like Melvin?"

Mamm shook her head. "It's not that, Ida. Just all the *kafuffle* that's been going on lately, with Lois and now Debbie's church troubles, has me distracted. But don't worry, Ida. I like the man — even though this whole thing of bringing you home seems kind of quick."

"He needs a *frau,* and he has six children who need a *mamm,*" Ida said.

"*Yah,* but are his children reason enough to marry him?" *Mamm* regarded Ida for a moment. "You do love him a little, I hope?"

Melvin's face as he kissed her flashed before Ida's eyes. She must have turned bright red, because a slight smile played on *Mamm*'s face.

"He must have made some kind of impression on you, it seems."

"He's strong, and decent, and has a tender heart," Ida managed.

"Okay, okay." *Mamm* waved her hand. "You don't have to tell me the details. If you're happy, I won't complain. But I do wish people could keep church things out of love."

"Melvin was just trying to help," Ida said. "He asked me to marry him last night, *Mamm*!"

"I was wondering what this was all about. I figured it would come sooner or later. You accepted, I assume?"

"*Yah.*" Ida hesitated. She made no effort to keep the dismay from her face. This was not how she had imagined the moment when she would tell *Mamm* the news of her upcoming wedding. "You don't seem overly happy. You surely don't object?"

Mamm reached over to touch Ida's arm. "Of course I don't object. Melvin's a *gut* man. I just want you to be happy. But he does have six children, you know."

"I know that." Ida paused. "That's why we're getting wed in May."

Mamm jumped up. "In May! Ida! That's in two months! What were you thinking?"

"It doesn't have to be a big wedding! It really doesn't." Ida clutched *Mamm*'s arm. "Melvin's perfectly happy with almost nothing. This, after all, is his second wedding, and he has his children's needs on his mind."

Mamm collapsed into her chair again. "Ida, it's just so much happening so soon."

Her *mamm* seemed close to tears, so Ida thought it best to let the topic rest. "Here, *Mamm*. I'll take the hamper down and work on the wash. You sit and rest.

When *Mamm* didn't object, Ida rushed down the basement steps dragging the hamper behind her. She checked the load of wash. It had been ready to take out ten minutes ago, but their conversation had delayed that. This load of *Daett* and Emery's work pants could probably use extra time in the washer anyway. Ida spun the wringer around and began to run the heavy pants through. She watched the slow turn of the rubber wheels and thought about Melvin.

Mamm's unenthusiastic approval of her plans had shocked her but it hadn't taken her feelings down like she would have expected. Perhaps she'd matured or gained confidence in her own decisions recently. And she could understand that *Mamm* had reasons for her lack of excitement. Lois weighed on *Mamm*'s mind more than she admitted. Debbie's recent problems didn't help either. But no matter what else was going on, Ida had a right to happiness. Wasn't this what she wanted? Peace, the chance to fall in love with a husband who was kind, and a life she could share with him that had purpose? Melvin with his six children supplied all that. *Mamm* would get used to the idea. Ida decided she'd keep the wedding small. That ought to compensate for the short notice.

Ida reloaded the washing machine and went up the outside basement steps. The air had warmed some since breakfast, but it still carried a nip. The sun would be out of the clouds soon, and a fine springlike day was on the way. Ida was halfway through clipping the heavy pants on the clothesline when she heard a car pull into the driveway. She glanced up and almost dropped one of Emery's denim pants. Debbie's old car had stopped by the hitching post, right near where Melvin had kissed her last night and asked her to be his *frau.*

This couldn't be Debbie. Debbie had given away her car. It had to be Lois. And how like Lois to show up on a morning like this even after what *Daett* had told her. Hopefully Lois had enough decency to dress properly this time.

The car door swung open, and Lois hopped out. She hollered across the lawn, "Howdy there, sister. Up early, I see."

Lois knew their schedule well enough having grown up on the farm, Ida told herself. Her sister was just nervous — as well she should be. But at least she was dressed properly this morning. Perhaps that much of *Daett*'s lecture had soaked in.

"*Gut* morning!" Ida answered with a warm smile as Lois approached.

"*Yah,* I'm decent," Lois snapped as Ida's eyes surveyed her appearance.

"You don't have to get short with me," Ida said. "You had it coming. You know that."

"It's still not right." Lois sighed. "But what can you do with hide-bound people like the Amish?"

"Speak for yourself." Ida glanced toward the house. Hopefully *Mamm* wouldn't see that Lois had arrived, but what hope was there of that? This would only add an additional burden to *Mamm*'s already-rushed morning. "So what are you doing here this morning?" she tilted her head. "And how did you learn how to drive that thing anyway? Doesn't that take a while?"

Lois looked hopeful. "Did you want to learn?"

Ida laughed. "*Yah,* I can just see myself whizzing around the community scaring everyone half to death."

"It's not that hard," Lois assured her. "I studied hard and practiced a lot. Debbie's mom, Callie, has been most helpful. I never could have done it without her. And now she's helping me with my schooling. It's so wonderful to have someone appreciate who I really am for once."

Ida gave Lois a sharp look. "You were loved well enough, if I recall correctly. You chose to walk away from us, Lois."

"I can't change who I am," Lois countered. "And I got tired of trying." Her face lit up again. "But I do have great news to share."

Ida waited.

When Lois remained silent she finally asked, "And what would that be — as if I really want to know."

"You don't have to be so mean, Ida," Lois said. "A *wunderbah Englisha* man I met at a party Debbie's mom took me to last week asked me out on a date. He took me to this fancy restaurant, and it was so . . ." Lois gazed toward the sky, apparently lost in the memory.

"And you came to tell us that?" Ida remembered Melvin's kiss last night, but pushed the thought away. Lois probably got kissed too, if she didn't miss her guess. But Lois's didn't seem decent in a way. Melvin's kiss would lead to wedding vows and the care of six needy children. Lois's kiss was for the fun of it, if the look on her face was any indication.

Lois came out of her reverie with a sigh. "He's such a nice man, and you don't have to knock him, Ida. I know what you're thinking. Love's the same out there as it is in here. Although I have to admit that I never felt this for an Amish man — not like I do for Doug."

"You could have *tried,* Lois." Ida busied herself with the last of the heavy pants. Lois could offer to help, Ida thought. She did know how to hang out wash, but there were obviously more important things on her sister's mind.

"So, how's life treating you?" Lois ignored the wash. "Still going on with old maid plans on your mind, hanging out clothes on a wash line when you could be drying them inside in a proper electric dryer?"

Ida ignored the insults. At least Lois had shown a concern for their lives. "I'll have you know I'm getting married in May."

Lois gasped. "You're getting married? To whom? And why haven't I heard about it?"

Ida let a smile fill her face. "Melvin Kanagy asked me to wed last night, and I accepted."

"But . . ." Lois clutched Ida's arm. "Not Melvin Kanagy! He has six children!"

"*Yah,* he lost his *frau* last year. And he has six lovely children. They are perfect dears." Ida hung the last piece of wash on the line. "And Melvin's a decent man. Don't you go saying he isn't."

"Decent or not, he still has six children, Ida. I know you like to sacrifice, but such a high number and right off the bat!"

"Well, it suits me." Ida picked up the hamper. "Do you want to see *Mamm*?"

A cloud crossed Lois's face. "Perhaps I shouldn't. But it's been *gut* talking with you, Ida. I do so appreciate that. Maybe we can do this again sometime?" Lois glanced around. "I do so miss all of you. More than I care to admit sometimes."

"You can come back, you know." Ida allowed hope to stir inside her. "That would be such a *wunderbah* day, Lois."

Lois shook her head. "I can't, Ida. But chatting from time to time I can do."

Ida thought for a moment. "Will you come to Amish weddings?"

"Oh!" Lois beamed. "You're inviting me? Of course I will come."

Ida glanced toward the house again. "Go then before *Mamm* sees you. We'll talk about this more later."

Lois ran across the lawn to the car, hopped in, started it up, and drove out the lane. Ida walked toward the basement steps, but she turned to watch Lois's car disappear from sight. It was *gut* that Lois had stopped by, even if she never came back to the community. Lois would always be her sister. Maybe she wasn't supposed to have them, but warm circles ran around her heart at the thought. Ida began to hum.

TWENTY-SEVEN

The afternoon sun cast fast-moving shadows across the lawn. Ida removed the clean wash from the line in the brisk wind. She filled the hamper to overflowing before she ducked her head and made a dash for the house. Once there, she emptied the sweet-smelling wash onto the couch in the living room before she went outside for another load. The wind was at her back now as she ran across the lawn. There was no rush really, Ida told herself. *Mamm* had begun the supper preparations in the kitchen, and she wasn't behind schedule. But she felt up to a good run at the moment.

Debbie would be home soon from her job in Ephrata, and Ida still hadn't spoken with *Mamm* about her detailed wedding plans. Not that she feared *Mamm*'s further disapproval, but now didn't seem the right time. Lois's visit hadn't helped. From the troubled look on her face, *Mamm* must have spotted Lois from the living room window as she left.

"Is Lois in trouble?" *Mamm* had asked.

"*Nee.* I think she stopped in because she's lonesome," Ida had replied.

Mamm appeared ready to say, "Then why doesn't she come home?" But instead she'd said nothing as she continued to knead the bread dough on the kitchen table. The counter was now lined with fresh loaves — enough for a week.

When would the wounds of Lois's departure heal? They couldn't go on like this forever. Each visit from Lois couldn't stir up this kind of pain or they would never find peace and happiness at the Beiler home again. At least her conversation with Lois hadn't been a disaster, Ida told herself. Lois didn't need unpleasant experiences every time she visited home. Not that she blamed *Daett* or *Mamm.* They were doing the best they could. Perhaps things would go better as time went on. But now Lois dated an *Englisha* man. Ida sighed. That was one thing she hoped *Mamm* wouldn't find out anytime soon.

In the meantime, life continued. And it had a right to, Ida told herself, even if she felt a little guilty. Without a doubt life improved for her each Sunday evening she spent with Melvin. Ida allowed a smile to creep across her face as she took the last hamper of clean clothing across the lawn and bent her head in the brisk wind. She entered the house and was ready to empty the load onto the living room couch. She paused and then took the wash into the kitchen instead where *Mamm* was working on supper. Ida set the hamper on the table and seated herself.

Mamm glanced at her.

"I'm going to fold them in here, if it's okay with you. I'd like to speak of my wedding plans."

"I've been thinking about them," *Mamm* said, keeping on with her work. "I don't need to tell you, Ida, how uneasy I feel about all this. It's too soon — and to a man with six children!"

"But, *Mamm*!" The words burst out of Ida. She didn't intend such intensity, but the objections from *Mamm* caught her completely by surprise. "You never said anything before! And Melvin's brought me home from the hymn singings several times. Why didn't you say something sooner?"

"I guess it happened too fast." *Mamm* sighed over the soup she was occasionally stirring. "I suppose I never thought it would go this far. And I've had Lois and Debbie on my mind. Then here you up and announce your wedding plans. And to a man with six children. It's a lot to deal with."

That was the problem, Ida told herself. She should have given *Mamm* more warning, but how could she when it all had happened so quickly, even for herself. Ida glanced at *Mamm*. "But you're not forbidding this, are you? Seeing that *Daett* has no problem with Melvin. And you know I'm plain looking, *Mamm*."

"Is that why you're taking Melvin? Because he's your only choice?" *Mamm* gave Ida a quick glance. "And you know *Daett* would approve of Melvin being he's Minister Kanagy's brother."

Ida sputtered a protest. "*Daett*'s not like that. Melvin's a decent man, and so what if I wasn't looking for Melvin's attention. At least the man loves me, and I'm falling in love with him — I think."

"You *think*?" *Mamm* paused to glance in the soup kettle. "You'd better know by now if you've promised yourself to the man."

"I do know," Ida said at once. And she did, Ida told herself. Look at the way she blushed at the memory of Melvin's kiss last night. Even now it sent shivers through her whole body. So far she liked everything about Melvin, and she would like the rest of him. Enough that she wished to spend her life with him — if *Da Hah* so willed it.

Mamm turned to face Ida. "It's his children, I guess, that really bother me. They've been without a *mamm* for a year now. Melvin's not the best disciplinarian from what I've heard. Not like his brother."

"And we can thank *Da Hah* for that," Ida said, before she thought how the words might sound.

Mamm didn't appear impressed. "Just because he's helping us out with Debbie doesn't make a man's easy ways the right thing, Ida. I hope you know that. Those children will be a handful. The oldest, Willard, isn't but nine years of age. The youngest one is only two. And none of them are yours, Ida. Do you know what that means?"

Ida swallowed hard. "Are you saying I'm not up to this, *Mamm*?"

A gentle smile spread across *Mamm*'s face. "You'd be up to it if anyone would be, Ida. And that's saying a lot. But I wish you'd know a little more about what you're getting into before you say the wedding vows with the man. There's no going back after that."

"I know the man. That's *gut* enough for me." Ida busied herself folding the wash.

This wasn't how she had wanted this conversation to go. But *Mamm* had a right to ask questions, and there was little she could do until *Mamm* was comfortable with the answers.

"Is Melvin being appropriate with you?" *Mamm* fixed her gaze on Ida.

"Mamm!" Ida gasped. "You don't really think that do you?"

Mamm shrugged. "He was once a married man, Ida. I don't expect he'd do anything very wrong, but he could be leading you on by . . . could that be influencing your mind?"

Ida knew her face blazed red, and *Mamm* probably thought this was evidence of her guilt. So she might as well not hide anything. "He kissed me last night. After I said *yah* to marrying him. Is that a sin? And I liked it. I'm hoping that's not a sin either."

Mamm relaxed a little. "And is that all?"

"He held my hand." Ida tried to breathe evenly. "Really, *Mamm,* must we speak of this?"

"Then keep it so until you've said the vows with him." *Mamm* turned around to stir the soup again. "This still doesn't solve my concern about his children."

Ida protested, "I'm almost an old maid, *Mamm*! I'm over twenty-four! Just be thankful I have an offer like this. And from a man I like, at that."

Mamm ignored the comment. "I think you need to visit his family — with someone along, of course. And spend some time with his children. Maybe make supper for them a few evenings. That will give you a chance to see what you're getting into."

"I'm not going to change my mind." Ida's voice was firm.

"I'm not saying you will," *Mamm* said. "But I won't rest easy until I know you've seen what you're getting into. And Debbie would be the perfect one to go with you. It will keep anyone from thinking there's something inappropriate going on. The two of you could be back home by nine or so, and that should work out just fine."

"Who would have thought you'd object," Ida groused. "After *Daett* finally likes a man his daughter is dating."

"Things don't always turn out like one plans." A wry gleam played on *Mamm*'s face. "And someone has to look out for you if *Daett*'s eyes are blinded by church business."

Ida kept silent. There really was nothing more to say, and *Mamm*'s requirement wasn't that unreasonable. She was Melvin's promised one, and this would improve their marriage in the long run. The children would get to know her better by the wedding date, and it wouldn't be as much of a shock once she showed up fulltime.

"You will do this then?" *Mamm* interrupted her thoughts.

"I'll ask Melvin on Sunday evening. I can't imagine he'll object. Now, can we do the real wedding planning?" Ida got up to take the folded pile of clothing into the living room. She returned with a fresh hamper of unfolded wash.

Mamm spoke before Ida sat down. "You say you want a small wedding, so we should only invite our church district and the immediate family. Even then there will be more than 200 people. And we'll ruffle some feathers by omitting the cousins, I'm afraid."

"It'll just have to be." Ida's tone was certain.

"*Nee.* I disagree." *Mamm* turned to face her. "You've been decent with my fears. You've agreed to do the extra work it will take to visit Melvin's family and prepare supper for them. Now I'm going to do what's best for you. You're going to have the same size wedding as Verna had." *Mamm* held up her hand as Ida opened her mouth to protest. "You're just as much our daughter as Verna, and these are circumstances beyond your control. There's no dishonor in taking a widower as a husband. I will not have it look like we think so. And I'm sure *Daett* will feel the same way."

"But . . ." Ida got her protest in this time. "But I don't feel that way at all."

"That's because you don't think of yourself like you ought to sometimes, Ida. Your heart is set on serving other people. That's why I'm looking out for you, and after you're married to that man he'd better not take advantage of your good nature." *Mamm* shook her finger in Ida's direction.

Ida laughed. "You don't have to worry about that. Melvin does love me. I know that."

Mamm raised her eyebrows. "Why? Because the man kissed you? That's not enough for me, Ida."

Ida looked away. Her cheeks burned again, and it was clearly time to move on. "Will you have the wedding here then? Like Verna and Joe did?"

"Of course. I wouldn't have it any other way." *Mamm*'s voice was firm. "All my daughters will get married in this house."

"Even Lois?" Ida regretted the question as soon as she asked it.

Mamm was silent for a moment. Then she

313

said, "I pray so. If not, I fear Lois is going to ruin her life. Oh, where did we fail her, *Hah*? *Daett* and I tried so hard, but it was as if her heart was turned from us even in the beginning. As a small girl she'd stand and admire *Englisha* dresses in the shop windows in Mifflinburg. I used to think it was cute until the truth dawned on me. How could I not have seen what was happening sooner?"

"You did all you could do," Ida said. She got up to slip her arm around *Mamm*'s shoulder. They clung to each other for a long moment.

"At least Lois is not in the *bann*." *Mamm* wiped her eyes and returned to the stove and her supper preparations.

They comforted themselves with small blessings, Ida figured. But there was nothing wrong with that. A vision of Alvin Knepp and his awful spiritual condition while under the *bann* flashed through her mind. If Lois were in such a state . . . Ida pushed the thought away. She didn't even want to think such thoughts! Should she tell *Mamm* more about the talk with Lois this morning? Ida decided to remain silent. *Mamm* had enough problems right now, and so did she. Debbie would be home soon, and she would ask if Debbie would go with her to Melvin's place. Debbie shouldn't have any objections. Not after she explained why *Mamm* wanted these visits. And if there were, she could tell Debbie about the part Melvin had played in her being allowed to remain in the community. Debbie would want to help out after that.

Mamm interrupted her thoughts. "I'm glad you're not doing what Lois is. I want to be sure you know that."

"Thank you," Ida replied.

She never would follow in Lois's footsteps, and *Mamm* knew that. *Mamm* attempted a smile as Ida left with the pile of folded wash. She put the laundry away in the bedroom dressers and then finished the rest of the wash on the dining room table. Mamm continued supper preparations . . . both women quiet in their thoughts.

TWENTY-EIGHT

On Friday night of that week, Alvin paused at his mailbox at the Park Heights Apartments. He took the three envelopes out and turned them over in his hand. One looked like a credit card application, one had no return address, and the third letter he slid into his pocket. His parents' return address was written on it. He'd open it once the pain in his chest subsided. The news from home couldn't be *gut.* On top of that, he was much more homesick than he'd ever imagined he'd become. Going back wasn't something he could do. There were simply too many unresolved issues.

Alvin pushed open the door of his apartment and turned on the lamp near the couch. His gaze took in his surroundings for a long moment before it settled on the electric stove with the microwave above it. He'd become more *Englisha* each day, and now used both with regularity. Though these objects of the world no longer caused him pause, inside he was still Amish enough to know he didn't really belong here. And yet where *did* he belong?

Alvin flopped down on the couch and ripped open the letter from home. He might as well face whatever accusing words were written there. This would be from his *mamm,* he knew. His *daett* wouldn't even think to write — even if they'd been close, which they hadn't.

Dear son,

I hope this finds you well. We've survived the winter okay, and spring is slowly trying to break out. Hopefully the city doesn't spread germs and infections around like I've heard it does. I can't imagine you being affected much anyway, having been raised on the farm like you were.

With the coming of spring, our financial problems on the farm are fully out in the open for all to see. I'm ashamed, as is your *daett.* In a way I'm glad you're not here to experience this. Although I do so wish you wouldn't have chosen this way out — that of being cast out of

the church. My heart breaks just thinking about your spiritual condition. Please
reconsider what you're doing. Nothing
could be as bad here as being outside
Da Hah's will there. We have relatives in
Ohio, Alvin. You can visit them for a few
months and make things right with the
church from there. Anything would be
better than being out there in that awful
world. Think about this, would you?

I've also continued thinking long and
hard on what went wrong that caused
you to leave because I know something
did. Something you haven't told either
your *daett* or me. Even with my continued ill health I've spent hours in prayer,
asking *Da Hah* to show me what it could
be. I've asked Him to tell us where we
offended you. And I believe I'm beginning to see that the farm problems you
had with *daett* certainly do lie at the root
of this matter. I haven't yet spoken to
your *daett* about these thoughts, but I
will when the time is right.

I don't know much about farming,
Alvin, and that's perhaps why I've never
paid much attention. I've preferred to
allow your *daett* to run things as he

pleased — and is that not how things should be? Yet, this financial ruin we are under has changed a lot. I've had to sit in the living room while a committee of men — of which Deacon Mast is the head — sit at the kitchen table with *Daett* going over the operations of the farm. I tell you, Alvin, it is a shame no one should have to bear. I now walk into the Sunday morning meetings with my head bowed. And I wouldn't even think of attending the monthly sewings — at least not until this is over. And from the looks of things, it won't be over for a very long time.

These past evenings I've listened to the committee talking with *Daett,* and I've heard them say things that you've said so many times that *Daett* never paid attention to. I'm sorry, Alvin. I never thought things were in a serious enough state to intervene. But the matter is becoming as clear to me as daylight. You knew how to farm with the newfangled ways the committee keeps bringing up and your *Daett* would never allow. Now they are forcing him to change. He fumes and fusses, sometimes right to their faces, but they don't back down.

Am I not right in thinking this was the primary reason for your leaving, Alvin? Did you perhaps see this coming? But surely this alone wouldn't have been enough to drive you away from us. And yet, perhaps it's more serious than I imagine. I lie awake at night wondering, doubting myself, wishing I could have done things differently. Where was I anyway? You were so different from the other boys, Alvin. I should have done something sooner. I should have spoken with *Daett,* but it seemed too difficult. Especially after your brothers grew up in front of you, all of them caring little how things were done around here. I guess I expected things would turn out the same. Then when *Da Hah* sends us the one boy with the answers, we were too blind to see it. I really do think we have wronged you greatly, Alvin, and now we are paying for it with this great shame that hangs over our heads. *Daett* isn't even allowed to buy a dollar of seed without the committee's permission.

I fear that *Daett* will never change. I don't think he's able, Alvin. He's too old. He has to listen to what the committee tells him, but he won't do it right.

I know he won't. He might try because he has to, but it's not in his heart.

If we are to save the farm, you must come home. Can you forgive us enough to consider this?

This brings me back to my original question. Was this the only reason you left? I used to think Debbie was partly to blame. You loved her, didn't you? You always seemed so taken with her. I saw how much it meant when you were asked to be a table waiter with her at Verna's wedding. That set-up was Debbie's doing, wasn't it? I think so, and I wish to ask your forgiveness on that matter also. I once imagined ill of her, but Debbie is a much better girl than I thought she was.

Alvin put the letter on his lap for a moment. He wiped his eyes with the back of one hand and stared at the blank wall. This was not what he'd expected. What had come over his *mamm*? Was it the shock of what the family was going through right now? Could he believe what he was reading? Did his *mamm* really understand him? And now she was even apologizing for her objections to Debbie? He picked the letter up again.

I probably shouldn't tell you this, Alvin, because I do want you to return to the community for the right reason. But I'm also your *mamm,* and I hope *Da Hah* understands that I'd do almost anything to bring you back. Not just because I want you back, but because returning to the faith is the only way you will ever be happy. I know you well enough to know that, Alvin. I'm your *mamm.*

There's been a fuss in the community lately about Debbie. I myself had things to say on the matter, but I freely admit I was wrong. The recent trouble with Debbie flared up when Bishop Beiler's daughter Lois left for the *Englisha* world. Many in the community blamed Debbie's influence. In the midst of all that, I heard that Paul Wagler made a move to win Debbie's hand. That sounds like he was trying to take advantage of the woman to me, since I know Debbie wished to stay in the community at all costs. But Debbie turned down his request to take her home from the Sunday night hymn singing in the face of all that. I couldn't believe this when I heard the news. She turned down Paul's advances even though it would likely result in a denial of her heart's desire to stay in the community.

Doesn't that tell you something? Debbie's not going to fall for Paul Wagler under any circumstances. Take that into account, Alvin. And the fact that I now see the *gut* heart the woman has.

Again, I'm sorry about all this, Alvin. Hopefully you can find forgiveness in your heart for our shortcomings. Come home. We can work things out. Talk to Deacon Mast. Tell him you see your mistake. Tell him you know the *Englisha* world isn't the answer to your problems. If you return, your *daett* and I will move to a *dawdy haus.* I'll see that *Daett* gives you full control on the farm, and the committee will back me up.

You still have a chance with Debbie. I know you do. She has a heart that longs for what we have. Don't throw this chance away, Alvin. I know the road hasn't been easy for you, but you've done some things right — like not speaking evil of *Daett* during this time. So consider my words. Please? There's still time to make this right.

> With all my prayers and my longing heart,
> Your *mamm,* Helen

Alvin stood and paced the floor, the letter dangling from his fingers. Moments later it dropped to the floor and slid under the kitchen table. Alvin didn't notice. He came to a halt before the picture window overlooking the street below. The line of cars moved past as usual, but he wasn't seeing them. In his mind's eye he saw the rolling valley around the small town of Beaver Springs. A thin stretch of blacktop ran toward Lewistown in the west and east toward Middleburg, but in-between were the fertile farmlands where men grew crops like *Da Hah* had instructed Adam after he was driven out of the garden. "In toil you shall eat of [the ground] all the days of your life . . . In the sweat of your face you shall eat bread."

He'd known that kind of work all his life; from dawn to dusk, while spring broke across the land and summer lay just around the corner, in the long fall and winter nights he'd waited out the cold. He'd tended the livestock in the barn and longed for the sun's warmth to bring the land to life again. That was his world. And *Mamm* had figured out the main problem. All the years he had lived in the house, she'd tended to him like she had his brothers. But they had never spoken words like these before.

But now it seemed the thoughts had surely been near the surface. It was *Daett* who had kept them at bay. Alvin must mend that fence, but how? *Daett* would not look upon his return as a blessing, not while this shame hung over the farm. Not while he, Alvin, his youngest son, would side with the committee. Regardless of what *Mamm* said, *Daett* would feel betrayal far beyond anything that had happened so far. Alvin had said over and over through the years how things needed to change on the farm. That had been one thing. *Daett* could take or leave his advice, but now all that had changed. If he went back, his words would stand against *Daett*'s and win the day. *Mamm* would never fully understand what that would mean.

What was he to do? He couldn't rush home, and he did have an attachment here now. There was Crystal to think of. He couldn't just walk away from her. And he hadn't even thought of Debbie in some time. Not that long ago he would have felt a great shame because another girl had made her way into his heart. Somehow it had happened, and now it couldn't easily be undone. And Crystal planned to go out with him tonight for another walk to the park, as was their habit. He wouldn't stand her up. Not ever.

Alvin glanced around. His gaze finally found the letter under the kitchen table. He reached down and retrieved it. He slid the letter into the desk drawer. He had to eat supper and get ready. He would think more about this later.

TWENTY-NINE

Alvin was waiting in the lobby of Park Heights Apartments when Crystal came out of the elevator with Brutus pulling on the leash. Alvin greeted her with a slight smile, but it wasn't enough to fool Crystal.

"Alvin, you look worried. Did something happen at work?"

"No, just a letter from home." He held the front door for her, and Brutus rushed out, nearly dragging Crystal with him. She laughed and hung on. Alvin sprinted after her and caught up in the parking lot. When they were able to begin a restrained walk with Brutus, she pressed the matter. "Not good news, huh?"

"You could say that." He stayed on the street side as they made their way briskly toward Clovery Park.

"Parents not doing well?" she persisted. He'd given her only the briefest descriptions of where he came from and life at home. She knew he'd been raised Amish, but he avoided the subject whenever possible.

"A little trouble with money," he said.

She laughed again. "Doesn't everyone have that?"

When he only grunted, she probed. "You've never told me much about your family."

Maybe I don't want to, he almost said. When she looked at him, he responded, "They live in Snyder County."

She raised her eyebrows. "Is that the great secret? You can tell me, you know."

"Amish troubles," he muttered. He blurted the rest out. "I've been thrown out of our church. My *mamm* wants me home to straighten things up. And *Daett* is in trouble over his mismanagement of the family farm."

"Oh . . ." Her voice was sympathetic.

Alvin kept his gaze averted.

She pulled on his arm with her free hand. "I'm sorry. That must be awful. I hadn't imagined anything like that."

"It happens I suppose." He still didn't look at her.

"Thinking of going back?" Her voice cut into his thoughts.

Alvin flinched. "Not really."

"So what are you doing way out here . . . living in an apartment . . . all by yourself? That must have been an awful fight you had with your folks."

"Amish don't fight," he said.

She guffawed. "You don't say!"

Alvin felt the shame burn inside him. "I guess we do underneath where no one sees."

She was sympathetic. "Don't take me wrong, Alvin. I didn't mean that negatively. It's just my way of saying things."

Alvin knew he shouldn't, but he said the words anyway. "I suppose you think I'm a coward for running from my problems."

She pulled on his arm again. "Of course not. You don't have a cowardly bone in your body. That's what I like about you — a wholesomeness I haven't seen before. Maybe never. I don't know. But you have it. If you went off without a family blow-up, it must be for a good reason. You wouldn't do anything wrong, Alvin."

He glanced at her. "Thank you for believing in me." The shame burned a little less. She had that effect on him. That's what he liked about her. It had never been so obvious, but tonight when he needed words that healed, she'd spoken them.

"You're thanking me?" Crystal hung on to the leash. Brutus had caught sight of the park entrance and made a dash forward. She reached down to unclip his leash. The dog raced off, disappearing from sight. "There! Now we can talk in peace. Come . . ." She took his hand. "Let's sit on the bench."

Alvin allowed himself to be led, just as he'd allowed these increasingly intimate touches from her. They weren't wrong, he told himself. Dating couples at home touched each other in innocent ways. But he wasn't *really dating* Crystal, and yet it was as if he were. He couldn't be more confused if he tried, Alvin decided. He sat down on the bench beside her. Crystal smelled of flowers tonight. Roses, he thought.

She turned her head as if she knew his thoughts. "Do you like it?"

"It's wonderful," he replied without looking at her.

She laughed. "Don't the girls you know at home wear perfume? Or does the smell of the horses drown out everything else?"

Alvin managed to join her in laughter. "I guess I wouldn't know. I have no sisters, and I've never really dated."

"No sisters? And no dating?" Crystal's eyebrows went up. "You're an uneducated man indeed."

He knew his neck was turning bright red with the heat of his emotions.

She didn't seem to mind. "Tsk, tsk, Alvin. This does explain much. But wait — wasn't there a girl somewhere in your story?"

"Yah." She might as well know. He had no shame to hide when it came to Debbie.

Crystal frowned for a moment. "Was there news in the letter about her?"

He bit his lip and didn't answer. He didn't want to discuss Debbie with her. And how would she understand his complicated feelings when it came to Debbie when he didn't? Crystal might not be impressed with a man who left the girl he loved because he expected to lose out to another man, no matter what his reasons were. Perhaps it was more evidence of cowardice.

"Is she seeing someone else?"

"No, she . . ." He stopped. He wasn't going to tell Crystal more. It wasn't right.

Crystal already had it figured out from the look on her face. "Broken up with him, right? And now she could be yours . . . if you went back?"

He felt disconcerted. How did women know these things without being told? His mother had figured out most of his heart's secrets without a word from him, and now Crystal was doing almost as well.

"It's complicated," he said.

"It always is." She stood and whistled for Brutus. When there was no response, she sat down again. "Confound that dog! He'd better not make me run halfway through the park to find him."

"I'll do the running," he offered. This was a routine they'd fallen into. He used the excuse that he needed exercise, and she usually took him up on it. But she didn't look that pleased tonight.

"I hope you stay here, Alvin. You like your job, don't you? And I'm guessing you're close to a promotion. You should be, at least."

Alvin allowed a wry grin to cross his face. "I'm fixing half the hotel it seems — plumbing and anything to do with carpentry. I get double the wages I began with, which doesn't make much sense. I'm only doing what I always did around the farm, tinkering with things."

"See!" Crystal looked triumphant. "You're getting paid for once, unlike on the farm. And we could make something of this . . ." She paused to think for a moment, ". . . this friendship we have, Alvin. You're one of a kind. Solid, true, honest, hardworking, rising in the world. What more could a girl want?"

Alvin looked away and thought of Debbie and Paul. "Apparently a lot."

She hesitated. "You look really good to me. Or am I being too forward for you? I guess I have to start asking that question."

He shrugged. "I'm fine." She reminded him of Debbie. He gave Crystal a warm look. He liked forwardness in a girl, he decided. At least this kind of forwardness. Hadn't Debbie finagled the arrangement between them at Verna's wedding? He'd liked that. Or perhaps it was the ways of *Englisha* girls he liked.

"So you're staying then?" Her face lit up. "And you and me, we could . . ."

"Look, Crystal," he interrupted, taking her hand. "I like you as a friend. I'm not ready for anything else. It's complicated, remember? And your world . . . it's not mine yet. And I don't know if it can be . . . what you have out here."

Her face clouded even as her fingers tightened on his. "I think I understand, Alvin. That's okay."

He felt the softness of her hand in his. It would be easy to love this girl, he decided. He could *almost* let himself go. It would be like stepping into a rushing river. He would have to do little but hang on. And yet he couldn't. Not now anyway. And it wasn't fair to Crystal to say things he wasn't sure of.

"That's okay," she repeated. "Let's not ruin what we have." She regarded him for a moment. "You're a dear, you know. So innocent and unspoiled. You haven't seen much of life have you?"

He looked away. "I imagine not." He glanced back and met her gaze. "But I've seen you. That seems like a lot to me."

She threw her arms around him and hugged him. She didn't let go for a long time.

"What was that all about?" he asked, his hand lingering in hers.

She gave him a weak smile. "With a sugar tongue like that, you sure you don't know what it's for?"

He ignored the remark and tightened his hold on her hand. "Tell me about yourself, Crystal. You've not told me much."

She leaned her head against his shoulder. "You're not going to find out, Alvin. You're too dangerous."

"Why?" He looked down at her. "I've told you about me."

She laughed. "Not much, I'm sure."

Again she was right. His silence was answer enough.

"Some things shouldn't be told." She

moved beside him. "Not ever."

In the silence that followed, Alvin wondered what secrets Crystal had. He couldn't imagine she'd ever done anything wrong in her life, but then what did he know. He was from the farm . . . an Amish farm at that.

"We'd better be getting back." She was on her feet now. "Brutus is likely into some sort of mischief by now."

He kept her hand in his. "I love it when you're with me, Crystal. You do me good."

She pulled her fingers from his. "I feel the same way. You're good for me, Alvin. Very good." Her gaze lingered for moment. "Now, where's that dog?"

"Let's see if this will bring him." Alvin whistled twice, and a few seconds later Brutus bounded out of the bushes.

Crystal turned toward Alvin. "What are you, a magician?"

He laughed. "I'm afraid not. I can't even fix my own life." It would take *Da Hah*'s help for that. But he didn't tell that to Crystal. She might not like his mention of God, and he hadn't really prayed much for a long time. But perhaps it was time he began. There was an awful lot that needed to be fixed in his life. That much he knew.

Crystal snapped the leash on Brutus, and the dog followed the couple without fuss, apparently worn out from his long run in the park. Alvin led the way as they walked down the street.

Crystal seemed tired . . . even subdued. She didn't say anything, and Alvin didn't know what should be said.

"Can we do this again soon?" he asked as they paused when they reached the apartment steps.

She didn't hesitate. "I'd love to, Alvin."

She moved on into the lobby toward the elevator. He wanted to ask her to wait, to share with him what was bothering her, but he didn't.

He followed her inside, and they silently boarded the elevator. When they reached the fourth floor, he took her hand and gave it a squeeze.

"Good night now," she said. "I hope your troubles at home get solved."

"And yours," he said. "Whatever they are."

She got off and the elevator doors closed.

Moments later, Alvin entered his apartment. He took the letter from his *mamm* out of the desk drawer and read through it again. Then slowly he slipped the paper back inside. He would have to write home soon, but he couldn't until he knew for sure what his answer would be. That might take some time. He also had to make sense out of what had happened between him and Crystal tonight. That might take even more time.

THIRTY

A week later, on Friday morning, Debbie drove Buttercup and the buggy toward Melvin Kanagy's place. Ida was seated beside Debbie, offering advice on handling a horse. Debbie needed the practice now that she had definite plans to become part of the community. Ida hadn't minded in the least when she'd asked for the reins once they left home. Ida was too thankful Debbie had agreed to take off from work and come along to complain about who drove. At least Ida didn't seem nervous that she'd run into the ditch while she drove the horse.

In fact, Ida wasn't nervous at all about going to Melvin's place either. She felt she knew the man well from their Sunday evening dates. And even the fact that Ida would see Melvin's family at their home for the first time tonight didn't have her in a tizzy. Ida was a marvel indeed, Debbie thought.

"Going to Melvin's to spend the day with his family is *Mamm*'s idea," Ida said. "It's part of the plan and shouldn't be a big deal at all."

It was also a decent plan, Debbie acknowledged. Ida would have more work than she could possibly imagine once she married Melvin. It would be a giant task taking care of another woman's six children, even for a dedicated and hard-working person like Ida.

Ida seemed deep in thought. Likely she was mentally working out a schedule to run the house for Melvin and his children. Debbie gave her friend a quick glance. "Plans churning around in your head?"

A quick smile flashed across Ida's face. "You know me well. But what about yourself? Have you thought of another visit to see Alvin?"

Debbie started. "Of course not!" Visions of Alvin dressed in his *Englisha* clothes with an equally *Englisha* dressed woman by his side flashed through her mind. That the woman was pretty only made matters worse. Debbie was going to forget Alvin and go on with her life. Alvin might be part of the reason she originally wanted to join the community, but she didn't need his love to continue her quest.

Ida was still on the subject. "I'm surprised

Verna is letting you give up on him now that Paul is no longer in the picture."

Debbie kept her eyes on the road. There was no way she would tell Ida or anyone about what had happened in Philadelphia. She kept her voice steady. "I haven't stopped at Verna's lately. I don't have my car anymore, and I'm on thin ice with your dad and everyone else already. That's plenty of reason right there to stay away from Alvin. With Alvin being in the *bann,* if the ministry even thought I was considering seeing him again . . ."

Ida sighed. "I suppose you're right. But it's still a shame. You lost both of them now — Paul and Alvin."

"Maybe that's the way it's supposed to be." Debbie worked hard to keep bitterness out of her voice. "I'll just be an Amish old maid. Isn't that what you call them?" Debbie jiggled the reins, and Buttercup increased her speed.

Ida didn't sound convinced. "Someone as *gut* looking as you, Debbie? Don't worry. Some young man will be calling on you soon."

"Maybe I don't want them calling," Debbie snapped. She wished at once she hadn't said anything, especially when she saw a cloud of sorrow cross Ida's face.

"*Da Hah* has His ways," Ida said before pressing her lips together.

Debbie held the reins with one hand and touched Ida's arm with the other. "I'm sorry I said that."

Ida nodded. "I know. Thank you for coming with me. I love Melvin, and I think I'll love him even more as I get to know him better. And his children, of course."

"Have you had any doubts?" Debbie asked. "The wedding's coming up quickly."

Ida chuckled. "I admit I had butterflies in my stomach for Paul Wagler once, but that's over with. I'm very content with the man *Da Hah* has sent me."

That's a nice attitude to have, Debbie almost said. But that might have sounded sarcastic to Ida's ears, and she really was here to support her. Especially with the favor Melvin had done for her. She likely wouldn't be in the community if Melvin hadn't prevailed with his brother on her behalf. She ought to cook and clean for the man every week for a year to express her gratitude.

"Do you disagree with my choice, Debbie?" Ida sounded worried. "Do you think I'm being silly . . . or wrong?"

"Of course not!" Debbie pulled Buttercup to a stop at the intersection. "I was thinking

I should help Melvin with his housework every day for a year in gratitude for what he told his brother."

Ida relaxed on the buggy seat. "*Yah,* it showed the kind heart Melvin has. And the *gut* judge of character he is. He saw what kind of girl you are. He's going to be a *gut* husband for me, Debbie."

"I'm sure he is," Debbie agreed. "Now, where is his place?"

"Up ahead a mile or so." Ida motioned with her head. "You'll like it. Melvin keeps it up nice considering . . ."

Debbie kept quiet as Buttercup's hooves beat on the blacktop. As Ida's friend, Debbie only cared about Melvin's place because of her. He seemed nice enough to Ida, and that was the important point. But another troubling thought raced through her mind. Had Ida's tender heart been swayed by Melvin's kind act of speaking up? Enough that she based her decision to marry the man on that reason alone? Surely not! Debbie decided.

"Melvin's sister Lily helps out when she can," Ida continued. "But she can't do much more than the housework. Melvin does the rest. I'll have to see today if we can at least begin a garden. Melvin told me on Sunday he'd have the spot plowed and disked, and that Lily wouldn't mind."

"She shouldn't!" Debbie exclaimed. "You're marrying the man."

"It's just that I didn't want Lily to think we considered her incapable of . . ."

Debbie laughed. "I'm sure Melvin made things clear to his sister." But Debbie's face darkened as her unspoken question returned. Finally she said, "Ida, I hope you're not being influenced to marry Melvin because he spoke to his brother on my behalf. Your mother does want you to use our visiting as a kind of trial run, you know. It's not too late for you to back out if it doesn't go well."

Ida's voice was sober. "I wasn't influenced by Melvin's kindness to you. Well, except to love him more. And you shouldn't take *Mamm* too seriously. She's worried about all the work in raising six children, I suppose. And about me becoming a widower's *frau* since I've never been married. But those things don't bother me. I know I'm not Melvin's first choice in a *frau,* but he wasn't mine either. *Da Hah* has worked things out as He sees best."

Debbie glanced at Ida. "Maybe your mother does have a point?"

Ida shook her head. "Now look who's on whose side."

"You know I'm always on your side,"

Debbie asserted. She motioned with her head. "Is that the place up there?"

Ida's face broke into a smile. "*Yah.* Pull up by the barn so we can unhitch."

Debbie took the turn into the driveway with care. She noticed a patch of freshly worked ground behind the house. Clearly Melvin had kept his word about the garden. She pulled the buggy to a stop, and the door of the house opened. Two small boys raced out.

Ida stepped down from the buggy and met the boys as they arrived. She greeted them cheerfully. "Hi! Is your *daett* around?"

The oldest dug his bare big toe around in circles in the driveway dirt. "He's in the back field now, I think. Although he was working on his tractor in the barn." They had turned shy now that they'd finished their wild dash to the buggy. Ida gave both of them quick hugs, which brought embarrassed looks to their faces.

"We'll go talk with Lily first then," Ida said as Debbie tied Buttercup to the hitching rack.

When Debbie finished, Ida was already on her way toward the house. She held the hands of the young boys, one on either side of her. She would make an excellent mother for these children, Debbie noted as she followed them. Ida obviously knew what was up. She was following her heart. *Just like I did in rejecting Paul's attention,* Debbie decided. Such things weren't always easy to explain or for others to see.

Lily met them at the door with a glow on her face. Melvin must have been right on that point also. Lily carried no hard feelings over this early foray of Melvin's *frau-to-be* into his home. Lily appeared frazzled, in fact, and tired. The woman probably wished her brother's wedding would be next week, if the truth be told.

"This is so *gut* of you to come," Lily told Ida. "And for you to come along," Lily said, turning her attention to Debbie. "That's such a special blessing."

"Thank you," Debbie replied. "It was Saloma's idea. I came along to help." Lily certainly did her best to make them feel welcome, and her words seemed sincere enough.

"*Ach!*" A pleased look spread over Lily's face. "You know it would have been perfectly decent, Ida, since I'm here."

Ida returned the kind look. "I know, but maybe we can get more work done. Melvin said he'd get the garden ready, and I see it's all disked. Shall we start there?"

"You don't waste any time, do you?" Lily

smiled as she tussled the hair of one of the boys. "You'll be making Melvin a decent *frau*. I don't think I could have made a better choice myself."

Ida colored and dropped her eyes. "I hope *Da Hah* will bless our life together."

"I'm sure He will! Let me show you around the house since you'll be moving in soon," Lily continued. "And you can talk to the children — the ones who are home from school, anyway."

Ida's neck burned bright red, but Lily didn't seem to notice. Both boys looked up at Lily with expectant looks on their faces. Lily laid her hands on the head of first one and then the other. "You know this is Amos, the oldest of these two. He's five and can't wait to attend school next year. This is Ephraim, the mischievous one. But aren't young ones all that way?"

"He's not the youngest!" Amos protested.

Lily didn't seem to hear as she led the way toward the kitchen. Ida followed, leaving the two boys with Debbie.

"She knows I'm not the youngest," Ephraim spoke up. He gave his brother a pleased look.

"Let's go out and play," Amos announced.

Both boys gave Debbie only the briefest of glances as she held the front door open for them. They dashed out and were gone. The two were nice enough children, Debbie thought. They seemed okay with the idea that Ida would be their new mother. Likely Melvin had told them all about Ida. Even then, she didn't envy Ida the task ahead of her. The responsibility of this household was immense. Ida had tackled more than Debbie would have. But then that was Ida.

Debbie found Ida and Lily in the kitchen with an even smaller boy on the chair beside them. He was all smiles as he listened to the chatter around him like his life depended on it. A little girl sat on Ida's lap — the same one Debbie had seen with Melvin at Sunday meetings. Lily beamed above them all, obviously thrilled the children were taking so well to Ida's presence.

"I've been telling Lonnie and Lisa, as well as the other children, all about you," Lily said. "And about my leaving this fall. I might even leave earlier now, which will be so much better than bringing in another relative who would only be here on a temporary basis."

Lisa reached for Ida's *kapp* strings and pulled hard.

"Lisa, don't!" Lily intervened.

Ida motioned to Lily. "She's not doing any harm. She just wants to know me better."

Ida gave Lisa a quick hug.

Lily stepped back with a pleased expression. "Well, we didn't get very far around the house yet. Shall we go on? The children can stay in the kitchen."

"Lisa's coming with me," Ida cooed as she got to her feet. "Aren't you, my little girl?"

Lonnie leaped to his feet. Obviously he assumed the invitation included him too. Lonnie grabbed Ida's other hand. Both Melvin and his sister must have done their jobs well. Whatever they'd said about Ida had stuck. The children thought she was *wunderbah.*

Debbie followed the two as they toured first the downstairs with Lisa in Ida's arms. Lonnie tagged along behind. Debbie gave the little boy a smile when they reached the top of the stairs, but he didn't return it. He looked at her as if she were a stranger. Obviously no one had talked her up to the children, so she would have to turn on her own charm. Debbie kept up her smiles, and by the time they finished the tour of the upstairs, Lonnie had managed a shy smile in return. Ida was clearly better at this than she was, Debbie decided. Which was how it should be. She would not be these children's new mother. That would be Ida.

THIRTY-ONE

Debbie dug the hoe into the soft garden soil as her friend worked beside her. Out of the corner of her eye, Debbie saw Ida pause.

"He's coming from the barn!" Ida whispered.

That could only mean one person — Melvin Kanagy! Debbie turned around to check as Ida rushed toward the approaching figure.

"I see you've come!" Melvin's deep voice rumbled. He reached out for Ida's hand.

Ida took it and stood for a few seconds to gaze up at Melvin's face. It was clear she loved him, Debbie thought as she looked away. This was Ida and Melvin's moment. She went back to work until the two came up beside her, still holding hands. Ida had a fading blush on her face.

"It's *gut* that you could come," Melvin greeted Debbie.

"I was glad to," Debbie responded. Should

she thank Melvin for his kind words to his brother on her behalf? She decided she shouldn't. The Amish had reservations about speaking too openly about such things — at least to the person who had done the favor. She was here to help Melvin and Ida with his farm, and he'd take that as thanks enough.

"Don't you have a job in town you have to be at?" Melvin asked, a puzzled look on his face.

Debbie laughed. "Yes. But my boss is allowing time off for . . . well . . . for your wedding preparations. One day a week is what I asked for, and Mr. Fulton agreed."

Melvin grinned. "That's *gut* and kind of him. And I for one am thankful." Melvin turned his attention to Ida. "And so you've really come. I'm still finding that hard to believe."

Ida gave him a shy smile. "You shouldn't be. I was glad to come."

After a brief silence, Melvin changed the subject. "Did you find the seeds in the basement? I told Lily where I stored them. Do you have any questions?"

"*Nee,* we're fine," Ida said. "Just tell us where you want the different seeds planted."

Melvin thought for a moment. "Well, I don't know much about garden planting. I

350

can do the hard work, but managing the garden takes a woman's hand."

Ida nodded, a touch of red back on her cheek, "I'll do my best then. *Mamm* taught me everything I know."

Melvin grinned. "That's what I was hoping for — not that I ever had any doubts. It's just that some girls never learn these things."

Ida didn't know what to say, so Debbie spoke up. "Ida, he's teasing you."

Melvin chuckled.

Ida said, "Oh!" She smiled at Melvin.

Apparently Melvin didn't tease a lot on their Sunday evening dates, Debbie decided. Saloma's idea for these visits had already borne fruit. And from Ida's pleased expression, she liked what she'd just learned today of her husband-to-be.

"By the way," Melvin said, "I hate to ask this of you women, but could you help me with something in the barn? I'd like to put on some new tractor wheels, and I can't seem to manage by myself." Melvin looked apologetic.

Ida wasted no time before she answered. "Of course we can! We're here to help you . . . whatever is needed."

"I know this isn't women's work," Melvin said as he glanced over his shoulder while leading the way to the barn. "Mary used to help me in the barn, but Lily has her hands full in the house. She does too much for the children and me already."

"It's not a problem," Ida assured Melvin, with a glow on her face.

Ida would flourish on this farm, Debbie thought. She'd feel fulfilled and satisfied as Melvin's *frau* in a way she never could have with Paul Wagler.

Melvin held the barn door for them and motioned toward the interior. "It's the back wheel. I have the jack under the axle, but I can't get much further. If the two of you would take one side, I can handle the other."

Amos and Ephraim appeared from somewhere. Melvin shooed them back. "The women are here to help. There's not much a five-year-old and a four-year-old can do."

Both boys were disappointed.

Ida patted their heads, but they still looked glum.

Debbie gave them both smiles before she turned to follow Ida's lead. Ida seemed to know what needed doing without instructions.

"Easy now, easy now . . ." Melvin said repeatedly as they maneuvered the heavy wheel. "Up, up just an inch, and there! We're in."

There was a metallic click, and the wheel lurched forward. Melvin was all smiles as he rushed to turn the wheel fasteners. Amos had picked the nuts off the floor and handed them to his father. Ida brushed the dirt from her hands. She looked pleased. Debbie also rubbed her hands together.

"We'll be getting back to the garden then," Ida said.

Melvin jerked his head up from where he was bent over the wheel. "Thank you so much, Ida . . . and Debbie. I so appreciate this. I was struggling for a few days already. There's not that many of the community men who stop by that I could ask for help."

Ida retreated and whispered to Debbie once they were outside. "The man needs more help around here than I imagined."

"Looks like you'll have your hands full," Debbie agreed. "Now you have farm work to add to your duties, besides a husband and six children."

Ida's face glowed. "I will be doing *Da Hah*'s work by taking care of a man who needs me."

"He'll have you up before dawn and working till the sun goes down," Debbie said with a smile. But that was typical Amish life, and she knew that if this were Alvin instead of Melvin she would be gladly getting up with him at four in the morning and working until the last rays of sunlight. Her smile would be just as goofy as Ida's was right now. Debbie pushed the thought away. Alvin had left for the world she'd retreated from.

And Alvin would never have a chance to run a farm like this, especially now that his dad's place was under the church committee's direction. There was even talk on Sunday that the committee might force Edwin to sell his place. That would be the ultimate shame, judging from the sound of the whispered women's voices who shared the news with each other. Debbie supposed she shouldn't have eavesdropped, but the women had become so used to her presence they no longer made any attempt to keep appearances up and their words quiet when she was around. Maybe it was another sign she was being accepted into the community. Her thoughts brought a feeling of peace to her heart — even if Alvin wasn't here to enjoy this life with her.

They arrived back at the garden, and Ida contemplated the strings they'd set up to mark the rows. When she didn't move for several minutes, Debbie tapped her shoulder. "Wake up, dreamer!"

Ida laughed. "*Yah,* that's what I was doing. Who would have thought *Da Hah* would give me a gift like this — a husband who wants me to work alongside him? I'll be so happy here, Debbie!"

"I'm very glad for you," Debbie said. "We'd better get busy or this garden is never going to get done."

That galvanized Ida into action. "We'll do carrots in this row, followed by two rows of red beets." Ida's voice choked for a moment. "Oh, Debbie, just think how *wunderbah* it's going to be. And once I can't help in the fields . . ." Ida colored again, but she continued on. "The oldest boy, Willard, will be able to help his *daett* with the evening chores by then. And he'll be out of school before we know it. Have you noticed how strong the boy is and how tall? He'll reach well above his *daett*'s height before he's done growing."

"Yes, that's fine, Ida. But please, let us focus," Debbie said. "We have to get this garden in."

That seemed to rally Ida's attention, and it didn't waver until Lily brought out glasses of lemonade for them. Lonnie and Lisa were along too. Lily left them to play in the dirt when she went inside again. From the wearied look on Lily's face, the chance to leave the two children with someone else for a few moments was as great a relief as the knowledge her brother's garden was being put in.

Ida cooed to Lisa every time they came near that end of the garden, but the children didn't need much attention, Debbie noticed. They seemed able to entertain themselves. They were sweet children, that was obvious. It was no wonder Ida had fallen in love with them and this place, just as Ida had fallen in love with Melvin.

When Lily hollered from the house that she had lunch ready, Melvin came in from the barn with Amos and Ephraim in tow. Ida and Debbie joined them, Ida walking at Melvin's side as the two boys tagged along with Debbie.

"Ida's nice," little Amos said.

"Of course she is," Debbie said. "Your father wouldn't marry anyone who wasn't."

Melvin stopped at the washroom door. His smile was grateful. "Ida tells me the garden's coming along well."

"Ida's a hard worker," Debbie said.

"She's *wunderbah,* I know." Melvin gave Ida a loving glance, and then motioned for the women to go inside first. Ida blushed as they entered and washed their hands. Amos and Ephraim waited patiently for their *daett* to finish and did a good job with their hands and faces. Ida stayed behind to fuss over the two boys as Debbie followed Melvin into the kitchen.

Lily had sandwiches and a delicious-looking soup set out on the table.

Melvin took a long whiff over the bowl before he sat down.

"Don't do that!" Lily protested. "They'll think you have no manners."

Melvin laughed as Ida joined them in the kitchen with the two boys in tow. "I'm just a farmer, Lily. Nothing is going to change that."

"Debbie's been college educated." Lily gave Debbie a quick sideways glance.

"That makes no difference," Debbie said.

"What were you talking about?" Ida asked as she settled into a chair.

"Melvin sniffed the soup bowl," Lily said.

"I hope he likes mine that well!" Ida said, not missing a beat.

"You'll be spoiling him silly, I see." Lily took her place at the table. "I, for one, will be glad to see it. Melvin's been alone with these children for much too long."

Gratitude for Lily's praise flashed across Ida's face as Melvin bowed his head and led out in prayer. When he finished, Ida made sure the children were served before she took any food for herself. Debbie noticed Melvin and Lily exchanged pleased glances. She was so glad for Ida. Now if the Lord would bless her with such love for a man — and one who would love her back. But she mustn't complain. She'd already been blessed above what she deserved.

THIRTY-TWO

Two weeks later Debbie drove Buttercup toward Verna and Joe's place. The previous evening Saloma had heard Debbie mention how she longed for a long talk with Verna. Saloma had insisted on the spot that Debbie make plans to drive over in the morning.

"But I need to help with the Saturday cleaning!" Debbie had protested. "And all the work for the wedding, which is coming up soon, remember!"

"Sometimes other things are also important," Saloma replied with a tender look.

Debbie figured Saloma knew how much this visit would mean. This last month hadn't been easy for Debbie, what with the rush at the Beiler household over Ida's wedding preparations. Plus the other things that crowded Debbie's mind — the continued heartache over Alvin and the pressures that came with attending baptismal instruction classes. The first class had been last week.

Debbie thought her knees would give out once the moment came to stand up in front of the congregation and follow the other applicants upstairs with the ministers.

Three boys had risen to their feet first, all of them much younger than she was. Before she stood, Debbie had left a decent pause to make sure no other boys were attending the class that morning. Ida had told her no one knew exactly who would apply to join the church until it happened. Debbie had dared take a brief glance over her shoulder as she followed the boys up the stairs. "Please, *Da Hah,* let there be another girl following me," she'd whispered. Apparently the Lord had other plans because there had been none.

Debbie had taken her seat across from the ministers and moved her chair so there was a wider space between her and the obviously nervous boys. She relaxed once she knew she wasn't the only tense person this morning. Though her facial muscles had almost gone into knots when she'd caught Minister Kanagy's gaze upon her. She guessed he was noting her appropriate dress and the space she'd created between her and the boys. He smiled slightly, so he must be pleased with both of her choices. Perhaps she hadn't done all that bad.

Debbie jerked herself out of her thoughts and back to the present as she approached a stop sign. She pulled Buttercup to a stop and checked carefully for cars before she asked the horse to move forward. As the steady beat of hooves filled Debbie's ears again, her thoughts drifted. That first morning in the baptismal class Bishop Beiler put his baptismal applicants at ease.

"This is all a little new for you," Bishop Beiler had told them with a smile. "We ministers have been through this before." Here the bishop motioned toward the other ministers with a nod. "Everyone has always gotten out of here alive."

This produced a few chuckles from Minister Graber and Deacon Mast. Minister Kanagy had even cracked a smile, although it quickly vanished as he studied the baptismal articles of faith he held in his hands. It was out of this little book, Ida had told her, that the applicants would be instructed. Bishop Beiler cleared his throat and had taken a moment to hand them all their own copies. He asked all of them to give a brief reason why they wished to join the church.

The boys had answered in the shortest of terms, words to the effect that they had now come of age and had the desire to make things right with God and the church.

Debbie thought she should make a stronger case for herself. She took a deep breath and began. "I've lived next door to Bishop Beiler all my life, growing up around his girls and the rest of the family. For years I longed for something more than I was experiencing. I wasn't sure what that was, so I followed the instructions of my family, which included attending and graduating from college."

Minister Kanagy frowned at the mention of college, so Debbie had rushed on.

"Mom was most insistent that I attend the university even though I didn't wish to." That she'd graduated with top honors she didn't mention. Minister Kanagy wouldn't be happy with that information. His frown had faded at the reference to her mother, Debbie noticed. The Amish had great reverence for the wishes of parents, even when those wishes disagreed with their values. She'd scored a point on that one, Debbie told herself. Thankfully she knew enough about Amish ways to know some of the things that held value to them and some of the ones that didn't.

"After I finished college," Debbie continued, "I faced life in my world and things became clear to me. I didn't want to live in that world, even if that was what my parents wanted. The time had come for me to make my own choices."

Minister Kanagy nodded.

"I asked Bishop Beiler and his wife if I could board with the family. I didn't ask to join the church right away as I felt my way along. I wanted to feel certainty about my decision to join the community. I didn't want the decision to be based on the emotions of the moment."

Minister Kanagy, Minister Graber, and Deacon Mast had slight smiles on their faces. Debbie decided she was hitting the right buttons this morning. Now if she could just make it to the end. If she didn't stop this speech soon, they might think her too forward. She took a deep breath. "The Lord has been with me and has blessed me. I've gotten rid of my car, and now I am ready to go all the way in making a commitment to the Lord and to this community. That is, if you will accept me."

"Thank you, Debbie," Bishop Beiler said. "I know your story well, but it's *gut* that you've told the others."

She purposely hadn't mentioned anything about Alvin Knepp, and she hoped they wouldn't either. For now, Minister Kanagy wasn't frowning, and Debbie wanted to keep it that way. She also realized she needed to get her mind off worrying what

Minister Kanagy and Minister Graber was thinking. She couldn't go through six months of instruction classes analyzing the men's every move. She didn't know Minister Graber well, but she had to push thoughts of Minister Kanagy out of her mind to focus on Bishop Beiler as he read the first article of faith from the instruction booklet.

When he was finished, each minister commented on what was read, and 30 minutes later Debbie followed them and the boys back downstairs. Everyone was staring at her, she was certain. But she kept her gaze appropriately downward and hoped her ears weren't burning bright red.

Again Debbie brought herself back to the present when Buttercup made a sharp turn on the road. She hung on to the lines until the road straightened out again. Buttercup settled into her normal pace, and the miles continued. Something Ida had told Debbie last week buzzed in her head. Lois was dating an *Englisha* man named Doug. Could that by chance be the Doug who had been her boyfriend? That seemed unlikely, but yet how like her mother it would be to introduce Lois to Doug. That was perfectly possible.

Did Saloma know Lois was dating? Debbie doubted Ida would have told her mom something like that. Ida would save her mother from that shock for a while yet. But it would only be a matter of time before Saloma found out. It seemed like Lois was a problem for which there never was a solution.

Debbie pulled on the lines and guided Buttercup down Verna's lane and pulled to a stop by the hitching post.

Joe came out of the barn, happiness written all over his face. "*Gut* morning, Debbie! It's great to see you again."

"And it's good to see you." Debbie climbed down as Joe waited by Buttercup's bridle. She tossed him the tie rope.

"On a Saturday morning, how did you get away?" Joe asked. "And with the wedding preparations in high gear too! Verna was talking of going over to help, in fact."

"Then I won't stay long," Debbie said. "When Verna comes over, we can chat some more."

"Always talking." Joe grinned. "I suppose the women have to get their time in together."

"Well, we are female," Debbie said.

The front door opened and Verna came out. She ran across the lawn and gave Debbie a hug. "It's so good to see you, Debbie! And on a Saturday morning at that.

I was thinking of going home myself to help with the preparations."

"That's what Joe told me, and you still can," Debbie replied. "I shouldn't have come to begin with, but your mother insisted."

A knowing look crossed Verna's face. "Then you must come inside. We'll talk while I finish cleaning the living room."

"I'm helping!" Debbie said without hesitation as the two walked to the house.

"Have a good talk!" Joe hollered after them.

Debbie thought he was looking a bit forlorn when she glanced over her shoulder.

"Oh, he's not neglected, let me assure you." Verna chuckled as she held the front door for Debbie. "He'd be bored with our chatter in minutes."

Debbie doubted that. Unless she missed her guess, even a man would find his interest held by the intrigue swirling around the Beiler household at the moment.

Verna busied herself with the broom and pointed toward a bucket of warm water with a damp cloth hanging on it. "You can wipe the furniture down while we talk."

"Well, first tell me how the baby . . . er, the *boppli* is coming," Debbie said as she tackled the rocking chairs first.

A pleased look crossed Verna's face. "I had my first visit from the midwife this week. She claims everything is fine. It's our first child, and everyone knows that can be difficult."

"You'll do fine," Debbie assured her.

"How was the baptismal class on Sunday?" Verna asked, resting her broom for a moment.

Debbie wrinkled her face. "Your father was nice enough. I think I'll make it."

Verna grimaced. "Minister Kanagy wasn't so supportive, I assume. Minister Graber was probably noncommittal."

"Minister Kanagy was okay. I shouldn't complain about one of the community's ministers, even to you." Debbie gave Verna a quick glance. "You know that."

Verna didn't back down. "You don't have to be coy with me, Debbie. I know enough already about the man. It's not going to be easy with him. It's just the way he is."

"I suppose so." Debbie sighed. "He did keep his eye on me Sunday, looking for any *Ordnung* transgressions, I think. But things seemed to go over well enough."

"You spoke a few words to the ministers then?" Verna asked before continuing. "But of course you had to. They always ask the applicants their reasons on why they want to join."

Debbie laughed. "I'm afraid I went a bit longer than maybe I should have. More than the others, that's for sure."

Verna's eyes grew big. "In front of Minister Kanagy?"

Debbie shrugged. "He was there, and it seemed appropriate. I wanted to let them know where I came from."

Verna's voice was tinged with horror. "You made a long speech? You're a *woman*, Debbie."

"It wasn't *that* long. Besides, he seemed to like it." Debbie shrugged. "Maybe Minister Kanagy has a softer heart than he lets on. His brother Melvin seems nice enough."

Verna's broom swept the same spot on the floor repeatedly. "Now I've heard everything. You sticking up for Minister Kanagy!"

Debbie glanced toward Verna. "I'm just saying. The two men do come from the same family. Maybe they both have soft hearts."

Verna's voice was clipped. "I don't believe that. Not after the way Minister Kanagy treated Joe before we were married. Remember? I went over to speak with the man myself. There wasn't a bone of softness showing in him that day."

"Maybe it's because I'm *Englisha*," Debbie offered.

Verna snorted. "*Nee!* That makes it worse, I'm sure."

"You would think so, but maybe not," Debbie defended. "I do know Melvin spoke to his brother on my behalf. But I don't think that would have been enough if Minister Kanagy hadn't been disposed to see me in a good light to begin with."

Verna's broom moved again. "I must say you're seeing something in the minister I never saw. But maybe you have a point. I hope things go easy for you in the instruction class. It's not every day that we have an *Englisha* girl wanting to join us."

"That proves my point!" Debbie pressed. For some reason she felt the need to drive home the fresh insight. Then she changed the subject. "Are you serious about returning home to help with the wedding preparations?"

"Certainly, if I'm needed."

"I'd love that! And, yes, there will be plenty of work to do. But we should finish your work here first."

"You're an angel!" Verna gushed. "We'll clean the basement yet and talk. I know you haven't told me why you really came."

Debbie looked the other way as she began work on the second rocker.

THIRTY-THREE

Debbie swept the concrete floor of Verna's basement. She would like a house like this someday. It was built on a hillside but was surprisingly airy down here. Half the back side of the house overlooked a small yard and walkout. But a house needed a husband, didn't it? And she had little prospects on that score. Debbie brushed the thought aside. There were worse things than the life of a single Amish woman. And the Lord might have another plan for her that was just as exciting as marriage — although that was difficult to imagine. Amish life was designed around family and children.

Debbie's thoughts turned to Verna, who was across the room also sweeping. Her friend had been silent ever since they came down here. It was just as well. Debbie needed a breather. She knew Verna would start coaxing her to talk eventually. She wouldn't be satisfied until she got to the bottom of Debbie's troubles. Debbie gave a dry chuckle at the thought.

Verna looked her way. "What's so funny? Did I do something?"

Debbie laughed. "No, of course not. I was just thinking about my troubles, that's all."

Verna paused. "Are you ready to talk then? You know I like to solve problems, including yours." Verna chuckled too. "It's about Alvin, isn't it?"

"Partly." Debbie sighed. "I've given up on Alvin. My trip to see him sure didn't do any good."

"There's another one of my plans that went into the ditch," Verna said. "Seems like nothing I came up with for you and Alvin worked. Getting the two of you together at my wedding, that failed."

Debbie wanted to protest that Verna wasn't to blame, but her friend had already moved on. "Oh well. One must try again. If the trip didn't work, we'll come up with something else." Verna was now sweeping the wall with vigorous strokes. "By the way, how did your meeting with Alvin go? He was bull-headed about coming home, wasn't he?"

Debbie looked away. Did she want to share this with Verna? It couldn't make things worse, could it? She blurted, "Alvin was walking with another girl when I got there. I never spoke with him."

Verna gasped. "You don't say! *Nee*, Debbie! Oh, this is worse than I imagined."

Debbie leaned the broom against the wall and wiped her eyes to head off the quick sting of tears. Memories of that morning in Philadelphia flashed through her mind. She saw again the scene as Alvin walked up the street with the *Englisha* girl and her dog. Debbie choked back a sob.

Verna appeared beside her and put her hand around her shoulder.

Debbie managed a wry grin. "It was just such a shock. I was waiting outside the apartment, and Alvin arrived . . . with . . . with this woman. She was *sooooo* pretty, Verna! And she had a dog — a big dog."

Verna was dumbfounded.

"I know," Debbie continued. "The dog should make no difference, but somehow it did. I guess that's one thing we didn't try. I should have gotten a dog."

Verna made a choking sound. "You poor thing!"

"Listen to the two of us," Debbie finally said, bursting out in laughter.

Verna soon joined in. "Are we losing our minds?"

"We could be." Debbie wiped her eyes.

"People who go insane don't know they're going insane, do they?"

"*Nee,* I guess not." Verna composed herself. "This is terrible though. We have to do something."

"Like what? I'm not throwing myself at him again." Debbie's eyes blazed. She could still feel the fire of shame consuming her heart.

"You weren't throwing yourself at him. But never mind that." Verna appeared resolute. "We must pray — hard!"

"I suppose so," Debbie allowed. She didn't wish to insult the Lord's power. Perhaps she needed to be resigned to the fact that He might have other plans for her.

"*Yah,* you never know," Verna said as she nodded, seemingly reading Debbie's thoughts. "There has to be something we can do."

Debbie grabbed her broom again. "Right now I'm ready to forget the whole thing. I've already taken up way too much of your time today. I should be getting back home to help. Your mother was more than kind to allow me time to come in the first place."

"But this is important!" Verna insisted. "You had to share what was on your heart. And this wasn't something you could have told me anywhere else. I'm thinking *Mamm* knew something was upsetting you."

Debbie swept while Verna continued. "You know, there's so much about this situation that makes little sense, Debbie. I suppose I shouldn't be telling you this, but I think you have some right to know . . . since you do love the man."

"Please, Verna . . ." Debbie shook her head. "I don't know what you're thinking, but don't make this worse by telling me something you shouldn't."

Verna shrugged off the protest. "Joe's on the financial committee, you know. The one that's helping sort through the Knepps financial mess."

"Verna, you shouldn't."

Verna ignored her. "Joe's the youngest member on the committee," Verna said, her face glowing for a moment. "That shows you the quality of man I married! But that's not my point. Joe says there's no reason the Knepp farm couldn't be one of the most prosperous in the community. He says it's been seriously mismanaged for years, and that old Edwin is dragging his feet every step of the way about making the necessary changes. It makes no difference what the committee suggests, they get the impression Edwin is disagreeing and working against them every chance he gets."

"What has this got to do with me?" Debbie asked.

"I don't know," Verna admitted. "But it has something to do with Alvin. Joe is sure of it. The committee is talking about getting in a hired hand soon — to make sure Edwin implements their instructions. There are no funds for the hired hand, but something has to be done. I'm wondering if Alvin has been objecting to his *daett*'s tomfoolery when it comes to farming for years now. Maybe that's one of the primary reasons Alvin left. Over the way his *daett* ran the farm into the ground."

Debbie wrinkled her brow. "That's a wild guess and sounds a little unrealistic."

"Maybe . . . maybe not." Verna sighed. "It would be nice if things were always simple, but they rarely are. And you're right about getting back to work. We'd better hurry and finish. I hope I haven't said anything that makes things worse for you."

Debbie forced a smile. "That would be a little difficult to do. But it does feel better to know that I can share my burden with you."

Verna stepped closer for a quick hug. They finished cleaning the basement and were on the way upstairs. Joe was seated at the kitchen table.

"Have you driven all the mice out of the basement?" he quipped.

"Joe, there are no mice that I know of!" Verna sputtered.

Joe laughed. "I'm just kidding! So what's for lunch?"

Verna gasped. "Lunch! I forgot all about lunch. What a lousy *frau* I am! Debbie and I were talking so much . . ."

"It's okay. I'm not dying — yet." Joe assured them.

Verna raced to the refrigerator. She sent Debbie a quick "help me" look.

"I'll set the table!" Debbie said. She quickly fell into the old routine they'd done many times when Verna lived at home. From the looks of things, soup bowls needed to be set out. Verna was pouring what looked like noodle soup from a large Tupperware bowl into a pot on the woodstove.

"Soup will be fine," Joe said in answer to the anguished look Verna sent his way. "It will stave off starvation for a few hours."

"He's teasing again," Debbie said when she noticed Verna's horror.

"I know," Verna managed, though she obviously didn't. She glared at Joe before continuing to get the soup ready to reheat.

Joe chuckled. "I think it's cute you forgot dinner."

"You just like to see me flustered!" Verna accused.

Joe regarded Verna for a moment. "You're pretty with red cheeks."

Verna turned brighter red. "Joe! We have a visitor!"

Joe looked smug. "It's nothing I wouldn't say anywhere."

"You just want to fluster me again," Verna shot back. "And don't you dare. Not in public."

Debbie smiled at their banter. She was sure Verna would kiss Joe right now if she weren't here. Their antics made cozy feelings rush around her heart. This was what Alvin and she could have had, but now that would never happen. At least the Lord saw fit to allow love into Verna and Ida's lives. What a privilege gaining the attention of a decent man must be. No wonder Ida had so willingly leaped into Melvin's arms even though it involved caring for six children.

Joe regarded Verna with a tender look. "You do make the best soup in Snyder County — even warmed-over soup."

"You close your sugar mouth right now!" Vern tapped Joe on the lips with her soup spoon.

Joe grabbed Verna's arm and squeezed it for a moment before he let go. "Is that soup

377

warm yet? I'm starving!"

"Then you should have hollered earlier." Verna could change from stern expression to teasing on a dime. "Tell Debbie about the Knepp situation."

Joe didn't appear pleased. "You want me to talk about Edwin Knepp?"

"I told Verna not to share with me," Debbie said, feeling a distinct need to clear her name on this point.

Verna waved her soup spoon around. "Debbie and Alvin. You know, Joe . . ."

Comprehension dawned on her husband's face. "Maybe that is different," he allowed. "But there's not much to say. Things are a mess, that's all."

"And you don't think Alvin was responsible," Verna prompted.

Joe shrugged. "I didn't know him that well, but my guess is Alvin wasn't. It's hard to judge a man without working with him."

"Alvin needs to come home!" Verna transferred the steaming soup to the table. "There! Let's eat."

Joe bowed his head, and once they finished the prayer and started eating, the conversation moved on to other things.

But Debbie didn't forget Verna's words. Did her friend have reason to hope that Alvin could return? Or was Verna being overly optimistic?

They concluded lunch with pieces of blueberry pie Verna brought from the cupboard. Then Joe dashed outside to harness Verna's horse to the buggy and Debbie cleaned the kitchen.

Verna protested, "There won't be much of the day left, Debbie. We should go."

"You can't leave your kitchen this way," Debbie responded. "My guess is your mother and Ida will have the house clean by the time we arrive. You know how they work."

"I suppose so," Verna allowed. "But surely there will be something we can do. If not, maybe today is a day for talking."

"It's been so far," Debbie observed. "And I needed it badly."

Verna rushed around even faster. "Let's get this over then, and maybe we can do both."

Debbie washed the last of the bowls while Verna dried them. They came out of the house to find that Joe had both of their buggies waiting. "I thought you were making another meal," he teased.

"If you're not careful you'll be eating supper by yourself," Verna threatened.

Joe laughed as the two women climbed into their respective buggies. He got Verna's horse going, and then stepped aside as Debbie gently slapped the reins against Buttercup. Verna leaned out of the buggy to wave goodbye as they went out of the lane. They made quite a sight, Debbie thought. Verna dashing down the road in front, both of them urging their horses onward.

As they drove along, an *Englisha* man ran out of a roadside stand to snap their picture. Verna pushed her buggy door shut, and Debbie did the same — once she saw what the man's plans were. Debbie lamented that some of the *Englisha* — her own people — didn't practice much respect of others. She used to drive past Alvin's place in the hopes she'd catch a glimpse of him at work in the fields, but she would never have taken his picture.

Debbie opened her buggy door to shake her head at the *Englisha* man as she went past him. He had his camera lowered at the moment and appeared tempted to try to snap another picture now that her buggy door was open. Thankfully he had the decency not to lift his camera again. He waved instead. Debbie returned the wave as they raced past.

THIRTY-FOUR

Fifteen minutes later, Emery came out of the barn to meet them. Debbie pulled to a stop beside Verna's buggy. Emery had a big smile on his face. "I thought I heard two wild women driving in."

"You thought nothing of the sort!" Verna shot back. "You thought, 'Oh, here comes my dear sweet sister on a greatly longed for visit.' "

"How could you read my mind?" Emery teased as he unhitched Buttercup.

"Now why don't I get any help?" Verna protested. "I grace the Beiler farm with my presence, and my brother doesn't even tie up my horse."

"You're no longer a Beiler. You're a Weaver!" Emery grinned from ear to ear. "Beilers get the deluxe treatment around here."

Verna laughed as she walked over to give Emery a hug. "You're still the same, I see."

Emery's grin remained, but he said nothing more.

Verna turned and tied up her horse. "That's a *gut* way to shut him up. Hug the man!" Verna told Debbie. "Come. Emery will take care of Buttercup. She's a Beiler horse, you know."

Emery was chuckling as the two women walked to the house.

Saloma held the front door open, and Ida rushed out on the porch to envelop Verna in a hug. "You've come home for a visit!"

"Yah." Verna held Ida at arm's length. "And you're to be wed to that dashing Melvin Kanagy. Now there'll be an end to our troubles with you having Preacher Kanagy's ear."

Ida blushed deeply. "You know I'll be doing no such thing, Verna. But Melvin's a *wunderbah* man!"

"With six children!" Verna observed. "Do you know what you're getting yourself into?"

Before Ida could answer, Saloma interrupted. "Now don't you be worrying yourself, Verna. We've got that all covered. Ida's been making trips over to Melvin's place to help out. And she's getting so *gut* at it that she's going by herself now and not taking Debbie along."

"Ida's in the house alone with Melvin?"

Verna questioned.

"Of course not!" Saloma said. "We have better sense than that. Lily's always there."

"I make sure of it," Ida added. "But I do help Melvin in the barn sometimes when he's fixing machinery."

"The man's good with machinery. I can say that much for him," Debbie got in.

"Well, let's hope he's *gut* with a *frau,*" Verna retorted.

Saloma gave Verna a hug and took her by the hand. "Come in and sit on the couch. I haven't had you home in 'who knows how long.' " Saloma wiped away a tear. "And to think you used to be here all the time . . ."

Ida hung back to whisper to Debbie as the other two walked inside. "Do you think Verna has doubts about Melvin and me?"

Debbie shook her head. "She's just teasing you."

"That must be it," Ida agreed. "Other than the workload with the children, I don't see how anyone could have doubts about Melvin. I'm handling the children pretty well, I think."

"I'm sure you are," Debbie agreed. She thought of how Melvin's three-year-old Lonnie already snuck over to Ida after Sunday services to climb into her lap. It wasn't approved behavior, judging by the looks several women gave. But no one said anything as Lonnie nestled in Ida's arms. She was going to make a great mother for Melvin's children. All that was needed now were wedding vows to seal the matter.

Ida disappeared inside the house, and Debbie followed. Verna was seated on the couch with Ida beside her. Saloma was ensconced on her rocker. The three looked the picture of health and happiness. Verna's face glowed as her sister and *mamm* listened with rapt attention.

"Joe hangs around the house in the evenings now, what with the baby on the way. He used to go out to work in the barn, but he's getting ready for the addition to our family. Getting himself used to staying inside, I'd say. He's going to be a great *daett*. I can't believe how I'm looking forward to the *boppli*'s arrival." Verna glanced down at her midsection. "Do you think I should stay home the last few Sundays from the services when the time comes closer? I know that's still a long way off, but I always thought it a little indecent . . ."

Saloma nodded. "It depends, I suppose, on how things are going for you by then. I attended services right up to the last week, but you'll just have to see. Bearing a child is no shame, Verna. You have to remember that. We're not among those who hide such things."

Now Verna blushed. "*Yah,* I know. But it's so new — and scary in a way. The midwife says everything's going along fine, and that we have nothing to worry about."

Saloma reached over to pat Verna on the arm. "*Da Hah* will be with you, Verna. I know He will. These are matters that lie close to His heart."

"I know." Verna exhaled slowly. "I suppose it's normal to fear. Joe gives me such peace with his words. He talks and reads to us every night — mostly a short chapter from the Scriptures with his *wunderbah* thoughts afterward. Oh, *Mamm,* what would I do without him? I've grown to love him so dearly."

"We must hold all things of the earth with a loose grip," Saloma said. "Even what we love. Please remember that."

Alarm flashed across Verna's face. "You don't think that Joe might be taken from me, do you? I don't know if I could bear it."

Saloma squeezed Verna's arm. "Nothing is asked of us that we cannot bear. Your body is going through a lot of changes, including emotional strain. You mustn't expect too much from yourself or pay attention to your fears. Life will look different once your *boppli* arrives!"

"*Yah,* it will," Verna said with forced optimism. "I know it will."

At the sound of a car in the lane, they all turned and looked out the window. Ida jumped to her feet and raced to the front door.

"It's Lois!" Ida announced.

Silence hung in the living room. Verna was the first to move. She rose slowly. She glanced at *Mamm.* "I'm going to welcome her. She's still my sister."

Saloma's voice was weak. "You haven't seen how Lois dresses now, Verna. She's gone completely *Englisha.*"

Verna hesitated. "At least she's not in the *bann* yet."

"For that I'm thankful." Saloma got to her feet with a sigh. "Does she look too awful, Ida?"

Ida peered outside again. "She's got pants on today."

"The girl has no sense at all," Saloma complained. "Well, let's go out and greet her. Hopefully *Daett* won't come back from town before she leaves. It would break his heart . . . again."

Debbie hung back at the front door as the three Beiler women went outside and waited together at the bottom of the porch steps. Lois came toward them and paused a few feet away. "Okay, you don't have to act so somber. I'm still me . . . and still part of this family."

"But you're wearing *pants,*" Verna said. "You know better than that. And I'm told you were a worse sight the other day."

"Don't get me started on that!" Lois didn't look too happy. "I am what I am, and you might as well get used to it."

"Then come inside," Saloma invited with a strained smile. "At least we can get you off the front lawn. What if someone drives past and sees you?"

Lois winced. "They'll think I'm an *Englisha* woman stopping to buy garden vegetables."

"But you're not," Saloma told her. "You're *my* daughter, and you'll *always* be *my* daughter. You should act like it."

"Like Debbie does, I suppose," Lois's voice carried a trace of bitterness.

"*Yah,* she does," Saloma agreed without hesitation. "And I wish you had the sense to follow her example. If ever *Da Hah* sent someone to guide your path, Lois, it was Debbie. She was straight from the *Englisha* world, and she spoke to you from her experiences. Why you insisted on ignoring

387

her advice and insights, I can't imagine. Debbie's got sense. She's joined the instruction class now, and even Minister Kanagy is seeing her *gut* heart."

Lois murmured something as Debbie stepped behind the front door and out of sight. She wished the floor would open up so she could disappear completely. That wasn't going to happen; she might as well face Lois. Debbie planted a smile on her face as Lois came through the front door.

"Hi, Lois!" Debbie said.

Lois looked at her. "I thought maybe you were off somewhere."

Debbie ducked her head. "No, I'm here."

Lois flopped down on the couch with a look of triumph on her face. "I'm dating now! In fact, he's Debbie's old boyfriend Doug. I guess Debbie and I really did change lives. I'm her, and she's me."

Saloma paled. "You're *what*, Lois?"

"Dating," Lois chirped smugly.

"Did you know this?" Saloma turned to look at Ida.

Ida glanced away and didn't answer, which was an answer in itself.

"What else am I not being told?" Saloma asked, her voice breaking.

"I'm not getting wed yet," Lois asserted, ignoring her *mamm*'s question. "I hear Ida is doing that though. And to old Melvin Kanagy with his six children. What on earth is wrong with you, Ida?"

"There's nothing wrong with her!" Saloma snapped. "That's the way of our people, Lois. Which is how *Da Hah* has taught us. We are to live sacrificial lives in the community. And what better task could one take on than caring for six young children who desperately need a *mamm*?"

Lois turned up her nose. "So love has gone out the window, Ida? I thought you had it bad for Paul Wagler."

Ida said nothing.

"I will have no such talk in my house!" Saloma ordered. "Ida is making a very wise choice. I was uncertain at the first, but *Da Hah* is clearly giving His blessing. I will not have you running Ida or her husband-to-be down. And with the way you're living, you shouldn't be casting stones."

Lois ignored the rebuke and addressed Ida. "Don't throw love away, Ida! Please! I know I'm not Amish any longer, but I'm still your sister. I hate to see you throw away your life and accept chains in place of love."

Ida finally spoke up. "I love Melvin, Lois! I really love him. He's kind and gentle. And his children will be a blessing to me, as I hope I will be to them."

Lois blew out her breath. "What a speech, Ida. Very dramatic. You must have spent hours working on that."

"I speak from my heart!"

Saloma silenced them both with an up-lifted hand. "Enough on that subject. We can't expect Lois to understand the ways of our people since she's rejected us. I only hope and pray that *Da Hah* will have mercy on her."

"He already has." Lois's face went into a pout. "There are many Christians out there, I'll have you know. The Amish aren't the only ones who love God. And Christians serve the same *Hah* you do."

"That may be," Saloma allowed. "But it's not for us to judge."

Verna cleared her throat. "Let's not quarrel, please. Lois is here today, and Ida's wedding is coming up soon. Let's talk about more pleasant things."

"I agree," Lois said. "Let's talk about Ida's wedding. Do I get to sit beside Ida as the witness for her side of the family? I'll even do so with an Amish boy — since Doug probably isn't considered *gut* enough."

"You'll do no such thing," Saloma replied. "You can possibly be a table waiter, but that is going a little far if you ask me."

"What does Ida think?" Lois had turned

to face her sister. "Am I such spoiled goods that I can't sit beside you on your important day?"

Ida looked from Lois to her *mamm,* from Verna to Debbie, and then back to Lois again. She said nothing.

"I take that as a *nee,* then." Lois sat back, defeated. "Why do you have to be so hard on me? I'm only doing what I believe is right for me."

"Lois, I'll ask Melvin," Ida said.

"You will?" A look of delight crossed Lois's face.

"Melvin will have the sense to say *nee,*" Saloma said. "Just like *Daett* and I do."

From the look on Ida's face, Debbie wasn't so sure.

Lois must have read the same message and wisely didn't press the point, other than adding, "I'll even dress in Amish clothing — for the entire day."

"That would be a miracle!" Verna muttered.

The conversation continued on about Ida's wedding day.

Eventually Lois announced that it was time she left. All four women walked to the front door with her and waved goodbye from the porch. Saloma sighed with relief as

Lois drove her car out the driveway without the bishop's buggy arriving.

Thirty-Five

Alvin paced the floor of his apartment. Outside the spring weather had warmed the streets. Gentle breezes brought the promise of fresh life and quickened his spirit as usual. It seemed so wrong that he wasn't living on the farm. Such weather shouldn't be expended on concrete sidewalks and paved roads.

On the way home through the city, a thought had rushed through Alvin's mind for the hundredth time this week. Oh how he longed to walk in the open fields at home, to feel the soft soil under the soles of his shoes, and to breathe in the bracing wind as it blew over the plowed ground. That was how spring should be met and enjoyed — near the land as a farmer. He was still one of them at heart. Then why was he still here, living and working in the city? Alvin had no reasonable answer.

In fact, his *mamm*'s letter was still on the

dresser unanswered. She'd be wondering what had become of him by now. Yet she probably knew him well enough to draw hope from his continued silence. Perhaps it meant he was thinking about the points she'd raised and didn't want to rush into a decision. *Mamm* would know that, just as she'd figured out that his departure from the community hadn't been done in the haste of the moment. It had happened after many years borne in silence under his *daett*'s strange ways. That and his doubts about his ability to love Debbie best in light of Paul Wagler's claims on her.

Now Alvin was beginning to wonder about things. Since he was out of the way, why hadn't Debbie taken the opportunity to commit to Paul? Paul's offer of a courting relationship should have been taken up by Debbie. A done deal. And yet, according to his *mamm,* that hadn't happened. Debbie had turned Paul down. Was it because of her feelings for him? The thought staggered his mind. If that were the case, what must Debbie think about his leaving the community? No doubt she'd been shocked. She'd probably set her mind against him by now. What a mess! And now there was Crystal to consider. His feelings for her were growing, a fact he couldn't deny. He even liked Brutus!

Alvin winced as he looked out the apartment window. The traffic tonight seemed heavier than usual, the cars lined up almost bumper to bumper. Others must also be afflicted with spring fever and were out to enjoy the weather in the *Englisha* way — taking drives in their cars with the windows open. He had no desire to join them. Alvin had his own problems. The large one right now was what to do with his life. He was seeing more of Crystal each week, though mostly by her design. She arranged their times together, and he allowed it to happen. Could he get serious enough with Crystal to consider marrying her? That's what his actions were boiling down to. When he thought of that, he couldn't shut off his Amish way of thinking. Walks in the park were nice, and Crystal was nice, but where was it leading. He couldn't quite see her as his *frau.* And he couldn't quite see himself with an *Englisha* life in front of him after they said marriage vows.

Perhaps this reluctance was something he still had to overcome. Alvin turned away from the window and went into the bedroom to change out of his work clothes. He was seeing Crystal tonight, and she'd sense his confusion, he was sure. Yet she continued to pursue a relationship with him. Tonight she'd invited him down to her apartment for supper. He had a feeling *Englisha* girls didn't usually cook for their boyfriends — if that's what he was to Crystal. But she'd asked him to show up for a home-cooked meal.

Alvin pulled on a clean shirt as he considered the situation. Was he Crystal's boyfriend? In a way he was, even if it had happened by default. And it had taken shape so easily. Was that something he ought to make note of? On the other hand, look how things had gone back home. Debbie had gone out of her way to pursue him. She'd driven past the farm even before she moved in with the Beilers. And Debbie and Verna had made the arrangements so he would be a table waiter with Debbie at Verna's wedding.

Although Debbie had told him these things, Alvin hadn't been able to see it this way. Maybe it took Crystal's attentions to bring clarity. Didn't *Da Hah* work like this? *Da Hah* wasted no experience — even bad ones. There would even be some *gut* that would come out of his time spent in the *Englisha* world. Perhaps a lot of *gut*. Was it wrong to think such thoughts? He shouldn't seek to justify his mistakes by depending on *Da Hah* to bring *gut* out of them. And he shouldn't be leading Crystal on. She was serious about him — unless he was totally misreading her intentions. He must decide what to do. He had to stay or leave. He couldn't do both. And *Mamm*'s letter needed to be answered. And soon!

Alvin left the apartment, making sure the door was locked behind him. He'd learned that from Crystal when she noticed he left his apartment door unlocked during their walks to the park.

"You have to lock your door, Alvin. Always!" Crystal had chided.

He had teased her. "I'm not from the city, remember?"

"This is no joking matter!" she told him. "You have to change your ways."

And so he had. But could he change more? For Crystal's sake? Change his life into that of an *Englisha* man inside and out? That could be the easiest choice. Crystal would love him, he was certain of that. And in time his feelings would grow even more for her. Whether they would reach what he'd felt for Debbie was something else entirely.

Perhaps when Debbie married someone else his feelings for her would go away. Surely she'd marry eventually, even if she'd turned down Paul Wagler. The other single men weren't as forward as Paul, but Debbie wouldn't lack suitors.

Alvin arrived at Crystal's apartment door and knocked.

"Come in!" her muffled voice sounded from inside.

He opened the door to find Crystal bent over the oven, billowing clouds of smoke filling the kitchen. Brutus peeked out from behind the couch, a mournful look on his face. The window was open, and a small fan was whirling on the counter. Alvin stifled a cough.

A shrill noise filled the room.

Crystal's flushed face turned to look at him. "Turn off that smoke alarm, Alvin! It's driving me crazy! Please!"

Alvin reached over the door arch and disengaged the alarm. He stepped back and looked at Crystal.

"Look at this mess, Alvin! I followed the recipe. I really did!" Crystal was waving her arms about in the smoke.

Alvin kept a straight face. "What are you cooking?"

"Some stupid . . . pardon that expression . . . Amish dish. It's something called 'Yum-a-setta' or something like that. Do you know how to cook it?"

"No," Alvin said, still stifling a smile. "I *farmed* at home. I didn't cook."

398

"Obviously I don't know how to make it either!"

"It's okay, Crystal." Alvin smiled helpfully. "Here, let's see if I can help." He took a look at the brown substance filling the bottom of the pan.

"No one can help with that!" Crystal wiped her brow. "This is unsalvageable. And it was all for you." Tears gathered in her eyes.

"You did this for me?" Alvin surveyed the kitchen with the humming fan and diminishing clouds of smoke.

"Yes! I wanted to cook you a proper Amish supper. See?" Crystal pointed to a cookbook on the counter.

Alvin stepped closer and flipped to the front cover. *Amish Cooking at Its Best.*

"If you laugh, I'll whack your head with it," Crystal threatened.

Alvin didn't doubt her words. He continued to hide his amusement. At that moment what he really wanted to do was hug her and give her a kiss. She looked so sweet and sincere. She'd gone to all this trouble for him. But he hadn't kissed her before, and starting now because of a disaster didn't seem right. He glanced away. "Tell you what, Crystal. Let's clean up and then go out to eat. My treat since you went to so much trouble to bless me."

A pleased look crossed her face. "Alvin, you're such a gentleman! I'll take you up on that offer. You pick the restaurant."

Alvin thought for a moment. "How about pizza? That place up on Chelten Avenue. The sign says the pizza is 'Germantown style.' Let's give it a try."

"Let's go!" Crystal splashed water into the pan, which sent clouds of steam into the air.

Alvin hid his smile as Crystal moved closer to the window. She grabbed her coat and snapped the leash on Brutus. "He can't go into the restaurant, but I can't leave him in this smoky mess. I'll tie him up outside while we eat."

Together they walked out of the apartment and rode the elevator down to the lobby.

Not until they were in the street did Crystal speak. "You probably think me a total flop because of supper tonight. And I was so hoping to surprise you!"

"You did! And I don't think you're a flop at all." He gave her a warm smile. "I'm honored you wanted to do this for me. You did look pretty cute and funny all flustered and ruffled."

Crystal broke into a sly smile. "Go figure!

Men like having their women at a disadvantage." She tugged back hard on the leash as Brutus surged forward. Crystal appeared pleased though. Brutus almost pulled her off the sidewalk.

It occurred to Alvin that even dogs liked to be out in the wonderful spring weather.

Crystal glanced at him a moment later. "Alvin, may I ask a favor of you? I know I said you could pick the restaurant, and pizza does sound great, but could we go to the lounge down the street? To Delmar's Place?"

"Sure!" Alvin didn't hesitate. This was his chance to do something for her. The supper fiasco had rattled her spirit. The other place would have sandwiches from the sounds of the name, and that was *gut* with him.

When Brutus slacked off on tugging against the leash, Crystal reached over to take Alvin's hand.

Alvin was sure he now looked the part of being *Englisha.* Here he was walking down the street with his *Englisha* girlfriend. Only he wasn't really *Englisha.* Not in his heart. And he doubted whether he ever would be. And was Crystal his girlfriend?

Crystal seemed to have no such doubts. She beamed up at him until Brutus lunged forward again. Her merry laugh rang out as she let go of Alvin's hand and ran to keep up with her dog.

Alvin sprang into a sprint and quickly caught up with them.

"At least I'm getting my exercise!" Crystal said, and her laugh sent pleasure all the way through Alvin.

But what right did he have to enjoy her company? None, if he were truthful with himself. Not if he refused to consider asking her to wed him. Alvin pushed the thoughts away.

Crystal had slowed down, and she pulled Brutus to a halt in front of a small restaurant. "Here we are!" she announced. "Thanks for agreeing to my choice. I know I don't deserve it. I know we should be going to the best restaurant in town — one much better even than pizza to ease the shock of you seeing me in that smoky kitchen."

"It's okay," Alvin said as he glanced through the glass windows of the restaurant. Several people inside were sitting on bar stools drinking from beer bottles or were having what looked like hard liquor-type drinks. Crystal had brought him to a bar. The thought burned all the way through him.

She noticed his hesitation. "You don't mind too much do you?" She clung to his arm for a moment. "I really need this . . . after that experience." Crystal's glance flew back toward the apartments. "And you are coming into my world, aren't you?"

He couldn't back away from this. Alvin knew that. This was Crystal's night, and he was in the *bann* anyway. What more harm could be done?

He nodded.

A pleased look filled Crystal's face. "Thanks. I knew you'd understand."

Alvin kept his gaze on the floor as they walked inside.

THIRTY-SIX

When they were seated at a table, Alvin glanced around and then picked up the menu the hostess had given him. He squinted at the words in front of him. It was so dark in here. He saw a waitress rushing around between tables and knew she would soon want to take their order. He glanced over at Brutus tethered by the front door. He was lying down and resting his head on his paws.

All around him were clear signs of things he'd heard of but never seen. Men and women were seated at the small bar. Most of them cradled dark bottles, wine glasses, or tumblers with their hands as they chatted with the person next to them.

Alvin involuntarily shivered. How had he gotten himself into this situation? It had been to please Crystal, he reminded himself. And doing that still felt like the right choice. His friend had suffered a traumatic experience when she attempted to cook an Amish supper for him, so he owed her this much at least. But going to a bar remained a problem no matter how hard he tried to tell himself otherwise. And what bothered him most was how comfortable and at ease Crystal seemed. From the smile on her face, this was a part of her life — and a right comfortable part. This was a side of her he'd never seen.

But then he knew little about Crystal. Alvin had been open about his prior life, even to the point where he'd told Crystal about Debbie. But she had never returned the favor. Maybe it was time now. If this was the life she was used to, he needed to know.

Crystal reached over to hold his hand. "Is this place bothering you, Alvin?"

He didn't look at her. "A little."

"Just relax. It's lovely, really. You'll like it." She breathed a long sigh. "It feels so good to just kick back and forget the battle I lost in the kitchen." A slight shudder ran through her. "Thank God that's over."

When he remained silent, Crystal squeezed his hand. "Alvin, please. I'm sorry, but I did try. Don't I get credit for that?"

Alvin smiled a bit. "*Yah,* thank you. But perhaps you shouldn't have tried. You're not

Amish, and it wouldn't be right to expect you to cook Amish."

Crystal looked hurt. "I did it because I knew how much it would mean to you."

Alvin looked away. Did home cooking really mean that much to him? *Yah,* he did miss *gut* cooking. He hadn't been able to fix a decent meal for himself in the months since he'd left the community. All his food was slapped together the best he could.

Just then the waitress approached. "Good evening, sir, and to you too, Crystal. Will it be your usual tonight?"

Alvin noticed Crystal didn't hesitate at all. "Yes, that sounds good, Betty. And I think Alvin will want the roast beef sandwich." Crystal gave him a quick glance, and Alvin nodded.

She'd ordered what he liked. That Crystal knew him well enough to order for him gave him a positive feeling for the first time since they'd walked in.

That feeling left seconds later when Betty asked, "And maybe a nice beer for Alvin? Or a decent wine?"

Alvin waited for Crystal to say no or order him a soft drink. When she didn't, he spoke up. "I'll pass. Just a Pepsi for me."

"Suit yourself." Betty shrugged. "We have some excellent wines. And our beer is locally brewed."

"I'm sure it's quite good," Alvin said. "It's just that I don't drink."

"I see."

Alvin caught the puzzled look Betty shot toward Crystal. He shifted on his chair, and stared at the table. Maybe he should have ordered a drink. But how could he? He'd never done anything like that in his life and wasn't sure he wanted to start now.

Crystal leaned toward him when Betty left. "You could have humored me, Alvin. What's a little beer? It won't kill you. And you're not going to get drunk — not on one beer, if that's what worried you."

Alvin glanced at Crystal's expression. Was she hurt or angry? He couldn't tell. "I'm sorry, Crystal, but I couldn't."

The silence that fell between them stretched into long minutes. Crystal folded her hands on the table. "Alvin, don't be so tense. Let's enjoy this evening. You seem so uneasy, and yet this is *me.* This is part of my world. If you don't like it, that's fine. But let's not let it come between us."

He forced himself to look at her again. "I suppose it's okay," he said. But inside he thought otherwise.

Crystal seemed to sense his continued tension and spoke again. "I'm sorry you don't feel like I do, Alvin. But consider my point of view. You drop in from who knows where — like from a town in medieval times. Sure, I like you. And your ancient ways hold charm, but I'm not from the world you left behind. I'm willing to make some changes . . . a little here and there. But you need to come my way too. And that includes this." Crystal motioned around the room with her hands "I suppose it's okay that you don't drink, but are you going to have a problem if I do? I know I don't want a disapproving man hovering over me every time I'm thirsty. Can you understand that?"

"*Yah,* I see. It's just not what I'm used to."

She studied him for a moment. "Then perhaps tonight can be a start. You can get used to something new. I suppose in a way this is my fault. I should have brought you here sooner, instead of springing it on you. This is one of my favorite places."

Alvin smiled, but the effort was weak. "You're not to blame, Crystal. You were trying to come my way by cooking me an Amish supper. That was good of you." He lapsed into silence. In spite of his brave words, his insides were in knots. He had no idea how he would eat the sandwich Crystal had ordered for him.

Betty returned beaming brightly as she set plates of food and their drinks on the table. "Here we are! Delmar's finest. Enjoy!"

Crystal took a long sip of dark beer.

Alvin grabbed his sandwich and tried not to stare as Crystal drank. The sight was almost too much for him. And praying openly for his food in this atmosphere was out of the question. Hopefully *Da Hah* would understand. How could Crystal do something like this? Yet he shouldn't blame her or judge. Wasn't he in the *bann* for choosing not to live in the ways of the community? What worse condition could one be in when it came to matters of the soul? Maybe he needed to get over these scruples since he'd been cast out of the church. A cold shiver traveled down his spine.

Crystal sighed as she set the mug down. "There. That helps settle the nerves."

"Am I that nerve wracking?" Alvin asked, attempting a grin.

Crystal gave him a wry look. "A little — but you're worth it." She reached across the table and squeezed his hand.

Alvin felt his pulse quicken. "You're serious, aren't you?"

"Yes. Are you having doubts about living out here?" she asked.

"Yah." He nodded slowly. "I won't lie

about it. But I do value our friendship."

"Is going beyond friendship with me . . . is that a problem for you, Alvin?" Crystal asked, looking at him intently.

Was it? Alvin's thoughts flew to his *mamm*'s letter. He pictured her sitting beside him now. What would she say? In a way she might be glad for this evening. She would be happy that he was seeing the *Englisha* world as it really was and that he wasn't comfortable with it. That he didn't go along with things out here very well. Pain throbbed in his chest.

"Is it?" Crystal insisted, interrupting his thoughts.

Alvin jerked his mind off *Mamm* and home and back to the present. *"Nee,"* he said. "I have never thought of you as a problem."

"Then perhaps it's just what I do?" Crystal took in the room with a quick glance.

"I suppose so," Alvin allowed.

"You're not expecting me to change, are you?" Crystal gave him a penetrating look. "I'm not a farm girl, Alvin. Nor am I a . . ." she hesitated, searching for the words. "A religious freak," she finished.

Alvin's face twitched. "Is that what I am?"

Crystal gave a short laugh. "I didn't think so at first. You seemed decent, solid, hardworking, and sweet. All of which is refreshing to see in a man. I just wasn't expecting this . . . this hesitancy about something so basic, so social." Crystal raised her glass and took a sip.

Alvin watched her and then looked away.

"I'm sorry this makes you uncomfortable, Alvin. But think about it. Think how very uncomfortable I'd be in the world you came from. Tell me something. Didn't you come here to get away from that religion and way of life? If so, why not let go and embrace your new one?"

Alvin thought for a moment. "I guess I really don't know the answer. I know I'm not living like I ought. The ministry back home put me in the *bann,* Crystal. They excommunicated me." He leaned forward to emphasize the importance of what he was saying.

Crystal appeared incredulous. "Why are you worried about what some priest says? And what on earth did you do to get thrown out?"

"I left the Amish community for the *Englisha* world."

"That's it? That's all? And they kicked you out of church for moving here? I thought maybe you did something really wrong."

"It is pretty serious," Alvin said. "At least

in my world. And we don't have priests."

Crystal shrugged and said, "Whatever they're called, Alvin, get over it. This is the world you're living in now. It's not perfect. It has sorrows, and woes, and broken hearts. Out here in this world, we find ways to get by." She glanced at her mug, lifted it, and took another sip of her beer. "Would you like to give this a try?"

Alvin didn't answer.

Crystal continued. "Yes, we have sorrows, Alvin. You very obviously have them too. So do I; so does everyone. You're not alone. We just learn to get past them the best we can. We move from one sorrow to the next joy. And then we wait for the next sorrow . . . and the next joy."

Crystal had a faraway look in her eyes. She seemed to be remembering something. Was it a sorrow of her own? Alvin wondered. But he just listened and waited. She went on and on, almost as if he wasn't present.

"Richard told me, 'You're the sweetest, my darling. But now is not the right time for us to have a baby. Let's lose this one, and we'll be okay. It's not even a baby yet anyway. We can have a hundred more when we're ready, when we're set financially and ready to settle down. Then, not now. We love each other, don't we?' "

Alvin reached for Crystal's hand, but she pulled away. "In the end, love wasn't enough. First it was the betrayals . . . and then the arguments . . . and then the silence . . . and then the lawyers. So much for love. But *you* . . . you're different, Alvin. You keep your promises, don't you? You love with all of your heart. Only . . . only . . . I'm not good enough for you to love, am I? I'm not part of your world . . . even if you think you've left it."

"Crystal, please!" He took her hand again. "You shouldn't talk like that."

She met his gaze. "I bet you have something against divorced women, don't you?"

Her words cut deep and he blinked hard.

Deep sorrow accompanied by tears filled her eyes when he didn't answer. "That's what I thought, Alvin. That's why I didn't tell you. But you might as well know. I need to know if it's something you can get past."

When he just looked away, Crystal pushed her uneaten food aside and got to her feet. "Let's go, Alvin. I know your answer."

Alvin paid the bill while Crystal went outside. He half expected she'd be gone when he stepped out on the street, but she was waiting beside the door with Brutus. He fell into step with them as they headed back toward their apartment complex. Alvin didn't know what to say. He felt an awful hollowness inside. He knew he needed to say something. "I'm sorry about this evening," he said softly. "I didn't mean for things to turn out this way."

"Perhaps it's for the best," Crystal said, her shoulders slumped. Brutus must have sensed her mood because he made no effort to tug at the leash.

"I wish I could change things, but I can't," Alvin offered.

"I wouldn't really want you to." Crystal managed a smile and took his hand for a moment. "I like you just the way you are. You're always a gentleman, Alvin."

He returned her smile. "Thanks, but I'm no gentleman."

She glanced at him. "Are there more like you where you came from?"

"I guess I'm not much different from the rest," he acknowledged. "Once I straighten things out with the church, that is."

Her face brightened. "Maybe I can visit your community someday."

"Maybe," he said, his voice low.

Crystal sighed. "I hope she's still waiting for you back there."

"Who would that be?" Alvin asked.

Crystal didn't answer for a moment. "You know who. And I envy her."

"I'm not sure she's still there." Alvin heard the tremor in his voice.

"Then shame on her."

Alvin kept his gaze on the sidewalk.

Her hand found his. "Don't leave for home without my phone number, Alvin. Just in case you change your mind." He nodded, and his silence said all she needed to know. Some things couldn't be changed. "But until you leave, Brutus and I are available for walks in the park. That won't kill you, will it?"

"No, of course not." He squeezed her hand as they approached the apartments again.

Brutus wagged his tail and tugged at the leash.

THIRTY-SEVEN

The following Sunday evening, Melvin drove Ida home from the hymn singing. As she waited beside the buggy, Melvin tied Red Rover to the hitching post. The moonbeams were so bright Ida could see the lines on her palms. Melvin finished with the tie rope and came back to stand in front of her. His face, half shadowed by his beard, glowed with happiness.

"You look beautiful tonight!" he whispered as his arm slipped around Ida's shoulders. He drew her close, and his lips found hers. They embraced for a long time, until Ida pushed away.

"It's not the wedding day yet," she said.

His smile spread over his face. "It soon will be! It's not many more weeks now."

"And so much work still needing done." Ida's voice caught, and her gaze took in the shadowed buildings around the farm.

"*Mamm* is worried we won't be ready in time."

"You will be, don't worry." Melvin took Ida's hand in his and led her toward the house. "You don't have to make such a fuss, you know. I've made that clear from the beginning."

Ida sighed. "There wouldn't be much fuss on my part, but *Mamm* won't hear of it. She says it's my first wedding even though it isn't yours."

A shadow crossed Melvin's face. "I know you deserve better than a widower like me, Ida."

"It makes no difference to me," Ida protested.

He silenced her with a touch of his fingers on her lips. "I'm glad you feel that way. I loved Mary dearly, but there's a new and precious love for you growing in my heart. Different, *yah,* but equally precious."

Ida leaned against his shoulder. "I don't doubt that, Melvin. And I will love you as if there had never been another woman in your life."

Melvin's hand tightened in hers. "My heart is warmed by your words tonight, Ida. I never dreamed I could feel like this."

"Do you think we'll have a long life together?" Ida asked as she glanced up at his face and opened the front door.

A kerosene lamp had been left burning on the mantle for them. Melvin's face was soft in the low light. "Surely you don't think I slay women by my very presence, Ida?"

A gentle laugh escaped Ida's lips. "Of course I don't. I was just hoping out loud."

"I pray that we live to see our old days together." Melvin led her to the couch and motioned for her to sit.

Ida resisted. "I have a piece of cherry pie for you — and a glass of milk. Let me get that first."

"The pie and milk can wait." Melvin sat down and tugged on her arm. "I want to look at you, you know, and maybe . . ." He let the thought dangle.

Ida sat down. "No more kissing tonight! Okay?"

He sighed. "You're right, as always." When Ida didn't answer, he continued. "You'll be a *wunderbah frau,* you know. The way you already get along with the children and with me . . . I don't know why I should be so blessed — and twice in a row."

"Maybe you deserve it." Ida reached up to touch his beard. "You've suffered, Melvin. With losing Mary and taking care of the children on your own. But *Da Hah* does give back what He takes away."

Melvin nodded. "This is the truth . . . and wisely spoken."

"Do you place much stock in dreams?" Her gaze searched his face.

Melvin shrugged. "*Nee,* but why? Are you a dreamer?" A smile played on his face.

"I'm afraid not. But when Verna was home the other week, she told me about a dream she had. It was quite vivid. There was a funeral, and Verna thinks it was Joe in the casket but she couldn't really see. When she awoke, her heart was all torn up. She hasn't been able to shake the memory. Do you think there's any truth to that sort of thing?"

"Of course not." His voice was confident. "*Da Hah* decides such things, and we shouldn't worry about them."

"That's what I told Verna." Ida settled into the couch.

"Was your sister talking about this in public?" Melvin had a look of disapproval on his face.

Ida hastened to answer. "*Nee,* it was in private. I don't think she's even told *Mamm* or Debbie. And Debbie usually gets to hear everything Verna thinks. The two of them have more schemes up their sleeves than one would think possible."

Melvin laughed. "I can imagine that. What are they up to now?"

"I don't know," Ida said, "but I suspect they have their heads together about Alvin Knepp. What they plan to do, I have no idea."

"But he's in the *bann.*" Melvin was horrified. "Surely they're not reaching out to him — two women like that?"

Ida touched his arm. "Look, it's harmless I'm sure. The two of them set Alvin up with Debbie at Verna's wedding, and a lot of *gut* that did them. They probably would do the same thing at our wedding if they could."

"They're not planning it, are they?" Melvin stared at her. "You know such a thing isn't possible."

Ida gave a nervous laugh. "Verna wouldn't — once it comes down to it. What I'm really worried about is Lois. She's asked to take part in the wedding — as my witness for the family. I told her I'd ask you."

Melvin was silent for a moment.

Ida worried that this had been the wrong time to mention this, but it was too late now. She finally ventured, "I understand if you don't agree to it. *Mamm* told Lois *nee,* but she begged so I consented to ask you."

"Would she agree to dress Amish for the day?" Melvin's face was stern. "I hear she's been visiting in some worldly clothes."

Ida blushed as she thought of how Lois

420

must appear to the community. She did dress badly enough when she visited. Ida's voice trembled. "She said she would dress Amish the entire day. But maybe we'd better not even consider it."

Melvin held up his hand. "Let's think about it. Maybe Lois's heart would be softened if she's allowed to be your witness — if she dresses properly, of course. And I'd like to have my brother Phillip as the witness on my side of the family." Melvin thought for a moment again. "If he'll do it, which he might not. He has issues with our family — Ben mostly. Phillip has always made a lot of noises about leaving the faith."

"I noticed you haven't mentioned him in a while." Ida was all sympathy.

Melvin nodded. "Phillip lives in Lancaster now. Hopefully he's settling down. Maybe if he knows Lois is being asked, it'll help him decide."

"I'm sorry about your brother." Ida kept her voice steady. "And Lois too. She'll dress properly. I'll see to that."

"Then why don't we ask both of them?" A smile crept across Melvin's face. "I kind of like the idea."

"You're such a kind man." Ida took both of his hands in hers. "I don't deserve you at all."

His head bent toward her but Ida pulled back.

"Oh, *nee*! No more of that, remember?"

Melvin laughed. "You don't forget, do you? But not many more weeks now . . ." He gave her a meaningful look. "I guess I'll have to be satisfied with thoughts of kissing you goodnight when I leave."

Ida didn't answer as heat rose up her neck. She jumped to her feet and rushed into the kitchen. She got out the pie and milk and prepared it for him. She carried his cherry pie on a plate and offered him a glass of milk when she got back into the living room.

He gave her another long look before he took the pie and milk and dug in.

"See, you were hungry!"

He grinned. "I just have to make sure you still know how to cook."

Ida changed the subject. "So how's the farm coming along? Has the corn sprouted yet?"

Melvin finished the last bite of his pie before he answered, "I see you notice such things." He appeared pleased.

Ida felt the heat rise again and glanced away. "I couldn't help but notice. You were in the fields with the planter when I came by some two weeks ago. And I did help you load the seed into the hopper after Lily fixed us lunch that day."

Melvin nodded. "I remember. And the corn is up. Did you see the tender stalks last week?"

"I guess I was looking at you and didn't notice the corn." Ida let the blush rush into her face this time.

Melvin reached for her hand. "That's sweet of you. Are you, perhaps, worried about the farm's financial condition? You've never asked, which is a compliment to your integrity, but what with the *kafuffle* going on with Alvin's *daett,* you must be wondering."

"I wasn't really," Ida protested.

Melvin glanced at her for a moment and then continued. "Either way, you have a right to know . . . what with six children and a hungry husband to feed. So here's how it is. All the loans are paid off on last year's crops, though the mortgage on the place is still there. Growing smaller each year, I have to say." A look of satisfaction crept across Melvin's face. "*Da Hah* has blessed me with a healthy body and a mind to work. Soon Willard will be big enough to work the fields by himself. That will mean we can finish sooner with the spring planting, and I can get more aggressive with the acreage. I could even turn that lower pasture into crops. We can always buy hay if we run short. Seems like I've had plenty each year now for a while, though a drought would cut back on that. But then a drought would hit everything hard."

Ida stroked his arm. "I'm not worried, Melvin. Believe me. You're a *gut* man, and I'm sure you've always been a *gut* provider."

"And you won't have to worry about the other children *Da Hah* might give us." Melvin's hand tightened around hers. "We can manage."

Ida glanced away as her face flamed. "I wasn't worried about that either."

"And my children will accept ours with open arms," Melvin added. "They all will be loved and prayed for."

Ida met his gaze even with her bright-red face.

Melvin didn't seem to mind. His fingers were tight in hers. When his head moved closer, she pulled back. He laughed. "Nothing slips by you — even when you're blushing."

She caught her breath and changed the subject again. "How bad are things with Alvin's *daett*?"

He studied her face for a moment. "You really want to know?"

"*Yah,* I'm concerned. Aren't you?"

He chuckled. "What a tender heart you have, Ida. You're quite some woman."

Ida tried to keep her voice stern. "If you think your smooth tongue will get you more kisses tonight, you can forget it." She surprised herself with her resolve. It just went to show how comfortable she'd become around this man. Not long ago she wouldn't have dared deny him the kisses he wanted. Not that he'd asked for many. Melvin had always been the model of decency around her — as a *gut* man should be. Even now he wouldn't take advantage of her. But she didn't want to tempt him either.

Melvin settled back into the couch with a sigh. "Edwin's not doing well at all with the discipline the church is placing on him. At least that's what Ben told me, which I guess isn't something I should tell around. It's pretty common knowledge, or soon will be. An overseer was installed this spring. A young man — Arthur Yoder — from up near Mifflinburg. That was all they could find, being as funds were so short so they couldn't hire an older man. Edwin's not listening to his advice though. He's doing whatever he wants even with Arthur standing right beside him. Arthur moved onto the farm this week, but who knows if that will solve the problem. It's a crying shame really, the way that place has been run into the ground. Edwin is the problem now, and that's plain enough to see since Alvin has been out of the way."

"Maybe that's why Alvin left," Ida mused.

Melvin snorted. "That's complicated thinking. Getting put in the *bann* for that reason."

"I'm sure you're right. I was just saying it's a possibility." Ida nestled against him. "But let's not think about other people's problems tonight. I feel so happy with you, Melvin."

Melvin shrugged. "You asked the question."

"I know." Ida smiled up at him. "And you told me, and there's nothing we can do about it anyway."

"That's right enough," Melvin said, beaming with happiness. "And on that note, I think I'll be off. I have that huge field of young corn to cultivate this week. Sleep is always in short order the way it is."

Ida followed him to the front door. Melvin squeezed her hand, and Ida laughed. "Okay, just one kiss. But then you have to go."

He drew her close and she didn't pull away.

"I said one," she gasped when she finally

pulled away.

"That *was* just one!" He appeared mischievous in the soft light of the kerosene lamp.

Ida shooed him off the porch. "Don't fall asleep on the way home, now."

"I'll be thinking of you!" he said, glancing over his shoulder at her.

Ida waved and watched him go toward his buggy in the moonlight. He untied Red Rover and jumped in. On the way out the lane he leaned from the door to wave again.

She was so blessed, Ida thought as she closed the front door. She didn't deserve such a *wunderbah* man. And yet she'd been given one. It was too much for her to understand. Such blessings simply had to be received with thanksgiving! She was thankful. *Very* thankful!

THIRTY-EIGHT

Late Wednesday evening at the Beiler household, Ida was humming a tune while she worked on the supper preparations. One of the young folks had led out the tune as the parting song on Sunday evening, and the memory of the words were still with her. One of the lines went, "God be with you till we meet again." It seemed so appropriate right now as she thought of Melvin and remembered Sunday night.

During their time together Melvin had agreed to give Lois a part in their wedding. He didn't have to, but his kind heart had won out. Ida still hadn't told *Mamm*. She hadn't dared, but the news must be shared soon. Perhaps right after she had a chance to tell Lois. Perhaps this gesture would be the next small step in the struggle to win Lois back to the faith. Weren't weddings often that way? A time to connect with family and draw closer to the faith?

Ida couldn't be happier about her life right now. How strange things turned out when one gave *Da Hah* full control. Here she'd once dreamed that Paul Wagler would ask her home from the hymn singing, and now her wedding with Melvin Kanagy was only weeks away. Already *Mamm* had made *Daett* and Emery sweep the yard clean of the few leftover winter leaves. And if the weather held, spring would be in full bloom about the time she entered her new life as Melvin's *frau*.

From the kitchen doorway *Mamm*'s voice interrupted her thoughts. "I've been meaning to ask you, Ida, are things still going well with you and Melvin? You haven't said much lately."

Ida allowed her feelings to show. "Things are going very well, thank you!"

"I'm glad to hear that," *Mamm* said. "You're getting a *gut* husband, Ida."

"*Yah,* I know."

Both women turned their attention to the kitchen window when they heard an automobile pull in the driveway.

"Debbie's home," Ida said, as they saw her hop out of her friend Rhonda's car.

"And there's Deacon Mast's buggy," *Mamm* said, almost in the same breath.

Ida leaned over the kitchen sink to look

further down the road. A shiver went up her spine. "I wonder what he wants?" Likely the deacon only wished to speak with *Daett* about some church problem that didn't involve her. She hadn't done anything wrong as far as she knew.

"Both you and Debbie are behaving yourselves?" *Mamm* asked rhetorically.

Obviously *Mamm*'s thoughts were following Ida's. "Not like Lois is," *Mamm* continued. "But then the deacon wouldn't be speaking with Lois here because . . ."

Mamm let the words hang as Debbie walked across the lawn toward the house. Ida pushed thoughts of Deacon Mast out of her mind and left the kitchen to greet Debbie with a hug at the front door.

"My, are we happy tonight?" Debbie remarked. "Wedding thoughts, have we?"

"*Yah,* I suppose I'll have them more and more until the day," Ida said, looking over Debbie's shoulder toward Deacon Mast, who was tying his horse to the hitching post. Fear raced through her with a rush. She had nothing to fear from Deacon Mast, Ida reminded herself.

Debbie followed Ida's gaze. "You don't think I've been doing something against the *Ordnung*?" The look of concern was heavy on Debbie's face.

"Of course not." Ida squeezed Debbie's hand as *Daett* came out of the barn. Deacon Mast waited for him beside his buggy and took off his hat well before *Daett* arrived near enough to speak with him.

Debbie turned and paused, her gaze fixed on the sight. The deacon never took off his hat when he arrived for his normal church visits. Why was he doing so now? Terror gripped her so tightly she could hardly breathe. Debbie stepped inside and looked out the front door. "What do you think is the matter?"

"Nothing, I think." Ida tried to control the beating of her heart. "I'm just a little jumpy right now."

Debbie kept her gaze on the two men. "Why do they have their hats off?"

Ida clasped her hands together, her face white. "I have no idea. It's not usually a *gut* sign. Perhaps we'd best get *Mamm.*"

Ida pulled herself away and turned. *Mamm* already stood there.

Wiping her hands on her apron, *Mamm* asked, "Is something wrong, Ida?"

Ida pointed weakly toward the deacon's buggy and the two men who stood with heads bowed.

Mamm took one look and motioned toward the couch. "Come! We must sit and pray, girls. Deacon Mast has brought bad news."

"It may not be as terrible as we think it is," Ida managed, but the pain in her chest was all the proof she needed that something awful had happened. But what? She didn't really want to know, and yet she would face whatever it was with courage. Surely this wasn't about Lois. If Lois were involved, the police would have arrived with the news of an accident. And in Lois's condition, *Da Hah* surely wouldn't allow Lois's soul to pass over without a chance at repentance. This must be news that involved someone else.

All three women sat on the couch praying, their heads bowed, until steps sounded on the front porch. *Mamm* said "Amen," and jumped up to open the door. *Daett* and Deacon Mast came in with their hats in their hands.

Daett finally broke the silence. "I'm afraid *Da Hah* has chosen one of our people to join the other side, and we must prepare our hearts to submit to His will."

Ida's hands turned cold as a horrible thought formed. Was Melvin dead? But how could that be with their wedding only a few weeks away? Surely not! *Daett* must be referring to someone else. But who?

Daett looked at Ida.

Ida couldn't keep her gaze from his face.

"I'm afraid this concerns you, Ida," he said.

Daett's voice went all the way through Ida. Her whole body throbbed with pain. "Not Melvin!" Ida heard her wail fill the room. *Mamm*'s hand clutched her arm. The strength of *Mamm*'s hold was the only thing that kept her on the couch. Ida struggled to control the sobs rising inside of her.

"Melvin has died." Deacon Mast spoke for the first time. "I'm sorry, Ida."

Ida struggled to keep silent. If she even breathed she might begin to scream.

Debbie's hand slipped around Ida's, but she was in a state of shock. Her body felt like it had left this earth. Only her mind had stayed behind. And even that wanted to escape, but she was earthbound. This couldn't have happened . . . it just *couldn't*!

"What happened? Has he gone? Surely there is still time for Ida to see him?" *Mamm* whispered.

Daett looked at *Mamm* with a puzzled face. "Deacon Mast said he has passed over. Melvin's gone, Saloma."

"Ida must see him," *Mamm* insisted. "She must see him before they take him away."

Daett and Deacon Mast glanced at each

other, looking for guidance neither of them had.

"She must," *Mamm* repeated.

"It can't be," Deacon Mast finally said. "Even I was not allowed near the accident until the *Englisha* undertaker had taken the body away. Only Willard and Lily saw him."

Ida forced herself to speak. "What happened?"

Deacon Mast stroked his beard as if questioning the wisdom of providing details. Finally he spoke. "The cultivator . . . Melvin must have slipped. After he stopped to let the horses rest and was climbing on again. The drag marks start near the back of the field, under the shade tree. The horses must have run for a long way. Melvin was using his young colt . . . apparently training him. There are rows of young corn torn up . . ." The deacon's voice trailed off.

"Melvin's children . . ." *Mamm* paused midsentence.

Deacon Mast met *Mamm*'s gaze. "Willard found him. I wish it were not so, but that's who went to tell Lily. She ran to check on Melvin while Willard stayed with the other children. Then Lily went to the neighbors' place to use the telephone."

Ida bolted to her feet. "I must be with Willard then. He must not be left alone. A young boy should not have found his *daett* so." Pain shot through her whole body now and broke in waves on top of waves. She pictured the face of Melvin's nine-year-old boy. A man dragged under the cultivator's prongs for any distance would not be a sight any nine-year-old should see, let alone if his *daett* was that man.

Sobs shook her body. Ida lunged for the door. No one made an attempt to stop her.

Mamm and Debbie finally moved and caught up with her halfway across the lawn. They held on to Ida's arms, one on either side of her. The three stood beside the hitching post.

Deacon Mast and *Daett* caught up with them. The deacon climbed back into his buggy and drove off.

Daett left and came out of the barn moments later with Buttercup harnessed. He had her hitched to the buggy with Debbie's help while *Mamm* and Ida climbed into the front seat.

"Stay as long as you need to," *Daett* told them as he handed *Mamm* the lines. "We'll be okay here."

"I'll take care of the house," Debbie added, her eyes bright with tears.

Ida hid her face in her hands and hung on as they raced out of the driveway and turned east. *Mamm* urged Buttercup on. The moments seemed to hang together. Numbness stole over Ida's body now that the first wave of pain had flooded her. Was this what others went through when they received such awful news? If it was, she would forever know what death brought in its wake. She'd never imagined it would be like this. Before her lay an awful darkness. Melvin was gone! And in the vast emptiness she could see nothing but the promises of what *Da Hah* had planned for those who believed in His name. Her dreams had been taken from her, but she must still believe those promises! Yet in this moment she felt only pain. She should be ashamed, but she wasn't. Too much had been lost not to grieve. It was as if heaven itself waited for her tears to flow. And Ida let them come. Did not the Savior Himself say that those who mourned would be comforted?

But right now she didn't want comfort either. Why would one wish for such a thing when she would never be allowed to stand beside Melvin and say the wedding vows with him. She would never know what it was like to live in the same house with his children and be their *mamm.* She would never know what it would be like to give Melvin all the kisses he wanted and feel no shame. She clung to the side of the buggy seat as the sobs racked her body. Why hadn't she kissed Melvin more on Sunday night? She could have. It would have done no one any harm, least of all her. But she'd refused him.

"Are you okay?" *Mamm* glanced at her.

Of course not! Ida wanted to howl. But she nodded through her tears. *Mamm* knew what she meant. Many a woman before her had walked through this valley of death. She was not someone special to think that the pain would be any less. She would be okay — eventually. It was the way of the community and the way *Da Hah* worked.

Ida collected herself as *Mamm* drove into Melvin's driveway. Groups of people stood around, and a few *Englisha* police cars sat in the yard. Minister Kanagy saw them first and came at a run across the yard. He grabbed Buttercup's bridle and tied him to the hitching post when *Mamm* handed him the tie rope. Minister Kanagy somehow made it to her side of the buggy by the time Ida managed to climb out. He took both of her hands in his as tears flowed down his face. "You must not allow bitterness to enter your heart, sister Ida," he whispered. "We do not know why this happened and may never know, but we must trust in *Da Hah*'s decisions."

Ida wiped her eyes. "Thanks for the admonishment, Minister Kanagy. I will grieve, but I will not allow my heart to grow cold."

Concern lingered on his face. "I so wish this had not happened, Ida. I want you to know that."

"I understand." Tears crept into Ida's eyes again. "I wish to see Willard. Deacon Mast told me he found his *daett.*"

Minister Kanagy hesitated. "You're not their *mamm,* Ida. You must understand that even in a moment like this."

Ida faced him. "You would keep Willard from me? I have been coming over one day a week for a long time now. I know the boy well." Ida knew her eyes blazed, but she didn't care. Death made one bold, and it was a strange feeling. Never before had she dared look at Minister Kanagy like this.

Minister Kanagy retreated a step. "Perhaps it's best that the boy be comforted. But after the funeral Melvin's extended family will take charge of the children. Remember that, Ida."

Ida nodded and swept past him on her way to the house. The crowd parted to allow her through.

THIRTY-NINE

Ida sat on the long bench near the front of the living room with all of Melvin's children on both sides of her. "It's only for today now," Minister Kanagy had reminded her again. Ida wished he wouldn't be so insistent on the matter. She understood that she had to leave Melvin's children after the funeral, but right now she didn't want to think about tomorrow or even about the next moment. Soon Melvin's body would be placed in the ground at its final resting place, and life would end for her. At least that's how it felt.

She comforted herself with the thought that Melvin wasn't really present now. Only his physical body lay in the coffin. Melvin's spirit was even now with *Da Hah*! What was buried would one day be raised out of death into eternal life. Yet, if she were honest, these truths meant little today. Even though they'd been whispered to her by family members and friends from the community a hundred times in the past few days.

And then there had been the news this morning whispered among the women. Minister Kanagy's *frau,* Barbara, had been told by her doctor yesterday, that breast cancer had been found. A serious case of it. Minister Kanagy should be in sackcloth and ashes himself this morning instead of being busy with his instructions to her about Melvin's children. But she mustn't think ill of the man. There might be more hope for Barbara than the women assumed. That's how those things went sometimes. People tended to think the worst.

One thing Ida did know — *Da Hah* was dealing harshly with the Kanagy family right now. Had she perhaps been at fault in some way? But how could that be? *Da Hah* made His own choices, and she must not doubt Him. There were reasons for what happened that man could not understand, and she must accept them. Today she would mourn Melvin's passing and comfort his children.

Ida hung her head. One arm was tight around the frail shoulders of Melvin's son, Lonnie. Lisa, Melvin's youngest girl, was seated in her lap, snuggled up tight like she never wanted to let go. Their parting would come soon . . . in only hours! Minister Kanagy would make good on his warnings even with his *frau* ill. His had not been idle words. Hearts would tear again soon, but it couldn't be otherwise. She was at least mature enough to know that. Even if she somehow kept the children with her, how would she support six young ones? If she were Melvin's widow, the community would rally. They would help her until she found another husband. Minister Kanagy would help see to that — the husband and the support.

Ida shivered at the thought. Perhaps it was best this way. If she'd said the vows with Melvin, Minister Kanagy wouldn't rest until some widower — from who knew where — made her a marriage proposal. And she would have had to accept whether she loved the man or not. One could always learn to love, Ida supposed, but so soon after Melvin's passing would be a struggle. So there was one thing she was thankful for today! If Melvin's death had been necessary, which *Da Hah* had apparently deemed to be so, she was thankful that it had happened *before* the wedding. It was an awful, selfish thought to entertain at Melvin's funeral, but she couldn't help herself. And this was also best for Melvin's children. They would be much happier with relatives than if they had to live with some unknown man Ida would have had to marry. All while she struggled to adjust to her new husband. Though there would surely be grace given, Minister Kanagy would say, and that was likely true. But still . . .

Ida turned from her dark thoughts with a sigh. She would return home tomorrow, and life would go on. The day would be a Sunday — the first day of the week, the first day of a new beginning. In reality her old life would resume. She must be brave for the children's sake and her own. Eyes that were cried out only did so much *gut.* She had discovered that upstairs in Melvin's house the past few nights. Lily had insisted that Ida rest when she came over since Ida refused to return home. Now she glanced down the bench toward Willard. He was the oldest, and the one who had found his father's body wrapped under the cultivator's steel teeth. Ida held still as a cold chill ran through her body. No boy should have to experience anything like that. If she had a complaint against *Da Hah* — even more than the fact that He took Melvin — it was that.

"You must not be bitter," Minister Kanagy had lectured her when she blurted out her objections. And he spoke the truth.

After she arrived at the house the first day

she'd rushed to Willard's side and tried to comfort him. But Willard wasn't willing. She found him on a chair in the living room. He was staring at the wall and as cold as ice. The attention and hugs she gave him didn't seem to reach inside him. Willard needed his real *mamm* at a moment like this, but that wasn't possible. It was a horrible, dark time. Ida felt tears run down her face. Somehow *Da Hah* would make sense out of it all, even if she couldn't see how things could possibly ever be right again.

Ida forced herself to listen to Bishop Troyer from a neighboring district. The Kanagy family had requested that he come in and preach the main sermon today. Perhaps the bishop would have some final words of comfort that would give her courage for the days ahead. She should have listened since the bishop began to speak instead of wandering off in her own world filled with her own pain.

"And now today we lay our beloved brother in the ground," Bishop Troyer said, as he lifted both hands toward the heavens. "But let us not forget the day that will come soon, a day of light and not of shadows, a day of joy and not of sorrows, a day when our cups will overflow and not remain empty. On that day, with *Da Hah* Himself, our brother Melvin will come back robed in all the glory of heaven to reunite with this earthen body of his. And so will all those who have died in the faith. They will be raised again or be changed in the twinkling of an eye if they are still alive. So let us comfort ourselves with that thought as we walk through the final steps of our sorrow today."

Bishop Troyer sat down, and wiped his brow with his handkerchief. His head was bent low toward the floor. To Ida he looked weary, as if a great weight rested on his shoulders. She couldn't imagine what it took for a minister to preach at a funeral, even if the deceased wasn't related to him. Ida waited as the ushers moved the crowd past the casket. Lisa climbed out of her lap and stared at the line. At two years of age, Lisa couldn't possibly understand what all this meant.

"Your *Daett* has gone to heaven," Ida whispered in Lisa's ear again, just as she had that first evening. She'd pointed toward the sky and tried to explain the tragedy in a way Lisa could understand. She hadn't succeeded though. Lisa had smiled and nodded. Later she'd asked when her *daett* would return from his trip to town.

Ida pulled the girl close. There would be

no return, and Lisa would eventually deal with the fact. But perhaps at two the events of today would forever be lost in the fog of unformed memories. It would be *Da Hah*'s mercy if this were true. Ida wished for foggy memories herself today, but she wouldn't have any. This moment would be etched in her mind for a very long time.

Mamm and Debbie appeared in Ida's side vision. *Daett* stood up from the preacher's bench to join them in the line. Where was Lois? Ida wondered. Surely she had come today. The answer came moments later, as *Mamm* and *Daett,* with Debbie at their sides, passed the casket. Verna and Joe stepped into view. Lois was clinging to Verna's arm. Ida let out her breath at the sight of Lois's black Amish dress. What if Lois had arrived in her pants today or even in a short *Englisha* dress? That would have been a shame the family might never have lived down. Thank *Da Hah* Lois had found it in her heart to make the right choice.

The opportunity to tell Lois that Melvin had approved of her as the family witness for the anticipated wedding day had never arrived. Ida choked back a sob and slipped her hand over her mouth. There were so many *gut* things that would never happen now. And each day would only bring more of them to mind. She would cry for weeks, if not months. Many had walked this path before her, and she must not think *Da Hah* would spare her the pain others had suffered.

Verna and Lois approached the casket. The two stood there for long moments as tears ran down their faces. Ida knew their tears were mostly for her — their plain sister. They probably figured she would never have another chance at happiness. At least not like Melvin would have given her. And this was true, Ida told herself. She buried her face in her hands as more tears came.

Little Lisa whispered in her ear, "What's wrong, Ida?"

There was no answer a child could understand even if she could have explained. Ida pulled Lisa close and said nothing. Someone touched Ida's shoulder moments later, and she looked up to see Debbie standing over her. Debbie motioned for little Lonnie to slide over on the bench. She sat down beside Ida. "Your mother said to stay with you," Debbie whispered.

How like *Mamm,* Ida thought. *Mamm* figured that someone Ida's own age would be the greater comfort as she faced one last look at Melvin's face. Debbie reached over to squeeze her hand. They sat in silence as the long line of mourners moved through. Which was worse? Ida wondered. The agonizing wait or the moment she would stand in front of the casket? Beside her on the bench, Debbie gasped and a startled look crossed her face. Ida turned to look in the direction of Debbie's glance. Her own emotions spiked. Alvin Knepp was in the viewing line! Why had he come to Melvin's funeral? At least Alvin had the decency to stand in line with his head bowed — a proper and fitting stance for a man who was in the *bann*.

Ida clutched Debbie's hand. What must Debbie think of Alvin reappearing at such a moment? Ida snuck a glance at her friend's face. It was pinched and pale, but the startled look was gone. What a shock this must be! What could it mean? No doubt the same question was racing through Debbie's mind. Alvin and Melvin hadn't been that close. Not close enough to bring Alvin home from the *Englisha* world on the basis of friendship. Not after all these months of silence.

Debbie lowered her eyes as the color left her face.

Surely Debbie must still love the man to have this kind of reaction, Ida thought. Oh, if only Alvin could see the wrong he had done and repent of his ways! Ida sat up straighter. What if Melvin's death brought conviction to Alvin for the life he was living? Did this tragedy make Alvin consider a reconciliation with *Da Hah* and the community? It was possible, but Ida wouldn't let herself jump to conclusions. Still, if *Da Hah* used Melvin's death to accomplish some *gut,* and not just any *gut* but the redemption of a soul that was lost, well that would surely soften the sadness.

Ida clasped her hands in front of her, as Lisa nestled by her side. Debbie was still looking at the floor, her facial expression frozen. This was such a sad day. Ida decided she was only grasping at straws in an attempt to find joy in the occasion. No doubt Alvin had simply been in the area for some reason and had decided to attend the funeral. But what if it were true that Alvin planned to come home? How *wunderbah* that would be — that something awful like Melvin's death might be used to heal Debbie and Alvin's relationship.

Hadn't Verna tried to use her wedding day to bring about the same thing? *Yah,* but it hadn't worked. Ida held her breath for a moment. *Yah,* Melvin would smile down from heaven if Alvin were affected in a positive way by his untimely death. Melvin must even now walk with the angels and bear the crowns *Da Hah* had given him. Why would it be so strange if some of that glory leaked back to the earth and accomplished a great *gut*? She must remember this in the days ahead, when the heartache of Melvin's loss became too much to bear. Alvin's presence today was a work of grace even if he never repented and made his peace with *Da Hah* and the community.

FORTY

As they approached the casket, Debbie stayed close beside Ida. The line had finally ended, and Melvin's brothers and sisters had gathered by their families. Each had taken what time they needed around the casket. Minister Kanagy had sat down moments ago and motioned toward Ida. It was time for her to go up with Melvin's children. She half expected Minister Kanagy to change his mind and substitute someone else. But she was glad he didn't. If she'd said the marriage vows with Melvin, this would be her responsibility, so it was appropriate that she act as *mamm* for these children today.

Debbie held little Lisa, and Ida managed to grab Rosa's hand. Rosa looked like she would resist as Willard had in the beginning, but then she didn't. Perhaps she was too numb to do so. Ida considered that it might have something to do with being the oldest boy and girl of the family that caused both Willard and Rosa to shoulder the level of responsibility they had. Both were trying hard to hide their intense grief.

With a great sob, the pent-up emotions spilled out of Rosa. She clung to Ida's arm and gasped for breath. Willard, standing in front of Rosa, stared straight ahead and ignored the commotion.

Ida moved forward, and a few steps later Melvin's bearded face lay before them. Ida's throat closed tight. She choked. When she could breathe again, she reached over five-year-old Amos to touch Willard on the shoulder. She had to reach Willard's heart so that his sorrow could be expressed. It wasn't *gut* that all this emotion was kept locked up inside him.

Willard didn't flinch at her touch, but he didn't do anything else either. His gaze over the coffin was glassy eyed.

Ida wanted to shake him, to break through his reserve, but this was not the place for a scene. She turned her thoughts to her own heart's sorrow. She looked long at Melvin's still face. She would never say wedding vows with this man she had grown to love. She would never touch his face again and feel the power of his strength, or the character of his life, or the depth of how much he loved her. Ida allowed her tears to flow freely.

Around her she heard the soft rustle of the congregation as they waited for her to finish. Debbie had stepped closer and now held her hand. The two of them leaned against each other. Ida stayed that way for several moments as time seemed to stand still. When she finally stirred, Willard was still staring sightlessly across the casket. It was time to move on. Ida nudged Amos, and he in turn nudged the others. As one group they moved back to their seats and sat down while gently sobbing.

When Ida looked up, the pallbearers had already closed the casket. She didn't avert her eyes as it was carried out and slid into the back of the open buggy. Minister Kanagy stood and led the way outside. Someone had Melvin's buggy ready; Red Rover in the harness. Their ride for the day. Sobs choked Ida's throat again as she helped the children climb in. She wished they'd used another horse for the trip to the cemetery, but that was not the way of the community. One faced the pain and so moved beyond it. She would have to see Red Rover one way or the other. She might as well begin now. It would be a long time before she wouldn't think of Melvin at the sight of him.

"Ride with us," Ida whispered to Debbie, who was still at her side.

"Is there room?" Debbie raised her eyebrows.

"For you, *yah,*" Ida replied.

Debbie seemed to understand. It would be best if they were crammed into the buggy than for Ida to ride without someone to comfort her. And it would also be better if Ida wasn't alone with the children for these last moments together.

"Shall I drive?" Debbie asked.

"*Nee.* Just be with me," Ida said.

Debbie climbed in. Ida took the reins and pulled into place behind the open buggy with the casket hanging partway off the back. They didn't have to wait long before the driver, Virgil, Joe Weaver's younger brother, appeared. He climbed into the wagon and took the reins. Moments later Emery came out of the barn and joined him. *Daett* must have told Emery to help out where needed. It was *gut* to see her brother riding ahead of her. This prepared her for the moment when she would return to the life she'd known before Melvin was part of her future.

Ida guided Red Rover as they followed Virgil's wagon and pulled out of the driveway. At the first stop sign, the *Englisha* cars stopped and waited until the long line of buggies had passed through. Ida wept as she thought of this courtesy provided her from people she didn't even know. No one had been asked to wait, and the people no doubt had places to be on a Saturday afternoon. Yet they paused to show their respect for the sorrow and grief in front of them.

"I can't believe you're holding up so well," Debbie said from the seat beside her. "And how you're ministering to others . . ." Debbie's glance took in the children.

Ida shook her head. Debbie was kind, but she was being too generous. She didn't have the strength to protest out loud. Nor did she have the strength to ask Debbie about Alvin. Debbie gave her arm a quick squeeze.

They soon arrived at the cemetery and the buggies pulled off the road. Many of the drivers tied their horses along the fencerow. Before Ida climbed down, Emery came from the open buggy to secure Red Rover.

"Thanks," Ida whispered as she helped the smaller children down. "It was *gut* to see you riding ahead of us."

Emery gave her a warm smile. "Take courage, sister. We're all weeping for you today. Even when our eyes are dry."

Ida gave Emery a grateful look. When he left, Ida led Lonnie and the others across the ditch line toward the gravesite. She was sure there had been tears in Emery's eyes, even with his protestations to the contrary. *Da Hah* had blessed her with a family who stood with her in this time of great sorrow. She couldn't imagine life after today, but at least her family would be there to help her.

A few people had arrived in the graveyard before Ida did, and they opened up to allow her and the children through. Ida walked up to the open grave. The sight was too painful for more than one quick glance into its depths. She wasn't supposed to draw back from the pain, but to bear up under it, Ida reminded herself. And yet she knew *Da Hah* would understand that there were limits to what she could endure.

Willard stared into the grave; his gaze no longer fixed but horror stricken. Ida stepped around Amos and Lonnie and wrapped her arms around the older boy's thin shoulders. For long moments she thought Willard would ignore her as he had done before. His gaze had returned to its fixed state, but as the prayers and Scriptures were read by Bishop Troyer, the flood gates of sorrow opened. Willard's young voice sobbed as he wept. At times it rose above that of the bishop's. Several people sent looks of sympathy their way. Others must also have noticed the young boy's lack of emotion before this and were thankful that Willard now mourned. By the time they lowered the casket and began to throw dirt into the grave, Willard leaned limply against her. Ida steadied him, noting Willard's frail frame was trembling.

"Please dear *Hah,*" Ida prayed silently, "don't let this sorrow be too much for this young heart. Heal the images Willard has seen of his father mangled in death. Give him hope for the future. Let Willard know that You are still a gracious God even though You must deal with us in our sins and trespasses."

When the grave was filled, Willard quieted down, his body no longer shaking. Ida waited until Bishop Troyer moved away from the gravesite before she followed with Melvin's children in tow. The rest of the family made way for her, as if they knew what her intentions were. At the edge of the graveyard Ida paused and went down on her knees in the soft grass. One by one, she hugged each of the children — even Willard, who still had tears in his eyes.

"I have to go now," Ida whispered. "Your *daett*'s family will take care of you."

"Won't we see you again?" Rosa's eyes shimmered.

"Surely you'll come around once in a while," Willard said, his voice catching.

Ida pressed back the tears. "I'll see you in church sometimes, but I won't be coming around the house anymore. Your *daett* and I weren't married. I wasn't . . ." Ida stopped, unable to go on. The words would have sounded harsh and cruel, yet they were true. She wasn't their *mamm.* It was perhaps better if someone else explained further. Someone who could say things better than she could.

Willard nodded, but it didn't look like he comprehended fully what she meant. But then who could completely understand this tragedy? "You'll all be okay," Ida told them. "It'll never be quite the same again for any of you — nor for me. But *Da Hah* will see that we're taken care of. His heart has a special place for . . ." Again Ida stopped. She just couldn't say the awful word "orphans." These were precious children, and she didn't want their minds seared with feelings that they were less than anyone else. Melvin's brothers and sisters would see to it that they were raised like they were their own.

Out of the corner of her eye Ida saw

Minister Kanagy approach. She rose to her feet, and glanced at him.

His look asked, "Are you done? Are you ready?"

Ida nodded. "Thanks for giving me this time with them."

Minister Kanagy's face softened. "You have given of your best, Ida. Even in this time of your own sorrow. I pray *Da Hah* will bless you with a full life. Now that He has taken, *Da Hah* will surely give again."

"I will pray for Barbara and you," Ida responded.

Gratefulness rushed across Minister Kanagy's face. "Thank you, Ida. Your kind heart is a credit to us all. We continue to hope for the best."

Ida hung her head and moved back a step as Barbara and Minister Kanagy's eldest daughter, Wilma, approached for the children. Another of the Kanagy sisters came up, and Ida turned to go. When she glanced over her shoulder, the women had their arms securely around the little ones. She mustn't look back again, Ida told herself as she forced her feet onward. Debbie was waiting when she arrived at the buggy. Emery had Red Rover untied.

"I'll follow you back to Melvin's place and help unhitch," Emery said as Ida and Debbie climbed into the buggy.

It felt good to be taken care of this way, Ida thought. It comforted her in a way, now that the load of the past few days was behind her. Loneliness rose inside of her, a dark, haunting force. She drew in a deep breath as the emotions flooded over her. This too must be faced. Ida took the reins in her hands. Emery slapped Red Rover's neck gently, and they were off. The horse's hooves beat on the pavement, but otherwise they rode along in a heavy silence. Even Debbie seemed lost in her thoughts.

Ida looked behind them and saw Emery following in his buggy. She was thankful he stayed close behind for the whole ride. It was as if Emery wished to carry her along by the strength of his presence.

Ida pulled into the driveway at Melvin's place and stopped beside the barn. Emery let his horse stand as he came over to unhitch.

"Are we staying for the meal?" Emery asked.

"I need to go home," Ida replied without hesitation. "But you and Debbie can stay."

"I'll take you home then," Emery said.

Debbie added her own decision. "And I'll go with you."

Ida didn't protest, other than to say, "It's

gut enough if I go with Debbie." It would be right to have Debbie with her. Tomorrow she would be strong again, if *Da Hah* gave her grace. She had said her goodbyes to Melvin's children, and it was best if she didn't see them again today. Emery nodded and took Red Rover into the barn. He came out moments later with Buttercup. Ida held up the shafts and Debbie helped fasten the tugs on the side opposite Emery. They were on their way moments later, Debbie at the reins this time.

"Thanks for coming home with me." Ida gave Debbie a weak smile.

"I'm making tea and chicken soup when we get to the house," Debbie said. "You're in for the collapse of your life."

Ida leaned back on the buggy seat. Her body and mind were numb. She allowed the tears to run down her cheeks. Sobs racked her chest. "I think it's already started."

Forty-One

Alvin drove his buggy into Melvin's lane after the burial service and caught a glimpse of Ida's buggy headed in the other direction. He sighed. Surely Ida would have Debbie with her. The two must have decided to leave at once rather than stay for the meal the community women had prepared. He could understand Ida's desire to leave. He'd seen her say her goodbyes to Melvin's children at the graveyard. The whispers around him had confirmed what he already suspected. The Kanagy family, not Ida, would take care of Melvin's orphans.

That he understood, although when Ida hugged each child in turn the scene had been a sad one. Several of the women who stood near him sniffled and wiped their eyes. Ida must have grown close to the children in the short time she'd dated Melvin. That was also something he could understand. Ida would have made a *gut mamm.* The whole situation was a tragedy beyond comprehension. But such were *Da Hah*'s ways, and His people would not question them. He hadn't been out in the *Englisha* world long enough to have taken up doubts. At least, not yet.

Alvin pulled to a stop beside the barn. Emery came out to help him unhitch. The people were kind to him today. Not that he had expected otherwise, but the *bann* hung over his head. If he stayed for the noon meal, the scene wouldn't be pretty. He would have to sit by himself in some corner. But it was the way it was done.

Emery greeted him with a warm smile. "Back home are you?"

"For now." Alvin let the comment stand, and Emery seemed satisfied. He held the shafts as Alvin led his horse forward. He didn't feel up to further explanations, and Emery didn't seem curious enough to ask more questions. Emery stayed behind as Alvin took his horse into the barn.

Last night Alvin hadn't given his *mamm* and *daett* much explanation for his return. They had their own opinion on the matter, he was sure, and he didn't want to start a disagreement. Their version was *gut* enough for now. They thought Melvin's death had brought him home. The truth was that

Melvin's death had affected him, but he'd been ready to return anyway. This had provided a better reentry point than he'd dared hope for. The community people liked to understand things, and when he arrived at Melvin's funeral the turn of events made a lot of sense to them. They thought the same as his parents did. He could tell by the looks they'd given him all day and by the occasional whisper he overheard.

"Thank *Da Hah* some *gut* is coming out of this tragedy."

"*Yah,* I think Melvin would be glad to see it."

Alvin's *mamm* had written on Wednesday night with the news of Melvin's death, and the letter had been in his mailbox on Friday evening when he arrived home early from work. He'd rushed about and caught the Greyhound Bus to Mifflinburg. He arrived by taxi at his *mamm* and *daett*'s place in the early morning hours.

They hadn't appeared surprised by his appearance. They'd assumed Melvin's tragic death had pushed him to think about the condition of his own soul. Alvin figured they hoped he wanted to repent and seek peace with the community. They were right in that he did want peace. And he did want a new start. None of which would be easy, but he

463

had to begin somewhere. If he accepted the shame of being in the *bann* in public like he had accepted it from his parents this morning, that would be the first step.

As much as he wanted to see and speak with Debbie, it was best if she weren't here to see his first humiliation in front of the community. Tomorrow there would be a repeat if he went to the services. And, *yah,* he would go, but by then the first blush of the shame would have worn down. The stares wouldn't be quite as intense nor would the emotions rise in his chest quite so severely. When Debbie saw his disgraced condition, she would have to decide what she wanted to do. She had plenty of reasons to never speak with him again. Regardless of that, Alvin was back to stay. He would not run again. Out there in the world was much worse than anything the community had for him. Crystal, with her kind looks and pleasing personality, had made that clear. Much sorrow and anguish lay hidden beneath the surface.

Alvin caught his breath when Deacon Mast stepped out from the shadows of the barn.

The deacon stuck out his hand in greeting. "*Gut* to see you back, Alvin. Are you staying for the noon meal?"

Alvin swallowed hard. The deacon was doing his duty, and this wasn't easy for either of them. Deacon Mast had a tense look on his face as Alvin answered, "*Yah,* I planned to."

Deacon Mast put his hands in his pockets. "You know, of course, Alvin, that . . . well . . . you'll have to sit by yourself. You're in the *bann,* you know."

"I know." Alvin nodded. "It's okay. I want to make peace with the community."

Deacon Mast's countenance lightened considerably. "You'll be at the ministers' meeting tomorrow morning then? We have the baptismal class, so they will have to listen in. It will be a *gut* lesson for all of them — seeing a man repent." Deacon Mast looked intently at Alvin. "So we can speak in detail then tomorrow? With the other ministers? You'll be there?"

Alvin tried to keep the dismay from his face. He would have to confess his sins in front of the baptismal class. This was almost too much shame to bear. Then he'd eventually have to confess in front of the entire community. Alvin worked at the lump in his throat. "I'll be there."

Deacon Mast almost glowed. "You'll not regret this decision, Alvin. Peace in one's heart cannot be purchased at any price.

Only *Da Hah* can give it when we change our ways and make our things right with our fellow man. Melvin would be glad to see you doing this."

Alvin hesitated. His mind whirled with the knowledge that Debbie would hear all his sins spoken out loud tomorrow morning. Alvin finally found his voice again. "I planned to come back soon, so it wasn't just Melvin's passing. But before my plans to return were finalized, I got the letter from *Mamm . . .*"

Deacon Mast slapped Alvin on the back. "I understand, son. We'll make things as easy for you as possible. Believe me, I'll do my part. Your *mamm* and *daett* need you back home. The farm's a mess, which you may or may not know about. You'll receive a great welcome from everyone — after you make things right, of course."

"I understand," Alvin said. Someone was walking past them with a horse, and Alvin didn't wish anyone to overhear this conversation.

"I will go in and personally see that a table is set aside for you." Deacon Mast didn't wait for an answer. He headed toward the house.

Alvin had no option but to follow. He would rather have sneaked into the house, but there really was no way to sneak around anyway. He was in the *bann,* and might as well have bright city lights flashing from the top of his head.

The deacon made a beeline across the lawn, not pausing to speak with anyone. Alvin felt the skin under his collar grow warmer with each step, but he stayed with the deacon as they entered the house. Deacon Mast motioned toward a bench with his hand. "Sit back there for now."

Benches had been set up in the living room, and a line of people were already filing past the big dining room table where the younger girls dished out the food cafeteria style. Several of them looked up at him.

Alvin ducked his head and moved to the far corner of the room.

Deacon Mast took his place in the food line, and everyone knew what his plans were. The plate of food the deacon filled wouldn't be for himself, otherwise he would have his *frau* by his side as they went through the line.

Alvin kept his gaze downward. No one made any move to approach him or sit beside him. They couldn't. He was in the *bann.* He fidgeted until Deacon Mast came across the living room with a plate of food. It looked *gut,* but Alvin wasn't sure he could get a single bite down. There were small children seated nearby. Most of them were staring at him openly. At least the adults were too well mannered for any lengthy looks.

"Here you are!" Deacon Mast announced. "It's already been prayed over."

"Thank you," Alvin said. He set the plate on his lap and stuck the fork into the potato salad. Slowly he lifted the fork to his mouth. He chewed and followed it with a bite of baloney sandwich. He was hungry and that helped. He would live through this, he told himself. Already the children had lost interest. Most of them had turned their attention back to their own plates. By the time he was halfway through, even the adults seemed wrapped in their own deep conversations.

Alvin gulped the last bites and took the plate to the kitchen where some of the women were already busy washing dishes. Bishop Beiler's *frau,* Saloma, gave him a warm smile and whispered, "I'm glad you're back, Alvin."

"How's Ida doing?" Alvin ventured. It didn't seem *gut* manners to ignore that question now that she'd made the effort to speak with him.

A shadow crossed Saloma's face. "She's

cut to the heart. Ida loved Melvin, but *Da Hah* has His ways. He knows best."

"Yah," Alvin agreed. He repeated the words he'd heard since childhood. "Even when we don't understand."

"Melvin would be glad to see you here today." A kind look crept over Saloma's face. "I hope you plan to stay."

Alvin nodded and retreated from the kitchen before an explanation came out of his mouth. It would be too cumbersome to explain that he'd already been planning to come home before he heard of Melvin's death. His attempt with the deacon had gone nowhere. He would just let the matter rest.

Alvin returned to the barn and retrieved his horse. Emery didn't show up to help with the buggy, and no one else offered. But it wasn't as if anyone stood around and watched either. He was in the *bann,* and most of the people would need to be cautious about contact with him until the matter was resolved. Well, he would begin that process tomorrow morning. Deacon Mast had made that part easy. Now if he could get past Minister Kanagy he'd have clear waters to sail in.

Alvin twitched the reins and guided his horse down the lane. Twenty minutes later he pulled into his own driveway. His parents' buggy was parked beside the barn, and Alvin glanced toward the house in surprise. Why were they home already? It wasn't their usual routine. Had they been ashamed of the scene they knew would play out at Melvin's place? Had they come straight home from the graveyard? Alvin's shoulders sagged. He hadn't even noticed their early departure. It was high time he paid more attention and perhaps had a long talk with them. He owed them that much. They had questions he needed to answer, and he had things that needed saying.

Alvin unhitched, put his horse in his stall, measured grain into the feed box, and walked to the house. His *mamm* and *daett* were waiting in the living room.

"Sit!" Alvin's *daett* ordered without any wasted time in small talk. "I want to know what's going on with you."

"Please, Edwin," *Mamm* begged.

The stern expression on *Daett*'s face didn't change. "The silence has been long enough, Helen. I want this explained. Alvin's not barging in here without some explanation. This is still my house, the last I checked."

"But the funeral was today," *Mamm* said.

Daett dismissed the objection with a wave

of his hand. He turned his attention to Alvin. "The funeral's over. Have you been speaking with the committee who's now overseeing my farm? Have they lured you back? Made you promises?"

"I don't know what you're talking about, *Daett.*" Alvin felt a chill spread through his body. He was going to stand up for himself, he reminded himself.

"I find that hard to believe."

But Alvin noticed relief spreading across his *daett*'s face.

"Well, then, perhaps you're home to supply some needed support for me," *Daett* continued. "I never thought the day would come when I'd need any." *Daett* paused and frowned. "Not that I can't handle things on my own. The committee has things all tied up so I can't move right or left, let alone straight forward. But they will listen if you speak with them for us, Alvin."

Alvin struggled to keep his voice even. "I'm not on your side, *Daett.* Not when it comes to the farm. You know I have ideas that should improve things around here."

"Edwin, please, must you do this now?" *Mamm* interjected again.

Daett didn't hesitate. "Later will make this no easier, Helen."

Alvin decided he'd better speak his mind.

It was now or never.

"*Mamm* wrote me about what's happening to the farm. She asked me to come home, and that's part of the reason I'm here. The other part is that I should never have left in the first place. I'm sorry I did. I'm sorry that I couldn't face the shame of what I knew was coming — once people found out the financial condition of the farm and decided to place part of the blame on me. But I'm back. Today I spoke with Deacon Mast, and I will have my situation straightened out with the church soon. Beyond that, I'm your son, *Daett. Yah,* I'm hopeful the committee will trust me. But that's because I'll do what they want done. We can save the farm, *Daett.* You know we can. But you need to let me run things."

"Just like that?" *Daett* leaped to his feet. "You think you'll just take over?"

Alvin swallowed hard. "Is that not better than having someone outside the family running things?"

Alvin waited for confirmation, but his *daett* said nothing. And that was answer enough. *Nee,* they would never see eye-to-eye regarding how to work the farm. Alvin would have to trust that things would change since the committee was keeping an eye on managing the work.

472

"I'm sorry." Alvin took his *mamm*'s hand. "I really am, *Mamm.* I tried to reason with him."

"*Da Hah* always makes things turn out for the best." *Mamm*'s eyes shone with tears, but joy glowed on her face. "And with my poor health, I'm so glad to have you home again."

"I suppose things had to come to this eventually," *Daett* muttered. He didn't move from his rocker or offer any further acceptance of the situation.

This is *gut* enough, Alvin thought. His *Daett* accepted his presence home and hopefully . . . eventually . . . things would go better between them.

FORTY-TWO

On Sunday morning Alvin sat on the hard, backless bench as the church service began with the first song. He kept his head down, only looking up often enough to keep track of Bishop Beiler. The bishop didn't appear very cheerful this morning, but the cause likely didn't concern him, Alvin figured. He did spot Ida seated among the young women. She looked drawn and pale. The funeral had only been yesterday. That alone was explanation enough for the bishop's troubled look. No doubt Ida still had a long way to go before she made a full recovery. Yet, she would make it. With *Da Hah* and the community's help, they all walked through whatever sorrow life handed them.

How foolish of him to have run away. He wasn't surprised that Debbie hadn't even looked his way this morning. She had every reason to doubt his intentions. He was the one who had bolted when the way became difficult. During his time away it seemed that Debbie had remained steady, making quite an impression on the community — even on Minister Kanagy — with the humility she displayed. Her gracious attitude had apparently won over the people's hearts.

"You should never have left," *Mamm* told him last night after the talk with *Daett.*

Alvin hadn't said anything but he hung his head in shame. He already knew he'd made a huge mistake. But he would make amends. Surely he would gain credit for that. Crystal had shown him what really was out there in the *Englisha* world, and now he wanted to return, save the farm, and win Debbie's heart back. Her affections had been in his hands once. He knew that now, and the knowledge stung. But regrets would only get him so far. It was time to take responsibility and make things right. First with the church, starting this morning in front of the baptismal class.

Alvin jerked his head up as Bishop Beiler rose to his feet and led the line of ministers upstairs. Alvin waited. Even though he was older than anyone in the baptismal class, it wouldn't be appropriate for him to go upstairs before they did. And none of them knew he was attending this morning's session except Deacon Mast. Unless the deacon had told Bishop Beiler, and he'd told Debbie, which wasn't likely. They would all be startled out of their wits if he rose and led the way upstairs.

Alvin kept his head low but watched three boys stand up, followed by Debbie. At least *Da Hah* spared him in one small measure. If there were another woman who would be listening in this first confession this morning that might be almost more than he could bear.

When Debbie was at the foot of the stairs, Alvin stood and found his way out of the bench row. He stayed an appropriate distance behind Debbie. She caught sight of him halfway up and whirled around with a startled look on her face. Alvin motioned for her to continue. A scene was something neither of them needed this morning.

Debbie just stared at him. "Why are you following us?" she whispered.

"Because I'm supposed to," Alvin whispered back.

Debbie was puzzled, but thankfully she moved on into the room the boys had disappeared into moments earlier. Alvin breathed a prayer of thanks and followed. The ministers sat on one side of the room, as he'd expected. The three boys sat on the other side, and Debbie had taken the chair beside them. The only empty place was next to Bishop Beiler. Alvin took a deep breath and sat down.

Bishop Beiler cleared his throat and said, "Let us open with prayer this Sunday morning. *Da Hah* has allowed a great tragedy to enter our community this week with the passing of our dear brother Melvin Kanagy. My condolences to you, Minister Kanagy for your great loss. My heart weeps for the family and for my daughter, Ida. I never thought to see death call at a more cruel time. Ida is a godly woman, and she will overcome this sorrow with *Da Hah*'s help. I hope all of you will join us in remembering the Kanagys and Ida in prayer in the months ahead as their hearts heal."

Everyone nodded. Bishop Beiler led out, "We give You thanks this morning, oh great and mighty Lord Jesus, even though our hearts sorrow and weep over what death has taken from us. Yet we know that all things are held by Your hands, and nothing is allowed that is not for the best in the end. With that confidence in our hearts we ask for Your blessing this morning. We ask for this class of young people who desire instruction in righteousness, and for Alvin, that he will be restored to You and to Your church. Amen."

"Amen," Minister Kanagy repeated in a loud voice. Deacon Mast echoed him. Minister Graber offered no verbal comment but nodded his agreement.

Alvin stole a quick look at Debbie. She was looking at the floor.

"First, let's take care of Alvin's matter," Bishop Beiler said. "Do you have anything to open the meeting with, Deacon Mast?"

Deacon Mast clasped his hands in front of him as he spoke. "I had a few words with Alvin yesterday at the funeral, and he expressed a willingness to make things right with *Da Hah* and with the church. I'm sure all of us are sobered by the great loss we suffered with Melvin Kanagy's passing. The time is short for all of us, and it would be well if we looked into our souls and made sure our hearts are right and humbled before *Da Hah*."

At least Deacon Mast was trying to make the way easy for him. Minister Graber would be supportive, but Minister Kanagy would be another matter, Alvin thought. Unless he missed his guess, Minister Kanagy wouldn't be satisfied until he'd heard every detail of the worst worldly transgressions Alvin had committed while out in the *Englisha* world. And Debbie would hear every detail. Likely she would never speak with him again after today. Not after she heard about Crystal. But he wouldn't lie. That road led to nowhere he wished to go.

"Thank you for that," Bishop Beiler replied. "I can say that I'm glad to see Alvin return home. We've missed him in the community. I'm sure his help will be greatly appreciated at home on the farm. Perhaps it takes a loss like we had last week to bring us all to our senses and appreciate the things that really matter in life."

Alvin opened his mouth to explain, but Bishop Beiler had already moved on. "I think we'll let our two ministers ask Alvin questions first. Deacon Mast may also speak again, if he wishes."

Minister Graber spoke first. "Perhaps Alvin would give us a short account of his time amongst the *Englisha*. I know we don't have much time this morning since the baptismal class still must be taught, but it would be in order to start with that."

Minister Kanagy nodded.

Alvin tried to block Minister Kanagy out of his mind as he concentrated on what to say. "I left here through no fault or leading of anyone but my own choice. I moved into an apartment in Philadelphia and obtained a job working at a motel as a maintenance man." Alvin gave a faint smile. "Seems my time fixing equipment on the farm did me some *gut.*"

None of the ministers appeared amused. He wished he hadn't said it, but the words were out of his mouth. He would be more careful.

"Did you purchase an automobile?" Minister Graber asked.

Alvin shook his head. Minister Kanagy almost appeared disappointed, Alvin thought.

"How did you get around the city?" Minister Graber continued.

"I walked," Alvin said. "And they have a public bus service that came within blocks of the apartment."

Minister Graber appeared to like that comment. "Did you wear *Englisha* clothing?"

"*Yah,*" Alvin admitted.

"How much of the time?" Minister Kanagy asked.

"All of the time I was gone." Alvin hung his head in shame.

Minister Kanagy dug in. "Did you date any *Englisha* girls while you lived in Philadelphia, Alvin?"

Alvin figured he was turning bright red. To make matters worse, Debbie was now staring at him. He forced the words out. "I did, although I'm not sure if they would be called 'official' dates."

"You spent time with a specific *Englisha* girl? You spoke of love with her?" Minister Kanagy asked, his shock evident.

Alvin tried to find his voice but couldn't. He would lose Debbie for sure now, but there was nothing he could do about that. He wanted to make his life right with the church and with *Da Hah.*

"Did you?" Minister Kanagy had grown impatient.

"Yah," Alvin said. "We did, and yet we didn't. We went for walks in the park with her dog, and we went to restaurants a few times. We talked of feelings of attraction, but not of love."

"There is more, is there not?" Minister Kanagy had his eyes fixed on Alvin.

Alvin sat up straight. "We did go to a lounge one night for dinner. Crystal told me about her past and that she was divorced. We both understood that our lives didn't belong together. That was the night I fully understood I didn't want to live in the *Englisha* world. I decided I would come home when I felt the time was right."

Minister Kanagy seemed satisfied with what Alvin had admitted. "I regret to hear what you've done, Alvin," he said. "But I'm glad to see you've come back."

Alvin waited for more, but apparently Minister Kanagy was done.

"Have you anything to ask further?" Bishop Beiler asked Deacon Mast.

Alvin didn't dare glance at Debbie. He didn't wish to see the anger in her eyes, the betrayal, the hurt. Why had he ever done what he did? No reason made any sense at this moment.

Apparently Deacon Mast had nothing more to ask because Bishop Beiler spoke again. "Let us pray and consider Alvin's matter for a few weeks. If any of us have any more questions during that time, Alvin will be available to answer them." Bishop Beiler paused and looked at Alvin.

Alvin nodded his agreement.

The bishop continued. "You may go back to the service, Alvin. If things go as I expect they will, we will hear your confession in front of the whole church next month. It will be a knee confession. Are you willing to do that?"

Alvin nodded again and got to his feet. In the face of the shame this morning and the pain that throbbed in his heart over his loss of Debbie, a knee confession was a small matter. Alvin slipped out the door and went downstairs. He found his seat among the congregation and joined in the singing, although he kept his head down. He also seldom looked up during the sermons. He didn't look up when Bishop Beiler dismissed the service. When the unmarried men filed out, Alvin found his way to the barn and stayed there until the call came for lunch. He swallowed hard but followed the others inside. He was given a small table by the kitchen doorway. He ate alone in silence and shame. It was as difficult as it had been yesterday, but he deserved every minute of this punishment. He'd lost the most *wunderbah* girl in the world and stepped outside the community. And he had no one to blame but himself.

When he finished eating, Alvin slipped out through the kitchen before the last prayer was called. He couldn't stand it any longer. Next Sunday he would do it over again because it had to be done, but this was enough for today. Alvin's hand was on the washroom doorknob leading outside when a soft voice called his name.

"Alvin."

He whirled around to see Debbie in the doorway on the other side of the little room. A slight smile played on her face.

"Alvin, I was proud of you this morning

up there." She pointed toward the room where the baptism class had been held.

"You were? Why?" Alvin felt like he couldn't breathe. She was such a vision of loveliness, and she was speaking willingly with him!

"I knew about Crystal," Debbie told him. "Well, about you being with a girl, anyway. I didn't know her name. It's a lovely one though."

"You *knew*? How?" Alvin didn't dare let go of the doorknob lest Debbie's face fade from sight. Surely he must be in a dream.

"I drove to Philadelphia to visit you one Saturday. When I saw you walking with her, I couldn't stay. I was so upset." Debbie frowned a bit. "But now you're here, and you've confessed before the ministry. That took a lot of courage."

He stepped closer. "I'm so sorry for everything, Debbie. Will you forgive me for leaving? For not talking to you first? Is there hope for us?"

Her face clouded for a moment. "Perhaps we'd better take this slowly, Alvin. You have a lot of things to take care of, with the *bann* and the situation with your *daett* and the farm. And there's Ida. I want to help her where I can. She needs time to heal from her great loss."

Alvin hung his head. "I saw Ida in the service this morning. I can't imagine the pain she's experiencing."

Debbie's smile was back. "It was good to look over and see your face again, Alvin. It was good to see you sit on a bench this Sunday morning."

"And it was *wunderbah* to see yours." He took a long breath.

Debbie glanced over her shoulder at the sound of someone approaching. "I'd better go, Alvin. You take care now."

"Yah!"

And Debbie was gone.

Alvin opened the washroom door and stepped outside. Debbie had missed him like he had missed her. Could that be? If so, surely they would find a way to make it work out between them! *Yah,* his wounds would heal, and so would Debbie's. After that anything was possible. Anything *Da Hah* had in mind for them. Alvin knew he would not run away again. Not after being given another chance like this.

"Heading home?" Emery asked when Alvin got to the barn door.

"I think so," Alvin replied, looking at the ground.

"I can understand that." Emery nodded. "I hope everything turns out okay."

It will! Alvin wanted to shout. Instead he slipped quietly into the barn to get his horse. He paused for a moment in the privacy of the stall. He knelt down. "Thank You, dear *Hah,*" Alvin whispered as he lifted his face heavenward. "You could have forgotten me, but You offered mercy instead."

Around him the barn rustled with its usual noises. Alvin stood and led his horse out to his buggy.

A few minutes later as he drove past the house, a hand waved from the washroom window and tears stung his eyes. He had seen Debbie's face again and she still loved him. That was more than any man deserved.

DISCUSSION QUESTIONS

1. What do you think of Debbie's desire to join the Beiler family?
2. Is Alvin Knepp with his hesitant ways a suitable match as a boyfriend for Debbie?
3. Was Alvin justified in his flight from home?
4. What would you have advised Lois as she struggles with her longing to join the *Englisha* world?
5. What are your feelings about Paul Wagler? Is he too bold? Should Debbie have accepted his attentions?
6. How would you have advised Ida as she first noticed Melvin Kanagy's interest in her?
7. Are the actions of the community towards Alvin too severe? Should he have been placed in the *bann*? What other course of action would

have served the community better?

8. Should Debbie have gone to Philadelphia in her effort to win Alvin's return? What is your opinion of Verna's advice to Debbie?

9. Was Saloma wise to suggest that Ida spend time with Melvin's family before the wedding? How did this affect her loss?

10. Should Alvin have been more open to Crystal's world after he discovers she's divorced and he realized the range of her lifestyle choices?

11. What do you think lies ahead in Ida's future?

12. Will Alvin be able to maintain his newfound strength as he settles back into the community?

ABOUT THE AUTHOR

Jerry Eicher's bestselling Amish fiction (more than 500,000 in combined sales) includes The Adams County Trilogy, Hannah's Heart series, The Fields of Home series, Little Valley series, and some standalone novels. He also writes nonfiction, including *My Amish Childhood* and *The Amish Family Cookbook* (with his wife, Tina).

After a traditional Amish childhood, Jerry taught for two terms in Amish and Mennonite schools in Ohio and Illinois. Since then he's been involved in church renewal, preaching, and teaching Bible studies.

The employees of Thorndike Press hope you have enjoyed this Large Print book. All our Thorndike, Wheeler, and Kennebec Large Print titles are designed for easy reading, and all our books are made to last. Other Thorndike Press Large Print books are available at your library, through selected bookstores, or directly from us.

For information about titles, please call:
  (800) 223-1244

or visit our Web site at:
  http://gale.cengage.com/thorndike

To share your comments, please write:
  Publisher
  Thorndike Press
  10 Water St., Suite 310
  Waterville, ME 04901